A Dangerous Bargain

ALSO BY ERIN COTTER

By Any Other Name

A Traitorous Heart

A DANGEROUS BARGAIN

ERIN COTTER

SIMON & SCHUSTER BFYR

NEW YORK AMSTERDAM/ANTWERP LONDON
TORONTO SYDNEY/MELBOURNE NEW DELHI

SIMON & SCHUSTER BFYR
An imprint of Simon & Schuster Children's Publishing Division
1230 Avenue of the Americas, New York, New York 10020

Jacket design by Sammy Yuen

Interior design by Hilary Zarycky
The text for this book was set in Garamond.
Manufactured in the United States of America
First Edition
2 4 6 8 10 9 7 5 3 1
CIP data for this book is available from the Library of Congress.
ISBN 9798347103966
ISBN 9798347103980 (ebook)

To the artists reluctant to share their work,
please do—the world needs it more than ever.

And to my dear friend Carlie,
who believed in my art first.

FLORENCE, ITALY
JANUARY 1469

CHAPTER ONE

The morning light's gone from pink to lemon before Leonardo finally decides to grace us with his presence.

I always notice him first. It's the barely there squeal of the door hinges, a pause as long as a heartbeat, then the shift of a familiar shadow in the corridor, followed by his too-long legs and shameless smile when he strolls into the workshop.

The other apprentices' heads snap to Leonardo.

But their eyes slide toward me.

Cristo santo, why does he even bother showing up this late? We'll be done in ten minutes. Leonardo's looking at me too, a sideways glance from beneath his eyelashes that makes me bite the inside of my cheek. At this point, the only person not looking at me is the workshop angel, his ancient eyes open and staring at nothing. Occasionally an awful wheeze squeezes from his chest, the only sign he's different from the half-finished statues surrounding him.

I drop my charcoal and rub my temples. "Third time this week, da Vinci." The vivid purple mark on his pale neck tells me why he was late without me having to ask, but I do anyway, just to see what he says. "Is someone . . . *distracting* you?"

Leonardo winks. "I did find something better to do than drawing old, moldy fruit this morning, yes."

That cursed wink feels like catching my toe in a dip on the floor. I glare to hide how something inside me stumbles. "If you won't practice, then you can do chores today. You know Verrocchio's rules."

Unlike every other master artist in Florence, Verrocchio forces his apprentices to sketch together each morning. He claims it's good for us, but I think all it's good for is wasting work time and sowing resentment between co-workers. Enduring the exercises used to feel like going to mass: necessary to keep the peace and good for me in some cloudy way I'm too unlettered to entirely appreciate. But now that Verrocchio's ordered *me* to lead the morning exercises, they've become downright torturous.

Leonardo bows, red-gold hair tumbling over his shoulders to hide the love mark. "Whatever you say, Virgil. I'm yours to command." He winks again, doubtlessly because he's noticed it irritates me. My eye gives a traitorous twitch.

Who was it this time? What boy was worth the drudgery of grinding pigments all day? It better not be an apprentice from another workshop. I want to goad him into revealing more—anything to wipe that pleased smirk from his face—but the other boys' stares feel like a ring of torches, too hot for me to tease him about anything without getting burned myself.

Leonardo cups a hand around his ear. "Were you going to speak? I heard the gears grinding away in your empty chest."

A machine joke, how original! I scoff and return to my work. If Leonardo wants to squander his time and shove his tongue down someone's else mouth all night, fine. Someone has to make sure these exercises get done, and sadly, that someone is me. What an appalling workplace—I really deserve a raise for all that I endure.

The blessed quiet lasts five minutes before a giggle breaks it.

My charcoal stick snaps when I throw it down this time. "What now?"

The other apprentices blink, eyes far too wide and innocent for me to believe it. All of them except Leonardo, that is, who stares at the lofted ceiling like he's being paid to do it. His shoulders shake with silent heaves of laughter.

"Are you capable of not being a nuisance for a single second?" I snap.

He thumbs a tear from his cheek, voice cracking. "It's not me this time, I swear it!"

Only then do I notice the huge, diabolical grin taking over the face of the apprentice sitting beside him. Giorgio, my second most annoying co-worker. An absolute menace who's done nothing but terrorize me from the moment he joined us last fall. Curious, the apprentice on Giorgio's other side leans in for a look. He slaps a hand over his mouth at the sight of Giorgio's sketch and dissolves into helpless giggles.

Glaring, I rise from my seat. "What's so amusing?"

"Nothing you'd like!" Leonardo sniggers.

I storm across the room, snatching the sketch from Giorgio before he can crumple it up. "Penises! How original."

The apples we're drawing today are there. Except great, quivering phalluses jut from each pair. Giorgio wriggles his fingers, and they *swell.*

I suck in a scandalized breath. "You made a bargain for this?"

Giorgio smiles, admiring his obscene artwork like a beloved pet has done a marvelous trick. "Aye. Gave up the memory of my nonna's house for it."

This is one of the worst bargains I've ever heard of. "Don't you spend feast days with your nonna? What happens next time you try to visit her?"

He lifts a finger to me, and then taps his chin with it instead, frowning. "Hadn't thought of that."

I choke back a frustrated scream. *This* is why apprentices should be barred from making bargains until they're at least sixteen! Otherwise, the magic they ask for is ridiculous, and the things they give up for it absurd.

This has, unfortunately, become a teachable moment, and our master has made the grave mistake of making me a teacher. I stride to the massive in-progress painting of the Last Supper and slap the sketch just beneath Jesus's face. He looks at the phallic fruits with a saintly, patient expression I've painted a hundred times over.

"Does this look like the sort of art that belongs here?"

"Sometimes." Giorgio keeps a straight face and points to a half-finished statue that—oh no—is male, naked from the waist down, and completely undermining the point I'm trying to make.

The other boys make an *oooo* sound before breaking out into hysterics.

Their laughter bounces off me like hailstones. I close my eyes, the pain in my temple blooming into a proper headache.

If Niccolo were here, my brother would say not to let them bother me. He'd listen when I'd confess I've allowed every worry to trouble me my entire life, and I don't know how to stop now. He'd help me find a way to deal with the hot, swirling feelings that fill my chest like smoke.

But my brother disappeared two years ago and took the best parts of me with him.

And if I hear them laughing at me any longer, I might burst into flames.

Stone-faced, I crumple up the sketch and stomp toward the workshop door.

"Wait!" Giorgio cries. "Where are you going?"

"To Master Verrocchio."

Giorgio gasps. "You can't! He said if I mucked around again, he'd kick me out."

"Should've thought of that beforehand."

The laughter dies, but it doesn't make me feel better.

Giorgio sniffles, his face white now. "Please don't tell him. I'll do your chores for the rest of the month!"

The other apprentices glance around nervously, as if they'll be next. Everyone knows if someone displeases Verrocchio, they're gone the next day. There's always another apprentice to take his place. I want to tell them that they're fine, that I'm only bluffing with Giorgio to teach him a lesson, but the words get stuck. How can I back down now without them laughing at me again?

"If you jest like this, you'll never amount to anything." Oh hell, that's not great. I clear my throat and try again. "Don't you want to be the best artist you could be?"

"Maybe he doesn't." Leonardo levels me with a judgmental glare. "Not everyone wants the same things."

I don't think we're talking about Giorgio anymore. My gut twists, like when the Santa Croce priest's stare lingers on me after a particularly soul-withering sermon, but worse, because Leonardo has no sway over my stupid soul, so why do I care at all what he thinks of me? "Actions have consequences," I say sullenly.

Leonardo throws his arms wide, exasperated. "Does it really

matter if we paint apples for the third sodding time this week?"

It doesn't. But I'd rather pour hot oil into my eyes than say so in front of everyone else. "It's what Verrocchio asked—"

A chilling, bone-grating noise cuts me off.

The angel is wheezing again, his bony shoulders shaking. The boy closest to him shoots up from his stool so fast, it falls over.

"It's all right!" I call, even as my skin prickles uneasily.

The angel doubles over with a vicious cough. A wet, gleaming stickiness drips from his mouth to the floor.

"Summon the physician!" Giorgio cries.

"Idiota!" another boy shouts. "Angels aren't people!"

The angel jerks up. Suddenly alert eyes latch onto Giorgio.

I step forward, a hideous feeling bursting through me—

Too late.

The angel crashes across the room, his hands already around Giorgio's neck.

"Give me a taste of your life, ragazzo. You have so much of it!"

Giorgio screams, flopping like a rag doll. Blood wells on the skin of his neck where the angel's sharp nails dig in. The other apprentices swarm, sobbing and yelling, pulling and tugging on the angel to no avail. The angel looks like an old man, but he isn't one. He's stronger than all of us.

A sour taste surges into my mouth. I need to move. I need to distract the angel with blood. I'm the one in charge this morning. It's my job to do *something*.

But I can't.

I'm paralyzed by a swirl of red against white, the last time I failed someone who needed me.

A guttural roar rips me from the memory. Leonardo has

stabbed a palette knife deep into his own arm. Blood flecks his freckled cheeks.

The angel drops Giorgio with a sickening thud. His eyes—too bright, like candles at the end of their tallow—take up his entire face. "At last. A taste of *you*."

Leonardo lifts his arm, teeth gritted. "I've been told I'm delicious."

The angel leaps forward, pointed teeth bared.

But mid-stride, his body spasms.

Then falls.

Master Verrocchio stands behind the angel, his brown skin gleaming with wetness. A slick sword trembles in his hand.

The angel splays on his back, his fingers twitching like insect legs. I finally snap into action and skid to his side, take the head into my lap.

The angel's rheumy, bloodshot eyes latch onto mine. He brushes the scars inked into my skin with something like tenderness. "Such a lovely life!" His jagged nails stroke me too hard, leaving behind angry pink lines. "So lovely."

He twitches one final time. Goes still.

Noise and movement erupt. Hands surround me, one bigger and more freckled than all the rest.

But I don't take it. I can barely see it.

All I can see is the blood on the dead angel's chin.

His blood isn't red, but a deep, dark gold.

CHAPTER TWO

The church bells toll for the angel's death.

I open my window to better listen to them. Verrocchio's attic is cold in the winter and sweltering in the summer, so no one wanted it. After Niccolo disappeared, I claimed it as mine. I relish the frigid air on my face and try my hardest to crush the twinge of dread I haven't been able to smother since the angel attacked.

Six priests came, four for the angel's body, two to interrogate Master Verrocchio, because it's a capital offense to harm one of the holy beings. The priests looked unhappy with Verrocchio, even after all of us had assured them he had only done it to protect us. I was unhappy too, but I kept it to myself. It's not my fault the angel attacked Giorgio, but the way the other apprentices refused to make eye contact with me afterward made me feel like it was.

I shiver. Not wanting to brood any longer, I latch the window shut and leave.

Verrocchio's house sits beside his workshop. As the person who leads the morning exercises, I'm the only apprentice with a key. I patter across the courtyard and its dead gardens to the workshop door. When I move to unlock it, a shadow charges from the darkness.

"Wait! Not without me!" Leonardo pants, catching himself

on a wall a second before smacking into it. He's inexplicably shoeless, clad only in tight-fitting hose and bare-chested underneath his wool cloak. He looks like a ridiculous pagan sorcerer.

My eyebrows pop up. "Were you spying on me?"

"No, I was watching for you. It's completely different."

"No it's not!"

"Of course it is. How else was I supposed to find you? Lurk outside your horrible attic? The younger boys all think it's haunted, you know. Are you going to let us in, or not?" He flaps his hand. It collides into mine and knocks the key flying.

I roll my eyes and look pointedly at the fallen key. "Gesù Cristo. Must you tonight?"

He stoops so suddenly to pick it up, my own stomach reels. He offers me my key with a flourish. "Yes, I must! Because *someone* ordered me to do chores all day, and now I'm behind in my work."

"Right, yes, it's all *my* fault you refused to practice this morning," I grumble.

He hadn't even attempted to sketch before Giorgio's outburst. He'd sat there twirling a curl of hair around his finger instead. A token from his new lover? Madonna santa, I hope not. If he's the reason we endure another plague of lice, I'll shear off his fetching waves myself.

Sometimes it feels like Leonardo da Vinci joined Verrocchio's workshop just to punish me. I'll never forget the first day his red-blond hair was bobbing around. He was showing his portfolio to all the artist workshops, trying to get one to bring him on as an apprentice. When I saw his sketches, it felt like a gut punch, because they were so good. Better than everyone else's. Including mine.

The next day he was circling my workshop, being all handsome and jovial, the other apprentices already hanging on his every word, welcoming him like he was the most interesting person they'd ever met. I hunched on my stool, quietly and inexplicably furious, working on a tiny detailed part of my painting so I had an excuse not to say hello.

But then he sat on me. Yes, *on me*.

"Oh, sorry," he said, laughter on his lips. "I didn't see you there."

He's been sitting on me ever since. Metaphorically, of course. I hate it when we touch.

He's always late, always behind, never around when you need him. And Verrocchio lets him get away with it because when he does work, everything Leonardo touches sends our patrons to their knees. Last year, he put finishing details on a David statue that were so vivid, so exquisitely rendered, the lady of the house had to cover it with a sheet to keep her daughters from swooning over it.

Despite all his feckless loafing, his inability to meet a single deadline, and what a disgraceful role model he is for the other apprentices, when Leonardo actually tries, he's the best artist in the workshop without ever making a bargain with the angel. Even though thinking the very thought makes me want to rip off my fingernails, it's still true, and having fewer fingernails won't make it less true.

And so, with a roll of my eyes, I usher him into the workshop with a sarcastic *after you* gesture. Leonardo doffs an imaginary cap as he sweeps past me, and my eye twitches.

Tragically, despite me subtly and not so subtly begging him

not to, Verrocchio has assigned Leonardo and me to work on the same painting.

Like all Florentine workshops, most of Verrocchio's commissions are collaborations between artists. It allows workshops to work harder, faster, to more quickly quench Florence's endless thirst for beauty. The breathtaking magnificence is what makes Florence so special, what draws the angels to our city and our city alone.

God-blessed, the church says of Florence. The angels flock here for beauty, and the magic they provide in return lets Florence strengthen her walls, keep gold in her coffers, heal the sick. Florence's wealthy families surround themselves with beauty in the hopes of attracting an angel of their own, to show their allies and enemies alike that even among blessed Florentines, God smiled on their name. After all, who wouldn't want their daughter to marry into a home where an angel walked? Who would dare attack a family so favored by God? What merchant wouldn't want to bargain for an internal whisper that said whether or not a deal was good or bad, if the price of silver would rise or fall?

But sometimes I wonder if the wealthy take things too far. Last week, I painted gold cherubs on a chamber pot. *An actual chamber pot!* Shitting gold seems preferable to shitting *in* gold, but to each his own, I suppose. It's not like my family would ever be well-off enough to dream of having their own angel.

I unroll the damp linen protecting my painting palette. "You know, if you spent as much time working as you did fooling around, you'd have your own workshop by now."

Leonardo shields his eyes from an imaginary sun and pretends to look for something. "Oh yeah? Where's your workshop, then?"

I scowl at my paints. His question makes me feel like the

grayish greenish brownish smear at the palette's edge. He's right. I should have my own workshop by now. 'Tis none of his business why I don't. Unlike me, Leonardo doesn't have anyone depending on him. He can mess around, do whatever he wants when he wants, and there'll never be any consequences for him. We're the two oldest apprentices in the workshop by several years. I'm still here because I have to be. He's still here because he can't be bothered to do anything else. The unfairness of it twists me up in knots.

"Can we start?" I snap. "I'd like to sleep before sunrise."

Tobias and the Angel has the marks of a good painting, but not a great one. I stare at the half-finished image, trying to diagnose what's amiss. "The fish in Tobias's hand."

Leonardo gags. "It looks like a slug. A horrible, turgid slug."

I bite my lip. I will *not* smile at him when we're working. It's a rule of mine. "Do you think you can improve it?"

He rolls up his sleeves, cracking his long, thin fingers. "For you, Virgil? I would happily banish this tumescent slug."

We lift our brushes. Even if I hadn't seen Leonardo's narrow shoulders hunched over the workbench all day, I would've known he mixed the paints. There's no grittiness, and the egg tempera's stink is tamed by smoky myrrh. When I offer a begrudging compliment, he beams like I've just proclaimed him the greatest artist of our generation.

"So I've been having thoughts," Leonardo begins.

"Must you share them now?"

"I've been thinking of centaurs."

"Centaurs?"

"Yes. Half man, half horse. Surely, you're familiar with them."

My eyes dart again to the purple mark on his neck. "No. Please tell me—"

Leonardo flaps his hands, his brush dripping on his lap. "Get your mind out of the gutter! I was thinking if a centaur has one pair of arms and four legs, then that would mean it has six limbs total—"

"That is how counting works, yes."

"So if there's *six* limbs, this would mean that a centaur is an insect, would it not?"

I turn—fully turn—toward him. He's near breathless, eyes huge with excitement. To my surprise, the slug-fish is almost fixed. It's not the first time his mind has spun off in one direction while his hands went off in another. Despite my best efforts to stop it, my mouth bows, a barely there bend.

"Would this mean a man riding a horse would be a spider, then? Because of the eight limbs?"

Leonardo rubs his chin pensively, smearing it with paint. "Now that's a *very* good question."

I turn my laugh into a snort, and then, miracle of miracles, the painting transforms from good to great as blue moonlight spills through the workshop. It's so cold, I can't feel my toes, but the sounds of Leonardo's breathing, the quiet shift of his body, are something like warmth. I slowly grow aware of him watching me.

The sleeves of my chemise fall to mid-forearm, revealing the black lines scoring my skin. Each one is the mark of a bargain I made with the angel. Each one represented a day, a week, or a month, of my life. There are hundreds of them.

When a workshop is blessed by an angel, the angel's magic can be borrowed by artists, for a price. Part of the artist's life or a memory for a taste of magic. Big bargains backfire, but small ones strike gold. There is an art to making bargains, and I'm a master.

A month of my life to never have my hands shake while painting with ultramarine, the most expensive pigment in the workshop. A day for the perfect memory of a snowy tree in mid-summer. Half a year to never have my paints go dry, even if I forget to cover them all day. The moment where the image is still caught between my head and my hands is no longer one of frustration. The magic smooths it, soothes it, and without it, everything would take me six times as long. I don't know how many years of my life I've bartered away at this point, but it might be decades.

"Be careful," Verrocchio warned me at the last Epiphany feast. His charcoal-stained finger skimmed down the latest mark on my flesh, still tender and raised. "You don't want to forget how to make art without magic."

I just shrugged. If I could afford to be sparing with my bargains—if my family could afford to keep the roof over their heads without the money I earned—I might've listened.

Niccolo wouldn't have wanted this for you, a vile, soft part of my heart whispers before I can strangle it.

No. If my brother hadn't wanted this for me, he wouldn't have left me to carry the weight of supporting our mother and sisters alone.

"Are you all right?" Leonardo says.

This close, it's impossible not to notice his arms are free of bargain marks. No magic steadies his hand or clears Leonardo's mind. Every other artist in the workshop has bargained with the angel, but years into his apprenticeship, he still refuses. Whenever someone asks him why, he smiles mysteriously and changes the subject.

I admire and resent him for it. If he gave an angel perhaps even a year of his life, how much more could he do? If I had his talent with my magic, I'd be the most successful artist in Florence. Perhaps even in all of Europe. My family's money troubles would be gone. I'd finally have a life free of worry and other people's expectations.

I flick my wrists. My sleeves flutter lower, hiding the marks. "Why wouldn't I be all right?"

Leonardo nods toward the painting. "Because that dog looks like a tasseled pillow."

I startle and pull back just enough to get a better look at what I've done. And . . . merda, he's right. "Looks more like a spider to me."

"Yes, but not a horse-man spider." Before I can tell him not to, Leonardo runs his fingers over the brushstrokes. "It's already dry."

I bite the inside of my cheek so hard, I taste copper.

"It's all right," he says hurriedly. "It's just a mistake."

"It's not." I *never* make mistakes. Not on almost finished paintings as important as this one. The next morning unspools itself with awful clarity. Verrocchio entering his workshop, his horrified scream when he sees the mess I made. Cristo santo, I won't be paid this week now, will I?

Leonardo's long fingers hover before me. "Can I have your brush to fix it? My fish turned out."

My fingers won't loosen. Everything in me goes against

letting the other boy take over. "Dogs don't have scales," I snap.

"They're not covered with a thousand little millipede legs either."

The cursed millipede dog swims before me. The first bargain I made after my brother left was a decade of my life for a sense of when a painting was going wrong. The staggering price should've frightened me—when I told Verrocchio, he had to sit down—but instead, it felt like freedom. Art always takes something from its maker. Your time, your eyesight, a piece of your heart—why not give it ten years instead? At least then I'd know exactly what I was losing.

"Virgil," Leonardo says, not looking at me. "What happens to the bargains you make with an angel when he dies instead of going back to heaven?"

Every black mark on my skin burns like a bargain newly struck. I inhale sharply, the horrible truth worming through my veins. Human life keeps the angels alive, but Verrocchio's angel was killed. Which means—

All the magic, all the power I bartered away my life for, is gone.

CHAPTER THREE

I stand outside my family home and feel like a stranger.

Casa delle Volpi looks no different from any other of the merchants' houses save for the pair of marble foxes bracketing the front stairs. I place my hand on one of their heads, thumb brushing the familiar chip in its ear.

Verrocchio gave everyone the week off. I'm not the only artist who's missing his magic, and he saw no point asking people to work when it would take twice as long and be half as good. Most of the other apprentices have gone to visit family for the unexpected holiday—even poor Giorgio found someone to take him to his nonna's house—but I stayed behind, until it was time for me to visit the bank.

"Fret not," Verrocchio said as I left. "We'll get a new angel soon, and then we'll all redo our bargains, and everything will go back the way it was."

When I hear the soft sounds of life from inside Casa delle Volpi, I sigh and trudge to the door. The sooner I go in, the sooner the nerves twisting in my belly will disappear.

"My boy." I'm greeted by my mother's camphor-scented embrace. Her too-powerful perfume hits me like a gut punch. I hug her back and breathe through my mouth.

"Hi, Mamma."

She holds me out at arm's length, frowning at the paint on my skin. "Could you not have scrubbed this off before you came?"

I flex my stained fingers. "Still worried about what the neighbors think?"

She scoffs and lets me go. One son disappearing was bad enough—but then the one left is an *artist*? Mamma has never gotten over the scandal of it, as if I chose my career on purpose to annoy her. As if we both don't know the real reason why a wealthy merchant's son left home at thirteen for a tradesman's apprenticeship across the river.

Mamma spots my gift. "What's that?"

"I stopped by the flower stall on the Ponte Vecchio."

One of her dark eyebrows rises. "And you bought *stinging nettles*?"

Feeling nettle-stung myself, I fling the plants onto a sideboard. In truth, they were the only thing I could afford, and it felt rude to show up empty-handed. "I thought the cook could use them. Elisabetta likes nettles." I hate how defensive I sound. Coming home always turns me into the worst version of myself. Perhaps I should step out and come back in. Start on a fresh page like this visit is a sketch I've already botched beyond saving.

Mamma's smile glitters. "Of course. How practical. I have something for you, as well."

She leaves me under the foyer's three monstrous, overbearing portraits, all of them Niccolo Pitti, because either my father was cursed by a primordial deity on a trading trip to name all his sons after himself, or because nine months was somehow not enough time for him to come up with another boy's name.

My father's portrait is the biggest: a glaring, gray-bearded man. He was old before he married my mother and older still when I was born. He died when I was fourteen.

The second portrait is my brother, Niccolo. My sight goes fuzzy when it passes over it.

Last, and smallest, is the portrait of me.

I was in the throes of puberty when it was painted, and dear God, does it show. My face is entirely round, a burst of pimples scattered across my forehead that the painter tried and failed to transform into charming freckles. I'd begged Father not to make me sit for him. I wasn't daft. I knew what the girls were giggling about when I was forced to dance with them. I didn't want a record of the ugliest, most insecure period of my life hanging where everyone could see it. Father had laughed and said it was his house and he could do as he pleased with it. I've since grown into my looks, but I've never been able to fill the part of me he hollowed out.

Mamma returns in swirl of crimson brocade. "Your father's solicitor stopped by. He's done up the papers for you."

I whip toward her with a skeptical, narrow-eyed look. "What papers?"

Mamma's eyebrows lift. "Shall I read them to you?"

The implication that I'll take forever to read them myself—even though it's true—stings worse than the nettles. I take the stack and slowly leaf through them until three things become clear. The word "marriage," Giovannia's name, and a rich old man I vaguely remember nodding off at my father's parties.

"An ancient man wants to make a bride of my baby sister? Absolutely not!"

"She's fifteen. Hardly a child anymore. It gets her out of the house and cuts our expenses."

"Over my rotting corpse it does."

"Niccolo, you're nearly eighteen. You're the only man in the family. You've had your time to play at being an artist, and now it's time for you to be head of this household. It's what you were born to do."

Merda, not this again. "Don't call me that." I mean it to be a growl, but the words are a whisper. "It's Virgil."

We've been over this a dozen times, but she still doesn't get it. None of father's old business associates want to work with a boy who can barely read and do his sums. I've asked them. A job working with my hands is the best I can do, and it wouldn't be an issue if Father hadn't magnificently fucked us all over.

Before he died, my father had struck a deal with the Medici bank. Mortgaged Casa delle Volpi to pay for his final trading voyage, promising them a handsome cut of the profits. He was so confident it would work, even though other merchants had told him there were rumors of bandits in the mountains.

And when it didn't?

The Medici bank was more than happy to come collecting. They demanded the first payment the day after Father's burial, colder and less forgiving than winter's first frost. It was grueling, but when Niccolo had still been around, when he was running what was left of the family business, we could make the payments.

Since he's been gone? I'm barely keeping us afloat.

There's a series of frantic thuds overhead before my two younger sisters burst from the staircase. They tackle me from either side, shrieking. "You're back!"

I laugh and hug them. At fifteen, Giovannia looks more like a young woman than a girl, and Elisabetta is going through her own mortifying adolescent journey. And, Madonna santa, has she gotten taller? *Again?* The hem of her dress barely goes past her knees. "You need a trip to the tailor," I say, tapping her on the nose.

Elisabetta scrunches her face and pulls away, revealing my brother's old practice sword in one hand. "Mamma has already bought me dresses, but I don't like them!" She spins away, thwacking a chair with the flat of her blade. "No one's going to slay Cerberus in a *dress*!"

I swallow and try to keep my voice light, teasing. "Fighting is no pastime for young ladies." What would the neighbors think? Two of Lucrezia Pitti's children have already caused enough scandal. There doesn't need to be a third.

Elisabetta stops, cheeks going pink with anger. Giovannia tugs her arm before a fight can break out. "Mamma also bought us more poetry. Let's show Virgil, shall we?"

New dresses? New books? I bite the inside of my cheeks, feeling the expenses pile up like bricks.

"You were like that too, once," Mamma chides when the girls disappear. "Be more patient with them."

Niccolo would be.

Mamma is always making comments like this, not comparing me outright to Niccolo, but letting the words hang unsaid like rotting figs. The worst thing is that she's right. Niccolo would know what to do with Giovannia and Elisabetta, how to care for them and give them room to grow. The panic simmering in my stomach billows to a boil.

The first fall he was gone, I had dreams that he came back whole and unharmed. Sometimes he was married to a Napoletano princess. Sometimes he'd return with ink-stained fingers, a famous poet from the royal Valois court of France. In my dreams, he clasped my face and kissed my brow. I imagined him saying, *You were right, Virgil.*

But I always woke up before he could say the words. Even dream Niccolo knew the truth that I would never, ever share with anyone.

It's my fault Niccolo is gone.

Mamma's cold fingers are a jolt on my skin. For the first time, she appears concerned for me. "You could look for Niccolo again—"

I laugh bitterly, because of course she'd suggest that. Niccolo was as good at doing the right thing as I am at doing the wrong thing. If he were here, he'd find some handsome, age-appropriate boy for Giovannia to marry who just happened to be a minor prince.

But he's not here. He's either dead, or he's not coming home, and Mamma refuses to believe it.

"We all wish it was me missing and not Niccolo," I say. Mamma flinches like I've stabbed her with her own sewing needle. "But unfortunately, you're stuck with me, and I'm not marrying my sister off to a lecherous old geezer so she can be miserable like you were with Father!"

Mamma's mouth flops open like a dead fish's.

Behind us, a throat clears.

I turn around, and guilt runs me over like a wagon.

My sisters stand in the parlor carrying shiny new books. I can tell from how Elisabetta clutches Giovannia's elbow that they overheard all sorts of things they weren't supposed to hear.

Giovannia crosses her arms. "Sorry, who's getting married off to a gross old man?"

I choke and flush from head to toe.

Luckily, I'm spared from having to explain anything by a knock at the door. Mamma nods curtly to me like I'm one of her long-dismissed footmen. I open the door to a courier boy, his light brown cheeks pink with cold. "I bear a message, signore! Master Verrocchio bids you to return to the workshop. The new angel is arriving, and he requests your presence for the blessing."

Gesù Cristo, about time. The news stops up the cracks in my composure, lets me breathe fully for the first time since I saw the stone foxes.

Elisabetta's shoulders slump. "There's no time for poetry, then?"

"A pity, isn't it?" Mamma crumples up the betrothal papers with a shaking hand. Without my signature, they're useless to her.

My smile is brittle. "Perhaps next time, cara. Quick visit. More of an errand, really. See you soon?" Ignoring Elisabetta's shrieks of protest, I kiss her on the cheek.

"You'll come back next week?" she begs, her eyes two little moons.

Behind her, Giovannia turns away, already knowing my answer.

I try not to let it cut me. How the way I disappoint her is becoming so familiar, she knows precisely how I'll let her down before it happens.

I smile at Elisabetta instead, infusing the expression with all the aching, terrible warmth I can never quite put into words. "We'll see, all right?"

Hopefully, next week I'll have new bargain marks racing across my skin, and I'll be too busy to do anything other than work.

I'll be the breadwinner my family needs and not the brother they want.

'Tis the best I can do.

CHAPTER FOUR

Verrocchio's new angel is nothing like the old one.

My master turns to the priest, his bottom lip near torn to shreds. "Are you certain this is the angel for my workshop?"

The new angel hisses. All the men flinch. I can't exactly blame them.

This angel refuses to wear clothes and refuses to use a knife, choosing to bite everyone instead to draw their blood for the blessing that would bind her powers to us and us only.

The former might not have been a problem if the new angel had had the body of a wizened old man like the old angel, but she's female, perhaps about my age. Not even one of the apprentices can look at her without blushing furiously.

Tangled blond hair falls to her waist, mostly concealing her breasts but not nearly enough. And—dear God, are those *lice*? I shudder, feeling phantom insect legs on my scalp, but I refuse to look away like everyone else. The fairness of her hair is unsettling against the deep gold of her eyes. She reminds me of the nursing wolf Niccolo and I found in the hills outside the city walls. How the wolf rose, ghost-pale and still, her white teeth gleaming sharp in the den's darkness.

The old angel stuck to the shadows like a shade himself.

There is something wild and beating and *alive* in this one.

The priest's eyes flick toward the street. "If you are displeased with her, perhaps you should not have killed your previous angel."

Verrocchio's mouth thins. "He attacked my apprentices. I had no choice."

The priest flaps a hand, his meaning clear: *And your workshop has many apprentices but only one angel.* "This is the angel who came when we prayed for your workshop. She is young and powerful. Her magic will be worth the trouble of keeping her."

None of the other workshops have a girl angel. Is her rareness a mark of God's favor for Master Verrocchio or a sign of harrowing times to come?

Judging from the crooked frown on his face, I'd say Verrocchio is puzzling over the same question himself. He swallows and speaks carefully, not wanting to give insult to the holy priest and the church's work. "We are thrilled to receive such a . . . vivacious spirit into our midst, Father. I'm just not sure it's going to work out."

I suck in a sharp breath. Is Verrocchio thinking of sending this angel away for a different one? He can't! When the angel at Antonio del Pollaiuolo's workshop was taken away, it had taken *eighteen months* to bless them with a new one. My mother and sisters will be fighting rats for scraps on the streets long before that. I dig my paint-stained thumb into the stinging bite wound on my palm, thinking quickly. "Master Verrocchio! I would be glad to take over the angel's care until she's settled."

He spins around, his face brightening with hope. "Truly, Virgil? You would do this?"

"Of course, anything for the workshop." Behind Verrocchio,

Leonardo catches my eye and mimes gagging. My fingers itch to make a rude gesture back at him, but I heroically resist. So what if he thinks I'm currying favor? God knows he doesn't need any magic!

Besides, angels won't strike bargains with just anyone, and this angel looks very much like she'd love to set the workshop on fire and then dance barefoot in its ashes. It can't hurt to have her like me.

As if realizing that her fate has been decided, the angel turns to me and grins a scarlet-slicked smile.

I smile back and hope I'm not making a mistake.

CHAPTER FIVE

I hold up the length of emerald brocade again, hoping the fourth time will be the charm. My voice is cajoling, an inch shy of despairing. "This is a dress. You must wear it, please."

The angel's nose wrinkles. "Why?"

"Because you'll get cold."

"I do not get cold, see?" She grabs my hand and presses it to her bare shoulder. Her skin burns fever-hot. I jerk away, eyes sliding toward the kitchen door. There's no doubt all the servants are gathered behind it, listening and waiting to gleefully share every embarrassing failure of mine with the entire workshop as soon as possible.

"Well, perhaps you won't get cold, but it makes everyone feel better," I say.

"Why is that?"

"Because . . . people don't show their bodies to one another."

Her eyebrows rise incredulously. *"Ever?"*

I grimace, the purple mark on Leonardo's neck popping into my head. An image both unwelcome and unnecessary. "Only . . . only during very special circumstances."

She drums jagged, dirty fingernails against her chair's arm. "And what are these special circumstances?"

A blush finally overtakes my cheeks. "You'll know when they happen."

She lifts a finger and pokes my face, eyeing my blush with a frank, blunt curiosity that would be unspeakably rude coming from anyone else. "It seems inconvenient to have a body."

Well, there's no counterargument for that. I mash a hand against my brow. My sister Elisabetta refused to wear clothes for an entire summer, and I've drawn more nude women than I can count, but none of that prepared me for *her*.

"What about your name? Could you tell me that?" I ask, more than a bit desperately.

She sulks and hunches farther into her chair. "The man in the robes gave me a name. It is a bad name. I don't like it."

I smile coaxingly. "It can't be all *that* bad."

She plucks a loose thread on her chair and pulls. An embroidered rose slowly disappears from the fine upholstery. I watch it unravel with hopeless resignation, wanting to tell her to stop it, but afraid of what she'll do if I say so. "He called me Maddalena, but it is not my name. It belongs to someone else."

"Many people have the same name." Surely she knows this already . . . right? There are four Giovannis in the workshop.

She hisses and rips out the entire rose with one savage yank. *"It's not mine!"*

"All right, good God, I'm sorry! We'll—we'll call you whatever you want, then."

The angel stops assailing the embroidery, anger replaced by suspicion in an instant. "How do *you* know God? You're no angel."

"You're not the first person to say so." I swallow a smile. She's an angel, but there's nothing saintly or holy about this half-feral creature. It's . . . amusing, when it's not terrifying, or teeth-squealingly frustrating.

I realize I don't know what the old angel's name was and feel a pinch of guilt that I never thought to ask. He was so *different* from her. It's hard to believe they're the same type of creature at all, were it not for the gold gleam that shines in her irises when the light strikes them the right way. I can't stop thinking of the snarling wolf from my childhood. "Can I call you Lupa?"

"Lupa?"

"It means she-wolf. A wolf is an animal, a predator." I pause, not sure how honest I should be. "You remind me of one."

She unspools from the armchair, a muscle moving in her jaw. "Men fear this animal?"

My thumb runs along the tooth punctures on my palm. "If they know what's good for them."

The angel smiles delightedly, the expression baring each one of her pointed teeth. "I like Lupa. Choosing one's own name is allowed?"

I think of the day I shed being the third Niccolo Pitti like it was a too-small coat. Niccolo had read the poet Dante's *Inferno* to me and my sisters so much, the book's parchment had grown puppy-ear soft in the corners where we turned the pages. The ancient poet Virgil was Dante's companion through the underworld. I liked the idea of being someone who led people through the darkness. I like thinking I can still be that person.

I worried Niccolo would see the name I told Master Verrocchio to write in his ledger as a rejection of him, but he hadn't. He hugged me so hard, my bones cracked, and said, "I love it. You deserve to have something all yours."

What would he think of this girl angel?

Sometimes I miss my brother so much, the pain feels like a

gaping hole inside me. Even though I'm angry he left, ashamed I'm the reason why, bigger than the bad feelings is the ache of his absence. Each time I turn to him and he's not there is a savage kick, but the day turning to him isn't my first instinct anymore? It'll be a knife through my heart.

My voice grows rough. "I don't care if it's allowed or not! You can be whoever you want to be." Not wanting the angel to notice I'm shaken, I close my eyes and let out a long, measured breath. "I'll support you, even if you insist on being covered in lice."

The angel—Lupa—throws back her head and laughs. The sound comes from deep in her belly and fills the entire room, wild and impolite and so utterly right, that I feel my mouth lift.

There's a knock. Verrocchio's housekeeper stands at the door. "Signore, I have drawn water for a bath."

Lupa freezes. "What is a bath?"

My smile grows wider. "It's a very special circumstance. I think you'll like it."

Lupa settles into the hot water with a contented sigh, even uses the soap and washrag with my instructions. I take on her snarled, lice-ridden hair myself, letting the soap sink into the brassy strands before attacking them with a comb.

In the fire-warmed kitchens, surrounded by the scent of sage and lemon, I can almost pretend she's one of my sisters and not a divine being strong enough to tear out my throat with her bare hands.

"And you must scrub a body every week?" Lupa asks.

"Just your *own* body," I clarify, lest she get the wrong idea. "You must always ask someone before you touch them. That's an important rule to remember."

Lupa *hmms* and sinks lower into the bubbles. I brush her hair and pause. There's a ropey spiderweb of scars behind her ear, the tissue still pink.

A cold, uneasy feeling swirls through my chest. "What happened here?"

Lupa touches the scar. "I don't know."

"You don't remember? Or you don't know?" I fight to keep my voice even.

The quiet stretches longer and longer. Lupa keeps tracing the scar, one jagged fingernail digging in too deep. A bead of dark gold blood wells up.

"I think I was created this way." She twists to meet my gaze, unease on her face. "Is it wrong?"

Wrong? 'Tis impossible. I have never heard of an angel needing to recover from anything. Every time the old angel injured himself—often, in a workshop filled with knives and fire and jagged bits of marble—his wounds closed up with a gleam of gold, leaving behind nothing. This wound is obviously still healing.

I trace the scar, my touch featherlight. Why does she have this?

She's not yours to look after. This isn't your problem.

There must be a perfectly acceptable reason for it. Perhaps Lupa has not fully come into her powers yet. Didn't the priest say she was young? It must take time for angelic powers to settle. It would explain her feral nature, how she seems at once both so much wilder and so much more human than the old angel.

I begin to braid her hair. "There's nothing wrong, but if it bothers you, you tell me. All right?"

Lupa dips her head forward, pressing into my touch like a purring cat. "All right."

The pink, raw scar disappears beneath the braid. As her hair flies through my fingers, I can't help but wonder:

Why is Lupa so different?

And how soon will it be before I can make my next bargain with her?

CHAPTER SIX

Where's your shadow today?" Leonardo lifts on his toes and searches the street. "I thought you weren't allowed to go anywhere without her."

The city's artists have been summoned to attend a grand meeting at the city hall—the Palazzo della Signoria—to learn what sort of beautiful wonders the Medici seek for their latest celebration. Wedding bells will soon sing for the marriage of Lorenzo de' Medici, the twenty-year-old heir to the family's vast fortune and power.

This walk is the first bit of peace and quiet I've had for days, so of course Leonardo has to come and ruin it for me. "We both know angels aren't allowed to leave their workshops," I say crossly. "And Lupa isn't my shadow."

Except she *is.*

I thought getting the angel settled would mean giving her clothes, showing her where she would sleep, where we took our meals, but no. Lupa has become my full-time job.

She lurks outside my door each morning and follows me around all day, asking endless, unceasing questions.

Who painted the sky blue?

Why do humans eat deer but not dogs?

Why do your insides smell so sweet?

The last question stopped me the week before. I was despairing over the damn *Tobias and the Angel* painting, still unable to make the dog resemble anything approaching canine-like territory. Verrocchio had started asking pointed questions about what was taking me so long.

"It's my blood. You need it to live." I turned to Lupa, tugging up my sleeve to bare my black marks. My pulse lurched nervously, as if I were on the verge of my very first kiss. "Would you like to make a bargain with me? I want to make one with you." My voice lowered. "I could give you a day, a week. A memory, if you like that more."

I felt Leonardo go still behind me. I wished I could tell him to go away without revealing that I was paying attention to him.

The angel stepped closer, nostrils flaring. There was a scrape on my arm, a casualty of brushing too close to a jagged, unfinished sculpture. I gasped when her tongue flicked against my broken skin, quick as a cat. She pulled away, wiping her mouth with a grimace. "I don't want to right now."

My heart fell. I tugged my sleeve back down, feeling exposed, as if Leonardo had witnessed something embarrassingly intimate. "That's fine," I lied. "I'll ask again later."

We burst out from the narrow streets into the city hall's piazza. The sunlight flooding the open square blinds me.

"I finished the Tobias and angel painting," Leonardo says abruptly.

I stumble. "When?"

He grabs the back of my doublet, keeping me from falling. "When you were explaining to Lupa the difference between butter and gold during breakfast."

That sly stronzo! Master Verrocchio told *me* to finish the painting. If Leonardo did it instead, then the money from the commission will all go to him. Was this his plan the entire time? Distract me until the old angel died, and then swoop in to steal the glory and coin for himself?

This close to his face, his stupid freckles look like gold dust. The observation is a stone in my shoe—I can't ignore it again now that I've noticed it. Freckles are too friendly, too sweet. How can you hate someone covered in *freckles*? I push away from him with a growl. "Thanks for stealing my commission."

An unreadable expression flits across his face—one that looks awfully like hurt. "I told Verrocchio you did it."

My heart wrenches in the opposite direction, all my anger and disappointment crashing into nothing. *"Why?"*

Leonardo tugs a hand through his messy hair, mouth twisting. Only now do I notice the purple marks under his eyes, like he hasn't been sleeping. He's wearing the same tunic he wore yesterday, the one with the dark blue stain near the collar. He's not lying; he was definitely up early.

But he still hasn't answered my question.

My body winds tighter and tighter the longer he stays quiet. I start to wonder if he needs a physician. If he can't talk, something is wrong. He never shuts up, even when I beg him to.

His shoulders hitch with a big breath. "Because it matters more to you than me," he finally says.

Heat squirms under my skin. I didn't want—*hadn't* wanted—anyone to see what finishing this one project meant to me. How much of myself I was pouring into it, how little of a difference it was making.

I scowl up at him, resenting for the thousandth time the few inches he has over me. "I didn't need your help."

Leonardo laughs carelessly. "Too late."

My heart pounds furiously. "What do you want from me? No one's this self-sacrificing without a reason. What's yours?"

He surveys me, head tilted to the side. A breeze whips his hair across his face, and I want to push it aside to see his expression. We work together. We eat together. We're cursed to spend most of our waking hours together. But we're not friends. Friendship means laughter and ease, a slice of focaccia pulled apart by too many hands. It's not this itching, wretched feeling of *owing* someone. I haven't had a friend since Niccolo disappeared.

"I'd tell you," Leonardo says slowly, teasingly, "but I don't think you'd believe me."

Frustration slams though me. *"Why are you like this?"*

Pigeons scatter at my shout. A few people turn to look at us. Leonardo's smile tangles and falls. "You know what? I don't think I'll tell you after all."

"Fine!" I snap, like I don't deserve the cold treatment he's giving me. "Thanks for finishing the painting for me. It was nice of you."

Leonardo pats my head—*pats my head!*—and smiles again, bigger, brighter, and more irritating than ever before. "That was a very good first apology. Practice a bit more and I might even believe you next time."

Oh, damn his need to have the last word every single time! "Did you know that you are the most annoying person I have ever met, and I have *younger sisters*?"

I can count every tooth in his smile now. "Your compliments

could use some work too." He turns and gasps, grabbing my sleeve like I haven't just been a beastly shrew to him. "Do you see that?"

Too late, I realize it's not the sun that's blinded me, but bronze.

More than I've seen in my entire life.

CHAPTER SEVEN

A parade of bronze statues prances through the piazza—gods, warriors, lions, wolves—forming a path leading to the Palazzo della Signoria's open doors. A shadow flies overhead, a bronze stag whomping inches away. I see my shocked expression reflected in its blank eyes before it scampers off to join the others. I click my jaw shut, not wanting to gape like a peasant. This is . . . a breathtaking amount of magic. A Medici display of power and might if there ever was one.

The Palazzo della Signoria's rough-stone face juts into the piazza like a jaw braced for a fight. It's one of the oldest buildings in Florence, built long before the angels blessed us with beauty. Inside the interior courtyard rich blue-and-gold frescos adorn the walls behind the loggia. If I tip my head all the way back, I can just glimpse the palazzo's austere clock tower piercing the winter sky: the Torre d'Arnolfo.

Niccolo told me the Medici patriarch was once a prisoner inside it. 'Tis hard for me to believe there was ever a time when the Medici didn't rule our supposed republic. Their immense wealth has shaped Florence for years—making the city theirs in practicality if not in name. The thought leaves me sulky and bothered.

After Niccolo disappeared, I lurked outside their bank until the owner, Piero de' Medici, appeared. I threw myself on my knees and begged him for relief with Casa delle Volpi, but he only laughed and ruffled my paint-speckled hair like I was dog. "Your family made a deal with us," he said bluntly. "Pity it was a bad one. Let it be a lesson to you."

If the Medici can waste their money feting their son for his wedding, why couldn't they forgive the money a dead man owed them? What does adding one more crumbling house to their vast investments do for them? Owning Casa delle Volpi would mean nothing to them, but it would mean everything to us.

I can't help feeling there's a slimy, rotten core in their hearts. It must be why the Medici have never had an angel of their own. The holy beings must sense the wrongness in them too.

The artists mill in the palazzo's courtyard until after the church bells strike the hour. Then, with the chiming still humming through the air, the doors to the palazzo's innards burst open.

Piero de' Medici, the family patriarch, stands with his son Lorenzo. The crowd explodes into cheers; some artists even bow to the old man like he's a king. Piero indulgently lifts both hands, a grandfather welcoming his grandchildren. "Gentiluomini! My eldest son is marrying this summer. To celebrate this occasion, we need a wedding portrait, one worthy of the Medici name and gorgeous enough to make the angels weep! Each morning, we will unlock the palazzo's doors, and my Lorenzo will sit in this courtyard. Every workshop will send their very best artists to capture his likeness, and Lorenzo's bride shall choose the portrait she most likes when she arrives. Whoever paints the winning portrait will become my family's own personal painter and receive one hundred florins for his work!"

There's a feeling in my stomach like I'm falling. I sway, catching myself against Leonardo's arm. The courtyard's noise fades away, my head echoing with Piero's words, so loud, there isn't room in me for anything else.

One hundred florins?

It's an unthinkable sum. Far more than I've made after almost five years in Verrocchio's workshop. Even after the workshop's cut, it would be enough to buy Casa delle Volpi. Enough to dower my sisters with gold to marry princes.

Enough to change my life.

And to be the Medici's personal painter . . . it's not opening my own workshop, but 'tis close to it.

"Lorenzo will sit his first hour today, starting now." Piero's teeth flash. "I hope you came prepared."

Chaos unleashes. Some artists draw out linen and charcoal from their bags, others bark at their boys to sprint back to their workshops to grab supplies. Master Verrocchio circles his index finger, gesturing for us to flock around him.

"Ragazzi, this is a chance to prove yourself. Anyone who wishes to be considered will give me a sketch by the end of the week. The artist of the most promising one will enter the Medici commission." He takes a bag of charcoal from his belt with a wink. "May the best artist win!"

We fall upon the bag with a flurry of excited whispers and furtive glances.

"Four months isn't much time to complete a painting." Leonardo frowns.

Merda, I'm still leaning on him. I back off quickly and snag a charcoal stick. "Perhaps not for you."

Leonardo's eyebrows rise, and a lick of guilt lashes me. He fixed my millipede dog in a single morning. The same one I couldn't complete for weeks. Had *never* completed, because he did it for me.

"Sorry. That was uncalled for."

"It *was* rude," Leonardo agrees breezily. "But your apologies are getting better, so I'll forgive you if you give me your charcoal."

Master Verrocchio's bag is empty.

I clutch my stick tightly. Not sketching Lorenzo's likeness now will cost me a day, but Leonardo did do me a favor, and I've done nothing but snarl at him for it. It was, objectively, a nice thing for him to do, even though I hate that he did it.

A bargain can help you make up for the lost time.

Perhaps a month of my life for a week of perfect memory. Then I'd only need to see Lorenzo once.

I unclench my fist and let the charcoal fall. "Happy to."

Leonardo catches the stick with a smirk. "Why, thank you, Virgil. Has the new angel broken the curse that turned your heart to stone?"

I turn away with an annoyed wave and try not to let the words slip under my skin.

A lesser artist would give up, but not me. The Medici have been de facto rulers of Florence for so long, some of their personal art collection must have snuck its way inside the government palazzo. I can look at it and get a better sense of what they like, learn how to create something that feels familiar yet fresh.

When no one is looking, I go through the unlocked doors into the palazzo's halls. I have a feeling I'm not allowed here, but I wasn't explicitly told *not* to explore either.

I scurry down the corridors, poking my head through the open doors. Endless offices and parlors and receiving rooms, the stone walls outside them bare and boring. Finally, two grand double doors etched in filigreed gold catch my eye. With a surreptitious look over my shoulder, I test one of the handles.

Unlocked.

This room is the largest one and filled with dark wood benches, enough for a hundred people. I ease inside slowly, grinning at the rows and rows of portraits on the walls. Finally!

They aren't exceptional pieces, but it's striking how similar they are, all of them squares in simple wooden frames. Some are so old and dusty, I can barely make out the faces, but a few still stink with the egg smell of fresh tempera paint. The subjects themselves are . . . interesting. Most of the men look frightened or angry, or both. Are these portraits of politicians? It would explain both the ugliness and the location, but there are more than nine portraits here, and only nine elected officials hold office at once. They must be of something else, but what?

The opening and closing of a nearby door tugs me from my thoughts. It doesn't matter who these men are. The portraits aren't the inspiration I'm looking for, unless I want Lorenzo's bride to feel sad and bored when she sees my painting.

I move to leave, but a flash of red catches my eye.

I turn.

And gasp.

I lift trembling fingers and trace the familiar cheekbone, the smile I know better than my own. The one I'd recognize anywhere.

Niccolo.

My missing brother.

On the wall of the most important building in Florence.

CHAPTER EIGHT

Niccolo was *here*.

My hand clenches the canvas, as if I can reach in and pull him from the frame. Every punch of my heart scrapes bone.

It's unmistakably him, down to the red cloak he wore the day he disappeared.

I will never forget the swirl of red against the snow when I last saw him. Even then, I wanted to take every horrible word I'd said and stuff them back into my lungs. But pride had grabbed my throat and held me still.

I trace the lines of his face. Without the cloak, I still would've known the sweep of his jaw, the green in his hazel eyes, the very same as mine.

Hope, raw and wild, claws through me, tears open my mind to a possibility I smothered long ago.

Is he still alive?

My knees thud to the floor, unable to hold me up.

It makes no sense for him to be alive, but not to be with us.

Niccolo knew how bad things were after Father's death. He would never have left us to face them alone. He knew I couldn't do it. He's better than me, kinder and stronger in all the ways that matter. It's why I never believed Mamma when she said he was still out there alive. He'd never leave us alone unless he was dead.

But impossibly, a portrait of Niccolo is *here*. Why?

"Signore, may I help you?"

A man hovers over me, clad in the red and ermine-trimmed robes of an elected official.

I scramble upright and away from the portrait like I've been caught palming a rich woman's jewels. I want to flip the canvas over to see if there's an artist's signature. I want to demand why the portrait is here, ask this man if he knows or has ever heard of Niccolo Pitti.

"Well?" the man demands. He glares at me like I'm in trouble, but behind his annoyance, there's a keen, near fevered curiosity. A wrongness whispers across the back of my neck.

"I got lost," I lie, lifting my charcoal-stained hands like, *Just a feckless artist over here!*

The man's smile curves, his eyes flicking toward the two green-liveried guards lurking near the entrance. "The doors were closed."

The guards inch closer.

I bow, clasping my hands to hide how they tremble. "Forgive me. I'm searching for inspiration worthy of a wedding portrait."

The man's expression hardens. "Come with me. You've seen enough of the palazzo for one day."

Having no choice, I follow him, head bowed, murmuring apologies. I don't dare glance at Niccolo's portrait on the way out, even though every single bit of me screams to turn around, tear the canvas from the wall, and start running.

I need this man to assume I'm just some lost artist, cloud-brained and harmless.

I need to be forgotten so I can come back.

I *need* to earn the wedding portrait commission now. It's the only way back into the Palazzo della Signoria. Everything in this building is here for a purpose: the beautiful frescos in the courtyard, the statues guarding the doors.

There's a reason Niccolo's portrait is here, and I'm going to find out what it is.

And then . . . maybe I can find him.

The thought snatches the very air from me.

The man takes me down a long staircase and opens a side door. He tips his chin toward the piazza beyond, mouth still hard. I bow once more, trying to make the gesture look extra penitent.

I wait until I hear the snick of the door locking behind me before I start running.

Pigeons erupt into panicked flight, curious heads turn to follow me, but I ignore them all. I race back to Master Verrocchio's workshop as fast as I can, my lungs ragged sacks of linen, my heart near thundering out of my chest. When I burst through the studio's door, the workshop is empty. Everyone else is still at the palazzo.

Except for Lupa.

The angel uncurls herself from her place near the fire. "Virgil?"

I stagger toward her, tugging up the sleeve on one forearm, slipping the knife from my belt with the other. "Make a bargain with me," I pant, each word tasting of blood. "A month of my life for a week of perfect memory." Verrocchio needs to pick me for the wedding commission. I need to be able to paint again. I need my magic back.

A soft breath shudders from her. She traces the black marks

along my forearm, lingering on the most recent one. I press the blade to the empty space beside it. My skin whitens under the pressure. "I know you hunger for life. I've seen the way you look at me."

Lupa's fingers skate along my blade. I wince as the knife sinks into me under the barely there pressure. I bite the inside of my cheek, bracing myself for the welling blood, the heady rush of magic. Striking a bargain always feels like holding my breath underwater for a second too long. A blackness in my vision—and then a fierce golden light.

Lupa eases up her touch before my skin breaks. "No."

"Why not?" I can't fail again. Niccolo, my future, all of it hangs just out of reach. A single kiss of the knife is all I need to seize it. I'll give Lupa whatever she wants. A year of my life, five of them. I need the edge magic will give me over everyone else. I need to be the best.

My entire world spins around Lupa's gold-green irises. Her hands rise to cup my face. Her thumb brushes away the dampness from my cheeks. "I can't do it, because I like you more than anyone else."

That's why she won't do it? From some softhearted desire not to hurt me? "Angels don't have feelings!"

She flinches like a frightened hound. I should apologize, but I don't. Everyone else knows I'm cold, and it's about time she learns it too.

Lupa's fingers trail down along my neck, her pointed nails lingering on the leap of my jugular beneath the tender skin. Her eyes darken hungrily. I swallow and lift my chin higher. I press her pointed nails into my hot skin, yearning for the ache of my own splitting skin. I would give her anything, everything.

And then, impossibly, she steps away.

Each one of her next words drops like a stone into my soul. "I won't do it because you have less than a year left of life. If you make another bargain, you will die."

CHAPTER NINE

After Niccolo disappeared, sometimes I'd go to one of the bridges straddling the Arno River and stare into the rush below. I'd wonder if it would be so bad if it sucked me under.

I wasn't going to act on the thought. But if it happened, if someone accidentally pushed me, I might not try to catch myself on the way down.

Having less than a year feels like staring into the darkness again. It's impossible to believe that next winter I won't be here, that each meal I eat or snowflake I catch on my tongue could be my last.

"What's wrong with you?" Leonardo demands after we spend an entire day sharing a workbench and I don't complain a single time. "You *hate* it when I bounce my leg!"

Was he doing that? I barely remember. "Are you . . . complaining that I didn't complain?"

He scowls and gestures to me with both hands, as if all of me is the problem. "For the past week, you've barely eaten. You've barely talked. You barely even work anymore, which is more my thing than yours, by the way. You're going around looking like someone died!"

I shrug and don't say anything. With a big, gusty sigh and

something that sounds suspiciously like "That's what you get for being a concerned citizen," he leaves me.

Being alone doesn't make me feel better. And he has a point. My moping is becoming noticeable, and I don't want anyone to know what I've done. Magic was supposed to save me, and now that it's damned me, I can't stop feeling a bit like a jilted lover, my betrayed shock a shameful secret to hide.

To show that I'm perfectly fine, I make sure to cheer extra loud when Master Verrocchio announces that Leonardo has won the Medici wedding painting commission, although the news makes my heart clench. I couldn't bring myself to start a sketch for it.

Even Lupa notices I'm not myself.

"You seemed to care about painting the Medici boy a lot, and now you do not care at all," she says. "Why?"

I kick a rock down Via dell'Agnolo, not looking at her. I'm heading to one of the apothecaries where Master Verrocchio sources his painting pigments. It's on a rougher edge of town, a fair walk from the workshop through narrow streets and hunched stone buildings. "If you must follow me, can you at least hide the fact that you're not human?" Angels aren't supposed to leave their workshops.

Huffing, Lupa flips up her cloak's wool hood. "Only if you answer."

"I didn't see the point."

Lupa's frown deepens. "Why? You are not dead yet."

I whirl to face her. "Right, but I *will* be. So why start anything new?"

She blinks, unfazed by my angry outburst. "Humans die so

easily, all of the time. If I had not told you how much time you had left, would you still be afraid of dying?"

I'm not afraid of dying! But I can't force it out. It's not a lie, but it's not the entire truth, either.

I'm afraid of leaving my family destitute. I'm terrified of not being able to find Niccolo before I'm gone. But the reason why I can't do more than glide through the remains of my life like a ghost? It's so shameful and small in comparison.

I thought I'd have a long, successful career as an artist, and now I'm going to die before I can sign my own damn name on a single painting.

Every time I want something for myself, it's yanked away as soon as it starts to feel like a real possibility. Opening my own workshop. Finding my brother. The moment I see a path forward, a gate with spikes on the bottom plummets in my way. I don't know why this keeps happening to me. The unfairness makes me want to scream.

"I'm afraid of failing my family." 'Tis the easiest answer: one I don't have to explain.

Lupa brightens. "Because of the gold! The kind you don't eat."

Never mind. Some explanation is obviously needed. "They need it to keep living in their house."

"Do they, though? We could gather sticks for them, like the birds in the workshop."

"No, bird nests and people houses are different."

Lupa sighs explosively and crosses her arms. "So many rules! It would be better if there were fewer of them."

"Undoubtedly." I gnaw my bottom lip, keen and frightened to ask the question that's burned through me for days. "On the subject of rules . . . you said I'm out of life. Would you take my memories instead for magic?"

For all my bargains struck, I've never once parted with a memory. Memory is too delicately stitched into the fabric of being human to be ripped out like a seam. One of Verrocchio's artists, wild with grief, bartered away the memory of his deceased wife for the ability to always know which colors a painting needed. But gradually, his vivid canvases grew dull, and by the end of the year, he could only paint in shades of gray. He cried softly at his easel, trying to remember what it was that once filled his life with brightness. He was gone a month later. Verrocchio never told us if he had quit or died, but I had my suspicions.

Lupa shakes her head. "No, they are not different like you think. Memory is life already lived. If I take anything more from you, you will die."

Angels can't lie, so I know she's telling me the truth, but I feel like part of it is missing.

"You should live as though you don't know you are dying," Lupa says. "That is what everyone else does."

"I don't know how." My confession is soft, barely a whisper.

She shrugs, as if the discussion of my untimely, tragic death bores her. "Ask the da Vinci boy to let you help with the painting for the Medici if it means so much to you."

My stomach jolts like I missed a step and everyone saw me stumble. "No jests. Haven't you heard I'm dying?"

"He likes to be helpful."

"He likes to be meddlesome. It's much different."

Lupa stares. An ancient, thousand-yard, dead-eyed expression we've been working on teaching her not to do because it unsettles people. "Be honest with him and he will say yes. You are like a cat everyone wants to pet, but who always has his claws out. Where is the harm in asking?"

I am supposed to drop dead sometime this year, so she has a point. But what Lupa doesn't understand is that there are a hundred other ways to die. Asking for help feels like one of them. Asking *Leonardo* for help feels especially horrible. He doesn't know what it's like to work hard only to fall flat on his face in the end.

If he had to, Niccolo would ask his least favorite person for help. I groan and rub my temples, feeling sulky and cornered. "What do you know about cats? You barely know how to use a fork."

Lupa's pointy teeth bare in . . . a smile? I'm not certain, but it's worse than her long, dead stare. We'll have to go over appropriate human facial expressions again. "If you do not do something to help yourself when we return, I will pee on your bed, also like a cat. Your moping bothers me."

"Oh, apologies my melancholy offends you, Your Holiness!" I place a hand on my chest, my face remorseful and penitent. "How rude of me. Your time on earth really should be all fun and games."

"It should be," she says without a trace of irony.

We emerge into a dead-end piazza. A cracked fountain sputters against the city wall at the end, its marble gray with filth above the water and streaked with green beneath. The Neptune in the center stares with dull, unseeing eyes. There's not a smidge of magic in this sculpture. Nor care, either, judging from the cracks already splintering through it.

But the fountain's state doesn't seem to matter to the dozens and dozens of people crushed around it, all of them filling up kitchen pails with the unclean water. A ripple goes through the crowd at the sight of Lupa, a rolling whisper that makes the hair on my arms rise.

"Angel, angel. An angel has come among us . . ."

Someone jostles me, sharp elbows against my soft side. "A girl," the woman whispers, lifting her dusty hands toward Lupa. "The angel is a girl!"

Mouth thinning, I push past her and place Lupa's hand firmly in the crook of my elbow. I don't like the shine in the woman's eyes. It reminds me of the priest's when he really gets going on a good bender about how all sinners are going to hell.

"We're going to leave."

Lupa peers into my empty basket. "You didn't get the pigments."

I keep a tight hold on the basket, angling it into the crowd. "Someone can get them later."

After I get her safely back to the workshop.

A woman in a torn skirt throws herself on her knees, a crying baby clasped in her arms. "Please, angel! My daughter won't stop coughing. You must save her."

Lupa recoils. Even in the shadow of her cloak's hood, her golden irises shine that unnatural green. There's no hiding what she is here or anywhere else in Florence. "What is this pink squalling thing? It is too loud!"

"Please!" The woman thrusts her baby closer. She uncovers one plump arm and sinks her fingernail into it until the skin breaks. The little girl starts screaming, a thin, high sound that puts a lump in my throat. "Let her bargain with you!"

The crowd spills closer, a sea of desperate faces and grabbing hands.

"We ran out of food already this winter—"

"His leg took a fever—"

"Bargain with me, please, angel—"

The demand grows like a rising tide. One man cuts his forearm, then another. The scent of iron fills my nostrils, a tang I taste as much as smell. The crowd presses closer, scarlet-slick wounds offered to the angel like shining, fat olives.

The tip of Lupa's tongue runs over her pointed teeth, her awful stare on everyone and no one. "Can you taste it too, Virgil?" She whimpers, her nails digging into my arm so hard, I gasp. "They taste *so good.*"

The lump in my throat hardens. Giorgio's terrified face flashes across my mind. I feel the awful spray of the old angel's hot gold blood on my face again.

Even though my brain screams not to let the angel go, I drop Lupa's arm and beat the crowd away with my basket. "She can't help you! Leave us alone!"

I don't know if Lupa would hurt anyone, and I won't find out. I told Verrocchio I'd look after her. It's the one promise I haven't broken yet.

The crowd scatters, only to regroup just out of range, surly and muttering.

A girl with soot-stained cheeks slinks forward. She sneers at the paint stains on my hands, the bargain marks disappearing up my sleeves. "It's not fair you artists can make bargains, but we can't!" There's a chorus of jeering agreement, the sound like a kettle approaching a boil.

My blood starts rushing. I get why they're angry, but it's not up to me who angels make bargains with. "If you're ill and hungry, there's a hospital nearby—"

She spits at my feet. A knife gleams in her hand. "We'll take her for ourselves!"

I throw the basket at her face, grab Lupa's hand, and run.

I hit the wall of people shoulder-first. Cries of pain and surprise surround us, then a clearing opens up. I take it, zigzagging past the final man who tries to block us with a jagged-toothed saw.

I don't stop running until we're outside the towering walls of the Cattedrale di Santa Maria del Fiore. I let go of Lupa and double over on the steps, hands braced on my knees, eyes locked on the street.

The crowd doesn't follow.

I didn't think they would, but Cristo santo, the *misery* in their eyes. Someone that desperate could do anything.

Lupa draws her cloak more securely around her body, her strange eyes flicking from me to where we came from. "What was that?" she demands shrilly.

"Oh, that? We call that one 'an angry mob.'"

She scowls. "It felt bad. Please don't create one again."

Right. As if I were the one they wanted. I will my galloping heart to slow. Each too-fast beat feels like a grain of sand tumbling from an hourglass, a pointless waste of life. "Were you going to eat those people?"

She bristles, offended. "Angels don't eat people."

"You know what I mean."

She shudders again, tongue tracing her teeth. "I wanted to taste their blood." A guilty look thrown my way. "But I wouldn't have."

Not quite the reassuring answer I wanted, but I let it go. "I suppose we learned the hard way why angels shouldn't leave their workshops."

"Why did you help?" Lupa demands.

I grimace and drag a hand through my dark curls. I don't like her tone—as if I'm someone who steals food from hungry children or kicks puppies. "They were trying to hurt you. Protecting the workshop's angel is a vital duty."

She pushes up on her toes and kisses my cheek. "Thank you."

My hand flies over the spot. There's a curious, helpless pull in my chest. "You're welcome?"

She nods like she's the one who saved me. "Stop this moping and choose to live. I like you, Virgil Pitti. You're my friend."

And even though her words are trite, even though I worry that the workshop's only nonhuman starting to feel like a friend isn't a good thing, there's a little burst of warmth in my chest anyway.

I offer her my arm to take her home. "I'll try."

CHAPTER TEN

After the plates and food are cleared from dinner, I go to Leonardo's room, but he's not there.

Although he *could* be. There is enough mess to hide at least three Leonardos. The desk is an unspeakable wreck of papers, charcoal, and old paintbrushes, some of them snapped, some of them ruined with dried-on paint. The bed is a snarl of blankets, pillows, and clothes, the linens stretching halfway up the wall. The floor is littered with torn bits of paper, crumbs. I even spot a spider weaving a web that rivals the grandness of the duomo itself. When I step inside, one of Verrocchio's garden cats leaps from its hiding place through the open window. Madonna santa, he lets them *sleep* here? I grimace and try not to sneeze.

It seemed better to talk to Leonardo here, where no one could see me or hear me, but being in his room feels too intimate, and waiting outside the door feels desperate.

I don't know why Lupa is so convinced he'll help me. Leonardo is many things, but I wouldn't say helpful is among them. Sure, yes, he helped me once, but *only* once. When it's time to rinse off the brushes, he's mysteriously ill. When someone must sweep the workshop floors, it's his day off. He does exactly what he wants to do, and nothing more. Begging him to make helping me one of the things he wants to do causes my palms to sweat, my heart to crawl along the bottom of my stomach.

What if he says no?

Then I'll have groveled for nothing, and he'll lord it over me forever. It would crush me.

I move to wait outside the door and knock into a bookcase I didn't see behind me. An avalanche of paper flutters to the floor, all of them sketches in various stages of doneness.

I kneel to pick them up.

And freeze when I see what they are.

Figure drawings, dozens and dozens of them. People in piazzas, people in cafés.

People in bed.

Those make my cheeks hot. There is nothing obscene about them, but the attention of each careful line, the delicacy of the details, feels astonishingly intimate, too private for my pillaging eyes.

So he *does* practice, even though he pretends not to. Is this what he does when he ditches our morning lessons? Why not just tell Master Verrocchio, so he'd stop punishing his lateness with chores? Each sketch is arresting, alive, even the half-finished ones. Sadness in the slant of the light, a declaration of love in heavy-lidded eyes. It's as if he captured part of his subjects' souls with charcoal and paper.

My insides lurch at the thought of what he would see if he ever turned his artist's eye on me.

I gather the sketches and return them to the shelf. But there are piles more, and my brain must be broken, because I can't stop from rifling through the others. One shelf is all insects. Another is different fish. One entire stack is different parts of a rose, rendered so clearly, I could be holding the flower in my hand. I sift through them all, brow furrowing. There are enough sketches here to paper the workshop's walls twice over. This must be a passion project of Leonardo's, one done at the expense of his actual, paying job.

Promising myself I'll be done after this, I lift one stack halfway, just barely glimpsing a familiar-looking face—

"Virgil!"

Leonardo explodes through the open doorway, his face wild.

I leap back from the bookcase like it's on fire. Madonna santa, there is no good reason for me to be in his room. Mortifyingly, it was I who created the rule about not trespassing in other apprentices' spaces without their consent. Leonardo thought it was ridiculous when it happened (*What if someone's hoarding all the best brushes, and I want to paint, Virgil? What then?*), so to mark the occasion he scrawled *ABANDON ALL HOPE, YE WHO ENTER HERE* above the door leading to my attic, which was undeniably rude of him, but at the same time, almost thoughtful, given how I felt about having my privacy.

Except now he's caught me snooping through sketches he doesn't want anyone else to see, or he would've shown them to us forever ago. If he did the same to me, I'd never let him live it down, and we both know it.

My nails dig painfully into my palms.

I've found my cause of death. Not a horrible accident or a wasting illness, but the humiliation of Leonardo rightly roasting me every day until I finally walk into the Arno River.

I lick my chapped lips and force my eyes to meet his. "Look. I'm sorry, I can explain—"

"I've been looking everywhere for you." He talks over me like I've said nothing. He stumbles forward, grabbing both my wrists. "I need your help."

I gasp at the coldness of his fingers. He's never touched me before, unless he was trying to jostle me out of the way for the best workspace each morning. Perhaps I didn't just bump into his bookcase: It fell down and crushed me, and this is the very first level of my own personal hell. "What are you talking about?"

He squeezes my wrists, brow divoting. "I need your help with the Medici wedding portrait. I can't do it alone."

I glance at the bookcase to see if it's still there and not pinning my broken body to the floor and drowning me in an avalanche of Leonardo's saucy sketches, but no, it's still standing.

"You want my help?" Because I'm supposed to be asking *him* for help.

Leonardo nods vigorously, red-blond hair flying.

We stare at each other some more while I wait for what he said to make sense.

"You remember I can't paint right now, right?" I say. There's no way I could possibly be useful to him. He's the one who bailed me out of my last deadline.

The stairs creak behind us. I yank myself from Leonardo's grip before someone sees us holding hands and making prolonged eye contact. Unlike the good God-fearing masses, no one in Master Verrocchio's workshop cares who fornicates with whom, but I'd rather die than have anyone think I might care for him that way.

"It's best if you don't pick up a brush or charcoal or anything. I haven't forgotten the millipede dog," Leonardo says.

"All right?" His explanation isn't making anything clearer.

He collapses against the wall, rubbing his temples. "I just need you there while I do it, really. Maybe offer some thoughts here and there."

"That doesn't really sound like me helping."

"No, it is," he says. "'Tis odd, but . . . I do my best work when another person is around. Trying to work on that portrait while the competition stares over my shoulder—" He blows out a breath and drags a hand through his hair. "I get all in my head about it and can't do anything."

This almost makes sense, except . . . "*I'm* the person who makes you relax enough to work?"

Unless I'm very much mistaken, our entire relationship is based on mutual dislike and a begrudging respect for the other's talents. I can't imagine a world where I'm the person Leonardo wants at his side, unless we're both being kidnapped by Venetian pirates, and he plans to use me as a convenient distraction to escape.

"Verrocchio also told me if I don't finish this painting, he might have to kick me out," Leonardo adds sheepishly. "I haven't finished any of my work yet this year."

Ah, so here's the real reason he wants me around. I snort, thinking of how many mornings I saw the love marks on his neck and his kiss-bruised lips. "Surely *someone* would take you in."

He crosses his arms and frowns. "If you're going to be a monster about it, don't bother." His eyes drag to mine. They're a deep umber, and the room is too dark for me to see what he's really feeling. "Will you come with me tomorrow or not?"

I tap my chin, pretending to consider the offer, then nod. I don't want to seem too eager to work with him, even though inside, I'm soaring. I didn't have to ask Leonardo for help—he begged me to help him. I sidestepped the whole being-honest nonsense and got what I wanted. About time some good fortune fell into my lap!

Someone coughs delicately.

Lupa stands behind Leonardo in the corridor, a grumpy tortoiseshell-colored cat in her arms. She must've been the person who came up the stairs, and she was clearly listening to our conversation. She catches my eye and lifts her brows meaningfully. She nods at the cat in her arms, and then toward the stairs to my attic. The threat is clear: If I'm not honest with Leonardo, she really will piss on my bed like a cat. Sod it all to hell.

Sighing, I drag my hands down my face. "I wanted to ask you for a favor too."

Leonardo's entire presence shifts into a higher key. "Oh, really now?"

Even with Lupa's threat, it's hard to force the words out. "I know I don't share much about myself—"

He snorts. "A grave understatement. You're a strongbox someone's chained shut and buried—"

"But do you remember when my brother disappeared two years ago?"

He sobers at once. "Of course I do. That was awful."

An heir's disappearance from a wealthy merchant's family was sensational news. Vanished, without a note or a record of where he'd gone! His poor mamma and siblings! Could you believe it? Verrocchio gave me the space I needed afterward, but the other apprentices hadn't. They were filled with questions, as if my brother's disappearance was a story they were eager to read, and not my actual life. I endured as much as I could before snarling that if anyone ever brought up Niccolo again, I'd snap their smallest finger. I immediately felt like a monster, but no one bothered me afterward. Come to think of it, I feel like I remember Leonardo shepherding more zealous boys away from me when they inched closer. The memory makes me feel awkward now—like I shouldn't have forgotten it.

"Right. Well, since then, I've been supporting my mother and sisters financially. If we won this wedding commission—assuming you're fine with splitting the prize money—it would help." Fifty florins isn't enough to buy Casa delle Volpi outright, but it would be enough for a substantial payment on the outstanding balance. "I think . . . I think if you're struggling to paint, and I'm struggling to paint, we could do better work together than we could apart." My throat tightens. I barely manage to get the truth out before I choke on it. "I needed this commission so badly, and I was too scared to even try to get it."

Leonardo doesn't need to know that my brother might be alive on top of this. This is quite enough soul-baring for today.

Leonardo's voice sounds far away, even though he's right before me. "Obviously we'd split the prize money, Virgil. I'm not interested in hoarding wealth like your merchant family is." The joke is gentle, just the amount of levity the situation needs to not be weird anymore.

I cross my arms with a huff. "You try telling your mamma to wear muslin instead of velvet."

His grin unspools like honey. "I wouldn't dare. A woman's will is not to be trifled with." He sticks out a freckled hand. "Seems like we got a bargain, then."

The word hits me strangely, the new context a shape the familiar doesn't quite fit into. It's hard to imagine a bargain made without blood, without me giving something up in return. I clasp Leonardo's hand and finally meet his eyes. "And we'll both get what we want from it." Ideally before this time next year, when I'll be too dead to enjoy our successes.

The corner of his mouth lifts. When he pulls away, his thumb brushes the skin on the back of my hand. "I certainly hope so."

CHAPTER ELEVEN

"So anyway, if humans can swim in water, then it makes sense there's a way for them to fly in air—oh, whoops!" Leonardo careens into me, and the charcoal bag tumbles from my hands. When he bends to pick it up, he drops a stack of paper. It hits the cobblestones and scatters, skittering toward a puddle of what we can only hope is water and not piss. I race to stop it, but too late.

I shake my head at the soggy mess. "It's all ruined."

It's early—far too early—for a full-energy Leonardo. The time just after dawn is for silence and contemplation, not whatever he's prattling on about.

"Well, I wouldn't have dropped it if you hadn't walked into me," he says.

Yes, 'tis far too early for this. "*You* were the one who walked into *me*."

Leonardo sighs. "Does it really matter if we both have to tell Verrocchio it's ruined?"

"Yes!" I say hotly, knowing very well that our master docks our paychecks for supplies ruined from carelessness. "Yes, it obviously does!"

Verrocchio was already annoyed we were both working on the Medici commission. I'd expected him to say no when Leonardo grabbed my sleeve and marched to his office, me protesting and dragging my feet the entire time, positive our plea would never work, but apparently, Verrocchio is as capable of being charmed by Leonardo as anyone else.

"As long as both of you get the rest of your work done." He made sure to make eye contact with me as he said it, which wasn't stressful at all. As if I were the person who was able to get Leonardo to do anything he didn't want to do.

"You're getting older, and it's time for both of you to think of the future," Verrocchio added.

Leonardo went still. "What do you mean?"

"Why, you don't want to be an apprentice here forever, do you?"

Forever. The word sank down into my soul, making me quiet for the rest of the day.

Four sour-faced guards let us into the Palazzo della Signoria. Even though we left early, the courtyard is already crowded with other artists furiously sketching a yawning, half-asleep Lorenzo de' Medici. Leonardo manages to smash the bag of charcoal and knock over his stool as he gets settled, earning reproachful looks from everyone else. When he finally sits down, he hesitates, eyes roaming over the other artists nervously. Instead of picking up his charcoal, he's twisting that curl of his lover's hair around his finger again. What does he do with it when he bathes? Put it on the floor beside him like a hair ball? Disgusting.

"I'm not sure I can get much done like this," he says a quarter hour later, having not drawn a single thing. "I don't think there's enough time."

A burst of annoyance goes through me. I've put in my own valiant effort to sketch the Medici heir, but my Lorenzo looks like he's in the final, excruciating stages of a wasting illness. Leonardo needs to draw *something* if we're to have any hope of winning. "This is why we practice every morning! If you ever came, then maybe you could do this. Or if you made a bargain with Lupa."

He shudders. "I'm afraid of blood. I've told you that."

He has, and I couldn't believe it. Angels and art went together like money and Medici. Like bread and butter. I'm beginning to regret not talking through the details of our so-called bargain before we shook on it. "You didn't seem afraid of blood when you plunged the knife into your arm to save Giorgio."

He lifts his index finger, mouth open. Then he shuts it, brushing the white scar on his arm. "That was different."

"How?" I demand.

Leonardo shoots me a rare frown. "You know, I think you're the problem today."

"Fine! I'll leave, then." I throw up my hands and walk away. He's impossible. Talented, but impossible. At least being his moral-support person is only half the reason I'm here. If he wants to be alone, then it's time to find my brother's portrait again.

I've worn my nicest clothes, and, after making sure the guards are all looking elsewhere, I slip through a side door leading deeper into the government building. There are hushed voices behind closed doors, men deep in conversation in shadowy corners. When I pass them, I nod confidently, shoulders high, like I belong there as much as they do.

A painting of a grisly battle hangs in the space between two offices. The men silently war on the canvas, wielding blades and shedding blood in an endless battle. I sidle closer to the magicked painting and whisper, "Pardon me, I'm looking for a big room with wooden benches. Do you know where it is?"

A wounded soldier raises his severed leg and points it toward a door behind me. I murmur my thanks and move on.

Down a hall, up a staircase, through another corridor, and—yes!—at the end are double doors etched in filigreed gold. My hand tingles when I grab the boar's-head-shaped knob. Anticipation surges through me as the door swings open—

I blink at the blank walls.

There are paler rectangles on the stone, the sign of frames recently taken down. There had been rows and rows of them. I could understand moving one or two, but *all* of them?

I walk to where I think Niccolo's portrait hung. I caress the empty space, as if the cold stone could give me answers, a chill prickling the nape of my neck.

It seems unlikely that the portraits were moved because I'd stumbled across my brother's, but . . . I can't shake the feeling that that's exactly what happened.

With one final glance at the barren wall, I slip back into the corridor.

I return to a room with broken chairs and tuck a busted wicker seat under my arm. Then I take a tapestry and wrap it around the chair seat.

I roam through the palazzo until I find the person I need.

"Excuse me!" I hold up the wrapped seat. "I found this portrait. It must've been left behind when the art was moved."

"What are you talking about?" The servant squints, as if he's trying to place me and can't. I swallow and keep my face bland. Agonizing seconds tick by before he finally sighs. "Oh right, that. Come with me, then."

He leads me upstairs—farther up than I've gone before—to another set of double doors paneled with exquisite wood carvings of the Last Judgment. Seems an odd choice for a government office. But perhaps God condemning people to hell is a perfect metaphor for our republic. I wouldn't know. I'm paid to paint, not do politics.

". . . so you're ready to go," the servant says.

Madonna santa, I've missed everything he said. He's already turning around, and asking him to say it all again would make me memorable, so I thank him and lift one of the heavy doors to slip inside.

High ceilings greet me, along with an excellent view of the piazza below. Rows of cabinets line the wall across from the windows, the shelves stuffed with fat ledgers. There's a throne-like chair at one end of the room and a circle of chairs and tables around it. Opposite the throne is a huge painting of a gray-bearded man emerging from pink-and-gold clouds. Something about his face looks almost familiar, but judging from how strapping he is, he must be God. Florentines love a muscular holy father, but even by their standards, this one's a bit tasteless.

The tables are chaos, every surface covered with loose papers, baubles, and—yes—a pile of linen-wrapped squares the size of my torso. I set my parcel down and unwrap the one closest to me.

It's a portrait from the other room.

Heart pounding, I carefully unwrap the corner of each one until I find Niccolo's. I only let myself touch his face once before I flip the canvas over and look for the artist's signature.

There's nothing.

Frowning, I return to the front to see if the artist hid their name in the portrait itself, but no. It's not unheard of for an artist not to leave their mark, but it is odd, especially for art that's important enough to hang it in the Palazzo della Signoria.

Someone left their work unsigned on purpose, but why?

My gaze slices to a ledger open on the table, the book half hidden under one of the other wrapped portraits. I set Niccolo's portrait down for a closer look.

It's a series of numbers paired with a date, some of them stretching back years, some more recent. A catalogue of some kind, the page only half full, as if someone was in the middle of doing their work and was called away. It reminds me of the inventory records from Father's trading voyages. The ones I could barely read.

I re-examine Niccolo's portrait even more carefully until I see them—three numbers so small, you wouldn't notice unless you were looking for them: 512.

A door opens in the distance, followed by rapidly approaching voices.

Merda! I hurry to rewrap Niccolo's portrait and accidentally knock a heavy iron key onto the floor. I wince at the loud thunk and shove it into my pocket. There's no time to put it away, no time to do anything except leave.

I push open one door as someone else pulls on the other.

Lorenzo de' Medici, heir to the ruling family's fortune and power, possible future owner of my childhood home, the man supposedly sitting for his own wedding portrait downstairs, smiles pleasantly even as his eyes remain two chips of stone.

"Why, hello," he says. "What brings you to my father's office?"

CHAPTER TWELVE

His father's office.

I'm in *Piero de' Medici's* office. The most powerful man in Florence.

And his son's caught me.

A dozen excuses well up, none of them good enough. There's no reason to be here. My fake portrait has outlived its usefulness. If Lorenzo discovers I've lied my way in here, there's a high chance I'll be acquainted with the sharp end of his sheathed knife. "I . . . got lost looking for the chamber pot?"

Lorenzo sighs. "Of course you did. Come along with me, then."

He snaps his fingers, and two guards appear. They flank me as Lorenzo marches me through the palazzo—so close, they nearly step on my feet. Why do they each have a sword and a knife? Seems like an awful lot of steel to carry around inside.

"Are you with the painters?" Lorenzo demands.

I'm not dragging Leonardo into this. He's an even worse liar than I am, and Verrocchio would make us both grind pigments for weeks if he learned we offended the Medici.

"What painters?"

Lorenzo's eyes flash. "You know," he says lightly, almost jovially. "Most people would agree it's unwise to lie to the Medici.

So I'm wondering: Are you very stupid, or do you have a desire to have your hands broken?"

My hands flex involuntarily. Lorenzo's mouth curls like a cutlass. I shove them into my pockets with a shudder.

My fingers collide with cold metal. The sodding key. What am I supposed to do? I didn't mean to take it.

One of the guards breathing down my neck shoves me. "Andiamo, ragazzo!"

Right. I'm sure explaining that I didn't mean to steal anything will go over as well as suggesting we all leave the palazzo and share a cup of wine together.

Perhaps I can use it as an excuse to go back. Graciously return it like a good citizen whenever it seems most useful for my schemes.

We enter the Palazzo della Signoria's courtyard, but there's no sign of the painters anymore. I must've been wandering around for longer than I thought if everyone's gone—no wonder Lorenzo found me.

Instead of dumping me into an unceremonious heap on the front steps like I expect and deserve, Lorenzo cuts right and heads toward a different, smaller door.

One that faces a narrow, dark alley.

My spine goes rigid.

There was an alley like this beside Casa delle Volpi. It was off the kitchen, a door no one used but the servants. When I displeased my father, whether it was fucking up my lessons or stammering something foolish in front of a client, he'd haul me out there. He never touched me—it was still public, after all—but his fury cracked over my narrow shoulders like a switch.

Hopeless.

An embarrassment to our name.

What did I do to deserve a son like this?

When Niccolo noticed my red-rimmed eyes, he started finding excuses to use the door before our father could really lay into me. He'd steal pears from the neighbor's tree overhanging the wall, sneak out to meet a girl. My father's scorching tirades were interrupted so much, he stopped dragging me out there entirely.

Niccolo's not coming to save you now.

If I go into the shadows with these men, a soul-crushing scolding will be the least of my problems.

I slow, looking for an escape, but there's nothing. I'll have to sprint for the piazza. They're armed, but I'm fast. 'Tis the best I can do.

We approach. Another guard opens the door. The sunlight burns so bright, I can't see. I brace myself, ready to run—

"There you are!" Leonardo whips around the corner, pink-cheeked and out of breath.

"Leo!" I cry out, relieved. Whatever useless thing he wants to prattle on about next, I'll listen without complaint. I hurl myself away from the palazzo's dark door, toward the light, toward him.

But an iron vise clamps around my elbow, holding me back.

Lorenzo frowns at Leonardo's charcoal-black fingers. "So you *are* with the painters."

I swallow back a wave of acid. "I—"

Leonardo interrupts with an *ehh* sound and a shrug. "Not quite. He followed me here. New apprentice. I'm afraid he's a little obsessed, trying to live up to me and such. Don't worry, it won't happen again."

Lorenzo's glare goes dark as pitch. He glances at me, then Leonardo, then the palazzo itself. He heaves a sigh and releases my elbow. "Keep your little pet on a leash next time."

Little pet! Never in a million years would I follow Leonardo around like a wide-eyed little puppy! I was an apprentice first!

I clamp a hand over my aching elbow, my mouth opening to protest—

A yelp comes out instead. Leonardo's stomped on my foot.

"Yes, of course, signore. See you tomorrow! I can't wait to draw your big, wide shoulders! Your bride shall swoon when she sees them!"

Lorenzo and his guards laugh good-naturedly. They slip back inside the palazzo, even giving Leonardo a jaunty wave before the door slams shut.

Without talking about it, I turn and start storming back to the workshop.

Leonardo easily keeps pace beside me, his too-long legs making it look effortless and graceful. "So, I take it things went badly for you and your mysterious errand?"

My face flushes, annoyance and shame and the oily feeling of failure all sluicing through me. "I didn't need your help."

"Oh no? Were you and Lorenzo going on a pleasant stroll? It certainly looked that way with all the scowling and guards."

My teeth grit. "All right, fine. I needed you. But you didn't have to do it like that."

I hate being compared to him. It makes me feel like a single thimble of his charm and talent counts more than anything I could offer.

Leonardo gives a smile. Not the cloying one he flashed the

Medici heir, but a wide grin that feels an awful lot like staring directly into the sun. "My apologies! I'll be sure to save your ego before your life next time." He pats my cheek and manages to dump all his sketching materials into my arms at the same time.

I stagger under the unexpected burden. "What are you doing?"

He tucks the charcoal bag into the pocket of my doublet. "Take these for me, will you? I think I've earned a day off." He turns west—the opposite direction from Verrocchio's workshop—and leaves me with all our things.

"Where are you going? We have work to do!"

Leonardo spins on his heel and points both index fingers at me. "Not telling you! When you're honest with me, I'll be honest with you!"

I scowl at his retreating back, almost too contrite to be annoyed. "Have fun with your centaur man, then!" I shout.

His laughter reaches me from all the way across the piazza.

But the sound grows hollow and distant when I take out the pilfered key and get a good look at it for the first time.

'Tis shaped like a skull with glaring ruby eyes.

CHAPTER THIRTEEN

The next morning, I resolve to be nicer to Leonardo.

I wake up extra early to leave him a slice of castagnaccio outside his door as an apology or a thank-you—whatever he needs to forget about yesterday—but he insists on making us watch a street performer's trained parrot on the way to the Palazzo della Signoria, and those excruciating ten minutes nearly burn up all my renewed patience for him.

So of course we're running late, and I make us jog to the palazzo, but none of it matters.

"Queuing outside the door!" Leonardo elbows me, smiling brightly. "See, we're not late after all. You didn't have to sigh so much."

The queue snakes from the palazzo's main entrance into the piazza. I join the end of it, unease humming beneath my skin.

I tap the apprentice ahead of us. "Excuse me, do you know what's going on?"

He turns, and I immediately wish I'd asked someone else.

It's Bartolomeo Rucellai, one of Botticelli's apprentices and the only other apprentice who hails from a wealthy family like I do. He sizes me up with a smirk. "Niccolo Pitti. I was sorry to miss you at the Strozzi wedding."

"It's Virgil."

Bartolomeo dips his head. "Sorry, I forgot about your affectation," he says sweetly, not sounding sorry at all.

I count to three and allow myself to have a very brief, vivid fantasy of watching his face crumple when my and Leonardo's wedding portrait wins over his. I give myself another two—to factor in the tears pouring from his eyes—but that's it! A boy shouldn't indulge too much.

And I've indulged *far* too much of Bartolomeo Rucellai in the past.

I made the mistake of kissing him when I was thirteen. An eager curiosity was growing inside me, and I wondered if kissing a boy would feel different from the girls who pressed their shy lips to mine in the garden's shadowy corners. Sodding Bartolomeo seemed into it during our sweaty, nervous moment, but then he soured on me and told his father, who told *my* father, and well, we all know what happened then.

Niccolo Pitti's enraged shouts filled Casa delle Volpi. If we open a rarely used cupboard, I'm sure one final, ghostly *no son of mine!* will wail out of it. He beat me so hard, Niccolo had to help me use the chamber pot afterward.

It's when I learned our father would never, ever accept the parts of me he didn't like. When I learned that keeping secrets would keep me safe.

"Yes, such a shame to miss it." I'd rather let Verrocchio's cats eat me one finger at a time than willingly mingle with the people from my family's world, especially Bartolomeo. "What can you tell us about the queue?"

"They're searching everyone for some reason. Medici guards are just inside the doors."

Every feeling abandons me except gray dread.

The key I walked off with yesterday winks on the floor beside my bed.

Another apprentice steps through the palazzo's door. He's swallowed by darkness at once.

Lorenzo de' Medici and his guards won't find the key on me. But if they see me, they'll find something far more damning: the memory of my face and the stumbling, clumsy lies I told yesterday.

They're not looking for some*thing*; they're looking for some*one*.

Me.

I take one step back. Then another.

"You know? I just realized we forgot charcoal," I say.

Leonardo frowns. "You made us go through everything twice before we left."

"Verrocchio . . . asked me for a favor."

He shrugs and turns away. "Better go deal with your problem, then."

He knows I lied to him yesterday and hasn't forgotten. Fine, that's fair. I wasn't that nice to him. Except he's made himself memorable to the guards and Lorenzo, too. If they see him, they'll remember that I was with him. I won't let him take the fall for my mistake.

I link my arm through his and tug. "Verrocchio said he needed you, too."

Leonardo doesn't budge. For such a tall, slender person, he's shockingly solid. "Is this some sort of prank? First, you howl all morning to hurry up and get here, and now you want to leave?"

Bartolomeo Rucellai bursts out laughing. "Cristo, you two bicker like old women!"

I flinch, and Leonardo's nostrils flare. "Actually, elderly women deserve a lot more respect—"

I tug Leonardo's arm before he keeps going, and he finally starts walking with me. I make a rude gesture at Bartolomeo with my other hand. "*Vaffanculo*, Rucellai! Seeing your tears when we win will be the greatest prize of them all."

I speed across the piazza. Leonardo follows, docile as a lamb, until we disappear down Via Vacchereccia.

Then he spins and cages me between his arms against a wall.

"No more lies!" His eyebrows are narrowed slashes over a serious gaze. They're dark brown, a contrast to his rust-gold hair. "Tell me what's truly going on."

My pulse stutters, then spikes.

Our art supplies scatter across the ground—he's dropped them to play prison guard—and I glance at the mess with a protesting sound, but he only draws closer to me, his nose inches from mine. God, there are even more freckles on his face than I thought. A truly hopeless amount. I couldn't count them if I tried. I shut my eyes so I don't give in to the urge to start.

"Virgil." My name is a command, an admonishment, and a plea all at once. "I won't be upset, but I need you to be honest with me. I know that's hard for you." It sounds sarcastic, except there's no mocking edge in his voice, no cajoling mirth.

I crack one eye open, and he's just *looking* at me, his warm breath gusting across my face. He smells like cake.

I stare back at him, the rush in my veins slowly falling, steadying out into something manageable, something safe. Someone catcalls and makes kissing noises from across the street, but for once I don't care what anyone else thinks about us.

I've done nothing but push him away, and he's still here.

My back goes soft against the wall. "I . . . may not have been entirely truthful about why I wanted to work with you."

He twists sideways, leaning against the wall with an elbow. "You? Being bootstrappy and secretive? I simply cannot believe it!"

Well, that hardly seems fair! There's nothing wrong with keeping my business to myself. I bravely resist the urge to snipe back, knowing I'll only prove him right if I do. "When we were inside the Palazzo della Signoria the first day, I found a portrait of my brother."

The teasing vanishes from his face. "You think he's alive and working for the government?"

"I don't know—but he might be. The wedding commission was the only way I could get back inside and see what else I could find."

"So you're using me, then." Leonardo's voice keeps its calm tone, and yet I wince and flush bright red like he's yelled at me.

"You don't have to help me anymore now that you know the truth. You could tell Verrocchio, get the commission fully for yourself, since it's not like I could help you paint anyway." My hands fist, and the black marks on my arms follow the movement. They cost me everything, and they're all useless now, a reminder of how I've already failed Mamma and my sisters and how I'll probably fail Niccolo, too. I wish I could scour them off.

"I don't need you to paint, remember?" Leonardo says. "In case you forgot, I also asked for your help with the wedding commission. I don't love that you lied to me, but I know what it's like to lose a sibling, and I imagine you still want the fifty florins. I'll stay in this if you do, but you can't lie anymore. All right?"

Leonardo had a sibling? I try to remember if he's talked about his family before: Nothing comes to mind. I nearly ask about it, but a warning glint in his eyes stops me. I run my tongue along my teeth and nod. "All right."

He opens his mouth and hesitates. "What was all that with the search today, then?"

I have a feeling this isn't want he wanted to ask me. "Oh, that?"

"Yes, *that.*"

"I . . . might've stolen something from Piero de' Medici's office?"

Leonardo smiles, a slow, melting expression he tries to hold back but can't. "Virgil Pitti *broke* a *rule*? His Highness is no better than a common thief?" He glances toward the slice of sky above us and cups a hand around his ear. "Do you hear that? Rushing wings! I think every angel just fled Florence because of your sinful, snatchy hands."

I wriggle out from under his arm, suddenly feeling very hot. "It was an accident!"

"I believe you, but your lies to Lorenzo were . . . how to describe them? Woefully inept, perhaps?"

"Yours weren't much better!"

His smile bursts out fully, the brightest thing in the street. "Give him a few days to forget your face. I'll say you ate moldy bread if anyone asks why you're gone."

"Oh right, *thanks* for that." Bartolomeo will bring it up every time I see him.

He lifts his hands placatingly. "Or I'll give whatever reason you want me to give. I'm not trying to humiliate you. You know that, don't you?"

I think of my hideous portrait in Casa delle Volpi's foyer. How Father sometimes lingered before it, grinning like it was the funniest thing he'd ever seen, and I stood next to him twisting my hands and staying silent because it didn't feel like I had a right to be upset. "You can say whatever you want. I don't care."

His response is instantaneous. "A family affair, then. Your house needed a repair."

Why is my throat getting tight? I quickly stoop to gather up our fallen art supplies. For some reason, I can't look at him any longer. "All right."

CHAPTER FOURTEEN

"Happy birthday, my boy. Eighteen at last!"

Mamma's kiss is too hot against my frigid cheek. I smile, trying to hide how my stomach slinks to the floor.

This is my last birthday.

I will never be nineteen years old.

The candelabras glitter around the opulent dining room, molten wax dripping down their golden arms like tears. The scent of citrus and browned herbs fills my head, but the sumptuous meal tastes like ashes. My family's voices wash over me. Mamma is thinking of redoing the garden. Elisabetta would rather take sword lessons than dance lessons, and why won't anyone listen to her? Giovannia has found a new bookstore with poetry from Venice. I try to take it all in, knowing it could be the last time, but the restless truth that's whispered through me all day grows louder and louder until it's a shout.

They don't know Niccolo is alive.

Keeping the secret from them feels terrible. But every time I try to say something, fear snatches the words back. I've let my family down before. What if I'm wrong about this, too? I couldn't stand seeing their hurt and disappointment.

The chime of silverware pulls me from my thoughts. Mamma

lifts her goblet toward me, smiling widely. "Volpacchiotto, your father would be so proud of the young man you've become!"

I start choking. My father? *Proud?* I doubt he'd be happy if I married a Medici, sired two dozen sons named Niccolo, and made a mountain of gold tall enough to fill the duomo's great red dome. I half expect his corpse to burst from its grave and shamble inside to say so.

"It's Virgil, Mamma," Giovannia says sternly as I get the coughing under control. "Only Niccolo can call him little fox."

I shoot her a grateful, surprised look. Is this the witchery of having a sister? They annoy you to the point of despair every day until they're fourteen, and then they'll go to war for you forever?

Mamma's mouth thins, but she doesn't push back.

The meal ends without dolci—I told Mamma I didn't need any so Giovannia could buy another one of her books—and more empty words about how promising my future will be.

A seasick feeling storms in my stomach, the few bites of food I've eaten churning and threatening to heave-ho. Even if I did have a future, it's not like it would be the one I wanted.

When Giovannia follows me outside after our goodbyes, I swallow back a wave of bile. "Did I forget something?"

Her eyes flick to the windows. We're beyond the stone foxes guarding the steps, far away enough for no one to overhear us, but her voice is barely above a whisper. "I have a gift for you."

Generally, I'm in favor of birthday gifts, especially since no one's given me any yet, but the way she's being all furtive makes me suspect this gift is among the Trojan horse variety that'll come back to betray me in some underhand manner. "No thanks. Seeing you today was all the gift I needed."

She pulls a wrapped parcel from the folds of her cloak. "Too bad."

It takes me longer than it should to tear the paper. Beneath is an exquisite red-leather-bound copy of Dante's *Inferno*. The gold leaf pressed into the illustrations glints from the closed book's edges. I bite my bottom lip. "Strange, I don't remember giving you a small fortune recently."

"It's not from me."

Holding my breath, I flip back the cover. My pulse stops at the handwritten dedication.

Happy seventeenth birthday,
Volpacchiotto!
Ti voglio bene, Volpone.

Niccolo.

My fingers trace over the letters. Each one is a memory, a marvel, a message for a past version of me who died a little when his brother disappeared. There's a splotch of ink around the exclamation point, as if Niccolo had been writing in a hurry, so eager to get the words down, he didn't care if he made a mess of things, because he knew I wouldn't mind.

Volpone and Volpacchiotto. Big fox and little fox. Our names just for each other. I liked being half of something with my brother more than I liked being a third of something with our father. Mamma refuses to call me Virgil, but every time she uses the name that my brother gave me, another bit of my soul burns off and blackens. I don't want anyone to call me Volpacchiotto ever again unless it's him.

Giovannia makes a soft, wondering noise and leans closer.

I jerk away from the book like it's a serpent. "Where did you get this?"

"It was delivered to the house a few months after Niccolo disappeared," Giovannia says. "It was addressed to him, so I opened it. I was going to give it to you last year, but . . ."

She trails off, both of us remembering how I refused to come home for my birthday. I was too filled with shame and self-loathing to look my family in the eyes, knowing more than they did about why Niccolo was gone.

The book feels iron-heavy, crushing. Niccolo must've asked the printmaker to create it months in advance, filled with all the memories of us reading the poem together, how we would share the same blanket and take turns reading the verses, our voices melting together until I wasn't sure if I was speaking or listening.

And then we fought days before my sixteenth birthday, and I never saw him again.

I slam the book shut and push it into my sister's hands. "Give this to Mamma. She'll love having a reminder of him."

Giovannia's mouth flattens. "He bought it for you."

"I don't want it." More like I don't deserve it.

Her face softens. "I know you don't." Her eyes are doe-dark and more perceptive than they have any right to be. "But he wanted you to have it, so I think you should take it. All right?"

She shoves the book into my arms and darts inside before I can return it again.

Grimacing, I move to stuff the unwanted book into my cloak, but a squall kicks up and peels back the cover. Rips out a page of loose parchment. I catch it before it dances down the street, heart hammering at the thought of losing more of my brother.

But when I turn the paper over, I nearly drop it again.

In familiar handwriting—spikier and even messier than before—there's another message.

Stay away. I know you'll try to follow, but I need you to leave me alone.
—N

It's dated two months after he disappeared.

CHAPTER FIFTEEN

Niccolo didn't only leave me a book; he left me a message. One he intended I receive when he was already gone. Which means wherever he went—whatever happened to him—he had a plan and knew what he was doing. At least in the beginning.

And wanted you to leave him alone. The thought knifes through me. *He didn't want you with him.*

A familiar helpless ache curls around my ribs. Is this message a warning or a command or angry hurt spilling over in the wake of our fight?

How do you read a message from a ghost?

I'm so stuck in my thoughts, I don't notice I'm being followed.

It's a shadow in the corner of my eye, there and gone so fast, I could've imagined it. A hushed *shh shh* of footsteps that mirror my own.

I suck in a soft breath. I lingered at Casa delle Volpi longer than I should've, and twilight drapes the corners with deep shadows. 'Tis a bad time to wander without a weapon, and of course I don't have one, because I sold off everything I didn't need ages ago. My shoulders hunch, and I walk faster, taking a different route back to the workshop than I normally do.

The footsteps follow.

But when I glance over my shoulder, no one's there.

My pulse skitters. At the end of the street, golden light flickers: the braziers warming the Piazza Santa Croce. It feels like a game of tag. If I can reach the light, I'll be safe. Another block, and I'll be surrounded by the open space and the people already there. A dozen more steps—

Darkness engulfs me from above.

I yell and throw myself to the side before a heaviness thumps to the street, landing exactly where I was.

Lupa straightens and tosses back her cloak hood, her hair wild and windswept. "What is a birthday?"

I brace myself against the wall, heart slamming against my breastbone. "Gesù Cristo, good evening to you, too, you horrible monster!"

"Good evening," she repeats diligently, impervious to my sarcasm. "Will you tell me what a birthday is?"

Why? Why must I be her favorite person? She won't give me magic, so she's got to claim me some other way? "You're not supposed to leave the workshop without Master Verrocchio's permission. You'll get me in trouble."

Lupa has been leaving the workshop whenever she feels like it—much to Verrocchio's chagrin. Without her, the paints grow tacky. Marble cleaves mid-sculpture. Artists go to make their bargains with her, except she's gone. It'd be cute, in an annoying-younger-sibling sort of way, if I didn't have two younger siblings already and Verrocchio didn't glare at me every time she returns to the workshop hanging off my arm.

An odd expression flits across Lupa's face. "You were missing all day."

"Yes, because I had the day off."

"But you did not tell me you had the day off!" Lupa stomps her foot. Cracks splinter through the cobblestones. "No one could tell me where you went. What if the angry mob returned because you upset them again? The girl who cornered you outside made you feel bad; I could smell it!"

An eerie glow starts to pool in Lupa's eyes. Dust starts to cyclone in a gust that didn't exist a moment ago. My skin prickles with warning. I catch Lupa's clenched fists in my hands, forcing her to look at me. "I'm all right, I'm here! I'm sorry I didn't tell you I was leaving."

She sniffs disapprovingly, the glow ebbing from her glare and taking the storm-feeling with it. "I accept your thanks. You are welcome."

"It's an apology, not a—you know what? Never mind. You didn't also ambush the girl you saw me talking to, did you?"

"No. But I can if you want me to."

I assure her heartily that I don't. The last thing I need is for Lupa to start menacing my family like a too-protective hound. Only then does she deign to come home with me. Along the way, I explain what a family is and why I was visiting mine.

"A birthday is a celebration of the day you're born. There are dolci and gifts. It means you're getting older." My thumb runs over the book spine beneath my cloak. The *Inferno* will be the last birthday gift I ever receive.

"You don't like that gift, though."

Guilt weaves between my ankles like a stubborn cat. "It's not that I don't like it. 'Tis more like . . . it makes me sad. It reminds me of someone I miss."

Lupa nods briskly, like the pieces are all falling into place for her. "I would also be sad to have a book and no dolci."

This time, I couldn't quite keep my smile back. "It's not usually an either-or—"

She fists a hand and lays it over her heart. "I will find you the dolci, Virgil, so your birthday is not so sad anymore."

Oh God, no. Verrocchio will be livid if she disappears again. "Please don't—"

Except she's already gone.

Not two minutes after I step inside the workshop alone, the doors burst open.

Lupa stands there, an entire zuccotto cake in her arms. "Everyone, it is Virgil's birthday, and we will celebrate!"

One by one, the other artists turn to look at her, then me. Their expressions range from surprise to confusion. I can almost see the same thought leaping from head to head: *Angels don't care about humans like this.*

I run my tongue along my teeth, hating being the center of attention. My gaze darts to the wood panel destined to become the Medici wedding portrait. Leonardo swore up and down he'd prep the wood for our painting himself, but of course he's not there. He's managed to leave out the bucket of glue, though. So much for hoping he's got a snide joke to diffuse the tension.

Lupa's smile wobbles as the silence stretches longer.

That goddamn wobble makes my chest clench. I push off my stool. "You heard her. Do you want dolci or not?"

"You want to celebrate with *us*?" Giorgio's eyebrows go high.

I shoot him a sly smirk. "If you don't want any, I'm happy to eat your share."

He bolts out of his chair with a snort. "Not on your life, Pitti!"

Slowly, and then with more enthusiasm, the other artists abandon their work to take a slice of the creamy sweet. Some even wish me happy birthday and seem to mean it.

When I take my own slice, I whisper to Lupa, "How did you get this?" Verrocchio's cook would never make a zuccotto for a lowly apprentice. Which means—

"I stole it."

Splendid! Now she's not just abandoning the workshop for me but committing crimes for me too. The pasticciere she stole the cake from is probably already in Verrocchio's office demanding their payment. Verrocchio's going to make me grind pigments for *weeks*.

Lupa sucks cream from her thumb. "No one will know. I used my magic to steal it."

"*Your* magic?" I thought angels' magic was limited to the bargains they gave artists.

"Yes. I made myself invisible and unlocked the door. It was easy."

A strange thrill goes down my spine. "You have magic of your own?"

"That is what I said." Lupa frowns. "Do you not hear me? Is there something wrong with your ears?"

My heart starts pounding unevenly. "So the time I saved you from the angry mob . . . you could've saved us instead?"

Lupa shrugs and licks more jam and cream from her fingers.

There's so much I don't understand about her. I thought I knew all there was to know about angels, yet each time I speak to Lupa, the mystery of her deepens. Perhaps I shouldn't trust her, but it's obvious she trusts me.

No, it's not that she trusts me. It's that I'm her *friend*.

And, despite the part of my soul that stills like a frightened rabbit when her eyes gleam in shadows, I think she might be my friend too.

I draw closer, speaking too low for anyone else to hear. "Could you use your magic to help me get past the guards at the Palazzo della Signoria?"

Niccolo told me not to follow him, but I don't give a damn about his message. It's been two years, and I'm not the hopeless little brother he left behind anymore. I might not deserve to have him back, but my mamma and sisters do, if he's out there to be found.

Lupa smiles, her pointed teeth stained red with jam. "Yes."

CHAPTER SIXTEEN

"You didn't come home last night."

Leonardo pauses on his way out the door with our sketching supplies. He turns slowly, a smirk unfurling. "Did you miss me?"

Even though there's no reason to be embarrassed—even though it's completely normal to notice whether or not someone is around!—heat fills my cheeks. I play it off with a shrug.

"You didn't prep the panel for the painting like you said you would." I finished up his abandoned chore myself after everyone else went to bed, sullenly slopping the glue on the wood and then pressing the linen into the stickiness.

Leonardo sucks in his cheeks, not quite remorseful enough to appease me. "I'll add the gesso tonight, then." Gesso is the last layer we need on the panel before we can start transferring our sketches to it. I should be happy we're about to move on to this stage of work—it means I'm closer to getting my hands on the Medici's golden florins—but my exasperation with Leonardo remains, a hissing cat that won't leave my lap.

"You also missed my birthday party."

His eyebrows shoot skyward. "Did you want me there?"

I sputter, thrown by the question. I *looked* for him last night, even saved a bit of cake for him, because I'd hear about it for days if I hadn't, but looking isn't the same as wanting. Suddenly self-conscious, I swallow and address the spot six inches to the left of his face.

"I needed to talk to you, was all. Don't go to the palazzo today. Let me buy you breakfast instead."

His eyebrows rise even higher. "You? Buying me *breakfast*?" He puts his hand against my brow.

I hiss and swat him away. "What are you doing?"

"I'm looking for fever. Something must be wrong if you're trying to do me a favor."

"That's not fair! There was the time you went off with the handsome blacksmith for three days, and I told Verrocchio you were caring for an ill relative."

He thumbs his chin pensively. "Oh yes. I forgot about that."

"You forget every time I'm nice to you," I grumble.

He glances at me, a sideways look through his eyelashes. "I don't forget. You're just so rarely pleasant, it's hard to remember."

I give up my fight with a frown. I can still feel the outline of each one of his cold fingers across my forehead. "This is important."

"More important than painting Lorenzo de' Medici's grumpy toad face for the opportunity to paint his toad-faced children? More important than precious *work*?"

I groan and look at the ceiling. "Please let me be nice to you."

He shrugs and tosses the art supplies back into the workshop. "All right, fine. I'm not the one who cares about winning."

I wince at the crash but don't tell him he doesn't have to throw things.

The city is painted ocher and bronze in the morning light,

the stone thawing in what promises to be one of the first warm days of the year. Leonardo takes me to a crumbling window that faces the Arno. An old woman with nut-brown skin hands slices of focaccia to a queue of workers. The entire time we wait in line, Leonardo twirls that lock of hair around his fingers, over and over again. Who *does* that? Isn't he worried about losing it or getting it all greasy? Did he pay a strega to put a curse on someone he hates? The hair color is close enough to mine that I pat my head to make sure I don't have a shorn spot.

The old woman has to yell at me twice before I realize it's my turn to order. Blushing for no reason, I order two slices topped with stracciatella cheese and roasted onions. Then, to really sweeten the deal, I buy a flagon of watered wine from the vintner just a few doors down. By the time we settle on the steps of Ponte Santa Trinita, Leonardo's skepticism is drawing the interest from the female *Primavera* statue guarding the bridge's northeast corner. She bends closer with a stony creak, eager to eavesdrop.

"Out with it," he demands. "You're obviously buttering me up for a reason. Breakfast and wine? I doubt you even do this for your lovers."

He's twirling the curl *again*. "Do you have a ragazzo?" I ask suddenly.

Cristo santo, that's not what I wanted to ask him!

His fingers freeze. "Are you asking me if I have a lover?"

My face is as hot as a kitchen fire, but it's too late to take the question back. We've never talked about both of us liking boys before.

Of course, everyone knows it about him—Leonardo maintains all the mystery of an unshuttered window that always has a candle burning in it so everyone can see inside—but I've only ever brought a boy home once.

He followed me up the stairs to my attic, shy and eager, but all I could think of when we tangled across my bed was whether or not Leonardo had noticed when we tiptoed past his open door.

I expected Leonardo to bring it up—it's the sort of thing he'd tease me mercilessly for—but strangely, he never did. "I'm only asking because what we're doing is important. You shouldn't let other people . . ." *Kiss you.* I bite the words back before I humiliate myself further.

His eyebrow lifts knowingly. "Distract me, as you're fond of saying?"

I nod and shrug, the movement jerky, and try to focus on the Ponte Vecchio upriver. 'Tis early enough that the butcher shops crowded along it haven't stained the water red yet. It doesn't matter who he talks to. It certainly doesn't sodding matter who he kisses. Why did I bring this up?

Leonardo slips the curl back into his pocket when he thinks I'm not looking. "No," he says finally. "I don't have anyone."

It's not the answer I expected, and he can tell. His long fingers flex, as if they can pluck the words he wants from the air. "Sometimes it's easier to let someone take what they want from you than to want something for yourself. Do you understand?"

I don't, but I'd rather die than admit it. "Sure." I shoo away the hungry pigeons already gathering around us and wait until it feels like I can ask the question I really wanted to ask him.

"Did you know Lupa has magic of her own?"

Leonardo takes an enormous bite of his focaccia. Steam wreathes his face from the warm bread, the sweet tangy scent of yeast enveloping both of us. He thumbs away grease from the corner of his mouth and leaves a smudge of charcoal there instead. "No."

"And you know how I've been struggling to get inside the palazzo?"

Leonardo's snort scatters the pigeons lusting after our food. "Struggling? You've barely tried! Every time you look at the guards, your face turns the color of spoilt milk."

He'd feel sick too if he remembered the casual menace of their grip. "Lupa offered to use her magic to get me inside. What do you think?"

I want to ask him to come in with me, but I can't quite bring myself to say it yet. I need to warm up to the question, like trying to pet a nervous dog.

Leonardo takes another bite and chews slowly. He still hasn't wiped off the charcoal near his mouth, and the smudge bothers me more than it should. After a century, he swallows and says, "I don't think it's a good idea."

My stomach swoops at his stern tone. "If you're worried about Verrocchio noticing Lupa's gone—"

His eyes snap to mine. "I'm not worried about Verrocchio. I'm worried about *you*. I don't trust Lupa."

I suck in a breath. "Are you jesting?"

He shakes his head, dark eyes never leaving mine for an instant. There's a ring of amber at the edges I never noticed before. 'Tis strange how you can see someone every single day for your entire life and still discover new things about them.

For example, the fact that Leonardo likes everyone, but not Lupa.

"She'd never hurt us!"

He runs a hand over a white scar on his arm. The wound he gave himself to save Gorgio from the ravenous, old angel. "You're the one who named her she-wolf. Does a wolf mean to kill, or does she kill because she's hungry? She'll hurt us if she has to."

I square my jaw and take a too-big bite of food and wash it down with a too-big wine gulp. He's wrong! How could he not see that Lupa is nothing like the old angel? She would *never* attack an apprentice. She's too strangely human. She cares about me.

"She uses her *teeth*, Virgil," Leonardo says. "If you watched her, you'd see."

I look away when Lupa makes bargains with the other artists, but it's only to give them privacy. Still, it's impossible to ignore how when people approach her with their knives, she shakes her head and leads them into the corner where the light doesn't quite reach. Cloaked in shadows, she splits their skin with her mouth instead, drinking tenderly. Sometimes a trickle of dark burgundy dries on her chin. Once, I reached across the table to wipe it away with my thumb before I remembered what the stain was.

"She won't hurt us," I insist, more quietly this time. "Not unless you strike a bargain with her."

The noise of the city settles between us. The rush of the river, the bustling bridge. Leonardo takes another thoughtful bite and wipes his mouth again, somehow still managing to miss the charcoal smudge. "You're not afraid of angels."

"No." I bite the inside of my cheek as I say it, because that's not the whole truth. Lupa doesn't drink my blood because she won't bargain with me. She can't hurt me because I'm going to die. There's nothing left of me for her to take.

Leonardo leans closer. "Most people are."

Our faces are close—too close for me to ignore it anymore. I wipe the charcoal smudge from his mouth. He flinches and I freeze, thumb lingering at the corner of his lips. Sudden understanding rushes through me. "The angels frighten you."

He laughs softly, but I can see the gooseflesh rising beneath his freckles. "Is it that obvious?"

"No." But it makes sense. He's refused to make a bargain with one; he never lets himself be alone with Lupa. Come to think of it, he tries to keep *me* from being alone with her too. How many bargains of mine did he watch me make with his heart in his throat, wanting to save me from myself?

My hand falls from his face. I should've noticed he was afraid sooner, but I couldn't imagine him afraid of anything.

"Verrocchio's old angel . . . he wasn't the first angel I knew." Leonardo braces his elbows on the step behind us and leans back. His long body fully takes up a third of the staircase now. People step over and around us, and we should probably move, but I don't say a thing. I'm drinking in his every word.

"I'm a bastard, as I'm sure you've noticed." His words are teasing, self-deprecating, but his smile doesn't touch his eyes. "When my father finally married, I loved my stepmother like she was my own mother. She was the one who taught me to draw, and then paint. She was the daughter of a painter, and she wasn't afraid to make bargains with the workshop's angel. I used to draw marks on myself with charcoal to look more like her. When she told me she was pregnant and I'd have a little sibling with red-gold hair like mine, I wept with excitement."

My lungs clench. His use of the past tense isn't lost on me. "What happened?"

His eyes flutter shut. His face lifts toward the sun, his freckles like flecks of cinnabar. If I painted them, it's the color I'd use, along with a hint of sienna earth. "There were complications. When they tried to stop the bleeding, they couldn't. She died, and my sibling died with her."

He's got that curl out again, twisting it tenderly between his thumb and index finger. In the light, it's shot through with chestnut. I picture him tucking it into his pocket each morning before he sits across from me at breakfast. Imagining him reaching for it and not finding it makes me tense. It's too easy to lose. He needs to be more careful with it.

"She should've lived, but she gave way too much of her life to the angel," I guess.

He shrugs, not saying anything.

I suck in a rattling breath, knowing I'm right.

And I've done the same thing to myself.

He can't find out what you've done.

I promised I wouldn't lie to him anymore, but if I had known his past, I never would've asked him to help me. Losing a beloved parent is awful—but losing his only sibling as well? Niccolo's disappearance was soul-rending. Trying to imagine life without Giovannia and Elisabetta makes my eyes burn. My siblings shaped the best parts of me. Without them, I'd be a lifeless lump of clay.

I never suspected Leonardo and I were both broken in the same places.

"I'm so sorry that happened." My voice catches. "And I'm sorry I kept telling you to make bargains."

He shrugs again. "You didn't know. I never trusted the angels enough to make a bargain, so at least some good came from it."

"You don't have to find the silver lining in something so terrible!"

At my sharp tone, his eyes fly open. "Virgil. Looking for the silver lining is what I do best. Life is too unbearable if we linger on the sorrow of it." He tips his head and smirks just a little, as if to suggest I could learn from him.

Well, I wouldn't go *that* far. Brooding is the respectable, honorable birthright of every artist. I scoff, but there's nothing behind the sound. We're Virgil-and-Leonardo, and this is how I'm supposed to react. If sadness is a place he doesn't want to visit, I won't make him sit there with me.

There's a sudden, dazzling burst of light. My arm flies up over my face, but the burning glare vanishes as quickly as it arrived.

"Lupa!" For fuck's sake, how long has she been there eavesdropping? "You're not supposed—"

The angel cuts me off. She doesn't even look at me. All her words are for Leonardo. "If I convince you I won't hurt people, will you help Virgil?"

Leonardo gapes. He startled so hard, his half-eaten focaccia went flying. Pigeons swarm on it—the cyclone of noise and feathers enough to drive everyone else away.

"I—yes?" His eyes slide toward mine helplessly. "Is that why you dragged me out here? You didn't want to search the palazzo alone?"

A blush bolts across my cheeks. Why is it so hard for me to say what I want? "If—if *you* want to help, then sure—"

"Great." Lupa snaps her fingers. An invisible hand pushes me upright, so strong, I nearly topple forward. "Come with me, then."

CHAPTER SEVENTEEN

Lupa parades through the Florentine streets like a queen, Leonardo and me trailing after her. Two bumbling, bickering attendants.

"Why is she taking us to the apothecary?" Leonardo says when we go north of the duomo. "You already got the pigments this week."

My insides tense when we pass people holding camphor-drenched rags to their noses and mouths. "We're not picking up pigments."

We're going back to the scene of the angry mob.

This time, when the people turn toward us, their eyes slide over Lupa and settle hungrily on me and Leonardo. I give away the last of my focaccia to the first child who begs for it, but my fine clothes still scream *wealthy outsider!*

I keep one hand on the knife at my belt. I barely know how to use it, but after Lupa startled me, I didn't want to be caught off guard and unarmed again.

The dirty piazza is nearly the same as before, except more crowded. People coughing on one another, breathing in the same rank air full of pestilence. I cover my mouth and nose with my hand to avoid inhaling the miasma.

Leonardo doesn't bother. "I'm not certain disease is caused by miasma, you know."

"We'll see if you still feel that way when you start choking on your snot."

A crowd gathers around the cracked fountain, filling up their buckets. Leonardo's nose scrunches at the green algae staining the white marble basin. "Are people really supposed to drink that?"

The water has a yellow tinge to it. "I think this is all they have."

The mob wasn't wrong to be angry with me before; I just didn't want to be their scapegoat. The Medici threaten to take my family's house, but how much more have they taken from these people, who have so much less to begin with? People forced to work for long hours and low wages in foul conditions? Florence is a republic, but the Medici might as well be kings.

"Come!" Lupa muscles to the fountain's edge. The crowd parts for her easily, their attention sluicing off her like water from glass. She must be using magic to make herself unnoticed.

The same can't be said for me and Leonardo.

"Come to gawk at us—"

"Eating fat figs in their golden halls—"

"The likes of them are not welcome here . . ."

The back of my neck stings. Clapping a hand over it, I whirl around, half expecting to see someone tickling it with a blade. "Hey, Lupa, remember what happened last time? If you're going to do something, think you could *hurry up and do it*?"

She hisses and flutters her hands over the fountain's filthy edge. "Give me your knife."

I'm not thrilled to hand over our only weapon, but the sooner we leave, the sooner I won't need it anymore. I offer Lupa my dagger.

She grabs it by the sharpened edge and *squeezes.*

"Oh God, oh God, oh God." Leonardo claps a hand over his mouth, gagging.

A gush of gold drips from Lupa's hand into the water. The crowd gasps and screams, half of them lurching away, half heaving forward for a better look. Someone pushes Leonardo from behind and nearly knocks him in. I steady him by the waist, snarling a curse over my shoulder.

"Look!" a child cries with a pointed finger.

As the gold eddies through the water, it doesn't dilute. Instead the water shimmers clear, then gold itself, a pale, translucent shade that reminds me of delicate gold leaf on the very tip of my brush.

A woman dips her palm into the glowing water and trickles it into the mouth of her coughing toddler. The pink flush of health fills her wan cheeks. She giggles, and the crowd hushes.

Tears sparkle in the young mother's eyes. "The angels have blessed our corner of the city at last!"

The cry zips through the crowd, catching faster than fire, swelling mightier than a flood.

Lupa's brow is beaded with moisture, her pointed teeth are bared in a grimace. She squeezes the dagger tighter and gasps as the trickle becomes a sickening gush. "Stop, you'll hurt yourself!" I grab her wrist, forcing her to release the knife.

It plunges into the water.

Lupa doubles over, tendons going rigid in her neck, her hands curling into fists. When they unclench, there's not a single mark on the skin, but her teeth chatter. She sways once, twice—

Leonardo and I catch her before she falls. He's breathing quickly, eyes bouncing from the golden fountain waters to Lupa.

"I thought angels could only make bargains with the workshop or house they were bound to?"

That was the entire point of the binding ceremony, was it not? Why else would Lupa sink her teeth into our palms and the priest proclaim she belonged to us and only us?

"This was no bargain. I asked these people for nothing," Lupa pants.

"Are you allowed to do that?" I harden my voice to hide the tremble. To hell with Verrocchio being cross with me for letting Lupa escape again. She's using magic in a way I've never seen before, never *heard* of angels using before. It feels wrong, blasphemous. A violation I should report to someone.

But as I watch the magicked water stop coughs and cure runny eyes, I can't deny that something about it also feels indeterminably right.

Why is she so different?

Lupa's eyes burn green-gold, the pupils nearly swallowed by the light. "I don't know," she says softly.

I shiver, unsure if she's answering the question I've asked aloud or the one I've thought.

Leonardo jerks his chin toward the duomo's distant shape, closer to home. The only thing that causes more of a riot than murder is a miracle, and we're in the epicenter of the biggest miracle Florence has seen since the first angel stumbled out the cathedral's doors.

We leave, fighting against an endless stream of people hurrying to the golden fountain, the rumors of a well that cures all illness already racing to every edge of the neighborhood. People fall to their knees, crying and giving thanks to heaven.

"See?" Lupa leans heavily on both of us. "I can help people too."

I open my mouth—but nothing comes out. What is there to say? Everything I thought I knew about angels has been upended. I don't know how I feel about it or what to think.

"I saw. I believe you." Leonardo tugs on his bottom lip, lost in thought.

A cicada-buzz chirrs in my ears. The longer Leonardo stays quiet, the louder it swells. He's never kept a thought to himself, so what's he thinking now? What did he see back there that I didn't? I need him to tell me so I can make sense of it.

"You all right?" I finally ask.

He shakes himself a bit. His gaze rises, full of resolve. "Will you make a bargain with me, Lupa?"

The buzz becomes a roar. "You don't make bargains!"

"I'm allowed to change my mind, aren't I?"

Obviously. I have no right to tell him what to do. But a hot feeling swirls through me, uneasy and wrong. It feels like a bad idea—one I need to talk him out of. "Why now? How can you trust it'll work?"

I gasp when his cool fingers trace my exposed bargain marks. "You trusted it would work. Over and over again."

Gooseflesh puckers my useless scars. *Perhaps I shouldn't have,* I want to say. "You didn't answer my first question."

His smile is sly, cajoling. One meant to make me forget. "Are you my mother now?"

"If I must be. Someone needs to talk sense to you."

He stops walking, slipping his arm around Lupa's shoulders so the half-conscious angel doesn't fall. His smile sinks into a long, dark look that makes me swallow. "I promise this bargain will help us with the Medici commission, but you've got to trust me."

'Tis not a question of trusting him. But how can I explain the anxious thrum rattling my bones? The horrible sense that this is somehow about me?

You know he'll never tell if you keep asking him.

Curse his stubbornness. I cross my arms with a huff, hiding my feelings behind a defiant chin. "Fine! I hope you don't regret it."

Leonardo laughs softly. I can't be sure, but I think I feel him brush my side as we start walking again. "I don't think I will."

CHAPTER EIGHTEEN

Easter in Florence always arrives with a bang. Quite literally. The streets are packed with jubilant crowds as the Carro del Fuoco lurches from the Porta al Prato to the Piazza del Duomo pulled by its six white oxen. The wagon looks like a tiered cake, each gold-and-green layer more exquisite than the one below. Sparklers fizz along its sides, and plumes of red and green smoke ribbon from its very top, a hint of the dazzling fireworks display to come when it reaches the Cattedrale di Santa Maria del Fiore.

"Have you ever wondered," Leonardo says as we weave through the packed piazza, "why we celebrate Easter by exploding a fancy wagon?"

"It's not like the wagon explodes. Just the fireworks it carries." Someone stomps on my foot, and I wince.

"Right, but why fireworks, specifically? Is there a bit about Jesus and fireworks in the Bible?"

"You really don't pay attention in mass, do you?" Someone else bumps into me, and I stumble. Leonardo grabs my wrist. He doesn't let go, even when I'm on my feet again. His smile is roguish and huge and only for me.

"C'mon, Virgil. The lecture isn't the most interesting part of church!"

I think of all the masses we've endured squashed together thigh to thigh on a too-crowded pew and frown. I don't think we're talking about Jesus anymore. Wait. Cristo santo, he's not . . . flirting with me, is he?

Of course he is. He flirts with everything that moves. My eyes flicker down to the fresh black line on his wrist. *But things are different now.*

No amount of wheedling will get Leonardo to reveal what Lupa promised him, even though I desperately, fervently want to know. For my own knowledge, of course. Not for any other reason. If he's gained an edge that can help us win the Medici wedding portrait commission, I deserve to know. My family needs the money more than he does.

"It's my own business, Virgil," he said bluntly last night, turning away from our painting to face me fully. "Or are you the only one allowed to have secrets?"

I sulked under his lifted, prim expression but refused to let him bait me. "Lorenzo's hand looks like he's trying to strangle his bride. Can you fix the fingers?"

The nights leading up to Easter all ran together in a sfumato haze of layering sketches on the Medici wedding portrait panel. My fingers were still clumsy, artless sausages, but my eyes worked just fine, and I'd convinced Leonardo to paint Lorenzo and his bride in profile, him coming to the window of her room: the opposite of the journey she will make to him. Not a marriage but a welcoming.

"That's good, I like it!" Leonardo exclaimed when I walked him through it. He didn't sound surprised, but he did sound proud, and I turned away before he could notice my unexpected smile.

Leonardo stops us against a wall until the crowd surges past, following the Carro del Fuoco rumbling down the street just ahead. When he finally releases my hand, it feels cold.

"Shall we?" He nods south, away from the cathedral and its Easter celebrations.

"Let's go."

Today is the day we break into the Palazzo della Signoria and go through Piero de' Medici's records. Waiting until Easter was Leonardo's idea. It's a feast day, so the palazzo should be less crowded, less guarded. And now that Lorenzo de' Medici is done sitting for his portrait, no one will suspect the artists of wrongdoing if we mess something up.

We melt away from the last of the crowd. Lupa waits for us beneath a street tabernacle, dressed in the trousers and shirt I loaned her. She grins and catches her fist in her hand at the sight of us. "Yes, it is time for crimes!"

I shush her. "Crimes are bad, remember?"

Her mouth pulls sideways. "If they are so bad, why does doing them feel so good?"

We take a roundabout way to the Palazzo della Signoria. There's an eerie, abandoned feel to the city, heightened by the distant roar of the crowd at the cathedral. In the absence of people, the shuttered windows overhead feel like judgmental eyes, all of them watching us with reproach. The feeling of being watched grows stronger when the Palazzo della Signoria's austere clock tower rises above the red rooftops.

I'm not doing anything wrong, I remind myself angrily. The palazzo is a government building. This is a republic. I'm merely trying to obtain information about a missing person. If answers about my brother lie within those stone walls, I deserve to know what they are. My entire family does.

"Here." I stop beside a wooden door. Flies buzz over barrels of food scraps. We're entering through the kitchens. Since today is a holiday, all the servants will have the day off.

Leonardo tugs the knob. "It's locked."

I straighten my shoulders and nod, my heart beating faster. "Lupa?"

She replaces Leonardo.

At first, nothing happens. But then an eldritch breeze lifts her hair. Gold glimmers in her eyes, the flash of a predator's stare in the dark. I can't feel the breeze on my face, but I can feel it inside—a whisper of wrongness just under my skin, the feeling of padding too close to a graveyard at midnight.

Something inside the lock clinks.

The wrong feeling lessens at once. I shake my head, ridding myself of its last dregs. "Let's go."

The kitchen is warm and dark, the fire banked to embers in the wide hearth. Bread dough proofs on a flour-dusted table and fills the air with a sweet, funky smell that's not entirely unpleasant. Lupa marches to the door leading deeper into the palazzo as Leonardo gently shuts the outside one behind us. He snags my sleeve when I go to follow her.

"Are you sure you want to do this?" he says, too low for the angel to hear us.

"Yes?" I don't understand why he's asking this.

He tips his head. The wind has had its way with his hair, and I can't read his expression. "You won't be able to unlearn what you discover."

I grimace, not wanting to talk about this now. "What do you mean?"

He loosens a breath, like he doesn't want to say it. "The Medici aren't good people, Virgil. If your brother is or was working with them in secret . . ."

Then your brother might not be a good person either.

The implication is a striking viper; I recoil from the danger instinctively. "You don't know the first thing about him!"

But I can't forget Niccolo's warning in the *Inferno*. The one I never told Leonardo about. My brother told me not to follow him, and here I am, doing exactly that. I assumed he was shooing me away from danger, but what if he had another reason? Like mold behind a gilded wall, once you peel back the wood, there's no ignoring the rot beneath.

Leonardo lifts his hands placatingly. "I can see I've overstepped. I'm sorry."

"You have." He's only looking out for me, but I never asked him to and I don't want it. I hitch my shoulders higher and cross the room, not waiting for him. There's a soft, frustrated sigh, and then Leonardo's footsteps are shadowing my own.

Outside the kitchen door is a dark, unadorned corridor. A servants' passage. When the door closes behind us, we're shut off in complete darkness. There's a faint noise, and I blink as a glow erupts on Lupa's hand.

"You can conjure fire from nothing?" Leonardo says, aghast.

She turns, frowning. "Yes?" A dying coal is pinched in her long fingernails. "Can't everyone with an ember?"

She touches the coal to a lantern's wick, and it sputters to life. The scent of burnt hair wars with the dampness, but she doesn't act like it singed her. "Lead us, Virgil."

It takes me a bit, but I navigate out of the warren of servants' tunnels and up the palazzo's endless steps to the offices above. Leonardo holds the lantern, and Lupa walks ahead, boldly rounding each corner with a confidence that makes my stomach curl. I know she's made herself invisible to everyone but us, but it feels *wrong* to see her walk like she has nothing to hide.

She guides us around a handful of guards, one on each floor.

Soon we're outside the double doors leading to Piero's office. The ones I've schemed and dreamed how to get behind for weeks. Leonardo runs a finger along one of the carved panels, frowning. "The Last Judgment is a grim choice, isn't it?"

That's what I thought when I saw the doors the first time. "Wait until you see the inside."

When we enter, Leonardo gasps with horror. "Dolce Gesù, he's *looking* at me!"

The wrapped portraits I found before are gone, as is the mess, but the muscular, menacing portrait of God still towers over us. Even though the painting isn't magicked, his eyes appear to follow me as I go to the shelves filled with fat ledgers.

"I don't like this. I don't like it at all," Leonardo mutters.

I've never agreed with him more in my entire life. "The sooner we find my brother, the sooner we can leave." I beeline to the one incompletely filled shelf and ease off the final ledger, flipping to the last page.

Someone has finished the portrait catalogue since I was here. My stomach sparks when I find the number on Niccolo's portrait—512—and show Leonardo the date.

"February 28, 1467," he says.

It's a few weeks after Niccolo disappeared, but there's nothing else special about it. I fist my curls, already feeling frustrated. "What am I supposed to do with that?"

Leonardo swoops closer. Ignoring my protests, he closes the ledger and taps a number stamped on its spine. "Seven one six. See how the ledgers on this shelf have three numbers on their spines and the other ones have nine on theirs? It's a cataloguing system."

It takes me a moment to catch up. "There's more information in another book?"

"Precisely!" Giddy with delight, he flies to another shelf. I slip the portrait catalogue back in its spot and follow just as he pulls a book with *716-459-840* on it from the shelf.

I groan when he flips it open. There are thousands of entries: births, deaths, arrests, job offers. Leonardo turns to the section numbered with *512* at the top, but there are at least ten pages with the label, all of them filled with handwriting so small, the thought of reading it makes me dizzy. I'm twelve again, a stammering mess before my tutor, my father a storm at my back.

"I don't see anything." He's reading the left page, but I can't force myself to make the words on the right page focus. Between God's judgmental, staring eyes and the imposing throne, it feels like we're not alone. When the churches chime the quarter hour, I flinch and nearly tear a page in two.

"Niccolo Pitti, right?" Leonardo's nose is an inch above a page, one finger keeping his place.

Hope bursts through me. "Yes!"

"Someone's coming!" Lupa whisper-hisses from her post outside the door. "Several someones!"

My pulse surges. I butt Leonardo out of the way, a familiar name in tiny script snagging my eyes just above his fingertip.

Niccolo Pitti, sworn into city service February.

Appointment status: current

Work address—

Lupa bursts into the room. "Hide!"

The address disappears. Leonardo yanks the ledger away and slides it back onto the shelf. I try to claw it from him, anger kicking through me. "I didn't get the address!"

I leap for the ledger. My fingers graze the spine, and it tumbles down.

There's a murmur outside the door. The knob starts to turn—

"I'm sorry, Virgil, I truly am." Leonardo tackles me and drags me under the table and its tablecloth, his eyes agonized.

Not a moment too soon.

The doors open with a swell of male voices, and footsteps shuffle into the room. I can just see their shoes through the gap between the tablecloth's edge and the floor. The fabric still trembles where we dove under it. Leonardo stops it with a single finger, his face stricken.

"Signori, seat yourselves. We have much to discuss before we're missed at the celebrations."

Dread bubbles in my gut at the familiar voice. I bite the meaty part of my hand to hold back a gasp.

It's Piero de' Medici.

And we're trapped in his office until he leaves.

CHAPTER NINETEEN

The chair closest to me pulls back. I only just manage to move away before it pushes in again filled with the lower half of a man's body. Leonardo squashes against me as the same thing happens to him. We're practically sitting on each other now, the red and ermine-trimmed robes of the elected priori brushing our skin, Leonardo's too-long legs scrunched a hairbreadth away from the tablecloth's edge.

His eyes meet mine, huge and ringed with white. One sound, one wrong movement, and we'll be discovered.

Merda! This is what we get for poking fun at God's muscular, glowering glory on Easter Sunday.

"Piero, what's the meaning of this? It won't be long before someone notices the entire city council is missing from mass." The man's voice is cajoling, but there's an edge of steel underneath it.

Piero de' Medici laughs. "Well, I suppose we should get on with it, then. Guards, seize him."

There's a stomp of boots, a flurry of gasps and murmurs, then the unmistakable sound of a body being dragged from a chair. Desperate to see more—and ignoring Leonardo's frantic gestures to stay still—I twist to press my face to the floor and peer underneath the tablecloth's edge.

The prior is on his knees before the blades of two Medici

guards' pikes, which gleam beneath his jaw. His shocked look is mirrored on the other men's faces.

"Tell us, Signore Soderini, why you haven't been able to find the person responsible for the fountain miracle. It's blasphemous that a human would attempt to parade as an angel and lie to all those poor people!"

My body goes statue still. They're talking about Lupa.

Except . . . Piero is saying it was no miracle, even though I saw the healing waters with my own eyes. Is he lying to his government allies, or does he not believe in the magic?

"Signore Medici, I can assure you, we have been searching for the culprit. It hasn't been easy. One man claims he saw a vision of the Virgin Mary right on the fountain's edge—"

"Liar. I know you raced to the fountain yourself to take some of its water. Don't try to deny it happened." Piero's voice is silk-smooth. "My son Lorenzo followed you."

The hair rises on my arms as if I'm scurrying through a piazza moments before lightning cracks through the sky. Why do the Medici care so much about what happened to people who needed help? What Lupa did was odd and unheard of, but angels and their magic are sacred. Their ways are not for people to question or control. That's what the church says.

I bite the inside of my cheek, sucking salt.

"Is he certain it was me?" Soderini says cooly. "He could have seen anyone."

Piero's voice grows cajoling, almost cloying. "And yet, he saw you. Come now, tell the truth."

The running-before-the-storm feeling grows stronger. I nearly yelp when a heaviness squashes my hand. Leonardo. I glance down at our hands pressed together, then up to his face. He's looking at me, too, face wide and frightened. His freckles are hidden in the darkness.

Those freckles are the only thing I want to draw. The wild confession surges to the tip of my tongue. I choke it back, appalled that my peach-fuzzy brain has decided now is the time to unearth this mortifying fact.

Leonardo's tongue darts along his lips. They part, as if he wants to say something too.

Pulse spiking, I clap a hand over his mouth, shouting at him with my eyes.

Whatever it is can wait!

He sighs against my palm. It warms my skin—and somewhere deeper.

"I went to the holy waters to study it." Soderini's voice is an anguished whisper, as if he's speaking against his will. "It felt like a true miracle, unlike the false ones you parade before us."

Piero's laugh holds no warmth. "How can you say that? My family is blessed with no angel of our own."

"And yet, I have lived long enough to notice how their magic always tips fortune in your family's favor. Why is that, Piero? You are hiding a secret from us, and I will find out what it is!"

The treasonous words congeal like a miasma, deadly and catching. I'd give anything to see the council members' faces. Are they leaning away from their ninth member, as if he'll poison them next? Or have they gone stone-still, too afraid to agree with their traitor in front of the Medici?

Piero makes a disappointed noise. "Thank you for your honesty."

A ringing rasp of drawn steel. With a gasp, Soderini falls, blood fountaining from his throat. It's a shocking dark red, spreading rapidly across the stone floor, pooling and racing along the cracks in the mortar.

Right under our table.

Leonardo flinches, only my hand over his mouth stifling his cry. The blood seeps beneath the tablecloth, reaching for him. He shudders closer to me, his panic a writhing, feral beast. All the man sitting closest to him has to do is cross his ankles, and he'll find Leonardo. Madonna santa, I thought he was jesting when he said he was afraid of blood!

Moving carefully, I wedge my body between him and the spreading puddle. I grit my teeth as it soaks into my trousers, lukewarm and sticky. The metallic scent swirls around my head, nauseating. I nearly gag, tasting it with each breath. I'm too close to the edge of the tablecloth, my smallest finger in the light. If someone looked, they'd see me. One glance, and they'd slit our throats too.

Leonardo's arm circles me, pulling me away from the damning sliver of daylight and against his side. I close my eyes and hook my chin over his shoulder, willing myself to stay still while the blood seeps up my thigh. He smells familiar, like the soap in Verrocchio's house, the nutty musk of linseed oil from the workshop, and a scent all his own, skin-warm and sweet. I inhale deeply, anchoring myself to the scent to crowd out the stink of blood, distract me from the fact that—dear God—the wetness is creeping up my *waist* now—

There's a sharp pinch on my earlobe. My eyes fly open, a shock jolting down my spine.

Did he just *bite* me?

Leonardo's mouth twists ruefully, confirming my suspicion that yes, he absolutely did, but he's nodding toward the center of the room, his fingernails curling into my bicep.

Stay with this. Pay attention.

"Does anyone else have a complaint they'd like to share?" Piero de' Medici sounds amused, of all things. As if he hasn't just ordered his own guard to kill a man in cold blood. As if he hasn't just violated one of the most sacred rules in our republic.

No one speaks up. A delighted clap rings out. "Perfetto," Piero says. "This meeting is over. If anyone finds out more about the fountain incident, tell me and me *alone*."

A murmur of assent goes around the room. Then the chairs boxing me and Leonardo slide backward. Footsteps grow fainter as the priori flee into the corridor. Leonardo moves away from me, unfurling his cramped legs with a long sigh. I clasp my arms around myself, cold without his warmth.

I'm about to crawl out from under the tablecloth when a hand appears inches from my face.

"What's this?"

My pulse *spikes*. The hand is unlined, young. A beat too late, I recognize Lorenzo de' Medici's voice.

We're not alone yet.

He picks something up. There's a *shhh* of flipping paper. Copper floods my mouth.

It's the ledger with Niccolo's name. The one I dropped before the meeting started.

They know someone's been in here.

"Leave it for the servants," Piero barks.

Lorenzo's voice grows surly. "What if someone was going through it for a reason—"

A *whump* of fist meeting wood. "I don't care! What I care about is how you managed to lose the key the one and only time I left you here unaccompanied."

I flinch, a wounded thing in my chest curling in on itself. *This isn't your father,* I remind myself. *This isn't your problem.* Even still, I can imagine Lorenzo's gaze sliding to the side, his shoulders rising as if someone else's disappointment is a physical thing he could protect himself from. I almost feel bad that I have his missing key in my bedchamber.

Piero continues berating his son, voice a low hiss. "Did you not hear Soderini? If someone learns the truth about angels, it's over for us."

"It's already happening," Lorenzo hazards to say, proving himself braver than I ever was with my own father. "What about Verrocchio's old angel? He attacked a boy. He tried to *drink* his blood. People aren't stupid. That's not the work of an angel; it's the work of a—"

Lorenzo cuts off abruptly. As if someone put a hand over his mouth.

"Do not *ever* say what they are out loud. Do you understand?"

The silence is knife-sharp.

After an eon, Piero and Lorenzo de' Medici finally leave, taking the book with Niccolo's whereabouts with them.

The body of the slain prior is left oozing and abandoned.

I barely even notice his cooling blood anymore. My pulse is a jagged, cutting quiver.

If the old angel wasn't an angel, then he must've been a—

We scramble out from under the table, shoulders bumping. Leonardo looks at Lupa and says it first, a whisper fringed with fear. "*Demon.*"

Lupa's eyes smolder a dark, glinting gold. She presses into the corner and *hisses*.

CHAPTER TWENTY

Leonardo races out of the palazzo, into the knotted streets. I chase after him, cursing his too-long legs. "Leonardo, wait!"

His feet churn faster.

He doesn't slow until he reaches the Piazza Santa Croce and stops on the steps of the stone-faced basilica. Chanting seeps from inside, low and soothing and entirely at odds with the air sawing in and out of my lungs.

"What are you doing? Anyone could've seen us running!" It's the wrong thing to say, but horror and shock have overwhelmed me, stolen away my better instincts.

Leonardo presses against the door and turns. His eyes are wild, rimmed with red. "Avoiding *her*. A demon can't step on holy ground."

Lupa freezes, her foot poised over the church's first step. Her face fills with hurt. "That is not true."

A high keening sounds escapes Leonardo. It pushes my pulse up to my skin, unearths some deep, defensive urge in me. I step between him and Lupa.

"Is it true? Are you—a demon?" It feels absurd to ask. Like wondering if the sky has gone green or hearing that the king of France demands my presence at his court.

Lupa runs her tongue along her pointed teeth, not meeting my eyes. "I don't know."

"You don't know, or you don't want to tell us?"

She shudders, tendrils of hair lifting around her face. "I don't know! I can't remember!" Breathing heavily, she folds in on herself: shoulders bowed, chin lowered. "Please don't be afraid of me like everyone else."

There's no sound but the Gregorian chant, its highest notes lifting like incense. I bite my lip and look away from both of them, blood rushing, heart torn. I don't know what to think anymore. I don't know what to believe.

If angels are demons, then the entire holy legacy of Florence, the city beloved by God, is a lie. It's demons whose magic infuses the streets and city walls. Demons who take our lives and memories.

And the Medici know. Whether they've known for days or decades, they knew and decided to let it stand. How could they let thousands and thousands of people believe such a lie? To let them worship demons instead of angels?

You know why, a cold, insistent voice whispers. *You've seen it firsthand.*

The Medici only care for themselves. I remember my and Niccolo's failed meeting with their bank, how we broke down into tears begging for them to forgive our father's debt. How their clerk flashed two sniveling boys a close-lipped smile and said, *A deal is a deal that must be honored.*

Leonardo snorts derisively. "I see you softening, Virgil. Ask her what she gets out of the bargains." He pushes off the door, fists clenched. "What do you take from us?"

The silence damns, the deepest note of a church bell.

"Souls." Lupa's eyes flutter shut, like she can't bear to see us. "We eat part of your soul with every bargain."

With a soft, brokenhearted sound, Leonardo opens the church door and slips inside. Even though he didn't touch me, it still feels like he's ripped part of me out along the way.

Lupa minces up the rest of the steps. I flinch away from her, the hair on the back of my neck prickling. Hasn't my body always responded this way to the angels? A mouse cringes beneath a hawk's shadow even if it's never seen its talons. Lupa says she doesn't know what she is, but part of me always knew I wasn't safe with her.

"Is that why you won't make a bargain with me? If you take the last scrap of my soul, will I end up in hell?" I whisper.

Lupa's face is a study in agony, more alive than I've ever seen it. A sorrow-stricken pietà. It cracks something in me, the humanity alongside the truth of what she is. "I don't know, but . . . I thought it might hurt you."

Her fingertips graze my wrist, as if to take my hand. I pull away. I need a human moment. I can't be the person she needs me to be right now.

Someone else needs me more.

The basilica swallows me without a sound.

Easter Mass is long over, but the monks are still chanting, devoted to their afternoon prayers. Even though it's light outside, the inside of Santa Croce is twilight dark. Gold glimmers around the high altar—a treasure trove of art telling the tales of the Bible. I shiver and cross myself. How much demon magic infuses the display? Does the holiness cancel out the profanity?

In the very last row, I spot a familiar red-gold head. Careful not to disturb the other worshippers, I tiptoe down the aisle and slip beside Leonardo.

His face is damp when he looks up.

I wish I had a handkerchief to give him, or the courage to reach over and rub the tear tracks from his cheeks. His face was sculpted for smiles; seeing him like this feels wrong.

He thumbs the wetness away himself. "We should tell the other artists. Warn them to stop making bargains with her."

I feel overspun, fabric with too fine a weave on the verge of tearing. Lupa is a demon, but she's still Lupa, the creature who wanted me to have dolci on my birthday, who worried enough to find me when I didn't come home. "I don't know if telling other people is a good idea."

Leonardo flinches. "Does a heart beat in your chest? My stepmother gave away all of her life to a soul-devouring *monster*." He ducks closer, lips nearly brushing my ear. "Don't you think everyone else should know?"

I shudder, the warmth of his breath too much on my icy skin. Do the other artists deserve to know the truth of their bargains? Of course, but also . . . would they want to? Would the truth stop them from seeking out magic?

I think of the portfolio I created to earn my apprenticeship in Verrocchio's workshop, how many nights I labored by candlelight until my head ached and my eyes strained. How when I struck my first bargain with the old angel, I was relieved that creating would finally be easier. Making bargains let me do what I loved to support the people I loved. Without my magic, my mother and sisters would've been homeless long ago.

I rub my fingers over my dead bargain marks, thinking of

all the power they gave me. I wait for the regret to well up like a rising tide . . . but 'tis more complicated than that. I regret how it's ending, but not what I did. Knowing angels are demons doesn't change anything that's happened.

"You once asked if a wolf means to kill or does she kill because she's hungry? I don't think we can judge a creature for trying to live." Leonardo scoffs and turns away, but I grab his thigh. He gives an annoyed huff, hard gaze striking against mine, but I don't let go. "I agree that Florence deserves the truth about the angels, but you heard Piero and Lorenzo. The Medici do know the angels are demons, and they've chosen to lie about it for a reason." The slain prior's blood has dried on my clothes, but the rust scent lingers. I can taste it with each breath. "Think about it. Who would you believe: the most powerful family in Florence or two lowly painter's apprentices?"

Leonardo jerks away, a hiss pushing through his teeth. The church door creaks open, sending a slice of daylight across his face. His frown is still there, but the lines are softer now, like he's turning over my words.

Lupa sits gingerly on my other side, a honey-scented pastry clutched in her hand.

My stomach sinks. "More stolen goods?" Now doesn't seem like a great time to remind Leonardo of her thieving fingers.

"No. I bought this with your money." Her brow furrows suddenly. "Is that stealing?"

I pat the coin purse at my waist—and yes, it's certainly lighter than before. "Not if you ask me next time."

Lupa offers Leonardo the cake. "I am sorry for making your face wet. Virgil has said the wet face—"

"Crying. It's called crying."

"That crying means I have hurt someone. You are not someone I wanted to hurt." She traces the ridgeline of a scar along the back of her head. "I don't know why I can't remember anything from before. But I wish I could."

I feel the quiver of her voice in my bones. Florence and her bargains. It's a handshake over a gilded desk, a knife biting into my skin. A banker with a predator's smile. Perhaps the true terms of what Lupa agreed to were hidden from her until it was too late to matter, just like they were from me.

"I believe you." Leonardo inhales sharply when I lay a hand along Lupa's face. "Do you know why you're like this?"

Her scar that shouldn't be there. The magic she uses outside of the bargains. Her girl-shape. Lupa has been so different from the very beginning. I shouldn't trust a demon, an eater of souls—the rabbit race of my pulse warns me away from her with every thump—but Lupa has never lied to me. She saved me when she didn't have to.

Lupa blinks, pinpricks of predator green flashing. "No. But I think . . . I think you make me different." Her lips part, pointed teeth sinking into the meat of my thumb without breaking my skin. "You make me want to be different."

I don't know what to think of that.

Leonardo's dark eyes lift beneath the fringe of his lashes. He traces the single bargain mark on his wrist, the scrap of soul he's pledged to this penitent demon. I bite my lip, half wanting to ask if whatever he asked for still feels worth it, already knowing he won't answer. He touches the pocket of his jacket, the place where he keeps the lock of his stepmother's hair. "I have to go."

"Wait, why?" It feels like I've gotten lost in a neighborhood I've walked through a hundred times before. "Shouldn't we figure out what to do next?" I don't want to puzzle it out myself. I need his quicksilver mind, his steadying calm.

Leonardo smiles, but the expression is as hollow as an empty heart. "Because my stepmother is dead because of demons. And you might be ready to forgive them, but I'm not."

CHAPTER TWENTY-ONE

"The Medici want to speak to you."

I flinch, sending my and Leonardo's painting palette crashing to the workshop floor. "Why would they ever want to do that?"

Verrocchio drags his frown up from the rainbow smear on his shoes. "Because you two are working on the workshop's wedding commission for them?"

I put down my brush with a shaking hand, trying to ignore the simmering panic in my belly. If Leonardo is also panicking, he's hiding it better than me, though his eyes have seemed unfocused lately, clouded with thoughts he doesn't share.

After making me scatter sawdust on the paint spill, Verrocchio motions someone at the workshop door forward. A solicitous little man with spectacles perched on the bridge of his nose comes forward, his wrinkled hands clasped behind his stooped back. Not Piero or Lorenzo, but someone employed by the Medici household.

I pull a hand down my mouth, shoulders relaxing. Cristo santo, Verrocchio really should be more specific with his Medici. 'Tis rude to frighten someone half to death.

The man presses his nose so close to the canvas, I expect him to come away with paint on it. "Hmm, no magic in this yet?"

I glance at Leonardo to catch his eye, but he's not looking at me. "Erm . . . no."

The man's spectacles magnify his stare, making my skin prickle. "Have you two worked with magic before? The Medici are eager to work with a personal painter who feels comfortable with the angels' gifts."

Oh ho, I imagine they are! I choke back a snort and hold out my forearms. "Yeah, I've made a bargain or two before."

The Medici's man examines the long rows of black marks scoring my skin, and bows with a supercilious smile. "My masters will be pleased to hear it."

As suddenly as he arrived, he's gone, walking out with Verrocchio. It's odd for a patron to send someone to examine their commission before it's done, odder still that the Medici's man barely looked at our painting at all. I think we could've shown him a painting of Giorgio's infamous phallic fruits and he wouldn't have noticed.

I slide closer to Leonardo as soon as the workshop door closes. "What do you think all that was about?"

He doesn't answer. He takes about a century filling in a detail on Lorenzo's collar with the tip of his brush before his eyes flick to mine, dark and unreadable. "C'mon, Virgil. Do we really need to talk about it? I think you already know."

His annoyance feels like getting snapped at by a friendly hound. "What's your problem these days?"

He bites his lip and drags a hand through his hair, clearly about to launch into a lecture of some kind—then he sighs and lets the red-gold mass tumble to his shoulders. "You know what? I'm not going to explain this one to you."

"Explain *what* to me?"

"It'll come to you or it won't," he says lightly, sidestepping me to go replace the paints I've ruined without making eye contact.

I gape at his retreating back. Unbelievable! What have I done to upset him?

Lupa slouches forward with a furrowed brow. She's sitting in a chair behind me, one of the garden cats curled around her neck. "Humans confuse me," she says. "He wants to spend time with you, then he does not suddenly. Why is this?"

"A very good question," I mutter darkly. There was a time in the not-so-recent past when I wouldn't have given a damn what Leonardo felt about me, but judging from the tight, buzzing feeling in my chest as I stare at him hunching over the pigment table, I now care quite a bit what he thinks of me. Sodding hell, I didn't ask for this!

I beckon Lupa closer, whispering so the half-finished putto statues can't overhear. Putti are terrible gossips. "I think I hurt his feelings."

She inhales deeply, nostrils flaring. "I smell no blood. What part of the body are the feelings in?"

"They're in your head."

"They are not real, then?"

"No, they are. When the cat purrs on your lap, what do you do?"

Lupa scoffs, as if my question is insultingly dull. "I stay still because the cat is on me."

"Right, but *why* do you stay still? Do you like it when the cat purrs?"

Her frown bends, becomes a pensive line. Her fingers sink

into the fur around the cat's neck, and the creature relaxes more blissfully against her. "I like it. It makes me want to stay."

"That's a feeling."

A spark of understanding strikes across her face. "I have tasted them in memories. All you need to do is find a way to unhurt the feelings, then! Where is the cure? The apothecary?"

If only it were that simple! Leonardo said he wasn't ready to forgive Lupa, but he's upset with *me*. I can't imagine why, because last I knew, I was not the dastardly villain lying about demons being angels—

My insides clench with a horrid realization.

His beloved stepmother *died* because of bargains. What if it had been Niccolo in her place? How would I feel if I learned demons had stolen his life? Leonardo was honest with me about the worst moment of his past—something he'd never shared with anyone else at the workshop—and when the moment mattered for me to remember, to care about how what we had just discovered might bruise his deepest, oldest wound . . . I said nothing. Didn't even think about it.

I groan, forehead thumping to the worktable. This is bad, even for me.

I've got to make it up to him.

Verrocchio's eyebrows rise at the plink of my coin purse on his desk later that afternoon. "I'd like to commission a bronze piece."

"Are you certain?"

It's not unheard of for an apprentice to place a commission, but I've never done it before, and he knows I'm supporting my family. Mamma could always use a spare denier: for my sisters, meals, entertaining other wealthy Florentines so she can preserve our family's reputation. She'd scream if she knew I had extra money and hadn't given it to her.

I push the coins closer to Verrocchio. "I am."

He sweeps my money away before I can change my mind. "All right. What do you want? I reckon I can get it done by next—"

"I was hoping to make it myself—if that's all right?" A nervy spasm tangles the statement into a question.

Is it my imagination, or does Verrocchio hide a smile in a cough? "Trying to impress someone, ragazzo?"

My blush blazes down to my bones. "No! Of course not."

Verrocchio waves me off, not believing me for a second. "'Tis none of my business anyway. Shall I go show you how to use the tools?"

"No, I'll work it out myself."

Verrocchio's eyebrows rise. I raise my chin so he knows I mean it. Then one of his eyebrows rises even higher, nearly touching his red cap.

I cross my arms, going for confidence and not petulance. "I can do it. Truly."

This time, my master doesn't bother to hide his amusement. "Suit yourself. It's harder than it looks."

He's not wrong. It takes me three days to get it right. The other apprentices ask me what I'm doing, why I'm working with metal and not paint, but I snarl at them to shut it and leave me. I don't want the surprise ruined. When my head is down, I feel Leonardo watching me from behind the Medici wedding portrait, his gaze a hand on the back of my neck, but he always makes sure I never catch him looking. His curiosity should distract me, but instead it feels like the vanishing point—the thing which all my time and effort race toward.

When it's finished, I return to my spot beside Leonardo and resume working on the wedding portrait. Now that we're working with paint, it's becoming glaringly, humiliatingly obvious that without magic, I'm useless. I glob the paint on too thickly, shade too heavily or not enough. A few days ago, I tried to blend a dab of white around Lorenzo's eye just to realize too late it wasn't paint at all: A sodding pigeon had shat on the painting from the rafters. Leonardo always waits until everyone leaves at the end of the workday to fix my errors so no one notices. He does it silently, neither of us talking about it, a snide comment never leaving his lips.

'Tis far nicer than I deserve, which is why my heart is pounding while I wait for the workshop to clear out for the night.

When the door closes behind the last apprentice, Leonardo breaks the taut silence first. "What's with all the fidgeting today?" He tilts his head, smirking. "Eager to tell me what I've done wrong with the painting?"

For the first time, I understand that his smooth smiles and witty words are a mask. He hides behind them just the way I do my frowns. "I like what you're doing. I haven't had anything to say about it for days."

"I noticed," he says lightly, carefully, those dark eyes never leaving mine for a moment. "What have you been doing with Verrocchio's metalworking tools? Giorgio's saying you're making a great, big golden phallus for Lorenzo de' Medici."

Giorgio would think that. "I was making you this."

He squints at the misshapen lump on my palm, an unreadable expression dashing across his face for a blink. "What is it?"

Why has my heart crawled up into my throat? "A locket. You're too careless with your stepmother's hair. You might put it through the wash, or one of the cats might eat it, and then you'd be all sad and demand that everyone poke apart their hairballs for *weeks*—" I cut myself off. Madonna santa. Why do my mouth and brain conspire against me? I'm supposed to be begging for his forgiveness, not telling him how he's doing everything wrong.

I swallow, chagrin and regret hot cinders shooting through my veins. "Sorry. I'm not good at saying the right thing."

Leonardo's mouth twitches. "You're really not. It's astonishing how bad you are at it." But there's no malice behind the words. Leonardo takes the locket from me. It looks ridiculous all of a sudden. Ugly, the edges uneven and jagged, the color somewhere between amber and gold. Because I couldn't afford a chain, it's strung on a leather loop that's already fraying. I was so proud when I strung the loop through it this afternoon, but seeing all its imperfections in his hand makes me want to snatch it back. "If you don't want it—"

"I do." He opens the back and plucks the dark curl from his pocket.

And hesitates.

The back of my neck cools with sweat. Is there something wrong? Did Giorgio add an embellishment to the metal when I wasn't looking? "Are you sure? Because you're not acting like—"

He puts the hair inside the hollow and snaps it closed. "It's marvelous. Thank you."

Marvelous? 'Tis serviceable at best, and we both know it. "But?"

He bites his lip. Then words spill out quickly. "I'm not careless. I just try not to hold on too hard to the things I cherish."

Wait, he *wants* to lose the last thing he has of his stepmother? I cross my arms and lean back on my stool. "You wouldn't happen to be like this about your money, too, would you? Because there's this house I'd *love* to buy."

He grimaces, like he'd rather not say more about it. "It makes it easier when . . . things leave. I can pretend I lost them instead."

"Instead of what?"

"Instead of them leaving me," he confesses to the painting.

"Your stepmother didn't mean to leave you. That's not why she made her bargains." I run my tongue along the back of my teeth, oddly angry. I can't tell if it's at him or for him. "That's a rubbish way to think. Does anyone deserve the people they cherish?" I think of my brother's face crinkled with laughter, the sea of kindness in him that had no horizon.

"Perhaps, but my father did leave me here and told me not to bother him until I finished my apprenticeship. And I know I can't stay in Verrocchio's workshop forever, but it's the only place that's felt like home for a long time." He slings the leather loop over his head, adjusting the fall of it just so. "People and places get all tangled up for me. I'm not sure that makes sense."

A strange softness fills my chest, smothers the anger. "Feelings don't have to make sense." I nod to his locket. "I hope this can feel a bit like home to you, then."

Leonardo touches the locket, peering at me from underneath his eyelashes. "I think it will."

That look of his makes my heart thud. I let out a long, shaky breath and say the thing I meant to say at the beginning. "I'm sorry for making you think I didn't care about your stepmother. I didn't consider how knowing it was demons who stole her life would make you feel."

He looks away again. "This whole time I've been able to imagine her in heaven, but what if I'm wrong?"

"You're not." Someone Leonardo loved could never be a bad person. It's simply not possible.

He gives me a small, fragile smile. "But we can't know. And Lupa doesn't either." He shrugs at my obvious surprise. "I believe that Lupa can't remember anything before she came to earth. More importantly, I don't think she's the problem. The Medici are playing with darkness and passing it off as holiness. They're the reason my mother gave up her soul for a lie. And I think you're right too."

"Me?" He's never admitted I'm right about anything.

"Yes, you." He pokes my chest with a sly, self-assured expression that finally feels like him. "We can't say Florence's beloved angels are demons without proof. Do you think your brother's disappearance and the Medici's lies could be related? Because I think they could be."

He's talking so fast, it takes me a moment to catch up. Then I laugh, the sound closer to a moan.

Niccolo didn't just know. He *told* me about it.

Leonardo grabs my shoulders, my answer clear on my bloodless face. "Show me."

CHAPTER TWENTY-TWO

The red leather cover of Dante's *Inferno* has an oily shine in the candlelight. "Your favorite book is horrifying. Drowning in rivers of boiling blood?" Leonardo flips through the pages. "No wonder you have such a melancholic disposition."

I make a noncommittal noise—not because I disagree—but because I can't get over the fact that he's next to my bed. *Leaning* alongside it, actually. He's practically under the covers!

Leonardo holds up Niccolo's warning note, one dark brow lifting. "You've had your brother's warning for two years and never thought to say anything about it until now?"

He doesn't need to know our thorny history. "I've only had it for a few weeks."

Leonardo closes the *Inferno*, marking his place with Niccolo's note. "Well, it doesn't get much more obvious than an ominous warning hidden in a book about voyaging to hell, does it? Your brother knew something."

Before I can stop him, Leonardo helps himself to my paper and half-filled pen. Then he rolls *onto* my bed, feet dangling off one end. I take a deep, long breath at the sight of his body dimpling my mattress.

"This is what we have so far." He sketches a familiar, grumpy face. "Lorenzo de' Medici is getting married, and the family is having a hard time keeping their supporters' loyalty . . ." Lupa appears next, her hands replaced with cloven hooves, the effect softening and not sinister. "Angels are demons, and no one knows but the Medici . . ." A startlingly fair likeness of me takes shape. "Last, we have your brother, who worked or is working for the Medici and sent you a warning." His hand moves faster, conjuring swooping elegant arrows connecting the three drawings over them, lines that transform the drawing into a tangled ball of rope. "The question is how are these three tied together?"

He glances up breathlessly as if *I* might know the answer.

I scoff. Trying to untie this Gordian knot is beyond me. Didn't Alexander the Great hack it apart with a sword in the end? "How should I know? We lost our only lead. I didn't catch my brother's work address because *someone* dragged me under a table."

Leonardo's bright expression dims. "What a pity *someone* saved your life, then."

I sigh guiltily. What's wrong with me? Even when I try to be nice, I fail at it. "I'm grateful for that. And I'm not trying to be a stronzo. There's a lot to take in, and we're running out of time."

It's not *I'm terrified I'll fail the people who depend on me before I die, and I worry you might be becoming one of them*, but it's still honest, which is big for me.

He takes in a deep, long breath and lets it go with a soft sigh. "I'm not just trying to help you. I don't want what happened to my stepmother to happen to anyone else. This is bigger than either of us."

"What do you mean?" That *us* of his puts me on edge.

He gestures to my window, the city skyline sweeping beyond

it lorded over by the distant duomo. "When we reveal the truth—when people learn about the lies—it could be the end of angels in Florence."

My skin erupts into gooseflesh.

A city without angels.

A city without *magic*.

"I don't think the Medici would like that very much," I whisper.

"I'd say the Medici can kiss my culo, but that's a pleasure, not a punishment, isn't it?" Leonardo winks.

I start choking. Leonardo slaps my back, but I'm not expecting it and accidentally kick the candle over.

His sketch catches fire immediately.

We bolt upright, stomping the flame until the room is left in darkness.

Wait, *complete* darkness? No, 'tis too early. Dinner hasn't even been served yet.

Leonardo screams and points at a shadow crawling through the window. He snatches a paintbrush from the floor and brandishes the wooden end at the writhing blackness. "Out, foul monster!"

The shadow thumps to the floor, letting in the orange-red twilight behind it. Lupa, her face scrunched in a determined grimace. "I want to help still, if you'll let me."

Leonardo's brush clatters to the floor. "You, a demon, want to help expose the truth about demons in Florence?"

It does seem odd for a creature who's said—more than once—how much she loves committing crimes.

Lupa hugs her knees to her chest, not quite looking at us. "If

I am not supposed to be here, then there's somewhere else I'm supposed to be."

Leonardo makes a disbelieving sound, but I don't join in. I think of Lupa's rogue magic, the Medici's reaction over what she did at the fountain. The Medici might be the reason why demons stroll the streets of Florence, but they're afraid of them too. Their house has never had a demon of its own. They know the dangerous game they're playing.

And they don't know Lupa's playing on our side of it.

"We'll need you, Lupa," I say. Leonardo's eyes start to roll, but I dive under my bed and pull out the key I stole from the Palazzo della Signoria. The little ruby eyes in the skull-shaped handle have a sinister gleam in the dying light.

Leonardo picks it up by the very end, like it's a stinging scorpion. "Where did you get this tasteless little trinket?"

"It's the key I accidentally stole. Piero was angry Lorenzo lost it." My empty hands twist together. "The Medici are frightened. Something's changing for them, and I don't think . . . I don't think it's impossible for us to take them down."

I can't believe I'm suggesting we dethrone the oldest, richest, most powerful family in Florence, but here we are.

Leonardo nods determinedly, like everything's already decided. "We'll try to see what else we can learn about your brother, and we'll finish the Medici wedding commission."

"Why?" My family could very much still use the money if we won, but I hardly see how it's going to help us expose the Medici as blasphemous scoundrels.

"Because when we drop off the portrait in the Medici's house, we can find whatever door that horrible little key unlocks."

"*You'll* finish it, then." My contribution to the painting will be minimal at best, ruinous at worst. "Or did you forget about the pigeon shit incident?"

"You made this, didn't you?" Leonardo flicks the locket.

"And it's terrible. Verrocchio might as well replace me with a dog."

The corners of his mouth kick up. "Don't sell yourself short, Virgil. A painting dog would be delightful, but your acerbic personality is irreplaceable. You used to paint without magic, and you'll remember how to do it again soon."

There's no point correcting him. His optimism is more stubborn than stone. He tosses the key and catches it with a flourish, taking my resigned sigh as an emphatic yes. "Excellent. We'll find your brother, avenge my mother, and along the way, perhaps Lupa will finally figure out what she's doing on earth. I think this is the beginning of a grand quest!"

"Or a triple murder." While I'm glad Leonardo isn't upset with me anymore, I'm not sure I like him pledging himself to my cause, either. "Perhaps we're rushing into this. I don't want anyone to get hurt."

"And I don't want to paint Lorenzo de' Medici, but alas, we can't always get what we want."

"These things are hardly the same," I say, voice tight. "No one is going to try to kill you in the workshop."

He grows serious in a second. "So it's all well and good for someone to try to kill you, but not me?"

The back of my neck prickles. Because the answer is, of course and obviously, *yes*, except I know saying it won't make any difference. Maybe it'll happen tonight, maybe it'll happen right before the bells chime midnight on New Year's Eve, but I already know death is coming for me; anything I do comes with some level of risk. I'd rather die knowing I did everything I could to find Niccolo than wait for death to find me. There's still time for Leonardo to avoid my fate.

"I'll investigate my brother alone. I don't need your help." I cross my arms and lift my chin.

"Of course you will." Leonardo smiles indulgently. "And when you leave, I'll follow you out, and you won't be able to stop me, because I'm much faster than you. We live together. You can't do anything without me noticing. You might as well let me help you from the beginning because I know you despise wasting work time."

Curse him, does he have to be right all the time? "Have you ever heard of boundaries?"

His grin is like staring directly at the sun. "I can't let you be murdered. Your glowering presence is the inspiration I need. You're like my own grumpy little angel, always sighing whenever I lose my focus."

"Don't you mean demon?"

"I said what I said."

"And you *like* this about me?"

He brushes the locket under his tunic. "I do. You just never believe me."

CHAPTER TWENTY-THREE

After Easter, there's a flood of commissions. All the wealthy families of Florence want to drape their halls with beauty, to welcome Lorenzo de' Medici's bride and earn the newly wedded couple's favor.

And if an angel should choose to bless their home as well? All the better.

"'Nubile Aphrodite'?" Giorgio reads the latest request, frowning. "What does 'nubile' mean?"

I snatch the paper from him. "I'll tell you when you're older."

Leonardo's mouth curves. Our eyes snag across the crowded workshop, an invisible rope pulling taut.

'Tis new, this sensation of being drawn to instead of away from him. As if I've stopped splashing upstream and finally allowed the current to take me where it will. I sincerely hope it's not to a cave full of flesh-eating spiders.

He mouths, *Tonight?* and I nod. He winks back, and for some reason, it makes me blush and choke and want to hurl myself into the Arno simultaneously.

The feeling only gets worse later when I usher him inside the empty workshop and lock the door behind us.

Instead of sitting before the half-finished Medici wedding

painting, he collapses on a stool by the workbench. He balances his elbows on the rainbow-stained table behind him, long legs crossed and stretched out to take up half the workshop.

"We're going to try something new tonight."

"We are?" Why has the air gone thin? Has he taken up half of that, too? I glance at Lupa's corner to see if she's noticed anything amiss, but she's already sleeping.

"You're going to paint."

"I won't! The whole point of working at night is to hide how I can't do it."

"I thought it was to discuss the very illegal murder and state secret we know about without anyone overhearing."

"That too, but—"

"No, Virgil. I'm getting tired of doing all the work myself. I know you can do it."

I shake my head. My morning exercises look like they were done by an untalented toddler. The paints run on my palette and smear into a color that could charitably be described as shit brown.

"It's faster if you do it alone."

"Just try."

Heaving a sigh, I uncover the paints and add a darker shade of green to a fold in the bride's skirt, only to realize too late that the existing color is purple and I've fucked it up *again*. I throw down my brush. "We don't have time for this."

His eyes snag on the part I've just ruined. "We do." He stands and draws closer. Even though we've worked alone in the dark dozens of times before, a spark crackles along my ribs. "You know how to do art without magic. I remember your stuff when I first started here. It was good. Really good."

"Great to hear I reached my creative zenith at fifteen."

His laugh is closer to a sigh. "You are incorrigible."

"I thought you liked this about me?"

"I said I liked your prickly personality. Not your aversion to anyone being nice to you." His voice grows softer. "That gets old."

I press my lips together and look away. The half-finished portraits and statues all seem to lean closer, listening. The magicked paintings actually *are*, nubile Aphrodite nearest, with her face in her hands and her ankles crossed behind her. She gives me a tiny glare when our eyes meet. *Be nice to him.*

All right, fine. I'm certainly in the wrong if even the paintings have noticed.

I gesture to the canvas. "Tell me how you paint without magic. Unless . . . ?" My gaze drops to the lone bargain mark on his wrist.

He smiles, the expression a slow, spreading slick. He swipes his fingertip through yellow paint and covers over the mark. "If someone had told me last year that Virgil Pitti would be so curious about me, I would've asked if they'd hit their head."

The slide of paint across his jumping pulse makes me swallow. I wish I could come up with a witty retort—he certainly would—but my tongue feels thick and clumsy.

He presses his yellow-coated fingers to Lorenzo's cheekbone. A smoky hollow takes shape, making his face feel alive in a way it wasn't before. "I like using my hands to paint. Ditching the brush makes me more aware of what I'm doing."

Without asking, he takes my hand and hovers it over the paints. "Which color calls to you?"

I fist my hand before he can tell how sweaty it is. "No. I'll make it worse."

"And if you do, I'll fix it. So I'll ask again: Which color?"

Cristo santo, he won't let me weasel out of this, will he? I don't know why he cares so much but . . . part of me also doesn't want him to give up on me. My eyes keep going to a purple so dark, it verges on black. "That one."

Leonardo nods to the bride's unfinished sleeve. "See how it feels."

I hesitate, the paint beading on my fingertip. "Maybe I should try on a different painting." I couldn't bear messing this one up any more. It needs to be perfect. Our plan hinges on getting close to the Medici.

Leonardo shakes his head, catching my wrist. "Try. It's just us."

He guides my hand closer, and I let him. When my finger is a hairbreadth from the canvas, I uncurl it with a held breath. I pull away and leave a tiny dot on the canvas where there was nothing before.

But Leonardo gasps like I've put the finishing touch on a masterpiece. "You did it!"

A baby could do what I did. On accident. I open my mouth to say so, but I can't bring myself to transform Leonardo's breathless smile into a frown. I don't want to be the person who dampens his fire tonight. He's helped me for *weeks*. I'd say it makes me want to be a better version of myself for him, but that's not quite right. Being exposed to his relentless warmth has thawed a part of me I forgot was there.

"I did." I smile shyly, but the grin he beams back magnifies mine tenfold.

"Keep going."

I dip into the paint again. This time I drag my fingers along the lines of sketch just visible beneath the yellow-gray base layer. The texture snags on my finger pads. The bride's dress slowly fills with a rich plum color. It feels *good*, right. After a few minutes, Leonardo lifts his brush and fills in a more detailed section.

Sitting side by side with him feels right too. His breathing follows the ebb and flow of my pulse. The sky goes darker as the scent of the night-blooming flowers tumbles through the open windows lining the workshop's second-floor gallery.

The dark makes me feel brave enough to tell him something I should've said a long time ago. "I've always admired the way you paint faces." Their expressions are alive in a way mine never are. "How do you do it?"

He blinks, as if my question is reaching him from the end of a long tunnel. "I always start with a real person. Not how they look, but how they make me feel." He drags his brush through ocher and adds it to the panel. "I'll sketch them over and over again until they possess me, the smallest details taking up my entire mind. Lines in a brow, the curve of eyelashes."

The word slips out unbidden. "Freckles."

His cheeks go pink, highlighting his damn freckles even more starkly. I drag my tongue along my teeth, embarrassed, but not enough to take it back.

"Freckles," he agrees quietly.

There's a squeal as his stool scrapes closer. I'm facing him now, our knees touching. Heat roars off him like a furnace.

"If I were drawing you, I would do the cheekbones first." His fingertips slowly drag along the ridges under my eyes. I shiver at the whisper of coolness where the paint sticks. "Then the eyes." He traces my brow bone tenderly, his finger lingering at the corner of my eye. "They're the most interesting color, did you know? A burst of copper ringed in green."

My heart is a storm raging beneath my ribs. After several ragged breaths, I cup his jaw in a trembling hand. "It's the freckles for me." My smallest finger presses against each one I can reach, gentle as a snowflake. "How many do you even have?"

A laugh rumbles deep in his chest. "Would you like to count them all?"

"I've tried." I press into the one at the edge of his mouth. It might be my favorite. "But you're so distracting, I always lose count."

"I distract you?" He tilts his head, lips against my thumb, eyes heavy-lidded and low.

It's not a kiss, but it could be.

My thumb drags downward, tugging on his bottom lip. "Always."

I feel his sharp inhale, the hitch in his breath, a jerk in my lower belly.

"Virgil," he whispers, barely loud enough for me to hear over my rioting pulse. "What are we doing?"

Dear sweet Cristo, what *are* we doing?

I lean backward slowly, wanting to put distance between us without hurting his feelings. A tumult of emotions charges through me—but none of them are shame or regret or anything that would douse the hunger in my soul and remind my traitorous, grabby hands that *kissing your colleague and co-conspirator is a very, very bad idea!*

I'm not allowed to have this. We need to go back to where we were before.

I wipe my shaking, stained hand on my trousers. "You do this a lot, then? Make up stories about strangers?"

His mouth presses together, the movement almost imperceptible. "Perhaps. Why do you ask?"

There's no point lying. Not when I've nearly *kissed* him and the alternative might be having to talk about that instead. "I . . . might've seen your drawings."

"Snooping in my room? I thought a rule book brought to life like you would be above such scandal."

I let out a breathless laugh, relieved he's letting me change the subject. Him teasing me is safe. It's something I can handle. "It was an accident, I swear. I went in because I feared your giant mess had finally suffocated you."

"As you've noticed many, *many* times, I find it hard to draw when I'm asked to." He glances aside, turmoil in his eyes. For one heart-stopping second, I think he's going to bring up the almost kiss. "I . . . don't think my mind works like other people's."

What an odd thing to say. "What do you mean?"

"When I'm assigned a project, I can't work on it, no matter how much I want to. There needs to be a pressure—a deadline or a person—to force me to do the work. Sometimes even that doesn't help. I get sucked into a new idea, and I can't climb out of it. Here, come look at this."

He stands abruptly, paint-sticky fingers dragging me along to the worktable. He fans a series of strange blueprints across it, hidden beneath everything else. They're . . . wagons? Wagons with wings?

"Flying machines," he says. "Verrocchio told me to come up with ideas for a church fresco, and I spent the entire day doing this instead."

The blueprints are incredibly detailed and involve an upsetting amount of math. I trace my fingers over the lines, feeling timid and tongue-tied. This glimpse into Leonardo's rich, frenetic mind feels like a gift I don't deserve. "They're good. You should keep working on them."

He laughs again, the sound bitter. "Sure. Until they put me behind on my next deadline and Verrocchio's glaring at me again." He shoves the blueprints away roughly. I want to say that I'd like to look at them for longer, but I'm not sure I've earned the right to. A cold feeling trickles down my back.

Leonardo says Verrocchio chides him for not doing what he's supposed to be doing, but I've done the same.

"My stepmother told me the way my mind worked was a gift, and it would take me far in life. But after four years here . . . I'm not so sure it's true." He tips his head toward the lofted ceiling. "There's so much I want to do and not even time to do it all. Perhaps I should've just picked one thing and stuck to it."

I hate the uncertainty in his voice. I want to tear it out and stomp on it.

"I love how your mind works." Oh no. Did I just say I loved him?

I keep talking before the embarrassment can catch up, before it leads me to make a joke or self-deprecating comment that undercuts what I want him to know. "I'm sorry if I made you feel smaller." I think of how long it takes words to make sense when I read. How sometimes I can't make them make sense at all. Father screaming at me that no son of his would be illiterate, me crying back that I wasn't, but I needed more time to do it.

"What makes you different is what makes your work so good. If other people can't see that, to hell with them." I make a rude gesture, and he laughs. "If you opened a flying-machine workshop, I'd be your first patron."

I never will—I'd be gone by then—but he doesn't need to know that.

"I know you will." He smiles. The soft caress on the back of my hand could be an accident, but I know it's not. "I can't promise they'll work, though. You might condemn yourself to a painful death."

"Better death by flying machine than by Medici."

A realization comes over me—not a new one, but one I'm immediately, excruciatingly aware of. The feeling of standing too close to the fire and not knowing until you're already scorched.

I have a *thing* for Leonardo.

For his cunning, quick brain that moves so fast, I can barely keep up.

Sure, yes, the rest of him too—I have eyes, I was trained to appreciate a good aesthetic—but this: him stripped down and vulnerable, that shy smile lighting up those goddamn freckles like flecks of gold—it fills my chest with such a big bright feeling, I could burst.

God, no wonder I was ready to kiss him.

How did I ever think it was jealousy that made my heart riot when his dark gaze brushed mine? That I couldn't stop thinking about him because he was my *rival*? He hasn't been for ages. Perhaps he never was.

There's a whole, secret world in him, and even though it's a terrible idea, I want to explore every inch of it. I wet my lips and lean forward.

"Leo—"

"Yes?" He's never said anything faster.

My hand travels the space I put between us, reaching for his. Our fingertips collide—

A scream shatters the silence.

CHAPTER TWENTY-FOUR

The scream comes from Lupa's corner. She thrashes, grappling with a dark, hooded figure. They careen into the storage cupboards. Pigments and brushes rain to the floor.

She screams again. This one has an unearthly deep note underneath it that rings my head like a bell. Leonardo claps his hands over his ears and sinks to his knees. The scream fills up my skull, throbs in the spaces between my bones. An agonized moan slides past my lips, then I'm slipping to the floor myself.

One by one, Verrocchio's statues shatter.

The magicked ones turn to me with silent screams in stone mouths before their faces explode.

The figure quails away from Lupa. It looks human, but the arms and legs are cloaked in shadow, nothing but swirling darkness where the head should be. Madonna santa, what is it?

The scream stops. Suddenly I can move again. I grab a splintered marble forearm from the floor and rush Lupa's attacker.

Its legs bend, then snap. It lands in the second-floor gallery. I blink, and it's out the open window.

There's nothing left but the wreckage of the statues, the bellow of my frantic breath.

"Are you all right?" Leonardo helps Lupa up. A cut weeps scarlet down his cheek.

The demon's chest heaves. "What was that?"

"You don't know?" I look at the ruined marble, the open window. No human could jump like that. No human could attack Lupa and be her equal in strength.

She shakes her head, face crumpling with rage-induced tears. "No! The magic felt like mine, but it was *wrong*."

Voices pour from the courtyard, followed by pounding footsteps. The commotion must've woken up the house. The workshop door slams open to reveal Verrocchio in a nightdress, a sword in his hand. His mouth drops open.

"My statues!"

A layer of dust velvets every surface, a haze of gray still caught in the air. I pull the collar of my shirt over my mouth and nose. The back of my throat already tastes of stone. A fortune of marble and commissioned work, lost in an instant.

"Something attacked Lupa," I explain quickly, as if saying it can undo any of the damage. "She defended herself."

Verrocchio surveys the destruction. The tip of his sword plinks to the floor. "At what cost?"

The other artists swarm inside, until the workshop is filled with anxious murmurs and weeping. Some of the sculptures were already done, months of work gone. Verrocchio might have insurance for the marble, but the hours of time and craft that went into shaping it? Gold can't replace that. I turn away from the destruction, a horrible darkness pulling at the edges of my vision, clawing the bottom of my stomach.

Leonardo grabs my sleeve, his whisper hot against my ear. "You know what this means, don't you?"

Someone—or some*thing*—is onto us.

• • •

The next morning delivers a barrage of questions from the city guard and Verrocchio, none of which I can answer in a satisfying way.

Yes, I saw someone with the workshop's angel. No, I couldn't see their face.

Yes, the door was locked. Yes, they came through the window.

I don't tell them what Lupa told me. That her attacker felt like they had her magic, but wrong. If they cared to know her side of things, if they cared about her wellness at all, they could ask her themselves.

At the day's end, Verrocchio looks a decade older. He crooks his finger. "Can I have a final word with you?"

A feeling of dread settles in my stomach. "Of course."

He closes the door to his office and slowly sits down, as if delaying the moment he has to speak for as long as possible. "Don't throw away your future, Virgil."

I rock backward, surprised. "I'm . . . not?"

But the painting master has found his stride and talks right over me. "You need to remember that angels aren't people. It's impacting your work."

He thinks *Lupa* is the reason why I've been furtive and weird, unable to focus?

"She's not distracting me, Master."

His bushy eyebrows lift. "Then why are you missing your deadlines? Why are you always gone when I need you? Why is the angel with you and not in the workshop for artists to make their bargains?" He smacks the desktop. I jump. "No matter how much this creature looks and acts like a human, she's not one. You're letting your affection for her blind you to what she really is."

I think of the crimson trickle down her chin, those too-sharp teeth and too-bright eyes.

Do you know what she really is, Master?

A hot rush races through me. I don't like Verrocchio's implication that Lupa is somehow less than any of us. "She's a part of our workshop, is she not? The most valuable member, given her magic. Perhaps someone was trying to steal her for themselves." It's the only explanation that makes sense. The man Piero killed wanted an angel of his own. The people at the golden fountain would've hurt me to take Lupa.

Verrocchio watches me carefully; his stare is a palette knife, scraping through all my layers to the bare canvas beneath. "She has value," he agrees. "Much like the horses that bring the marble to the workshop, or the cats that keep mice from the kitchens."

"She's no animal!"

"No, she's even more dangerous. See that you don't forget it."

What does he mean by that? My fingers tighten over the armrests of my chair. *Does he know the angels are demons?* If anyone else in Florence did, it would be the workshop masters. For the first time, I find myself edging away from my mentor, doubting him.

Verrocchio's mouth twists. "I'd like your key to the workshop, please."

My hand darts to the slender silver length. "My key?"

He gave it to me over a year ago, the day after Christmas. It wasn't a gift, but it felt like one. After months of putting my head down and working when Niccolo disappeared, Verrocchio giving me the key felt like a sign that my sacrifices were paying off. Like the future might finally work out for me.

"I'll lead the morning exercises myself from now on." He holds out his hand. "If Lupa leaves the workshop again, you'll be leaving too. Do you understand?"

My fingers are fat, clumsy salumi. It takes a few tries to untie the key and drop it into Verrocchio's palm. "Yes, Master."

Watching his fingers fold over it feels like bargaining away the last bit of my soul.

CHAPTER TWENTY-FIVE

"What a stronzo!" Leonardo shouts so loud, several people give him scandalized looks. "Verrocchio didn't threaten to evict me from the workshop, and I was there with you!"

"That's because you're too valuable for him to lose," I say miserably. The day matches my mood. Sullen rain has pummeled the streets all day, turning Florence into a drab smear of gray brown.

"Where did you go last night?" I looked for Leonardo after Verrocchio snarled at me, but he wasn't around. I waited up for him in the workshop, scraping off the bits of marble and dust that had stuck to the Medici wedding portrait. I would've stayed up even longer except Verrocchio kicked me out after dinner. I tried not to sulk when I saw him lock the door with my old key.

Leonardo's hand twitches guiltily, making it halfway to his neck before dropping. "Visiting a friend. Why does it matter?"

My temper flares. A friend? He was out with *a friend* last night? I know exactly what kind of friend this is because I've heard him give the same excuse a dozen times before. My teeth grit at the thought of Leonardo sharing a flagon of wine with this so-called friend. My insides seethe imagining him leaning in close and laughing when Leonardo whispered a joke. I don't want to meet this friend. He's not allowed to come to our home and be confused by Lupa or pet one of the sodding cats.

Cristo santo, perhaps I should be grateful. If Leonardo hadn't crawled into someone else's bed so soon after I realized I have feelings for him, I might've acted on them in a fit of mortifying weakness. I kick a loose cobblestone more savagely than it deserves. "It matters because what we're doing is secret! And you have a habit of . . ."

A sideways look from him. "Talking too much?"

"*Being* too much." He recoils a bit, and I hurry to clarify. "Being too much the sort of person people want to talk to. Know more about." Where is this coming from? I need to be stopped. "It'd be easy to let something slip."

"I wouldn't," he says. "Even if I did, my friend's a chambermaid where I'm taking us. She's discreet."

His friend is a *girl*? I swallow, cheeks flaring hot. I pray that he doesn't notice so I don't have to explain myself. "Where are you taking us?"

Leonardo goes guilty-still. I shoot him a sideways glance, and he bites his lip. "Remember how you wished you'd caught the address your brother worked at? I have a very keen memory. I see something once and remember it for years."

I glare to hide my jealousy. Bargaining for a power like that would take at least a decade, and of course he gets to have it without sacrificing anything. "You've known where my brother works for *days* and you *didn't tell me*?"

He lifts placating hands. "It was written in a shorthand that I couldn't figure out. That's why I met my friend. I wanted to be sure before I promised you anything."

I know he's trying to be helpful, but all it does is add thunderclouds to my dark mood. "I said I wanted to investigate my brother *alone*."

Leonardo runs his hands down his thighs. There's a nervous edge to his disarming smile. "I know you did. But—well, the thing is, we're already there."

I tilt back my head—up and up—to take in the massive building dominating the entire block ahead. I'm confused, until my eyes snag on a stone shield adorning the building's corner and its five red balls. "Oh merda."

It's the Medici's private home and the headquarters of their bank.

Niccolo works here? For *them*? After they hoodwinked our father, threatened to take our home?

How could he? A grief that's as much anger as sadness washes over me.

I knew he was in their employ, but it's one thing to be tangentially employed by the Medici and another to be working at their goddamn house.

"There's a party." Leonardo nods toward the snaking queue of coaches. Guards dressed in Medici livery attend a side door, helping elegant patrons inside and checking their names on a list. Each time the door opens, a slice of gold spills across the street, a release of spice and laughter that chases the shadows away. On principle, I hate every person inside already.

"We could get in." Leonardo suggests this like it's perfectly reasonable.

"Absolutely not!"

"Why not? There's dozens of people here. I doubt they'd notice two more."

Before I can stop him, he's striding across the street. A guard notices him with a scowl. "Begone!" He shoos us, like we're two sad-eyed dogs hoping for a biscotti crumb. "This isn't for the likes of you."

Leonardo's smile is big and bright and utterly mesmerizing. He sidles closer, hands clasped penitently. "We were hired to help serve."

The guard takes in the charcoal under Leonardo's nails and crosses his arms suspiciously, weighing whether or not we're lying against how upset the Medici will be if they have to wait to have their wine cups refilled.

The movement draws my attention to the sword at his hip. It's shockingly nice for a guard's blade, the crosspiece a wonder of twisted silver. It has an unnatural shine in the dull twilight. Is the blade magicked? I can't recall if I've heard of an angel being pledged to a silversmith before, but an artist's workshop could've done it just as well. The design on the pommel is oddly familiar, a stylized skull with two red gems in the eye sockets—

I gasp. 'Tis the same design on the key I stole from—

". . . Lorenzo de' Medici. He's the one who put this together to welcome Signore Soderini to Florence," the guard says.

Leonardo and the guard are nearly brow to brow now, the man sucked in by Leonardo's easy charm. I grab his arm and *tug*.

"We've gotten this all wrong," I say.

Leonardo's brows shoot upward. "We have?"

I tug him again, harder. He's more solid than marble and apparently, in this moment, just as dense. "Yes, wrong house. Let's go."

I yank again, and Leonardo finally stumbles after me. I don't let go until we round the corner, well out of the guard's sight line. He crosses his arms and scowls. "Oh, come now, I almost had us in!"

"The guard's sword pommel has the same design as the stolen key."

"So?"

"I had a bad feeling about it!" I flap my hands, unable to explain more than that. "And Lorenzo has seen us before. If he recognized us there . . ."

Leonardo sighs and massages his temples. "He probably wouldn't have." But he doesn't argue with me further.

I fist my hand and lay it against a slick wooden door, feeling like a failure.

Even though I've wanted to find Niccolo, even though unraveling the mystery of his disappearance is all I want, the prospect of having answers—or even coming face-to-face with him—terrifies me. Leonardo created a chance for me to learn, and I couldn't take it. My old fears spilled out, coins from an unfastened purse. All I could do was collect them and run.

I squeeze my eyes shut and force myself to say the words I can barely think. "What if Niccolo got in trouble?" I can't stop hearing the thud of the prior's body as it hit the floor, his blood soaking my clothes. "What if the Medici hurt him?"

I already thought he was dead once.

What if I find him only to lose him again?

You're going to lose him no matter what. You're going to lose everyone.

Leonardo drapes his hand over mine, grounding me. I don't realize until then that I'm panting, short hard bursts like I'm running for my life.

"Piero de' Medici wouldn't keep a portrait of a troublemaker in the Palazzo della Signoria, much less care enough to move it." He doesn't gentle his voice. It comes out the way he'd say anything else, like it's a fact, and it's unreasonable for me to argue with his facts, because he knows about a million more of them than I do.

I suck in a big breath, my fingers shifting under his. I ought to pull away, but I can't bring myself to. "Niccolo's older than me. Big fox and little fox . . . they're our childhood nicknames. I used to hate it, because what kid wants to constantly be reminded that he's younger and smaller than his brother? But when he called me little fox, I didn't mind."

Why am I telling him this? There are reasons I chose not to, but I can't remember them anymore.

I feel Leonardo's heartbeat in the center of his palm, starwarm and steady. "You looked up to him. He was your world." His other hand lifts to my cheekbone, brushing away a rogue tear. When did I start sodding crying? He tilts my chin up, so I have no choice but to look at him.

"What happened between you two?" His hand is soft against my icy cheek. "I promise, I'm not trying to pry. I just want to understand." His throat hitches when I say nothing. "You don't have to tell me if you—"

My heart roars, even as my body freezes. "No, I do."

He's touching me. *He's cradling my face.*

And I finally feel brave enough to spill the shameful story I've shared only once before, in the darkness of the confessional.

"My brother said he was leaving for a job that would buy Casa delle Volpi twice over. I didn't trust the sound of that, so I begged him to take me with him. He took off his ring and asked me to keep it safe instead. He had to leave alone because I'd only slow him down." The snow was sugaring the street, his red cloak the brightest thing in the world, and for the first time in our lives, my brother told me he didn't need me. My breath stutters even remembering it.

"My brother was nothing like our father, but all I could hear was his voice, telling me I would never be enough. I knocked the ring aside and told him to go because I couldn't stand the sight of him." I'll never forget the answering hurt on his face, how he lifted his arms helplessly and asked if I'd at least hug him goodbye, just in case something happened.

I turned away instead.

And Niccolo left, but not in anger.

He left crying. His hot tears still couldn't thaw the ice in my chest. I didn't go after him or take the words back.

A week later, he was missing. Only then did fear slide into my anger, chisel out a nice little hollow to fill with curdling shame.

My brother was gone, and I hadn't hugged him goodbye when he'd begged me to. I'd turned my back on him instead. I'd made him *cry*. After all he'd done for me. This was how I treated the person I loved most.

I'm crying now. Big, ugly sobs that shake my bones.

I'm suddenly stumbling forward, a wall of warmth under my cheek. Leonardo has pulled me into an embrace so tight, it almost holds me together. He mutters a soothing stream of softness against my temple. Tender words I don't deserve. I'm the boy with the heart of ice, and he's the sun itself. I'll freeze him out too if he gets too close.

"You were upset, Virgil," he says. "Everyone makes mistakes when they're frightened."

"You wouldn't. All you ever wanted was a sibling with your rust-gold hair."

He squeezes me once, but doesn't deny it. His fingers trace patterns on my back. A circle. A star. A shape that feels like the very first letter of my name. The motion makes my blood slow, my hands unclench. I can't remember the last time anyone held me.

"What are you going to do after you find him?" Leonardo says abruptly.

"What?"

His face is sfumato through a gritty haze. "Sometimes when things feel awful, I imagine what happens next. For me, I'd like to open my own workshop. I've decided leaving Verrocchio's doesn't have to be a bad thing."

My stomach knots strangely. *Verrocchio's won't be the same without you.*

Which yes, obviously. There are two dozen apprentices; people cycle in and out of the place all the time. Leonardo was always going to leave someday. But . . . I can't imagine myself there without him.

You won't even be there a year from now. This is a good thing. The best thing. He'll never have to see you die. The thought is a heart-stopping kick to the chest—sobering enough to chase away the rest of my tears.

"That's great," I finally choke out. "You'd get the recognition you deserve, the chance to honor your stepmother's legacy. You'd finally have everything you want."

He smiles, the expression seeming to hide something else. "Would I?"

Is this a test? "You just told me it's what you want."

"Virgil." He looks down at me, his freckles dark little stars against his moon-pale skin. My eyes get lost tracking them, searching for constellations in the chaos. "Don't be ridiculous. I could never open a workshop alone. You'd have to be there too."

"You want a workshop with *me*?"

Did we trick our way into the Medici house after all and eat mind-bending truffles? Did unearthing my most shameful secret knock my brain sideways? I can't imagine why else Leonardo would say this. I can't paint anymore. He *knows* this. Even if I weren't facing an untimely demise, I'm the worst business partner imaginable.

And yet . . . there's a curl of longing cresting in me like smoke from a snuffed-out candle.

Before Niccolo disappeared, before I had to put my family's well-being ahead of my wishes, before I bargained away all of my days, opening a workshop had been my dream too.

A sudden movement at my side: an opening door. Leonardo tugs me from the path of a snorting horse that has no business being that big. My shocked face is reflected in its glassy eye. Sodding hell, it almost trampled me! Do the Medici not look before they unleash their monstrous beasts into the city?

"Gesù Cristo," an oddly familiar voice grumbles. "Move!"

Two pages lead out the enormous bay. Astride it glowers a handsome, bored young man.

I just barely get a glimpse of the rider's face before he gallops into the rain.

Shock kicks my mouth open. *"It's him!"*

My brother.

Alive and just ahead.

CHAPTER TWENTY-SIX

My heart slams against my breastbone, writing a frantic message: *Niccolo is here. Niccolo is here. NICCOLO IS HERE!*

My feet are flying. Leonardo falls behind, shouting. I don't pause to hear what he's saying.

The rain has stopped, and the narrow streets swell with people trapped inside until now. They just barely move aside for the racing horse. They definitely don't move aside for me. A frantic scream tears from my throat, and the crowd becomes a blur of shocked faces. No one wants to stand betwixt a madman and what he's chasing. It's just enough to let me keep the rider in sight, to not lose him down a sharp corner.

The horse pauses at the end of a distant block. I get close enough to see it's stopped in front of a grand house with an unfamiliar coat of arms hanging from its window.

Niccolo dismounts. He tosses the reins aside carelessly. A footman lunges to grab the horse's reins before they hit the filthy street. Niccolo climbs the wide stone steps.

I throw myself after him in one last, desperate rush. My fingers catch his finely embroidered sleeve. "Volpone!"

Niccolo turns, eyes wide. The air catches in my lungs at the tiny heart-shaped divot on his cheekbone—a scar from a rock when we were little. I thud to the stairs on my knees, all my strength gone. "It's you. It's really you."

He grips my wrist, the only thing keeping me from falling off the stairs entirely. His other hand is held palm-out to the footmen, motioning them back.

On his finger is a familiar ring.

A cluster of black garnets on a heavy silver band. I spent all of my first payment from Verrocchio on it. I couldn't fathom the extravagance now, but at the time, it felt right to spend everything I had on the person I loved most. He helped me convince our hidebound father that going into a trade would be good for me. He knew I needed to leave Casa delle Volpi before our father broke me. I wanted Niccolo to know how much his support meant.

Niccolo blinks, his mouth slack with shock. "Who *are* you?"

The words don't make any sense. "It's . . . *me*. Your brother."

A maelstrom of emotions swirls across his face—confusion, disbelief, and, finally, anger.

"I have no brother."

He lets go. I sprawl into the street, staring with horror as he disappears inside and the doors slam in my face.

CHAPTER TWENTY-SEVEN

The next day I tell Verrocchio I'm sick so no one will bother me. Nothing makes sense.

Niccolo is alive, but he says he has no brother.

But I know it's him. There's no mistaking his scar. Elisabetta threw the rock in anger, and then broke down sobbing when she saw the blood. Niccolo took her on his lap and showed her the cut and reassured her that it was an accident: Look, see how it was heart-shaped and becoming a mark of her love?

He's angry and pretending not to know you, an awful voice whispers. *You deserve this. This is* your *fault.*

I need to go back. I need to apologize and beg him to return to us. He can ignore me all he wants, but Mamma and our sisters will need him when I'm gone. I half stand, ready to leave right then.

Except . . . if he *is* angry, why would he still wear the ring I gave him? Why keep it at all?

"What if he's not angry or ignoring you?"

Leonardo's question stops me. I didn't realize I'd spoken aloud. I also didn't realize he'd slipped into my room like a flea-ridden cat.

I whirl on him, scowling. "Shouldn't you be working on our painting?"

"Last I heard, it was a group project."

"I'm sick."

He sits cross-legged on the floor. "Looks fatal. Shall I summon the priest?"

Must he make me spell it out? "I want to be alone."

He has so many smiles, they could be their own language. This one says I'm full of shit. "No, you don't."

If he'd asked if he could be here, I would've said no. But the fact that he's already here . . . it's like setting down my brush when it's too dark to paint anymore. A break I didn't want, but one I needed.

"If my brother's not ignoring me, then what do you think he's doing?"

Leonardo tips his head and taps the black mark on his wrist. "I think he made a bargain and gave up a memory for it."

A bargain. *Of course.* I collapse on my bed and release a long breath. "But the only people who can make bargains are in workshops and the Florentine families blessed with their own . . . demons."

It feels odd to call them demons still, even if that's what they are.

Odder still that Niccolo would make a memory bargain with one. When I came home from Verrocchio's workshop with my first mark, he'd given it a long, dark look and begged me to be careful. He didn't like the thought of me giving up my life for magic, even if it was just a day or week. His grim expression didn't change when I said it was expected, that all the other artists did it too.

Leonardo tugs his bottom lip thoughtfully. It's stained with the faintest brush of deep purple, the same color as in the Medici wedding portrait. I scrape my tongue along the back of my teeth and shove away the memory of how his plush lip felt under my thumb when I almost kissed him.

How it looked when he asked me if I wanted to open a workshop with him.

What did he mean by that?

I desperately want to know, but I'd rather swallow paint than ask. He was probably jesting. I was upset and he needed me to stop bawling in public like a child. He's my co-conspirator. All right, fine, a friend. A distressingly attractive friend, but still. There is no future for me, and I need to focus on what's important. I can't be distracted by him. I won't—

". . . could be hidden. What do you think?" He stops talking with a bright, expectant look.

Sod it all to hell! A mouth has no business being that distracting.

"Something on your mind?" Leonardo asks lightly when I stay silent.

I force my gaze up, making dedicated eye contact and everything. "No. 'Tis a lot to consider, that's all."

His mouth curls. "I *said* we've been told demons can only make bargains with the people they're bound to, but how do we know if that's true? Your brother could have a hidden bargain mark."

That's not a half-bad theory.

"We could bribe his valletto and ask if he's got any," Leonardo says.

I frown. Asking the person who dresses my brother questions about his body feels wrong. "Won't that seem . . . odd?"

Leonardo shakes his head emphatically. "You wouldn't *believe* the things people pay good coin to learn about the ladies and lads of the Baldracca—"

"And I never want to!" The absolute *last* thing I need to think about is Leonardo in the city's notorious bordello district.

He crooks a finger, beckoning me closer. Against my better judgment, I give in. "Promise me one thing."

"What?" His breath smells faintly of the fig jam from breakfast. I imagine he'd taste like it too.

"Don't try to visit your brother alone."

Cold souses my fantasy of kissing him. "Why not?"

Leonardo grimaces, like he'd prefer not to answer. "Because when you talk about your brother . . . you get this *look*."

"What sort of look?" I don't like the thought of him seeing things in me I can't see myself.

"Like it's life or death to you."

I cross my arms and look away, chafing warmth back into the skin. "I don't like it when you tell me what to do."

Leonardo grimaces. "I'm not. I'm just trying to look out for you." Hurt hovers behind the words, and I instantly feel bad.

But not bad enough to take it back. Niccolo is just north of the workshop. There's nothing stopping me from going to talk to him. It would be faster than all this talking and planning. Each tolling of the church bells feels like the start of a funeral. Every hour I wait is another hour of my life gone. What if Leonardo and I lose the Medici wedding commission and its winning purse? What if I die before I solve Niccolo's mystery? Who will take care of my mother and sisters then?

"I could help," a new voice says from the door.

Oh good, and now Lupa's here too, a white cat in her arms

and several more trailing her skirts. Am I the only person in this entire workshop who respects another person's right to sulk alone?

Leonardo's mouth drops open. "Is that Buttermilk? I haven't seen her for days!"

"Buttermilk?" I repeat, aghast. "You *named* them?"

"Of course." Leonardo strokes the head of a fluffy tortoiseshell, who hisses and swipes at him. "You'd name them too, if you opened up your heart to the joy of cats."

"I'm not—I don't—I'm allergic to them!" I punctuate this with a tremendous sneeze.

Leonardo's mouth quirks, and he tosses me one of my own stockings as a handkerchief. "The gray tabby is Prancer, this one is Fifi, and the brown stripy one is Mykee."

"Mikey is a terrible name."

"It's short for 'my kitty,' because he was the first one who liked me."

The cat in question bumps his head against the boy's hand, and I have to admit, something warm and soft crawls into my heart at the sight of their reunion.

Who wouldn't want to kiss a boy who cares for animals? a small, secret part of my heart whispers.

I promptly tie it to a chair. Then smother it with a sheet for good measure.

"Why do the cats like you? Is this some demon magic?" I ask Lupa. I don't actually care, but I need to think about anything other than softhearted boys with kissable mouths being kind and gentle to creatures that don't deserve it.

"Yes. Cats are descended from demons. They can walk between worlds."

Leonardo freezes, his hand still on the animal's head. "I thought you didn't remember anything of your life before you came to earth?"

Lupa lets the mean fluffy cat climb into her lap. "I don't. But I can recognize my kin."

Well, that's horrifying and certainly explains my dislike of cats.

"You said you could help." Leonardo sidles closer to Lupa. "How?"

Her too-long fingernails flick to the cats. "The same way I recognized them. If I smell or taste your brother's blood, I'll know if there's magic in it."

I bite the inside of my cheek, holding back a wave of frustration. "You're forbidden from leaving the workshop. If Verrocchio sees you've left again, he'll blame me." Being tossed out of the workshop would take up time I don't have to spare. I don't like our odds of breaking into my brother's fancy house at night, either, even with Lupa's magic.

Leonardo bolts upright, one finger lifted. The cats startle. "I have an idea!"

A fissure of hope darts through me. That quicksilver mind of his could come up with five ideas before I even came up with one. It once would've made me cross, but now . . . "What is it?"

He rubs the back of his neck, laughing nervously. "It's a smidge sacrilegious."

CHAPTER TWENTY-EIGHT

"Mass," I whisper-hiss accusingly. "You've brought *a demon* to mass!"

A finely dressed lady gives me a judgmental look down her long, pointy nose. Leonardo motions for me to be quieter. "We won't let her take the Eucharist; it'll be fine."

Fine, he says! I'm not someone who's fretted much about his immortal soul, but this seems like a step too far.

And a mass not just in any church, but in the Cattedrale di Santa Maria del Fiore, the place to be and be seen. The cathedral's red duomo is my north star, the landmark that takes me anywhere I want to go within the city walls. But walking beneath it today makes the huge red dome feel like a lid trapping me inside a boiling kettle.

I'm not doing a good job hiding my unease, because Lupa nudges me and whispers, "Am I doing this right?"

She's wearing an inconspicuous dress, a gauzy veil over her hair. There's nothing we can do about her eyes, though. They flash gold green when the burning braziers catch them at the wrong angle. My hand flexes, resisting the urge to throw the hood of her cloak up. She only needs to make it to the pew. Once mass starts, no one will care about a girl they haven't seen before.

"You're the very picture of piety." My smile is a limp dishrag.

She frowns. "Is that a good thing?"

"Right now it is."

I rise up on my toes, searching for a curly black head, a heart-shaped scar beneath smiling hazel eyes—

I flinch at a horribly familiar red cap instead.

"Oh merda."

Leonardo whips toward where I'm looking. His eyes widen. He drags us behind a Corinthian column. "What's Verrocchio doing here?"

The master artist smiles and laughs among the beautifully dressed crowd. He attends mass at Santa Croce with the rest of his apprentices, but come to think of it, I haven't seen him there in a few weeks. He must be here to glad-hand Florence's wealthiest into commissioning more art for the Medici wedding. It's why the workshop's been so busy. Curse his excellent business instincts!

"We should go," Leonardo whispers. "We can see if your brother struck a bargain another time."

"*You* want to *leave*?"

Usually, he's the one who goes charging in, and I'm the one pleading for caution. Past Virgil would both appreciate and applaud this unusual display of restraint from him, but that was before I knew Niccolo was alive. I don't have time for caution anymore.

There's a stirring at the church's doors. I turn, and my stomach swoops to see Niccolo entering the nave dressed in scarlet and gold. Is it my imagination, or does his appearance cause a ripple through the crowd? Is he as important to them as he is to me?

"You two can leave," I say, shouldering out from behind the column. "I'm staying."

Leonardo catches my sleeve, mouth tightening. "You won't even know if he's made a bargain without Lupa!"

Even in the dim church light, his freckles stand out. They're growing darker in the sunlight, more bronze than gold. Witnessing the change feels like my own private autumn here in the spring. Will I live long enough to see how brown they are in the fall? My hand fists, quelling the urge to trace them.

"I know. But I need to get closer to him."

I tug my arm free. I don't look back as I stride the marble floor toward the stranger shining in the splendor of it all.

Niccolo.

His hair is longer, combed back. The panes of his face are sharper, his jaw stronger. He's older, and he looks like it. My heart aches, soft and helpless, at all the changes I missed in him.

I hold my breath as he walks toward me down the aisle. I know I shouldn't stop and stare, but I can't help myself. When he walks past me, my eyes flicker to his.

A furrow appears in his brow, so brief and sudden, I could've imagined it, and then he's behind me.

My heart pounds like a drum. Maybe Leonardo was right. Maybe Niccolo's not avoiding me. Because surely if he recognized me just now, I'd see it on his face. I was always the better liar.

"Signore." Someone ambushes Niccolo. "It's a delight to finally meet you."

"The pleasure is all mine," my brother says in a voice both his and not. "Florence is lovely."

"You grew up outside of Bologna, did you not?" The man's voice is eager. As if he's fishing for information, just as I am.

There's a moment of hesitation, far longer than expected.

When Niccolo finally does answer, it's uncertain. "Yes . . . that's right. I've been living in the countryside for the past few years."

I gnaw the inside of my cheek. If that's true, it explains why I never saw him in the city until now.

"Such a pity about your uncle's death. You and he must've been quite close if you were named his heir."

This time, the silence stretches even longer. An anxious pang races through me. For some reason, it feels vital that Niccolo answer this question right. Something is . . . off about all this, in a way I can't quite place. It's like Niccolo doesn't know his own story.

"I miss him terribly. Now if you'll excuse me—"

The other man startles, his face the very study of shock. "Do you not mean to seek revenge for him? Everyone knows Iacopo Soderini's death was no accident!"

Soderini. Why is that name familiar?

A name from Father's merchant circle? But no, I feel like I've heard it more recently than that.

Niccolo leans away from the other man. His hands clasp behind his back. He rubs the black stones of my ring, spinning the silver band around his knuckle. The movement is fitful, nervous, at odds with the stiff set of his shoulders. The skin underneath the ring is rough and red, as if he does this often.

I gasp, the answer coming to me in a dizzying rush.

Soderini was the name of the prior Piero de' Medici killed. The one who accused the Medici of wrongdoing with the angels.

A force catches my shoulder and pulls me back. "What are you doing?" Leonardo says. "You're staring at the man like he owes you money. Don't be daft!"

An annoyed snarl builds in my chest, but it dies when I see he's right. We're some of the last people standing, and it's drawing attention.

I turn away before Niccolo notices, before he can recognize me from the steps of his house or in his own reflection.

Because Niccolo isn't Niccolo here, is he?

He's Soderini—the heir of the man Lorenzo and his father killed.

Leonardo strong-arms me into a pew beside Lupa. I turn to him breathlessly, even though the mass is starting. "Did you hear that?"

"I heard enough." He runs his finger over his lone bargain mark, brows drawn together. "Is that how your brother usually acts?"

I shake my head. Niccolo's halting answers. His fidgeting. He was like a player who doesn't know his lines. But if his lie is discovered, he'll be arrested and executed, Medici protection or not. Why would he do something so foolhardy and dangerous? Is this why he warned me not to follow him? Is that why his face was on the wall of the Palazzo della Signoria—to better sell the lie of him being a man named Soderini?

But my brother wouldn't do this. He's no criminal.

Or would he? My bargain marks prickle, each one a reminder of my own bad choices.

There's a spiking throb in my temple. It feels like I'm trying to guess what someone else's painting looks like before it's finished.

Leonardo's knee nudges mine. "You still want to go through with this?"

My brother is sitting somewhere behind me. His presence

feels overwhelming—like a mountain or a raging river. "Of course."

Leonardo's mouth thins, but all he does is nod.

When the congregation stands for Communion, the three of us don't file out with the rest of our pew. I watch the queue go to the priest, heart in my throat as Niccolo gets closer and closer.

When he reaches the end of our bench, Lupa slips out.

She slams into Niccolo.

He catches her. She pulls back with a gasp. "Apologies, signore! I am so hopelessly clumsy. It brings great shame to my family."

Niccolo frowns. "I—erm—yes?"

Lupa grabs his wrist and rightens herself. Niccolo hisses once and grabs his arm.

But Lupa's already pulling away, her index finger in her mouth.

She's tasting his blood.

My entire body strains toward her, desperate to know what she sensed. She finds my fervent stare through the crowd.

And does nothing but stare back.

I shake my head, then nod, raising my eyebrows. Did she forget what we discussed? She ducks her head and arrows over, knocking people out of her way. Annoyed grumbles fan behind her, and my temper spikes. What the hell is she doing? She'll get us noticed.

She thunks on the bench and speaks before I can tell her off. "Your brother has no soul."

"What?"

She's frowning like I've said something she doesn't like, but there's a frightful white ring around her eyes that doesn't match the expression. "His soul is missing. Gone. I tasted nothing."

I feel like a rock someone's skipped over the river's surface. Everything's spinning so fast, I can't get my bearings. I look to Leonardo, hoping he can make sense of it, but he's shaking his head, mouth paper-thin. "That can't be possible. Niccolo's right there. He's alive."

"Of course he's alive," I hear myself say. "What are you two going on about?"

Both of them turn to me, concern and fear warring across their faces. Lupa's words finally sink in, water closing over my head.

When my brother first went missing, my greatest fear was that he was dead.

The truth is worse.

His soul is gone. Stuck somewhere I can't reach. What if I found him but it's too late to save him?

"How do we get it back?" Curious heads ripple in my direction.

Leonardo motions for silence. "Virgil—"

"How do we get it back?"

Lupa blinks, biting her bottom lip. "I don't know."

"But you knew it was missing. You can figure out where it went, can't you?"

Leonardo grabs my elbow. "Be quiet and think." There's a wheedling edge in his voice that stings like nettles. I toss him an annoyed glare, but he doesn't stop talking. "Your brother is involved with the Medici, who are involved with—" He mouths the word "demons," hands twisting helplessly. "I'm sorry, but I think there's only one place it could be."

I gasp and shove away from him.

Hell.

He's trying to tell me my brother's soul is *trapped in hell.*

All at once, the cathedral is too crowded, the incense too cloying. I can't hear the priest prattle on about God and heaven when my brother's stuck in hell. I need to get outside, where there's more space and air, where my beloved brother can't look at me with nothing in his eyes.

Leonardo inches closer, his face so gentle, I want to scream. "Virgil, you can't—"

"Let's go." I take Lupa's hand and stand, pulling her with me.

Only to collide into someone returning to their seat from Communion. I've gone the wrong way out.

"Excuse me!" the woman cries.

Lupa turns, her face a full moon in the circle of her veil. Her eyes catch the candlelight—

A gasp, as loud as a scream, cuts through the quiet.

The woman's face goes milk-white. Her shaking finger rises.

"Angel." Her eyes are wide and shining. She pivots to the congregation and shouts joyously, *"An angel is among us!"*

CHAPTER TWENTY-NINE

"Angel!"

"A girl angel!"

The news ripples through the crowd, a wave that crashes into every corner.

I lace my fingers through Lupa's, wanting to drag her somewhere safe, even though every eye in the cathedral is on her. I can't forget what happened at the fountain, her eldritch scream and ravenous eyes. They don't see her as a person. They won't care if they hurt her.

And if they do, she might not be able to stop herself from hurting them.

"Lupa?" Oh God, Verrocchio. There's a bulge in the crowd ahead, as if someone is trying to push their way through. *"What are you doing here?"*

The demon's eyes flare with gold. She pushes me away. "He can't see you!"

I open my mouth, ready to protest, but Leonardo is already tugging me away, shouldering his way through the crowd and the double doors outside.

The piazza is deserted, save for coaches parked and waiting for their wealthy owners. The drivers' heads perk up curiously. They're gathered between the cathedral and the white-and-green marble bell tower. Mass doesn't end for another quarter hour.

Acid bursts in my stomach. This was a foolish, stupid idea. I should've listened to Leonardo. We should've scrapped the plan the moment I saw Verrocchio.

"Don't run. It'll look suspicious." Leonardo motions me down the steps, toward the coach queue.

"Is running away not exactly what we're doing?"

"Leaving mass early is a sin. Fleeing guiltily across the piazza is a crime and infinitely more interesting to anyone watching."

The clamor of voices swells louder from inside the church. Then a door slams open.

"Virgil!" Verrocchio's furious voice cracks across the courtyard. *"I know you're behind this!"*

Panic floods me like a slick of oil. If we run down the empty piazza, he'll see us. If we freeze on the other side of the coaches, the gossiping drivers will see us. There's nowhere to run.

But there's somewhere to hide.

Leonardo shoves me toward the nearest coach. "Inside, inside!"

My fingers fumble on the latch, and the door flies open. We tumble onto the bench.

Leonardo reaches back and closes the door right before a familiar silhouette appears beyond the linen curtains.

Leonardo watches Verrocchio's shadow, breathing hard. His hair is in my mouth. His elbow is between my ribs.

And his body, beautiful sweet Cristo, his body is spread over every single inch of me, hot and heavy and glorious.

I want him to move. I *need* him to move before it becomes glaringly obvious how I feel about him being on top of me, but all he does is sigh and rest his brow in the divot between my neck and shoulders.

Our ragged panting fills the tiny space, somehow louder than all the conversation happening outside. Yes, the drivers saw two boys leave mass; no, they didn't notice what they looked like. Do they look like they're paid enough to play driver *and* guard at the same time? Verrocchio's silhouette disappears, and even though I can still hear him arguing, my pulse starts to slow.

Leonardo fidgets and slips into the footwell. My arm shoots up and hooks around his waist, pulling him closer to me.

"Virgil." His nose traces a line along my neck. By accident, obviously.

Still, the movement makes my skin prickle with want. "Yes?"

"I think—" He tries and fails to move again. "I think this coach might've been made for one person."

"You don't say."

He laughs, and the warmth of the sound races down my entire body. "I also don't think we can move for a while. Not until Verrocchio leaves."

Someone will definitely notice a rocking carriage, even if it's rocking for reasons different from what they assume.

I make a noise of agreement—all right, you could call it a whimper—and stare at the dusty ceiling, my trousers growing tighter. The landscape of Leonardo's back presses against my hand with each breath, the furrows of his ribs, the deep channel of his spine. It takes all my self-control not to crook my fingers, trace senseless patterns across his jacket, ones he could imagine on his skin.

This is the punishment I get for bringing a demon to mass. I should've known better.

"Do you think Lupa is all right?"

Leonardo shifts the tiniest bit. His elbow slips off my ribs into my stomach. "It's illegal to harm an angel."

It's not the comforting answer I was hoping for. "Verrocchio already thinks it's my fault."

"And he's right, but he doesn't know that yet. We'll go to Santa Croce after this. Their mass starts later. If someone sees us there, he can't know for sure we were here."

I let out a shuddering breath. "We shouldn't have come here today. I fucked it up."

My brother is trapped in hell, and I'm trapped in some rich person's coach. Instead of finding answers, I'm hiding from the consequences of my own poor choices.

Leonardo elbows me again. I'm starting to suspect he's doing it on purpose. "No, we both fucked it up. And that's all right, mistakes happen. How were we supposed to know Verrocchio would be here today?"

I sigh and let my eyes drift closed. Try to focus on the bitter tang of old sweat and not the way Leonardo's scent swirls around me like summer flowers. How that "we" makes my insides twist. He won't let me blame myself for this, and I don't believe him, but I'd be lying if I said it didn't make me feel a bit better.

"You never answered me, you know." His voice is light, teasing.

"Answered you about what?"

"Opening a workshop together."

I stop breathing. I only start again when I remember that Leonardo is on top of me and definitely noticed.

His fingers race, featherlight, over the back of my hand, twine through my fingers. Even though I'm the one holding him, it feels like he's the only thing tethering me. "Why can't you answer?"

My mouth tastes like old blood. "I thought you were jesting about the workshop."

His hand goes cold in mine. "Jesting?"

"Weren't you? I thought you were trying to make me feel better. I was crying." *In your arms.* I swallow at the memory. I don't want to think about it when we're chest-to-chest again. "It was amusing. I mean, could you imagine it? We'd go bankrupt by the end of the first year."

He smiles against my collarbone. "I wasn't jesting, Virgil."

I stammer out a disbelieving noise.

He presses his lips to the spot over the frantic thud in my throat. "Is that all you're worried about, then?"

I gasp, the sound more like a groan. Us? Together? Has he swallowed all the workshop's white lead? It's a possibility. I've seen him drink rinsing water instead of drinking water by accident at least five times. I drop my arm, pushing myself up and away from him, damn the carriage rocking. "We'd get nothing done!"

Leonardo's eyes crinkle into crescents. "Probably not," he agrees cheerily.

I shake my head, trying to ignoring the firework feeling beneath my ribs. "You'd let a million cats live inside. You'd bounce your leg on the bench. You'd do that thing where you breathe all deep and distracting when you're concentrating, which would be almost never, because you miss every deadline!"

"I know." He's grinning, a huge Lupa-like grin. "What do you say?"

I let out a frustrated huff and jerk away. I will *not* look at him. I don't want him to know how much he's rankled me. "I don't think you have the slightest clue how much you get under my skin."

He laughs and skims a hand across my forearm, dragging his fingernails across the black lines there. "Do I now?"

My skin erupts in traitorous, damning gooseflesh. I keep my eyes six inches to the left of his like my life depends on it. "You know damn well you do. You do it on purpose. Sometimes it's all I can think about."

He smirks when he feels the bumps. "It seems like you think about me a lot, then."

"Yes." I shiver as his hand moves under my wrist, traces the blue veins. "I do."

"Look at me." He cups my jaw. My mouth parts, a shocked, airless gasp. His thumb traces just beneath my bottom lip, eyes dark as pitch. "Perhaps I should give you something new to think about."

Joke's on him. I've haven't gone a day without thinking about him since he set foot in Verrocchio's workshop, so bright-eyed, I couldn't look away. I thought it was because I hated him. I thought it was because he was an annoying fop whose art was better than mine.

"Yeah," I murmur. "I think you should."

He grabs my hips and crushes his lips to mine.

I kiss him back, my hands raking through his hair, dragging him closer.

It's the first gulp of air after bursting from the river. It's the first drop of honey after Lent, a taste so longed for and missed,

I'd forgotten how much I wanted it. He slots his body alongside mine, the too-small coach bench suddenly big enough for both of us.

It's all tongue, and a little teeth. It's him and me and *it's everything.*

"Virgil," he whispers helplessly, a hand below my doublet, tracing the curves of my ribs under my thin shirt. "Mi tesoro, you don't know how long I've wanted to do this."

My insides go molten.

My treasure.

Except I'm the one who's struck gold.

I whimper into his mouth and fumble with his laces. I need more of him. Even if I had all of him, it wouldn't be enough. How long have we been heading to this place? How long have I held back even thinking it, putting him on the list of things I wasn't allowed to have? I want to kiss him until the only word he can gasp is my name. I want to burrow beneath his skin exactly the way he's tunneled into me and show him the shape of my longing.

I've wanted him for so long, I don't even know when it started.

He pulls back slightly, hot mouth dragging over my rough skin, as if he can't bear to give up the contact. That's when I hear it too.

The creaking of carriage wheels. The clop of hooves.

Mass is over. I imagine whoever owns this carriage doesn't want a show afterward. I groan and let my head fall against his shoulder.

He laughs and nuzzles my temple. "Come on, now. We've got to go to Santa Croce. We can continue this later."

Later. The word thrills and terrifies me in equal measure.

After lifting the curtain to be certain no one's right outside the door, we sneak out and wend our way through the crowd. I can't stop staring at Leonardo, the riot of his red-gold waves, his kiss-swollen lips. When he catches me looking, his shy smile lights me up like a torch.

I'm so distracted, I don't notice the hooded figure waiting with crossed arms at the mouth of Via dell'Oriuolo until an arm blocks our path.

Verrocchio throws back his cloak hood, his face grave as sin. "Enough."

CHAPTER THIRTY

I won't stand for it any longer."

For a breath-stealing moment, I fear Verrocchio is on the verge of an aneurysm. He's almost wheezing, his face drenched and dripping into his collar. His red cap is crumpled in his hands.

Leonardo edges closer. "Master, are you—"

"Go home, Leonardo!"

He flinches like a startled dog. Verrocchio is hard on us, but he's not one for yelling, especially out in public. Nothing comes before his workshop's sterling reputation. Leonardo throws me a beseeching sideways look, as if I might know something he doesn't.

"Go home *alone*." Verrocchio's nostrils quiver.

His teeth sinking into his bottom lip, Leonardo reluctantly disappears into the crowd. His absence makes me feel cold even though the air is thick with moisture. I chafe my arms, trying and failing to banish the panic gathering around me like clouds. Is it my imagination, or are the people giving Verrocchio and me a wide berth?

Verrocchio wipes his brow with his cap, almost yanks it back on with a trembling hand, then crumples it again. "You're no longer part of the workshop."

My body goes rigid. "I'm . . . not?"

Verrocchio grimaces, like he hates having to do this. "You're fired. You've given me no choice. You were one of my most dependable apprentices, but now all you do is cause trouble." He scrapes a hand down his chin. A week-old beard clings to it. Marble dust packs the crescents of his nails like grave dirt. It's been hell on him recreating the statues we lost when Lupa was attacked. And I haven't made things easier. I run my tongue along the back of my teeth, feeling the tiniest pinch of guilt. My master has been good to me, and I've repaid his trust with lies, secrets, and a pile of art so terrible, I wouldn't even use it as privy paper.

A tremor shakes Verrocchio's body. A sickening jolt goes through me as I realize it's a sob. "We lost Lupa because of you," he says.

The bottom of my stomach drops away. "What?"

Verrocchio twists his red cap so hard, part of the brim rips off. "The church took her after mass. They said if I couldn't control her, the workshop didn't deserve to have her."

Panic crackles along my nerves, engulfing me entirely. I grab fistfuls of Verrocchio's cloak, yanking him closer. "Where did they take her?"

His eyes bulge with astonishment. "Virgil—"

"What are they doing with her?"

Nothing can happen to Lupa. She's the only one who can help me find my brother's soul.

Verrocchio yanks his cloak from my clenched fingers. A vein throbs on his brow, the *tick tick tick* of it like a warning. "You dare to make demands right now? What the church does is none of your business. Do you care nothing for what this does to the workshop? To your fellow apprentices? This will ruin my life's work!" His anger rises like a whale from the depths of the sea. "Do you care about a single person who isn't yourself? Are you suggesting *the church* is not a safe space for a holy being?"

A cold, sinking dread races along my bones.

Verrocchio can't help me. No one can except Lupa. I'm running out of time to save Niccolo, and she's not in the workshop anymore.

Words I never thought I'd say fill my mouth, glass-sharp and sour. "Fine. I'll get my things."

Verrocchio plants a hand against the wall, blocking my exit. "Giorgio will bring them to your family's house. It shouldn't take him more than an hour."

I think of all my blank paper in careful stacks, the nubs of charcoal and well-used brushes. It all belongs to Verrocchio, doesn't it? As an apprentice I was never able to put my name on a single painting. Six minutes will be the trek up and down the stairs; it'll only take Giorgio one to shove what's mine into a satchel.

Five years of my life, erased in ten minutes.

Everything's gone airless. I gave the place everything: my time, my eyesight, the rest of my very life.

And for what?

I tried to split myself into neat little boxes to please everyone. A diligent artist for Verrocchio, a dutiful son for Mamma and brother for my sisters. I tried to be everything anyone wanted me to be without questioning why. If I kept all the careful pieces of my life separate, no one would see how empty I was inside.

Except . . . not everyone was fooled.

A pair of eyes the color of rich earth flash before me, the wry smile beneath.

I take in a long, shuddering breath that breaks into a moan.

Leonardo's going to try to follow me. He's going to think me kissing him is a promise when nothing could be further from the truth.

Verrocchio sighs and puts his mangled cap back on. "You were good, Virgil. If things had worked out differently, you could've been great."

I watch Verrocchio leave, my insides numb.

He's right.

I could've been a lot of things. Now I've got no time to be any of them.

Leonardo slowly inches out from a corner ahead, racing over when he sees Verrocchio's gone. He gasps at the sight of me, the worry in his face gutting. "Are you—"

"I'm leaving."

He stumbles back at the bluntness of my words. "Right. That's all right, then. I'll get my stuff—"

"I'm going alone." Even though saying it feels like swallowing a bowl of nails. Even though following through on it will feel like walking with one in the middle of my bare foot all way to Casa delle Volpi.

Leonardo's skin goes milk-pale under his freckles. "If Verrocchio fired you for this, he'll fire me, too."

"He won't!" A tempest tears through me, a vortex of shame, anger, and fear. I need him to stay away. "We all know you're the person he really wants. You always are."

I don't need the workshop anymore, but Leonardo does. He

needs to build a life with someone who'll be there for him, not some boy who already has one foot in his grave. It was stupid to kiss him: It could only end with me hurting him. "We can stop pretending we mean something to each other."

For the first time ever, I've shocked him. His catches himself on the wall as if he can't trust his legs. "You really are leaving," he whispers. "Why?"

A single, breathless word with so many answers. He knows this isn't about me being fired. *Because you deserve more. Because I'm running out of time, and I don't want you to see what happens to me. Because I fuck everything up, and if you come with me, I'll fuck you up too.*

Instead I go with the far crueler truth. "Because I want to."

Leonardo makes a quiet, wounded noise and finally stumbles out of my way. I wait until I'm charging past him to scrub the tears blurring my vision.

By the time I gather the courage to look back at the end of the block, he's gone.

Just like I wanted.

CHAPTER THIRTY-ONE

The fox statues outside Casa delle Volpi fill me with a familiar sinking feeling.

But the silence after I knock? That's far worse.

I rap my knuckles again and wait, a high anxious whine in my head. The satchel with my pathetically few things bites into my shoulder, heavier than it has any right to feel. Giorgio caught up with me before I crossed the Arno River, his eyes wide like was seeing a ghost. Carrying the bag feels like lugging home all of my failures and disappointments. Every time I close my eyes, Leonardo's pale, shocked face is there. Knowing I've hurt him weighs on me heaviest of all.

The door cracks open.

"Virgil!" Giovannia hisses. "We expected you here an hour ago."

They . . . did? For one horrible moment, I fear Verrocchio has met with my mother and discussed what an utter disappointment I've been, but no, he wouldn't. Verrocchio isn't one of my old tutors who tattled to Father every time I misspelled the Roman emperor Titus as "tits."

"Right. Where should I go?"

She points me to the dining room.

A man wearing the insignia of the Medici bank sits at the

table's head, Mamma off to the side. Her face is huge with concern, moon-pale, almost frantic. When she sees me, she gasps, a beringed hand fluttering to her bodice. "I thought you couldn't make it."

"So did I." I sit down in the chair heading the opposite end of the table. Spread my legs wide. Seeing him in my father's chair stirs the dregs of my anger. This banker doesn't get to intimidate my mother just because he's a man. It's not his house; it's ours. "Where did you two leave off?"

Mamma gulps. The banker doesn't notice—he's busy rearranging his papers. "We were discussing your mother's line of credit and the second mortgage on the house. If she cannot clear her account with us by the end of the month, I'm afraid this fine house will belong to the bank."

The words jumble in my head. They don't make sense, but the sickening lurch in my gut tells me what I already know.

My family is losing their home in weeks.

And I just lost my job.

Numbness trickles from the tips of my fingers to my toes. I try to speak—to make my mouth move and form words and thoughts—but I can't.

We're going to lose *everything*.

When the banker leaves, Mamma closes the doors to the dining room before turning to me, her face so pale, it glows in the darkness. She hasn't even lit candles for this, as if the expense was too much. "I can explain."

"Can you?" She flinches from the gravel in my voice, and I clear my throat, angry with her even as I'm angry with myself for frightening her. I won't be my father. Mamma is an adult, much as the world pretends women are children. She must have her reasons for the debt. I'm going to listen to them.

"I know you've worked your culo off for this place. For us." Her hands twist together. "But it wasn't enough. Giovannia needs a dowry, and I didn't want to ask for more money when I knew you couldn't do it. Men don't care about marriage the way women do. You don't need it."

Actually, I care a great deal about my little sister being married off to a toothless man five times her age. "I thought we agreed Giovannia wouldn't marry this year?"

Mamma drags a hand down her face, smearing her cosmetics. She gestures to the unlit room, the moth-eaten drapes. "What other choice do we have? Do you want them homeless? No man worthy of Giovannia would look at her twice if he knew how far her family had fallen. A boy can forge his own future, but a girl can't."

The quiet despair in her voice ices under my ribs. Women aren't allowed to apprentice in the trades the way men are. If they can't marry, they're forced to work as laborers. My sisters would be at the mercy of men who looked down on them, men who thought they were only there for their own entertainment. Men who might be worse than the brother who can't protect them or an indifferent husband.

I didn't want to agree with Mamma months ago. I still don't. But I understand now that I simply didn't want to hear what she had to say.

Ever since Niccolo disappeared, we've been slowly sliding off a cliff, scrambling for purchase on the way down, but now the abyss yawns deep and horrible beneath our feet, and there's nothing we can do to stop the fall.

Mamma thrusts her hand under my nose. Pops the giant sapphire out of her ring. I catch it before it falls, only to gasp when I crush it. "Plaster and stone dust. I've been replacing all my gems one at a time. I'll smelt the gold next, but 'tis harder to hide what I'm doing from the girls." She gestures to the garden going rogue outside the windows. Not the roses she loves, but beans, fat, shiny pods hanging from their vines. "I tore out the flowers for food. Your sisters never come to this side of the house."

I see them outside now, skirts butterfly bright against the late-spring green. Elisabetta whacks a book from Giovannia's hand with a sword, screaming with glee. I plant my hands on the windowsill, knuckles white.

Mamma's done everything she could to protect them—protect *me*—and it's still not enough.

I take my mother's hand, rubbing my finger over her ring's empty setting. This whole time, I thought she was coldhearted and calculating for the wrong reasons. My ribs squeeze at how badly I've misjudged her.

"Why didn't you tell me? I could've helped." Taken on more commissions. Left Verrocchio's workshop for another job, a better-paying one.

Mamma's eyes fill with tears. There are more lines around them than I've ever seen. How long has the stress of all this hollowed her out? "I didn't want you to blame yourself. It's not your fault your father made a bad deal and your brother disappeared. You deserved to have a chance to live the life you wanted."

Not your fault. Not your fault. The words ricochet in my empty chest. At some point, I knew this, but I forgot after Niccolo disappeared. The responsibility and blame became one, a burden too big to carry alone, but that didn't stop me from trying.

I wrap my mother in a hug, a crushing one that says all the tender things I can't put into words without weeping. *Thank you for seeing me. Thank you for giving me a chance.*

She lets out a shaky breath. She feels like a reed under her dress, too thin and brittle. Have I always been this much taller than her? "If Giovannia is engaged before the month is over . . . if I rent out some of the other rooms, I think we'll be all right."

I don't correct her. She needs something to believe in, even if it's wrong. The Medici bank will always have their gilded hands around our necks. They've been trying to take our house for years.

Niccolo can fix this. I'll get him back. I cling to the hope, stubborn as dried glue. *Getting fired was a good thing.* I lock up the memory of a freckled face collapsed in despair in a place where it can't haunt me anymore. I had to hurt him. He wouldn't have let me go otherwise.

"The girls don't know?" I say.

"Not Elisabetta, but Giovannia . . ." Mamma doesn't need to finish the statement. My sister is too clever by half.

I nod and squeeze her one last time. "I need to see her."

Mamma darts her thumbs under her eyes, so quick, I almost miss it. "The garden wall needs fixing. I hate to ask, but . . ."

I bend down and kiss her forehead. Normally a request like this would rankle my pride. Earn a snippy comment about how working with statues is nothing like mortaring stone, and I'm a painter, anyway.

But this time I don't. "We'll be all right."

• • •

Giovannia is already perched on the crumbling wall outside. "You seemed surprised to see the banker."

Oh, she absolutely knows something's wrong. "What have you been doing lately? Working on becoming Florence's finest poetess, I hope?"

She rolls a stone under her slipper. Sends it flying with her toe. "No. I've been negotiating my own marriage. While you're here, I'd like you to sign the betrothal papers."

I rake through my curls, sighing. "I won't."

She makes a frustrated noise. "You will! I'm not daft. If I marry, then Elisabetta can have a chance to live the life she wants."

It feels like some sort of Biblical atrocity, the kind Verrocchio's workshop is always painting to terrify people into behaving. Each family member sacrificing themselves so the next one can do better, have more. I've been stuck in the cycle long enough to know that Giovannia's sacrifice isn't going to work.

"I won't let you do this."

Giovannia's eyes flash. "I don't care if I'm married to an ancient man if he leaves me alone to write. You got to choose your own path, Virgil. Or am I not allowed the same courtesy because I'm a girl?"

No! I want to shout. *You're not allowed to do this because you're my little sister, and I know that you deserve better.*

"Be honest. Does this plan truly make you happy?"

Her stare hardens into a stony mask I know all too well: the same one I've worn every day for the past two years. "Someone needs to make sure this family survives."

And that someone hasn't been you.

The unspoken words are a chisel to my chest, the single

too-strong hit to an incomplete statue that makes the entire thing crumble. I blink, the garden's colors smearing. "I've been trying."

Giovannia claps a hand over her mouth, eyes wide. "I didn't mean it like that." Her voice is ages younger, the little girl who cowered against my side even as she leaned breathlessly forward at the scary parts in Dante's *Inferno*. "I know you're doing your best. We all do. It's not your fault the bank is greedy and dreadful. I just want my brother back."

Soon, I think. *I'll bring him back soon; I promise.* "I know. I miss him too."

She punches my shoulder. "I'm not talking about Niccolo. I'm talking about *you*!"

"Me?"

"Yes, you! When Niccolo disappeared, you became a ghost." She wipes her own tears away with an angry, defiant gesture. "Sometimes it feels like I lost two brothers."

Slowly, slow enough that she can back away if she wants to, I gather my sister into a hug. She lets me, fists curling against my chest. I didn't know she was lonely like me.

"I'm right here. I've always been here for you. I'm sorry you didn't know that."

Her head notches into the divot between my neck and shoulder. "I know."

We have a nice, tender moment that lasts maybe half a second before she wriggles away, her look sharpening. "Now tell me what you're really doing home."

Curse those terrifying gears of intelligence in her skull! I've been away so long, I forgot she's smarter than me. I shift my weight from foot to foot, unsure how much to say.

Her eyes narrow. "Don't you dare try to lie—I'll know."

She's right. She's absolutely right, but there's still an anxious, scraping feeling inside me. If I tell Giovannia about Niccolo, I can't take it back. If I let her into the parts of my life I've tried my hardest to keep walled off, there's no asking her to leave.

But aren't my walls already crumbling?

Lupa crashed through the stones, and then Leonardo came creeping in after her, both of them like the horrible cats I couldn't keep from my attic. I didn't want them there, but after they insisted on it . . . I didn't want them to go.

I thought my distance kept my sisters safe, but it's hurt them instead. I don't want Giovannia to feel like she's lost me before I'm gone.

My throat squeezes around the impossible truth. "What if I told you Niccolo is alive, but doesn't remember a thing about us?"

She rears back, eyes going huge. "I'd say . . . it sounds impossible. A bargain?"

"Something worse, I fear." I'm not ready to share the truth about his missing soul and the demons. I don't want to put her in danger.

Elisabetta's voice rings through the garden, startlingly close. "Virgil, Giovannia! Where are you?"

Merda, she can't know the truth. I pull Giovannia closer, our brows near touching. "He's pretending to be a man named Soderini. Do you know anything about the family?" I've been out of the wealthy circles of Florence for ages, but my sister hasn't.

Giovannia drags her thumb across her bottom lip. "The family has been in power for ages and hate the Medici. The patriarch used to vote against Piero's wishes just to spite him."

"Vote against what?"

Giovannia frowns, her expression askance, as if I should know this already. "The priori have suggested Florence do away with elections for the Gonfaloniere of Justice. Soderini never let it pass."

"Which means . . . ?"

Giovannia mashes a hand over her brow and groans. "I cannot *believe* that you are a voting member of this city and don't—"

"Yes, yes, we all know you're the smart one, and it's entirely unfair. Take pity on your helpless sot of a brother, will you?"

"The Medici don't want a republic: They want to rule Florence outright."

My fingernails drag along my thighs, the memory of Soderini's blood drying on my skin a phantom itch.

The Medici murdered their most outspoken enemy and replaced him with Niccolo. I have an awful, certain feeling the new head of the Soderini family will be much more amenable to allowing the Medici to take over the city than the old one.

"The Medici are keeping Niccolo close. I need to get into their wedding next week to talk to him. Can you help me?"

Giovannia's breathless smile takes a moment to find its feet, and when it does, the look is worth more than all the gold in the city's cathedrals. "Depends, dear brother. How do you feel about thievery?"

CHAPTER THIRTY-TWO

Every church bell rings when Lorenzo de' Medici and his bride step out onto the cathedral's marble steps. The packed piazza roars when he takes his new wife's hand and kisses her knuckles. She blushes prettily, and they roar even louder.

Everyone except for me.

Mamma looks at me, her eyebrows high. "Stop scowling. We don't want him to see it. He might be kinder than his father."

He might let us keep the house, she means. Never mind the fact there's no way Lorenzo de' Medici can see my face from hundreds of feet away, much less would let us keep something his family could take from us.

Instead of arguing with her, I smile, fingers going to the skull-headed key hidden in my innermost pocket. "Perhaps."

A carpet of cloth-of-gold, its gleam nearly buried beneath thousands of rose petals, leads from the cathedral's steps to the Palazzo Medici. Two magicked papier-mâché unicorns, their sides woven with garlands of herbs and wildflowers, rear and charge down the golden road to the thrill of fifes to lead the couple to their new home. Lorenzo's bride gasps, both hands flying over her mouth at the sight. She's never seen magic before.

The crowd follows the married couple, and the scent of

crushed flowers fills the air, sharp and green. When I inhale it, even I'm not immune to the great excitement sweeping through the city like a fever.

Today Lorenzo de' Medici, heir to the family fortune and its vast power, has wed.

And tonight, I'm breaking into his house to find and share his family's dark secrets with the world, starting with whatever they've done to my brother.

The Medici's palazzo shines as bright as a bonfire. The stream of people moving to the garden doors makes nerves tighten in my belly, brings up the old fears of sitting down for an exam I didn't study for. To steady myself, I take in my reflection in a coach window.

An arrogant stranger in black velvet and gold glares back at me.

"You'll look good," Giovannia said as she helped me get ready this afternoon. "You'll look like you belong."

Except I don't want to look like I belong to the Medici's glittering, rotting world. In these fine clothes, I'm a version of Virgil who never discovered art, who never insisted on bucking my family's expectations to work in an artist's workshop.

I don't look like the boy who fell for Leonardo da Vinci and broke his heart.

Even though I'm not here for Leonardo—even though he'd *better* not be here for me—I can't help pushing up on my toes to scan the crowd for him. Did he finish the wedding portrait? Did Verrocchio have him hire a horse and cart to bring it over this morning? What did he think of all the grandeur?

"Your invitation, signore," the Medici herald says. The two-story garden doors are carved with images of Proserpina. Torches burn inside, beckoning like crooked fingers.

Niccolo's already inside. Three more steps, and I'll be there too.

I swallow and pull out the gilded paper. "Of course."

The herald frowns at the guest name. "Isn't he . . . ?" He trails off, doubtlessly unable to find a tactful way to say *about three inches from death* without being rude. My family might be too poor to make the Medici's guest list, but Giovannia's ancient would-be fiancé isn't.

"Yes. I'm his nephew. We have the same name."

People scowl and mutter behind me, sullen about what's taking so long. A guard whistles and makes a *hurry up* gesture.

The herald sighs, finally giving in to my plan. "Welcome, signore."

Two guards search me next. One frowns when he upends my empty sword scabbard and out falls a rolled-up paper. "What's this?"

The paper unfurls. The foxes look at me from the gravel path, a smaller one tucked into the bigger one's side. I snatch them up before anyone steps on them. "My sister must've hidden it there."

It was my first commissioned artwork. Niccolo bought it with a single coin. When I presented it to him, he hugged me to his side and whispered, "You're a real artist now, aren't you?"

It was the first time someone else wanted my art. The first time anyone stuck a name to what I could become. If this drawing can't get my brother to remember me, if it can't spark knowing in his distant soul, then nothing else will.

The guards shrug and motion me through the doors at last.

The courtyard garden is all a delightful fantasy. Vining roses wrap around delicate lattices and box hedges. Rearing lions and unicorns flank the paths, cut with such precision, I touch one just to be sure it's greenery and not another magicked object. Exquisite marble statues line the paths—prophets and kings and saints—who bow and usher guests deeper into the courtyard. Even the torches seem to glow brighter, little pops of gold and silver fizzing from them like bubbles in a pale gold wine.

Keep your mouth shut, I remind myself. *Don't gape like a bumpkin.*

This could be straight from a fairy tale, a dream. I grew up wealthy, but not like *this.*

I spot Niccolo in the crowd. He's deep in conversation with a man whose back is to me. My brother's wedding finery is black and gold, just like mine.

I tug my doublet's collar, the skin too hot beneath it. My brain insists it's a coincidence, but my heart whispers it's a sign. A hidden thread connecting us, one waiting for me to make obvious to him once more. The drawing of the fox burns like an ember at my side.

I take a step closer, then another.

The person talking to Niccolo turns.

And I freeze.

Lorenzo de' Medici.

The groom's dark eyes scan the room, as if searching for a threat. Pulse kicking into a higher tempo, I duck behind a lemon tree before he sees me.

"And you, signore." An older man with salt-and-pepper hair turns to me. A sapphire winks on every single one of his fingers, a gorgeous woman is under his arm. She's decades younger than him and so attentive, she must be a courtesan. "Do you make your gold from banking or commerce or"—he runs his hands up the woman's backside—"flesh?"

Gesù Cristo! I just bathed, but watching this man makes me feel like I need to scrub dirt off my skin again.

A silk-clad arm slithers around my neck. "Painting." Bartolomeo Rucellai grins. His dark blue wedding finery is working hard to make him look like a handsome young man and not a pile of rats in expensive brocade. "He's also a painter, Zio. The Pitti one."

His uncle? Splendid. I bet he heard everything about me snogging Bartolomeo as a boy.

The bordello owner ogles his companion's low-cut bodice, as if appraising a jewel. "I've always wondered what would inspire a man to paint instead of possess."

Bartolomeo smirks at the insult. "If you're smart, you can have both."

Gritting my teeth, I pluck a glass of wine off the lion's-paw table beside us and clink it against Bartolomeo's. It would be unforgivably rude to snub him, no matter how much I want to. Pitti isn't the name on my invitation here, so I need to stay forgettable. Pleasant. "It's very bracing to see you."

"Bracing?" He frowns like he's never heard that word before.

"Yes, just like running face-first into a wall."

He throws back his head and laughs. 'Tis a mean, grating sound, one that makes other people turn and look. I shoot a furtive glance at Niccolo and Lorenzo, but they're too far away to hear.

"Insult me all you want. I've won, and you and da Vinci have lost!"

It takes me a moment to understand what he's saying. "The wedding commission?"

Bartolomeo *won*? God, that's annoying. He'll be insufferable about it for the rest of our lives. For once, the fact that mine will be so short doesn't seem like a bad thing.

His smirk turns oily. "You didn't know? I thought you and da Vinci worked on it together."

"Verrocchio only let one of us attend today. I'm not here as an artist." I smile in a way that I hope reads as arrogant and not nervous. I can't reveal that I don't know the details about the wedding commission: Bartolomeo might figure out I'm not supposed to be here.

Bartolomeo's lip curls again. "No. You're here as a failure."

I run my tongue along the back of my clenched teeth, holding in the hot words that threaten to spill out. To this crowd, I'll always be Nico Pitti's second son, the spare heir who embarrassed him, the artist who fizzled like a wet log and went out before he was nineteen.

The bronze toes of the lion's-paw table wriggle at me, awfully close to Bartolomeo. Florence's wealthy love commissioning a magicked walking table for parties. Unfortunately, lion's feet develop a mind of their own and become more likely to trip people than listen to them.

Bartolomeo doesn't notice. He's already turning away with a horrible, gloating smirk. Fighting with him would be foolish, but ruining his night just a little bit . . . I give the table a nod and leave.

There's a hollow thunk of someone tripping, followed by a satisfying crash and scandalized gasps. I bite the pad of my thumb to keep from smiling, not daring to turn around.

You know someone's being a stronzo if even the art begs you to bully them.

"I shouldn't encourage you," a familiar voice says. "But I love it when you put Bartolomeo Rucellai in his place."

Leonardo's grin stops my heart.

CHAPTER THIRTY-THREE

Leonardo is here.

He's wearing his favorite pink tunic, except someone has found him a jewel-crusted doublet to wear over it. I have a horrible, certain feeling I've seen the doublet hanging in Verrocchio's workshop. My voice drops to a scandalized whisper. "Did you steal that?"

He loops his arm through mine. "All in good time, Virgil, all in good time."

"You're not supposed to be here."

He leads me around a fountain and into a loggia, its ceiling clustered with fragrant jasmine. Flower petals rain on his hair and shoulders like little stars. "And yet, here I am." The smile he gives me is sly, and it makes my chest squeeze so tight, I could burst.

"Why?" I was dreadful to protect him, and I don't have it in me to do it again. Seeing the hurt on his face and knowing I caused it was gutting enough the first time.

"Dance with me and I'll explain."

"No one else is dancing." *And I don't deserve this.*

"No. But the guards stationed here are kissing behind the fountain, so I doubt they'll notice."

I startle, glancing at the fountain, and . . . sure enough, there are two shadows tangled on the ground. Good for them.

Feeling lightheaded, I slip my hand into his. "I'll have to lead."

His fingers lace through mine. "I'm happy to follow you."

You shouldn't be, I think helplessly. *That's our entire problem.* I keep him an arm's length away, a stately pavane, but the loggia's too small, and he's so close, all my nerve endings feel like they're on fire. I didn't want him here. I did everything I could to get away from him, but he is here, and now my heart is *rioting.*

"You should go home. Someone's going to figure out you're not supposed to be here," I hiss.

"Do you think they'll toss you or me out first?" A familiar gilded paper appears in his free hand. "Because last I knew, your name wasn't Zanobi Ghirlandaio. Unless you have a secret third name you only use when you're being especially difficult."

I bite my bottom lip. The words are light and teasing, but the sentiment behind them is real.

"Why can't you listen? I said I didn't need your help anymore."

"Actually, unless my memory is wrong—which it's not, because I remember everything—you didn't say much of anything when you were fired. You just ran away."

No I didn't! The protestation is right there, but Leonardo's rising eyebrows dare me to say it. He catches my waist, reversing the lead. He dips me suddenly, my head and the flower-filled ceiling swirling. "Why did you do it?" His face is inches above mine, rust-blond hair brushing my face, my neck.

A wave of his scent dizzies me. "Verrocchio did me a favor. There wasn't enough time for me to work and find my brother."

He sighs like he's disappointed. "You're always saying things like that."

"Like what?"

He doesn't let go, even though he should. If this goes on for any longer, we won't be able to pretend we're dancing anymore. "That time is running out. There's plenty left to do what you want. You just don't let yourself believe it."

All the black marks on my skin burn, each one a tally toward the end. I tear myself away from him, terrified he'll see the truth in my face. "You don't know how much time I have."

But I do.

That's why I'm alone, a stolen key in one pocket, a childhood drawing on my hip. I'm not here to dance in ridiculously beautiful gardens with a boy I want but can't have. He comes in here, all handsome and slick, and makes me forget myself. This is why I left the workshop. This is why I left *him*.

"Where are you going?" he calls after me.

Despite myself, I turn. "I have a plan."

His mouth hooks. I feel the yank behind my navel. "So do I."

God, he's impossible! "Leo, you can't—"

He crosses the space in three steps. His index finger lights on my lips, thumb under my chin. "Did your plan involve sneaking into the house and then trying all the doors?" He caresses my side. The skull-headed key presses against my ribs. "Did you think everyone would be too busy to notice you?"

My tongue bumps the back of my lip. I want to taste him. "Getting in was the hard part. I was going to figure the rest out."

"I'm sure you would've." He lets his hand fall from my face, but not my side. "What if I told you I could make it easier? I've been here all day, talking to people, making friends."

I can feel every point where his fingers rest against me. I'm wearing three layers of clothing; it shouldn't be possible for my body to be this aware of him. "What sort of friends?"

He grins, the expression toying with a smirk, like he knows exactly how I'm feeling. "Ones who can help you."

I'd be lying if I said I wasn't intrigued. And yet . . . I swallow and force myself to hold his gaze. "All right. But it doesn't change anything. I'm not going back to the workshop after this. We can't . . . we can't be anything."

The brightness from his eyes vanishes, but his smirk remains. "Whatever you wish, Virgil."

His guarded eyes remind me of a room with nothing in it. I dig my nails into my opposite wrist to resist the urge to fill it up again.

He doesn't know why I'm pushing him away, but I know it's for the best. If he wants to be here, if he wants to help me, I won't say no. I'm too weak for that.

After making sure the guards are still very much preoccupied with each other, Leonardo crooks his finger, and I follow him inside the Palazzo Medici. With easy smiles and long, loose strides, he charms his way past second cousins and servants and footmen with an ease I could never muster. When a guard tries to stop us from going upstairs, he flaps a hand and laughs. "The signora is expecting us, but you can go ask her yourself if you'd prefer."

The guard accompanies us, and I silently thank Giovannia for having the good sense to dress me in black so the guard doesn't notice the ungodly amount of sweat I'm wiping off my palms. He knocks on a closed door and goes inside. The scent of frankincense floods the corridor, and then the guard pops outside again and nods for us to go inside next.

I gasp when the door opens.

It's the Medici private chapel, and every inch of it is exquisite. Gilded carved ceilings, gold dripping from every surface. A fresco of pilgrims spans all four walls, the scale and color of it so overwhelming, I feel like I've stepped inside a book of the Bible. The figures are still, unmagicked, but their realness is so breathtaking, it moves me. "Is this a Gozzoli piece?"

I reach up to touch the wall. Only then do I notice the robed and hooded figure sitting before the altar.

They're sliding the beads of a rosary between their fingers. The clicking rhythm matches the pounding in my temples.

Leonardo sweeps into a low bow. "Here he is, signora. The man I told you about."

The figure turns, revealing eyes wide with fear. "You know the truth about the demons?"

I suck in a breath and nearly stagger against the fresco.

I've only seen her once, on the steps of the cathedral that morning, but I recognize her anyway.

It's Lorenzo de' Medici's new wife.

CHAPTER THIRTY-FOUR

The church bells chime the hour. Lorenzo's wife ducks her head and counts out another bead, another prayer. When she closes her eyes, I see tears clinging to her lashes.

I glance at Leonardo, but he's not looking at me. He's watching her, with a patient, gentle expression I've only seen him use on me when I'm at my worst. He slowly settles on the pew beside the girl. *Clarice,* I remember. Clarice Orsini from Rome.

"I know that the angels are demons," I admit. "But that's all."

Clarice nods and squeezes her eyes shut even more tightly. "My husband tried to tell me that magic is what makes his family so powerful, that it'll make *me* powerful too, but I know it's wrong. He's been betrayed by evil just like his father."

"Tell Virgil what you told me," Leonardo urges gently. Only now do I see that he's covered up his bargain mark with a leather bracelet. I brush my long sleeves, making sure they haven't risen far enough to reveal mine.

Two tears roll down Clarice's cheeks. "How do I know I can trust him?"

I sit next to her. "You can't. Trust is earned, and I don't have time to earn yours." Leonardo lets out a dismayed squawk, but Clarice's eyes flick to mine. "I can tell you magic has hurt me. My brother has forgotten who I am because of it. If you can't trust me, fine, but you can trust that I agree with you that the magic can't be trusted."

Clarice's fingers pause their rapid counting. She searches my face for a long moment, then nods. "Piero de' Medici has been corrupted by demons. He moves things without touching them. When he speaks, I feel sick and have no choice but to obey."

"Do you remember when we were in his office?" Leonardo says. "And Piero demanded that Soderini tell him the truth? I wanted to . . . confess things to you."

I remember it too, his warm breath on my palm, how a feeling like a rising storm almost made me admit that his freckles were the only thing I wanted I paint. The desire seemed to come from somewhere outside of me. It's not something I would've said to him at that time no matter how true it was.

My mind starts racing, picking up the pieces one by one. The unnatural creature that attacked Lupa. My brother's missing soul.

'Tis all magic. Magic unbounded by art and bargains or anything I've ever heard of before.

Sod it all to hell, the prior killed by Piero was right. The Medici are getting *far* more from the demons than they let on. Their household never had its own angel because they didn't need one.

They found a way to wield magic on their own.

I swallow, a sick feeling coursing through me. "Do you know how Piero got his power?"

Clarice scoffs. "Isn't it obvious? The devil has turned his heart away from God." The rosary clicks faster, louder. No longer counting prayers but racing heartbeats.

Leonardo and I exchange an appalled look over her bowed shoulders. "You mean that . . . figuratively, right?" I say.

Leonardo's voice drops lower. "Can you take us to the room you mentioned before?"

She shakes her head, knuckles white on the rosary. "The chapel is the only place where I feel safe."

I suck in a soft breath as Leonardo touches her shoulder. "Please. I promise you we want the same things."

Her tear-filled eyes meet his for an eternity.

Then she nods once and stands.

We follow Clarice out of a second exit from the chapel, one leading to the Medici's private quarters. Here lies the most magnificent of the family art collection: paintings and statues and tapestries that all seem to glare at us as we pass by. Can they tell we mean their masters harm, like a pack of loyal hounds?

"How did you earn her confidence?" I say to Leonardo, too low for Clarice to overhear.

"She judged the wedding portraits this afternoon. Ours was the only one not magicked. She was frightened of the others, so I got her alone and asked why. I promised her we were trying to rid Florence of the demons, and if she picked our portrait to win, we could help her. She picked Rucellai's instead." He runs a hand down his jaw, frowning. "She wouldn't tell me why but insisted we'd be more useful if we didn't win the commission."

None of this sounds good. Except . . . "So she liked our painting more than Bartolomeo's?"

"Of course that's what you'd latch onto." But his mouth quirks anyway.

Clarice comes to an abrupt halt in the middle of a hall. At the end, two Medici guards flank a door. A torch burns close, its light catching strangely on their sword pommels.

I brush the skull-handled key hidden in my inner pocket. I'd wager anything it matches their swords.

At the sight of their new mistress, the guards square their shoulders. "Signora, what are you doing here?"

Clarice draws herself taller. "Step aside! These are my chosen painters." Gone is the terrified woman from the chapel. She strides forward, not waiting for a reply, but one of the guards stops her with a gauntleted hand.

"Your husband's instructions were clear, signora. No one is to let the winners inside except for him."

Clarice's nostrils quiver. "This is outrageous! I will not be denied."

The three of them begin arguing in earnest.

This close, I can see their weapons clearly: ruby-eyed skulls on both pommels.

Leonardo nudges me forward. "Go on." His hand lingers on the small of my back, brushes along the base of my spine. "I'll stay here and keep watch."

Too distracted by their argument to pay me any attention, I slip my key into the lock.

And the door creaks open.

CHAPTER THIRTY-FIVE

It's a workshop.

Or perhaps less a workshop and more a painter's studio.

A wooden canvas lies on an easel, waiting to be prepped. The workbench is bare of brushes and pigments, but I see the old stains. I drag my finger through a spill of cinnabar on the floor. It's gritty and dusty—too old to have been spilled recently.

The only window is located in the ceiling—a strange, slanted thing. Leonardo might know what it's called, but I certainly don't. A swath of stars is visible beyond. A sleeping pallet in the corner and a chamber pot beside it make up everything else in the space.

I spin around, trying to make sense of it. Why would the Medici hide this?

There's a creak, and a section of wall starts to *move.*

I scramble backward, needing to hide, but there's nowhere to go.

Niccolo, my brother, freezes at the threshold of the secret doorway. "How did you get in here?" His eyes snag on the still-cracked door behind me.

I should run. This isn't a place wedding guests are supposed to see. His growing frown confirms it.

And yet.

The weight of the scabbard tugs on my hip, reminding me he's the entire reason I'm here.

I bow, inflecting the gesture with every ounce of poise I've got. "I'm the painter Signora Medici has chosen."

Niccolo doesn't move. "Are you, now?"

Sweat slicks my brow. I flex my fingers instead of wiping it off, afraid he'll read into the movement. "She brought me here herself." I nod over my shoulder to where I came from and shrug. "You can ask her, if you'd like."

After a heart-stopping second of silence, Niccolo closes the door behind him. Its stone seams are invisible; no one would know it's not a wall unless you saw it open.

Why would anyone need a painting studio under guard with a secret door?

And why would only one of them open from inside the room?

The second the door settles, Niccolo shoves me against the wall, jaw gritted. "You don't look like a painter."

I inhale sharply. Familiar fingers of shame and fear wrap around my throat. *I'm sorry, Papà!* I get halfway to stammering out the apology before I pull it back.

This is Niccolo. Not Father.

I should pull away—he needs to let me go—but instead my fingertips nestle in the dips between his clenched knuckles. Wrongness worms through my chest, but I can't bear to leave yet. He's here, his heart so near to mine, I see its furious beat in his neck.

With the sort of haughty grimace I've seen Bartolomeo Rucellai wear, I unpeel his grip from me finger by finger, even though my own hands shake. "Not all of us are gutter filth, you know. Our lord's lady has taste."

He blinks, rage rinsing away like paint from a brush, filling with a desperate, haunted look instead. He lets go so suddenly, I stumble.

"I'm sorry." His voice is an agonized whisper. He starts spinning his ring, the silver band flashing. "Who are you again? I can't—I don't . . ." He trails off, glancing helplessly at the sealed door behind him. As if he can't remember how he got in here.

The wrong feeling digs deeper. My brother is one of the bravest, calmest people, I know. This haunted shade of a man . . . there's nothing of Niccolo here, even though the face is unmistakably his.

I should leave.

The thought is swift and sudden. I hesitate before it, as if a wild animal has appeared and there's nowhere for me to go.

But I'm so *close* to him. There's the heart-shaped scar on his face, the same sharp chin as mine, the same curly black hair. I reach a hand toward his shoulder, then stop, fingers knotting uncertainly.

He tracks the movement with sudden suspicion, a stiffened back. "Why are you here?" There's no warmth, no recognition in his voice. Just the cold command of a powerful man used to being listened to.

I bite the inside of my cheek, finger tapping the sword scabbard at my hip. The hair along my arms rises, a warning. *Leave now. Don't show him the drawing.* Even just looking into my eyes made fear cut through him like a frigid wind: What would happen if I showed him something else from his forgotten past?

But didn't I come here to make him remember me? I don't know when I'll be alone with him again. This could be my only chance.

Even though some deep instinct screams at me not to, I pull out the fox drawing. "I'm here to show you this."

Niccolo snatches it up. I flinch, a *Be careful with that!* on my tongue that I only barely manage to hold back. It belongs to him. He can do whatever he wants with it.

"It's us." The words are shaky. "I called you volpone. Do you remember?"

Do you remember, do you remember, do you remember . . . ?

The words tangle together, echoing against the stone.

Niccolo stumbles backward. The drawing flutters to the floor, face up. He stares at it, eyes huge.

My heart leaps, a desperate, searing lurch. "Father commissioned the fox statues because foxes were your favorite animal."

His breath comes out in short, sharp gasps. One shaking hand caresses the drawing, lingers on the smaller of the two foxes.

Then footsteps, followed by an odious voice.

"What's *he* doing here? *I* was the winning painter! How could you fools get it wrong?"

In my lifetime of hating Bartolomeo Rucellai's voice, I've never hated hearing it more. I shove the cracked door as hard as I can. Hear the outraged gasp as it slams closed. "This imposter is trying to take what's mine!"

This time the guards must assist him, because even with my entire body weight against it, the door flies open. The force sends me stumbling into Niccolo. He grabs my shoulders, holding me up as much as he holds me away. He glances at his ring, then his eyes meet my own for one searing second. "Volpacchiotto?"

Bartolomeo freezes like he's seen Medusa. "Niccolo Pitti?" His shocked stare bounces between us. "*Both* of them?"

My brother's eyes roll up inside his head.

Then he falls to the floor screaming.

CHAPTER THIRTY-SIX

Niccolo clutches his head and screams, his eyes ringed with white and shot through with red.

I lurch closer, wanting to help but terrified to touch him. What if I make it worse?

Lorenzo de' Medici and two more guards pour through the open door. Lorenzo balks at the sight of me. "You again!"

I sidestep them before I'm boxed in, racing through the door and back into the hall.

Leonardo and Clarice de' Medici are gone.

I make a split-second decision to go right, the opposite way of the grand stairs leading to the garden and the glittering party.

At the end of the hallway, another door bursts open, and out pour five more guardsmen.

I skid to a stop, choking back panic. The guards from the painting studio pound down the hall behind me; these are racing toward me from the other side, and there's no way to go. I have no weapon except the stupid skull-headed key, which will prove beyond a doubt that I've been sneaking into forbidden spaces. I should've slipped a knife in my boot; God, even a paintbrush would be more useful, but I didn't think this through, and now they're almost upon me. I can count the gray hairs in the first guard's mustache—

"Virgil!"

A hidden door thuds open from the wall. Leonardo is frantic, his face ghost-pale.

I dive into the space right before the guards reach me. Leonardo slams the door shut and kicks a splintered board between the door and the wall. When the guards slam against it, the board only lets it open wide enough for a single, furious eye to glare at us. "Come out, ragazzi! We only want to talk."

"The party is fabulous! What more is there to say?" Leonardo kicks the board again, and the eye vanishes.

We run down the pitch-dark servant passageway.

I hold my breath each time we pass one of the doors leading into the main house, but no one bursts through them. We stumble up a small staircase, then down another, and then the passage dead-ends at a door. It opens up to the hay-and-horse-smelling courtyard. Laughter and music reach us, the din of the wedding on the palazzo's other side.

How long will it be before the guards figure out where we ended up?

"Should we steal horses?"

Leonardo snorts. "You think I can ride?'"

The door from the palazzo bursts open, guards rushing out.

We dash into the street.

Each turn leads us to some new obstacle—chickens, kissing couples, drying laundry—and loses us precious seconds. The heavy footsteps behind us crescendo, angry voices nipping at our heels. I taste blood in every breath.

Unless a miracle happens, we're not going to outrun them.

We tear around another corner and stop short.

The city wall rises before us.

Yellow stone stacked fifteen feet tall. If I tilt my head back, I can just spy the merlons staggered at the very top.

A curious helmeted head peers down at me from between two of them.

Guards behind us, guards on top of the wall.

My jaw clenches so hard, I see stars.

There's nowhere to go.

"Virgil." Leonardo's eyes dart all around. "What do we do?"

A sour taste floods my mouth. There's nothing for us to do, but I can't be the one to dash his hopes. It should only be *me* caught alone at the end. He wasn't supposed to be here. This is why I pushed him away. Sodding hell, why can't he ever listen?

The Medici guards draw closer, bellowing for help from the men above. I hear the shift and clink of armor. Their attention sharpens on us, hands going to blades. Leonardo gives a soft cry.

I knot my fingers fiercely through his and yank him closer, wishing with all of my wild, racing heart that I could stand between him and whatever's next.

There's a dash of gold along the rooftop.

I jerk up, but it's gone.

Gold flashes again, right overhead. A scream pierces the night.

"Watch out!" Leonardo pushes me. A sword plummets to the spot I was just standing in.

Then something far larger thumps to the ground before us.

"Into my arms!" Lupa, her body alight with a green-gold glow. Her hair floats in an otherworldly breeze, the black of her pupils gone entirely in a gold haze.

The Medici guards stop, mouths hanging open. One of them drops to his knees and makes the sign of the cross.

"C'mon!" she shouts.

We throw our arms around her shoulders. Lupa starts running, not away from the approaching Medici guards, but toward them, the glow surrounding her getting brighter and brighter until I have to squint my eyes against it.

Most of the men cower, but one nocks an arrow to his crossbow. He levels it with the center of my chest. His finger twitches on the trigger.

Lupa leaps as the arrow twangs, lifting us up with her. The arrow passes under my feet.

And my feet don't touch the ground again.

Wings arch from Lupa's shoulder blades, a million golden filaments burning against the deep violet sky. They flare brighter with each downward stroke, showering little golden sparks on the red rooftops beneath us.

We're flying.

The whole city falls away. I feel like I'm looking at one of Leonardo's blueprints, an overwhelming whole broken down into its little details right at my fingertips. Terra-cotta roofs reduced to rectangles, steepled bell towers to marsh reeds.

The only thing taller than us now is the redbrick duomo. Lupa cants toward it, gaining more altitude.

"I've always dreamed of flying." The stars gleam in Leonardo's overbright eyes. He stretches out a hand, as if the distant lights are close enough to touch.

At least one of us is enjoying this. I cling to Lupa more

tightly, feeling like my stomach might fall out of me with each wing stroke.

"You escaped and showed everyone your strange magic. They know you're different now. This wasn't worth the risk!" I say.

Lupa's holding one of us in each arm. She turns her lips to my ear and my ear alone. "It was. It will be."

Brunelleschi's great red dome grows bigger and bigger. Catching a glimpse of the cathedral's marble walls at the end of a street always felt to me like stumbling across a sleeping giant, yet it somehow seems even bigger from the sky. Huge white ribs hold up the thousands and thousands of bricks that compose the dome. An octagonal white marble lantern tower caps the dome's very top, the highest point in all of Florence.

When Lupa dips toward it, I gasp. "No no no no no, you can't leave us there!"

Her feet land on the tower's flat bottom. She lets go of us. I scream and grab one of its marble pillars. There's no railing. *Of course* there's no stupid railing. Why would anyone want a railing around the pinnacle of the entire damn city?

Lupa crosses her arms. Her wings flare, sparks scattering. "I won't be back until you tell him the truth."

The blood rushes from my face. "The truth . . . about what?"

She can't mean that I've fallen for him, right? Because I was planning on doing that in a note. One Giovannia will find among my things when I'm dead. Lupa's rushing me, and I don't like it.

Lupa draws a finger across her throat with a raised brow. "Why you really left the workshop. He deserves to know the truth."

Oh. *That.* "I can't."

It'll devastate him. There's no reason for him to know. It doesn't change anything.

She cocks her head and smirks. "Then good luck getting yourself down."

And she steps backward off the ledge.

Leaving me alone at the city's peak to talk about the very last thing I want to discuss with the last person I want to tell.

CHAPTER THIRTY-SEVEN

"Tell me about what?" Leonardo says. Then he gasps, darting to the terrifying edge of the tower so suddenly, I scream, certain I'll see him dashed to his death on the greatest architectural marvel in the world, but no, he just points to the rooflines with an expression of absolute wonder. "Look at it!"

The city spreads beneath us, a softly lit maze of shadows studded with pinpricks of light. Beyond the arc of the city walls rise hills, undulating through the distance until they go black against the backdrop of the stars. Clouds blot out the sky to the southwest. A storm is coming.

Leonardo's fingers flex, as if clutching a charcoal stick, as if when confronted with such a stunning view, he can't help but try to capture it for later.

The sight makes me ache. No matter what else is happening, he's always so . . . *him*.

"Florence looks good from up here. Smells quite a bit better too."

Leonardo cackles, and I bite back a smile. When did his laugh become my favorite sound? I know I'm the one who should be answering his question, but I have one of my own. "Why were you there tonight?"

His fingers still trace soft patterns of nothing. "You're very predictable." He pauses, shooting me a knowing glare. "You've never listened to another soul in your entire life. I knew you'd find a way into the Medici wedding, and I knew whatever disaster happened, it'd be best if I was there too."

My heart is a cracked pane of glass. One touch would shatter me. "You came for me? Even after I was awful to you?"

He stops sketching the skyline. He won't quite look at me. "Of course, Virgil. I just wish you'd let me be there from the beginning. You *promised* me you wouldn't see your brother alone."

I cup his jaw, gently turning him toward me. He blinks, face softening even as his gaze grows darker, more intense. He places one of those long, elegant hands over mine, pressing my skin closer to his.

"I did want you there," I confess. "But I don't always know how to *let* people be there."

He tilts his head, pressing his lips to my palm. A butterfly-soft kiss. "I know, tesoro. That's why I found you."

The gentleness of those words! I don't know if I want to kiss him back or sit down and cry.

He makes a sound, a murmur not quite my name, and then both his hands go to my face, tracing tender paths of fire. "We figured it out. We're here now, aren't we?"

An exquisite pain spikes through me. I saw him every day for four years. We ate meals together, painted together, sat through mass together. I know the sound of his footsteps and the shape of his shadow. I would hear his voice in any crowd. How could I not have known what he meant to me for so long? I was spoiled with an abundance of him and didn't know it.

I would do anything to live through one of those mundane moments again. It all feels different now, pastel-toned and fragile.

I didn't know what I had until it was too late.

"Why are you crying?" He brushes the tears away, feather-light and tentative.

My ribs are cracking, and my body shakes. "I have less than a year to live. I made too many bargains, just like your stepmother. That's why I left. Why I pushed you away. I didn't want you to know."

I brace for his reaction, to watch the horrible surprise crawl across his face and settle into his bones as a gutting truth.

But there's nothing on his face except that tender, unbearable softness. "I know, Virgil."

I sniff, not understanding. "You know . . . what?"

He takes me into his arms, strokes a hand up and down my back to ease the shivers. "I know you're dying. I've suspected it for a long time. When your magic stopped working but you wouldn't make any bargains with Lupa . . . it wasn't hard to put together."

"Then you know why we can't be together."

A steely expression slips over his face. "I don't know about that."

"Do you think I never asked Lupa if she could save me?" I snap. "I'm not letting you ruin your life for me."

"Bold of you to assume you could ruin it better than I could myself."

He smirks, and I jerk away with a huff. How does he not understand? He has a future, and I don't. He deserves everything, and I can give him nothing. In a city full of dealmakers, he's the worst bargainer I've ever met.

"Virgil," he says cajolingly, the backs of his fingertips racing lightly down my jaw. I reluctantly face him again, trying to keep all the ice out of my expression. "You don't get to decide for me."

I lean away from him. "Perhaps I should."

He throws up his hands in frustration. "Do you know what I've always hated about you?"

"Quite a start to a romantic speech!"

He growls, yanking the edge of my doublet so we're chest-to-chest. "When I joined Verrocchio's workshop, there was no doubt who the best artist there was. But when I gave you competition for the title, when I first finished a piece that made Verrocchio look away from you to me . . . something in you gave up. You were still the best, but you acted like you had already lost. I saw you go to the workshop's dark corner, blood already welling on your arms. I watched the black marks multiply across your skin, and I wondered why. Why is this boy with so much talent retreating into himself, relying on magic he doesn't need?"

"I needed it," I say. "I wasn't enough on my own."

Why is he saying this? He knows my brother was gone. I needed money, not masterpieces. I did what I had to.

His dark eyes grow furious beneath the red-gold mess of his hair. There's no hiding from him like this, his glare pinning me like a butterfly to a book. Like I'm a rare specimen he's studied for ages and he's determined to tell me everything he's learned from his yearslong apprenticeship whether I want to hear it or not.

"But you *were*, Virgil. You always give up on yourself first, before anyone else even has a chance to be disappointed in you. I didn't pick Verrocchio's workshop because it was the best place for me. I didn't pick it because it paid better. I picked it because you were the one artist who refused to tell me I was already great, and I knew that meant only you could make me better. I had to see you again, no matter what." His nails dig into my skin, hard enough to scratch furious white lines. "I hate how you give up on yourself. I hate how you think you're not worth it. I hate how you insist on making yourself smaller when you're the biggest thing in my life."

A comet could smash me to pieces right then and I'd be less shocked. He joined because of me? All those years ago? "Having a crush is a terrible reason to pick a place of employment." I need to joke; I need to pull the bottom out from this moment to make it light enough to bear.

Because what he's saying . . . it can't be true.

I've never been the best at anything in my life. I'm the second son, the second brother, the apprentice you put in when your better one is busy.

He scoffs, disgusted with me. "That stubborn *mouth* of yours—"

Then his mouth is on mine, lips and teeth and tongue and, God, I feel it all the way in my toes. I bury my hands in his hair and pull, my core going molten when he gasps against me.

Even though he's cracked me open like some hard-shelled creature plucked from the sea, there's nothing soft about this kiss. It's hot and urgent, all roving hands and nipping teeth. He groans when I bite his bottom lip, and I sigh into his mouth when his cool hands sneak into my doublet. This kiss feels like a fight, and I've always loved fighting with him.

This is all we can ever be to each other. Right now—mouths and hands and bodies discovering how they fit together. He's going to be someone great long after I'm just smudged fingerprints on a forgotten canvas.

I hope some part of me stays in his heart forever, untarnished and pristine. Will he think of me when he limns an angel's hand with gold? Will he remember the bow of my lips when he paints them pink on a lovely face?

No longer afraid of falling, I deepen our kiss and let him push me against a column, only to gasp when wetness seeps through the back of my clothes. "It's raining?"

Leonardo blinks, puzzled. "But we're not getting wet."

Lupa crouches on the arch of the colonnade above us. I don't know how long she's been there, but it must've been for a while from the way her damp hair is plastered to her neck, how water drips off her nose. Those great golden wings still unfurl from her shoulders, their glow more subdued now, their edges blurring and sizzling each time a droplet hits them.

They're extended over us.

But she doesn't look down. Her stare is intense, furious even, trained on the too-dark horizon like it's personally wronged her in some way. Tears course down her face, mixing with the rain, but she makes no move to stop them.

It's the wildest and the most human I've ever seen her look.

Leonardo cranes his head back. The hand not holding mine rises, tentatively touching the gleaming gold feathers just barely in his reach. He flinches when the entire wing ripples, like the disturbed surface of a pond.

"Lupa," he says. "Do you mind if we stay here?"

"Why?" I demand, instantly anxious.

His stare drags back to me. He traces my jaw with the edge

of his thumb, sliding his hand around the back of my neck. "Because as soon as we leave this cathedral, we'll have to deal with the Medici," he murmurs, pressing his lips to mine again. "And you keep telling me you don't have enough time." One knee eases betwixt mine, slowly, tantalizingly. "So we might as well make the most of what time we do have."

A spark zips through me, then explodes. It's fire down a slick of oil, to a barrel, no, to an *entire warehouse* filled with barrels of oil, and Madonna santa, I think I might be dead already.

"I don't know how—"

"I do, if you're willing." He presses his lips to my neck and sucks. A bitten-off sound slips from me. I tilt my head back, giving him more access to my skin. Letting the full strength of my want course through me feels like releasing the sails of a ship in a storm. It should frighten me, but instead I want to follow it.

"I want you," I say breathlessly. "*All* of you."

His smile unfurls against my skin like a glorious sunrise. "I was hoping you'd say that."

CHAPTER THIRTY-EIGHT

I blink awake the next morning, rain dripping into my eyes.

And immediately choke at the face three inches from mine.

Lupa slaps a hand over my mouth. "Stop! You'll wake him."

Oh, so she's the one scolding *me*? "You can't do things like that!" I whisper-hiss.

Lupa scowls, as if I'm being unreasonable. Her hair's a tangled, sodden mess. The sky is gray, sluggish drops pattering across the lantern tower's marble floor. In the morning, the drop to the city below unsettles me more than it did at night. More exposed. It makes me want to cover sleeping Leonardo more fully with my ruined doublet, the world's soggiest blanket.

One of his arms is still thrown across my waist.

He hugs me closer to his warm, sleepy body, a sweet sigh feathering across my neck.

A tender ache opens up beneath my ribs.

Lupa stares at the place where we touch like she's tasting butter for the first time. Or seeing a kitten. Or one of her dozens of other firsts that give her that same fervently bright look.

It feels like too much.

I trust Lupa. I'm grateful she forced me to be honest with

him. But I'd gladly hurl myself off the rooftop before explaining what's happened between us to her.

Gently, oh so gently, I ease myself from under Leonardo's arm. "Have you been here all night?" God, I really, *really* hope not.

Her mouth twitches. "I gave you privacy."

Which is very much not a no, though I am squelching like a washrag, so she must've stopped sheltering us at some point. Heat bursts across my face, followed by an icy twist in my stomach. "You shouldn't have stayed. You need to leave Florence." If the church or the Medici catch her again, who knows what they'll do to her?

An unreadable expression flits across her face. "Perhaps."

She doesn't look well in the weak dawn light. It pools in lines on her face that weren't there weeks ago; it barely highlights her dull blond hair. Her wings are gone, her golden gleam limited just to the rings of her irises. Did the church refuse to let her make the bargains she needs to live? Is she starving? If I didn't know any better, I'd say she looks sick. Except . . . I doubt demons can get sick.

Unease spiders across my skin. "What's going on?"

She laughs suddenly. "Everything, Virgil, everything."

She's not making sense. I glance at Leonardo, half hoping he'll wake up.

Lupa's hand shoots out to cover mine. "Don't wake him. I have things to say to you."

I stare at the black claws tipping her fingers. They weren't there before.

"The priest will be up soon to unlock the door." She nods at one of the lantern tower's octagonal sides. In the daylight, I see the door seams that were hidden in the darkness last night. "Do you know why demons seek beauty?" she says.

"Because . . . the devil is an appalling decorator?"

Lupa throws back her head and laughs so hard, pigeons scatter from the cathedral beneath us. Her teeth. Are they pointier than usual? My unease sharpens into fear. "I thought you couldn't remember anything about hell."

"I can't. But when I look at this city, I know I've never experienced any of this before." Her gaze ricochets between the familiar landmarks: the bell tower with its lovely green and red marble accents, Palazzo della Signoria with its bronze statues, the crenellated tops of the magnificent houses with their hidden wonders. "I don't think I came here for the beauty."

What did you come here for, then? I want to ask, but I quail away. "Is that why you're different?"

She shrugs and doesn't answer.

Cold ripples across my skin. "You're scaring me."

She tilts her head—just a little too catlike to be reassuring. "Don't be frightened. Everything is as it should be."

Oh, I don't believe her *at all.*

The conversation feels like a riddle I'm too dense to solve. I glance at Leonardo again, but he's still sleeping, raindrops scattered across his face. The sweating air has transformed his hair into glorious chaos. Even if I tried for a year, I couldn't capture it on the canvas. Every shade of ocher and red and chestnut wouldn't do the color justice.

"If you're in trouble, Leonardo can help—"

She growls, claws nicking my pinned hand. "No! Only us."

I gasp, soul flinching, a mouse beneath the hawk's shadow.

Even though my body screams to flee and everything feels wrong-sized and uncertain, Lupa has never once hurt me.

She crashed into my life and refused to leave even when I begged her to. She saw what I needed before I could see it for myself. She took my hands and dragged me kicking and screaming through the darkness.

I'm suddenly on the verge of tears. "I don't know what's wrong, but I promise whatever you need me to do, I'll do it."

She gives a roll of her eyes and hugs me. Her claws prick through my thin, sodden shirt. "You're my greatest friend, Virgil. You always will be."

I squeeze her back, surprised and touched and overwhelmed. It's so . . . *human*, yet also something else, a feeling I can't quite name.

She presses an object into my hand. A tiny, sealed ceramic vial. "This is a bit of my blood. There's a second vial inside Dante's *Inferno*. Now you can make a bargain with me whenever you want."

This makes no sense. "I thought you needed *my* blood to make a bargain?"

Her tongue darts out, dabbing at the corner of her mouth. "I tasted you once. It'll be enough."

The hair on my neck ripples. "Won't one more bargain kill me?"

She folds my fingers back over the vial. "Yes." Her head jerks over her shoulder, as if she's heard a noise, but I don't hear anything. "Don't make one until I'm gone."

"What do you mean, gone?" Frustration kicks through me. She's being mysterious on purpose, and I hate it. She's got to let me help her. That's the entire goddamn point of being friends.

She kisses my forehead, and then her fiery wings reappear with a startling *whoosh*. She dives off the tower with a sparkling snap, leaving behind nothing but a single golden feather. It burns red, then blackens to ash when I touch it.

I stare at the mark it leaves scorched onto the marble and finally recognize the feeling I couldn't name when she hugged me, realize why it bothered me.

It felt like a goodbye.

CHAPTER THIRTY-NINE

Too late, too late.

The awful words echo, pounding in time with the thud of my feet down the duomo's spiral staircase to the cathedral below. Lupa's sailed west, toward the workshop.

Why is she going back there? Why is she doing the worst thing possible for herself?

Behind us, the shocked priest who unlocked the lantern tower's door calls for us to stop. It only makes me faster. When I trip and nearly tumble to my death, Leonardo seizes the back of my doublet before I realize I'm falling.

"She said goodbye?"

"Something like that." The ceramic vial digs into my side with every step.

Why would she give it to me if she knows making one more bargain would kill me?

We hit the wooden door at the end of the spiral. Leonardo wrenches it open. A black-robed priest jerks up from the altar. His look of open-mouthed shock is all I see of him before we're careening down the nave, heading toward the triple set of double doors at the end. I can't believe Lorenzo de' Medici married Clarice here yesterday. It feels like a lifetime has passed between those two moments, each hour stretching out into a year.

We race down Via dell'Agnolo, toward the workshop, every window in Verrocchio's house too brightly lit, like wide, staring eyes. We skid to a stop outside the courtyard door. Leonardo lifts the latch carefully, and then we're standing in the space betwixt the house and the workshop.

No one is there.

"The morning exercises. They're probably already working," Leonardo says.

I bite my lip and nod, opening the workshop door. But the space is dark and still.

I tiptoe inside, unease coiling in me. "Where is everyone?" It's just after or during breakfast time—the start of the workday. Even the candles are still snuffed out, the edges of the room hidden in shadow. "Lupa?"

Nothing.

Leonardo runs a finger down his bargain mark, *What the hell is going on?* written all over his furrowed brow. I lift a hand, urging caution. There's a reason for this. There must be.

But then a shadow grows sharper at the back wall, comes out into the light. My gasp of fear turns into surprise when I see who it is. "Master Verrocchio?"

Verrocchio slowly draws closer, a queer expression on his face I can't quite read. "She's already gone."

"Gone?" It doesn't make sense. We came here as fast as we could. Lupa's faster, of course, but Verrocchio wasn't expecting her: I thought I'd find them mid-quarrel. I rise up on my toes, searching the farthest corners of the workshop, as if Lupa's lurking just out of sight, waiting to play an unfunny prank on us.

"That's what I said, no?" The column of Verrocchio's throat pulses. Too late, his expression clicks into place.

It's one of fear.

Iron hands clap down on my shoulders.

The workshop floor is suddenly filled with Medici guards.

There are six of them, each one standing in a pool of shadow except for the one who grabbed me. The other five stand eerily still, faces hidden behind pewter helmets. I tear away from the guard with a snarl.

He doesn't try to touch me again. But the rest of them join him, stepping out from their hiding place to form a gleaming, deadly line.

Acid floods my insides, hot and horrible.

An ambush. But no. Lupa had to know I'd follow her. She wouldn't lead us into a trap on purpose. And six guards feels like a number you'd send to capture a dangerous, successful murderer, not a former artist apprentice who once accidentally stabbed himself with his own palette knife.

Unless they think I'm more than I seem.

The guards step closer. Leonardo sucks in a soft breath. I plant myself between the guards and him, thumb caressing the empty sword scabbard at my belt. It's nothing, laughably useless. I'd be better off throwing paint in their eyes. Actually, that's not a bad idea.

But the table that holds the paints is curiously clear. I blink, frowning. The last time that table was cleared off was the moment it was newly built into the workshop. There are crusty smears on it older than I am.

"Why are they here?" Leonardo demands, any authority in

the question undermined by the crack in his voice. "Where's Lupa?"

Verrocchio crosses his arms, then uncrosses them, eyes flicking to the guards behind us. "The Medici took her away. She was defective."

"Defective?" Anger sizzles through me, hot and smoldering. Only things are defective. Lupa isn't quite a person, but she's far from a thing. "You know better than that."

Leonardo's fingers are light on my elbow, holding me back. "Why would the *Medici* take an angel away? Shouldn't it have been the church?"

Verrocchio shakes his head. "I don't know," he says, confused, then frightened. "I don't know!"

A sharp breath straightens my shoulders. *My master doesn't know about the demons.*

It shouldn't matter to me right now, but it does. He didn't let the Medici into his workshop. He's not working with them.

Verrocchio's eyes meet mine for a breath. Then they flick behind me.

I tackle Leonardo to the ground just as the guards try to seize us.

But I'm not the only one moving.

"Leave them alone!"

Giorgio's face looms overhead. He's leaning over the narrow balcony that runs along the workshop's second-floor gallery. The other apprentices' faces pop up beside him, some fierce, some frightened, but all of them set with a frantic resolve.

I push myself up, gaping. How long have they been lurking there? Where was this fierce determination when it came to their lessons?

As if he can read my thoughts, Giorgio winks, an expression he absolutely, one hundred percent learned from Leonardo. "Now, everyone!"

As one, they upend the buckets they held behind their backs on the guards' heads.

The guards shout and shriek as watered-down paint pours through the holes of their helmets. Some of them double over with coughing; some rip their helmets off and rub frantically at their eyes. Verrocchio screams and leaps onto a stool to prevent a flood of paint from sloshing over his very expensive boots, only to scream again when he realizes it's ultramarine paint, one of the most expensive pigments in the entire workshop, used exclusively for Virgin Mary commissions. He grabs his face and howls, *"Anything but the blue!"*

Leonardo's freckles are sprayed with green flecks, an awed and delighted grin spilling across his face. He kisses his pointer and middle finger and turns them toward the balcony.

Giorgio salutes him and tosses another bucket over the railing. "Lupa warned us something like this might happen before she was taken away. Go get her back!"

We leap to our feet, sidestep the howling guards, and escape to the street.

Pedestrians gasp and leap aside when we pass them. I can only imagine what they think when they see us, dripping with a rainbow of colors, holding hands and running like our very lives depend on it.

They probably do.

"Here." I tug Leonardo down an alley filled with drying laundry. His eyes pop when he sees me tearing off my shirt. Then my trousers. "We're too easily spotted. We need to change."

A beat later, he starts shucking his clothes too. "Right! Of course."

I'm not sure the end result is less conspicuous than before. Leonardo's trousers barely go below his knees, and his red-blond hair might be permanently stained green. He examines one of the tresses and lets it fall with a resigned sigh. "Now what?"

"We need to find Lupa." The fact that the Medici took her and she warned the other apprentices to look out for them confirms my hunch that there's something she hasn't told us yet.

"Where would they take her?"

That I'm less sure about. "The Palazzo della Signoria?"

"I don't think they'd take her somewhere a lot of people have access to," Leonardo says. "The Medici wouldn't want anyone to see her captured. Angels are still sacred." He paces across the alley's narrow length, one finger tapping his chin, the other hand drumming along his long thigh in those ridiculous, too-small pants.

I look away, trying not to be distracted. "I don't understand how they were able to take her in the first place," I say. "She has powers. She can *fly*."

"Which means they'd take her to a place where no one could see her struggle."

A chill sinks into my bones that has nothing to do with the boots stomping through the streets or the distant shouts of "Avete visto due ragazzi ricoperti di vernice? Sono dei ladri!" Florence is a city of a thousand secret doors. Lupa could be anywhere.

A soft *mroow?* distracts me.

A gray-and-white cat perches on a rubbish pile. Its tail lashes over its feet, head tilted to the side in a way I don't like at all. Another drops from a second-story windowsill.

Leonardo kneels. When his knees hit the cobblestones, the first cat rushes over and brushes its head against him, circling him entirely before prancing to the next intersection. "The cats!"

"What about them?"

He gestures to the gray-and-white one. "I think they want us to follow them."

"Cats don't have *thoughts*."

But even as I say it, the second cat joins the first. And then a third pops out around the corner. They watch us with uncanny, glowing eyes: so much like Lupa's.

I braid my fingers through Leonardo's. "Let's go."

CHAPTER FORTY

The cats race toward the river, silent, seething shadows.

Leonardo and I run side by side, our shadows stretched out before us, the sun at our backs. It feels as though it's begging us to turn around, to go back to where we came from.

But I couldn't. Not even if I wanted to.

Lupa saved me so many times. She's why I know where Niccolo is now. She's why Leonardo's fingers keep brushing mine every few steps, his touch a constant reminder that I'm still here, I'm not alone, no matter how much time I have left.

I don't care who says there's something monstrous about her.

There's something monstrous in me, too. I feel it shifting under my skin, spiked and hot, ready to roar if I find out that anyone has hurt her.

I skid to a stop, eyes wide.

A flooded-out ruin of a church stands before us—a collapsing, moss-choked pile of stones, the gurgle of the river just beyond it—but we're not the only ones here.

Dozens and dozens of cats stare, their gold-green eyes flashing in the shadows. "This must be every goddamn cat in the city," I whisper.

Leonardo reaches down. A cat butts his hand, purring aggressively. "Thanks, Buttermilk. One day Virgil will appreciate your charms."

The stink of rot fills my mouth. This church must've been destroyed in a flood and abandoned. The Arno River is tempestuous and fickle. Its deadly presence cuts through the heart of Florence like a banked fire. Safe, most of the time. Until a storm ignites its destructive powers.

I square my shoulders and take a deep breath. Release it in one long shudder. Then I cross those last few yards and push open the church's door.

A shaft of silver light spikes in from the collapsed ceiling, illuminating a single chair.

Lupa is tied to it.

I cry out her name and rush over. She lifts her head groggily, eyes half lidded and slow. They sharpen when they see me. "Not you."

I fumble with her bonds. They've tied her hands with iron, not rope. The links have already bitten into her skin and left smears of gold blood on the metal. I'll have to break the chair back to free her. "We're getting you out of here, all right?"

She jerks away, hissing. "You shouldn't be here!"

"I'm not leaving you behind." I try to bend the chair's wooden slat and fail. "Leo, I need your help."

He's stopped behind me, transfixed by something. At my shout, he jolts, turning with awful slowness, his face white beneath his freckles. "You need to see this."

There's a portrait of Lupa on the wall behind her chair.

The chain slithers from my grip.

If I didn't know her so well, I'm not sure I would recognize her. The angel in the portrait wears her hair in a thick braid over one shoulder, the strands combed and glistening. Her teeth are blunt, not pointed. Her expression is guarded, like it's hiding a secret she's just daring me to ask about.

But it's her eyes that stop my heart. They're painted in bold, confident strokes, so lifelike, they seem to see straight through me. There's a faint shimmer in the irises that offsets their main color, a rich, smooth—

"Brown." I turn slowly, tearing myself away from the portrait. "Your eyes aren't brown."

She glares at me with those bright golden eyes I'd recognize anywhere. "I told you to leave!"

I flinch at the sound of a dropped object, the muffled curse that comes after it.

Niccolo emerges from the darkness. Gone are his fine clothes from the wedding. He's wearing the rough-spun clothes of a laborer, a disapproving frown growing deeper and deeper. A fresh cut weeps red down his cheek. Does he know the truth about what Lupa is? A good, God-fearing Florentine would hesitate before treating an angel like a prisoner.

"The Medici were supposed to take care of you two," he growls. There's no brotherly recognition in his eyes.

But he definitely remembers me from last night. "Surprise! They didn't," I say.

His frown turns ugly. He unsheathes a long, curved knife. "I suppose I'll have to do it myself, then."

The bottom drops from my gut. I'm suddenly ten years old, crying hysterically in Casa delle Volpi's garden because Niccolo's bruised my fingers with the flat of his practice sword. Father pulled me out of arms lessons the very next week, too embarrassed to have his youngest son crying in front of the hired arms master.

Niccolo is the one who stayed in the lessons. And judging from the way he holds the handle, some part of him remembers every minute of them. Even if I did know my way around a blade, I couldn't bear to hurt him. I need to do something else.

"Volpone. Do you remember me yet?"

He shudders. "You're a liar."

"I'm not. Your favorite food is coccoli. You used to sneak into the kitchen and try to eat them all before dinner."

Niccolo's eyes widen, revealing bloodshot, sleepless red where they should be white. He surges forward, blade first. "Shut up!"

I sidestep him, just barely. His knife snags on my stolen shirt, opening up a long gash. "This isn't your life. Do you remember your parents? Your childhood? I know all about it. You have two little sisters named Elisabetta and Giovannia. They love you more than anything."

Niccolo's face flushes burgundy, chest heaving. "You're lying!"

"I'm not." What goes through his head when I name these memories? A blank, opaque wall of nothing? An entire false life that was never real? My gaze drops to his garnet ring. "I gave you that because you saved my life. You helped me escape before Father could kill my spirit. Do you remember?"

He makes an agonized sound. *"Stop it!"*

He's rushing again—but not at me.

At Leonardo.

Niccolo crashes into him. Leonardo screams, doubling over. Red blooms on his arm.

My vision goes red too. Weaponless, I throw myself at my brother's back, arms noosing around his neck, kicking every part of him I can reach.

Leonardo grabs my shoulders. "I'm fine; please, Virgil, we've got to go!"

But it's too late.

The thud of footsteps approaches, followed by gleeful shouts. The guards from the workshop have finally found us. Rough hands surround me. I feel the skull-headed key pulled from my trouser pocket, hear the clatter as it falls. Fingers start to dig in the pocket containing Lupa's vial. I lunge forward and sink my teeth into the meaty palm. The guard curses and shrugs me off, banging my nose. There's a shock of pain, then blood pours from my nostrils, hot and salty on my lips.

"Gesù Cristo." Niccolo makes the sign of the cross against me. "This demon has cursed them! He thinks she's one of us!"

He called Lupa a demon. He knows the truth, just as I suspected.

I spit at not-Niccolo's feet, stumbling to Leonardo's side. "She *is* one of us!" He's all right, thank God. A thin coat of blood sheets down his arm. Niccolo's blade only nicked him.

"Why are you doing this?" Leonardo's voice is small and helpless.

Niccolo stalks to Lupa's side. "She's become too human." He tilts her chin with the knife. She hisses, and he flinches. He digs the knife in deeper, opening up a weeping gold line on her skin. "We knew a woman was not a worthy vessel."

Damp rot fills my mouth.

I've failed Lupa.

I've failed her just like I failed Niccolo. She told me to live, and now I'll be the one watching her die.

Lupa's eyes meet mine, fierce and full of resolution. Her mouth lifts. "Goodbye, Virgil. I'll see you on the other side."

Niccolo's knife arcs up over Lupa, a gleaming, glittering fang.

"Lupa!"

It slashes downward and rips through my soul.

Leonardo grabs my face at the last moment, tucking it into the crook of his elbow, sparing me from the horrible sight of the mortal blow. There's a terrible, wretched scream, and it takes me a moment to realize the sound is tearing from me.

Then an awful stillness.

I throw off Leonardo, rushing to the body slumped over and silent in the chair. I cradle her face, sweep away her tangled hair. Her eyes are shut, eyelashes fanned across her cheekbones. There's no blood, which surprises me. I feel lower, around her neck, her chest, and then her stomach, searching for the handle of the knife.

Leonardo steps beside me, his arm extended, fingers lighting on the knife's handle.

It's sticking out from the portrait just above her head.

The ruined canvas peels from its frame, one bold, brown eye staring back at me.

The girl in my arms wakes up and starts to scream.

CHAPTER FORTY-ONE

The girl kicks away from me, her screams quickly dissolving into sobs. Niccolo unlocks her chains. I half expect her to run, but instead she sags in the chair like she can't hold herself up. Her unsteady hand goes to the space behind her ear. Iron breaks on my tongue when she discovers the scar tissue there, when I see her eyes grow round with shock.

"Who are you?"

It's Lupa's voice, but . . . not. There's a wrongness, like velvet brushed in the opposite direction.

"We're friends," Leonardo says softly. "We're here to help you."

She smiles, a dreamy, half-asleep thing. Her beige skin is going gray—a sickly pallor spreading faster than any wasting illness. A trickle of blood weeps from her nose to her mouth, leaving behind a smear of red. I stare, cold sweeping through me. Just moments ago, it was gold. Just moments ago, she was Lupa, and now she's not.

"She's sick!" I cry. "Help her!"

"We have no more use for her," Niccolo says.

What do you mean? The question dies in my throat.

Because I understand now, with awful, heart-stopping clarity.

Demons don't visit Florence.

They possess it.

They inhabit the bodies of Florentine citizens while they're on earth.

Lupa's eyes flutter shut. Her head lolls to the side in the circle of my arms. Her body goes limp. I feel frantically for the pulse in her neck, but there's nothing. Only a horrible stillness that fills me with horror. Leonardo sinks to his knees, a soft, helpless whimper escaping the hand over his mouth.

The girl—Lupa—whoever she is—is dead.

There's a flash of scarlet. A crushing pain on the back of my head.

And everything falls away.

I wake to the faint scent of linseed oil.

I push myself up slowly, shading my eyes against the ruddy daylight filtering in from above.

A soft *tsk*ing noise sounds. "About time you're up. I was beginning to fear Father cracked your skulls too hard."

I'm inside the Medici's painting studio. Lorenzo de' Medici slouches against the back wall with a smirk. The second day of his family's elaborate, weeklong wedding celebration has him done up in white and gold, his hair carefully combed. Tormenting us must be his entertainment between stealing sweets from children or yelling at puppies or whatever else evil people do when they welcome their brides into their nightmare families.

Leonardo's red-gold head pops up beside mine. "What's this ugly little room?"

Lorenzo scowls. "My family's personal painting studio. It's where you'll be staying while you're with us."

I force myself to stand, wincing at the splitting ache in my head. My hand goes to the spot and comes away bloody. It's in almost the exact same location as Lupa's scar.

Is this how they took her? Cudgeled her in the skull, stole her away in the dark?

I drop my hand and fist it. "You're killing people."

Lorenzo scoffs, as if I'm being childish. "Did you think angels floated down from the clouds on little feathery wings?"

I couldn't say what I thought. I was told heaven and hell were real, but they felt as distant as the Arabian Sea or China—places I was told existed but would not ever see. Either way, I hate how Lorenzo makes me feel small. "They're demons. Call them what they are," I snarl.

"If you insist. The hosts consent to serving. Some consider it a great honor." His eyes cut to mine. Hold them as tight as the reins of an unruly horse. "Your brother did."

I slither to the floor. My head hurts too much to stand anymore. "My brother agreed to be one?"

It makes no sense. Niccolo isn't a demon. His soul is missing. Lupa tasted him and told me so. If he was a demon—if the demon isn't inside him anymore—

He'd be dead just like the girl.

I shiver and hug my knees to my chest. There's a sour vinegar feeling festering inside me. I don't know if I want to vomit or cry.

Lorenzo snaps two perfectly manicured fingers. The hidden door behind him opens, and footmen stream inside carrying two copper tubs, jugs of steaming water, marble trays of soap. I briefly think about making a run for it, but guards come in after them.

"Bathe and dress for dinner. My father will explain it all to you."

My belly fills with ice. "What if we don't want to?"

Lorenzo's smirk sharpens. "This is Florence. There's always a deal to be made if you're clever enough."

CHAPTER FORTY-TWO

The Medici's private dining hall is overwhelming. The floor is covered with dark, tasseled rugs. Gigantic tapestries of an Olympian symposium hang from the walls. A gold candle-branch hangs from the ceiling, all its lit candles glittering and reflecting off the crystals dangling from its arms. The table is stacked with delicacies, enough food to feed all the artists in Verrocchio's workshop for an entire week.

But there's only one person sitting at the table.

Piero de' Medici flashes a dazzling smile. "Thank you for joining me."

I hesitate when I see the two extra places set across the table on either side of Piero. When I don't move, a guard shoves my back. I hold my breath and perch on the very edge of my seat. I don't like being split up from Leonardo. Even this short distance from him feels like a trap, just big enough for something awful to slip between us like a knife betwixt the ribs.

There's a soft pressure against my booted foot.

Leonardo's eyes snag mine from across a platter of roasted meat. They gleam with a promise. *I'm still right here.*

I expect someone to set out a place for Lorenzo—mustn't they have miscounted, when there's four of us?—but instead he stands behind his father's chair like a sentinel. Or a servant.

Piero sips his wine. "So, you discovered our little secret."

"Which one? The fact that angels are demons or that you *kill people* so they can be possessed?" I hate how he talks about whatever we saw like it's an inside joke, when a girl died in my arms with no memory of what happened to her. I hate *him*, and I don't think I've ever truly hated before.

I lean forward, smiling viciously. I shouldn't say it like this—keeping it a secret might be more useful—but I want to anger Piero de' Medici the way he's angered me. "Or your own bargain with the devil?"

The old man's eyes flash red.

And then I start to choke.

I scramble to unclench the force around my windpipe. There's nothing there—no hand, no garrote—but the awful pressure builds, squeezing tighter until my vision tunnels, until all I can see is Leonardo's freckled face widening with a scream—

The strangling feeling vanishes as quick as it came.

I thud against my chairback, chest heaving. Lorenzo looks away from me, his jaw squared.

Madonna santa, Clarice de' Medici was right.

Piero flexes his hand. "My family owes much to the devil." His red-limned eyes go to the bargain marks on my arms. I fight the urge to yank my too-short sleeves lower. "I see you've taken much of the devil's magic for yourself, boy. You have no right to judge us."

Except I've only damned myself, not innocent people who believed a lie.

"Your bargain with the devil is different. You can wield magic." Leonardo is curiously calm. As if everything we're discussing is entirely plausible. "What did the devil want for it?"

Piero takes a sip of wine and slams the glass on the table. "You think us foolish enough to tell you?"

Leonardo shrugs. "Perhaps. Your ancestor was foolish enough to make a deal with the devil. It's not as if one of those has ever gone wrong."

The red in Piero's eyes pulses. The candles gutter, and a familiar incoming-storm feeling prickles my skin. It's like Lupa's magic but wrong, all wrong. No crackle of latent lightning—something more jagged, rotten.

Lorenzo grips his father's shoulder. Piero's hand twitches, like he'd love nothing more than to slap his son away, but instead he releases a long, low breath, and the candlelight steadies.

"You already know. What all demons want." Piero's voice has a sulky edge to it now. "Souls."

Leonardo flings an arm over his chairback, head tipping to the side. "Don't you care what the devil's doing with them? He must need souls for a reason."

Piero steeples his fingers, danger flashing in his eyes. "You are an annoying worm, aren't you?" A muscle strains in his jaw. The movement pulses through the room like a water ripple. "Do not mistake being here with being my equal. I will crush you the moment you stop being useful."

A blistering heat boils me from the inside. "Don't fucking *touch* him."

They took Lupa. They took my brother. They will not take him.

Piero recoils with surprise, but I barely see it. The edges of the room have gone hazy. I can feel Leonardo's gaze on me, but I can't look. I might vibrate out of my skin.

You have less than a year to live rattles around my brain like the last coin in a purse.

Perhaps it'll be too late for me, but it won't be for Leonardo.

I won't let anything happen to him.

Lorenzo lifts his hands for peace, speaking for the first time. His voice seems small compared to his father's. "Our ancestor tricked the devil and found a way to limit his power just as we limit the power of the demons here."

"It didn't work with Lupa, though. You couldn't control her." The understanding comes to me in a sudden rush. "That's why you attacked her at Verrocchio's."

Piero laughs, the sound harsh and grating. "We took care of her in the end, didn't we?"

I'm not so sure they did. Lupa's hidden vial presses into my thigh, hot as an ember. I kept it hidden in my smallclothes as I bathed, returning it to my pocket when no one was watching. She gave it to me before she left. She knew what would happen to her and went willingly to her fate.

There must be a reason for it.

Piero throws down his napkin. "Come. We'll show you how we do it."

Neither Leonardo nor I move.

Piero smiles. Then he says the words I can't resist. The ones that would get me to follow them anywhere.

"Don't you want to know what happened to your brother's soul?"

CHAPTER FORTY-THREE

Lorenzo leads us through the palazzo, to a door hidden behind an especially gruesome hunting tapestry. My pulse stutters when he takes out a key hanging from a chain around his neck.

The skull-headed key's little ruby eyes wink.

"It was so kind of you to bring this back." Lorenzo unlocks the door. "It's been hard to get in here and the painting studio without it."

"Wouldn't have been a problem at all if you weren't so goddamn careless," Piero hisses.

Lorenzo's smirk falls, replaced with an icy calm that's somehow worse.

The door opens silently into the dark room. Eerie green-gold light pulses to life inside at Piero's first step. He glances over his shoulder with another impatient sigh when he sees us hesitating. "Do you want to know, or not?"

Leonardo's hand lights on the small of my back. The single touch steels my courage.

It's an art gallery, but I've seen all the paintings before.

I spin around the room, a waterfall roar in my ears. It's all the portraits from the Palazzo della Signoria. There are even more of them here, so many, I can barely see the wall underneath.

They're painted in the same style—a face-on portrait, from the shoulders up—but the expressions are a spectrum of emotions. Fear. Resolution. Joy. Most of the portraits are slashed, a single cut bisecting the frame.

"The portraits are essential." Piero rights a crooked one with a single finger. "They serve as a tether that allows the demon to possess their human host by pushing out their soul. When it's destroyed, the demon leaves the body."

"*Kills* the host, you mean," Leonardo corrects.

I grow still when one face leaps out from the sea.

Niccolo.

I brush my fingers along the canvas, the paint's rough texture catching on my skin. The portrait on either side of it has been slashed, but his remains whole. It makes me want to tear it down from the wall. Hide it in an iron-banded strongbox so no one can hurt it, even though a stranger dwells inside my brother.

"Your brother begged to become a host. I've never met someone so desperate to escape their life."

A feeling like lightning splinters through me—the hot strike of surprise chased with burning pain. "Escape?"

You already know, an awful voice whispers. *You've always known.*

"The pressure of your father's terrible deals seemed to be crushing your brother, but of course, you'd understand that more than me." Piero's grin shows every single one of his teeth. Like he knows he's drawn my blood and revels in the taste of it. "Forfeit your life to send your soul to heaven. A lie, of course, but a necessary one if Florence is to keep her magic."

A disbelieving noise escapes me. I think of my brother's red-rimmed eyes the day he trudged to me through the snow and told me he was leaving.

He thought he was leaving to die.

He chose to die rather than ask for help. To be honest with me.

And I wouldn't hug him. Refused to say goodbye.

Now his soul is drifting in hell, lost for eternity.

I touch his face again, my fingers unsteady. Was he struggling that much? Was I such a selfish sibling that I couldn't see it?

"That's not true. Don't listen to him." Leonardo's voice rings like a sword being pulled from a scabbard. "It wasn't your fault, Virgil."

Piero's mouth pulls. "After your brother gave up his soul, a demon refused to possess him. It's happened before, but there was always a flaw with the host. Nothing was obviously wrong with your brother, but I suppose there must be a hidden defect in your family." He notes my clenched jaw with a satisfied smirk. "Your brother became a shell, an empty vessel who could remember nothing of his past, or even what he'd done the day before. What use did we have a for a boy like that? We almost killed him. But then we thought it would be useful to have an . . . ally of sorts. After Soderini chose to spread his slander instead of keeping his mouth shut, we thought it best to replace him with someone more sympathetic to our family."

Leonardo's arm wraps around my shoulder. He pulls me to his side, his entire body quivering. "Niccolo's not an ally. An ally can disagree with you, fight back. An ally is a person. You're *using* a boy who lost his soul. Who believes he is whoever you tell him he is. Who can do your dirty work and never complain. Why be a banker when you can be a king?" His fury picks up speed, a boulder crashing down a hill. I feel his warmth pouring into me. "Why be a king when you can be God?"

Lorenzo flinches, his eyes flaring wide and darting to his father. Piero's expression clouds over, his friendliness dropping like a mask. I hear a set of heavy footsteps approaching from the corridor.

"Can I interest you in a bargain?" The patriarch's voice is as soft as smoke and twice as deadly.

I slide closer to Leonardo, hands fisted and shoulders raised. "I think we've made enough bargains."

"I'm afraid it's not a request. We need a new painter for the angelic bargains." His chin dips to me. "And a new angel, since a workshop has so tragically lost one."

A shadow slinks into the room. A guard, a body in his arms. He drops it at Piero's feet. I flinch at the horrible thud. The corpse's head lolls toward me, eyes vacant.

Bartolomeo Rucellai.

"I'm afraid my daughter-in-law didn't pick a painter who could stomach the task."

A foul taste swells up my throat. The wedding portrait commission was an audition. A way for the Medici to admire a promising crop of younger artists without anyone knowing what dark prize awaited the winner. Is Bartolomeo's death our fault too? There's a jagged feeling in my chest. A knife of panic and guilt that plunges deeper and deeper.

"I'll give you three days. And if you can't do it, like he couldn't . . ." Piero nods toward Bartolomeo. His smile curves like a cutlass. "We'll kill you both."

CHAPTER FORTY-FOUR

I pace across the painting studio, a staticky, crackling restlessness racing through me. "We'll find a way out of this."

I won't let anyone hurt you.

The unspoken promise fills my veins with iron. It's not one I can keep.

Leonardo doesn't act like he's heard me. He sits on the edge of the pallet, his head in his hands, hair cascading to his knees. His back is to the canvas and paints on the worktable. Someone must've stocked it when we were out.

Leonardo's things are here as well. His extra clothes. A patched winter cloak. Most chilling is the stack of leather folders rising from the floor to the table. Leonardo opened the first one and then recoiled as if it were a striking serpent. They're all the sketches and machine blueprints from his bedchamber, organized and catalogued in a way he would never have done himself. A violence and violation of his very being. He hasn't looked at them since.

Nothing of mine was moved here. I might as well already be gone.

"How?" His question is a tiny, broken thing. It cracks something in me. He's all sunshine, my light. I don't know how to be the person who fixes things for him, even though I want to be.

"We can make a bargain." I settle on the bed beside him. The mattress dimples under our weight, pulling us together thigh to thigh. I pull out Lupa's vial and uncork it so he can see the gold blood for himself. "Lupa gave this to me before she left. She's not sure how it'll work, but it's worth a try."

Leonardo's eyes widen.

Then he pushes it away gently. "No."

"No?" I repeat, certain I've misheard. "It could be a way out. We might as well try it."

Niccolo's soul has been stolen. We'll be dead in three days. What else do we have left to lose?

He sighs at my furrowed brow. "Let's think through this. If we escape, what happens next?"

It feels like Verrocchio is peering over my shoulder, evaluating my work and finding it wanting. "We'd get far away from Florence. I'd tell my family to follow. We could open up your workshop."

Leonardo's mouth pulls ruefully, as if I've answered wrong. "What about your brother? Would he come with us too?"

I pull in a sharp breath, as if I've stepped on broken glass.

I don't know what to do about Niccolo. He's gone, but he's here. He's soulless, but alive. I found him, but he's never felt further away. I can't leave him here, but I don't know how to save him.

I don't know if it's possible.

Leonardo's fingers lace through mine. His pulse gallops in the hollow of his throat. "You know what would happen next. The Medici would find another unsuspecting painter to lock up. They'd find more desperate, innocent people to agree to end their lives and be possessed by demons. More people would make bargains. More people would *die*. I can't let that happen. My mother, your brother, Bartolomeo. How many more people will suffer? I can't run away from this now that I know the truth."

Panic lunges in me, a frightened, snapping dog. He can't ask me to leave him here. I won't. "If we escaped, we could get help. Tell people what's going on—"

"You said it yourself. Who would believe us over the Medici?"

Rage seethes through me, a bruising, wild river of it. I shouldn't be angry at him—none of this is his fault—but I've been so angry for so long, I don't know how to feel anything else.

"So that's it? You're just going to give up?"

His warm lips brush across my frigid knuckles. "It's not giving up."

I rip away from him, even though it feels like sinking a knife into my own skin. "You should do it, then."

"Do what?"

"Paint me."

His umber eyes pierce me, drawing the air from the room. "No."

"*Yes*. I was never going to survive this year anyway."

If Leonardo does what they demand—if he paints this one portrait—it might buy him the time he needs to come up with a way to tear it all down forever. The Medici only have need of one artist, and it's not me. I'm a spare, a body good for filling up with something more useful.

But not to Leonardo. Never to him.

A spasm shakes his body. "I won't end your life."

Why can't he see the obvious? I've been waiting for this moment the entire year. "Then someone else will soon!"

He makes a soft, furious noise and shoves me.

I fall back on the pallet, gaping at his blazing face. The dying sunlight has caught in his hair, spinning it all to glorious fire.

"You can't ask me to take a life. Especially not yours."

"It's the only way to save yourself and end this—"

"Then after, I'll do what? Live a life without you?" His breath is ragged, stirring up flurries of golden dust motes. The hand pinning me down is a brand, a stone, a cathedral over my heart.

"I thought you wanted to end the age of angels and magic?" Can he feel how I'm shaking? "I'm giving you the chance to do it."

As abruptly as it swept over him, the anger clears. Disappears into some distant part of him I've never seen before. He yanks me up roughly. "I need to show you something." He drags me to the worktable, flipping open one of the leather folders and gesturing for me to look.

I make eye contact with a sketch of my own face.

It's not the sort of image anyone would want in their house, certainly not one they'd commission. My brow is furrowed, expression angry, a paintbrush clamped betwixt my teeth.

"That's from when you were doing the Strozzi commission," he says. "You were fighting with the canvas the entire time."

I trail my fingers over the feverish lines of my face. Each one is rendered in exquisite, loving detail. It's like someone saw past my skin to the soul beneath.

His hand is a torch against my back. "Keep looking."

The folder is filled with drawings of me. At work, at the dining table, alone in my window overlooking the garden. There's even one of me holding up Giorgio's phallic apples.

There are dozens and dozens of sketches, in all stages of

completion. One for every day of the year, one for every time I scolded Leonardo for not getting his work done. One for every time I thought I'd never be happy again.

His voice is as soft and steady as a heartbeat. "Every time I kissed someone, I wished they were you. When I couldn't force myself to draw anything else, your face was the only thing I could finish." He laughs, the sound like the flash of gold leaf in the candlelight. "I always wanted to draw you during our morning exercises, but I was afraid you'd notice."

The words shift and crackle through me like a fire. All the sketches of other people I found in his room. All these of me lying just underneath. I was so close, but I didn't see them.

We've ended up back at the first sketch, the precise lines now blurred. "Why didn't you ever ask? I would've sat for you." Then maybe we would've realized sooner what we meant to each other. Then maybe we would've had more time together.

He brushes the dampness from my face. "I was terrified you'd say no. I dreamed of you for too long to let you go, even if it was only in my head." He traces my cheekbones, like he's putting the final touch on a masterpiece. "That's why I asked you to open a workshop with me. It was never about the sodding work. I wanted a life with you." He draws in a long, shuddering breath that I feel everywhere. "Whether we have months or years together doesn't matter. It won't change how I feel. Any time I have with you is worth it." He brackets my face like it's something holy, something cherished. His dark eyes burn. "You're wrong if you think you're giving me what I want by sacrificing yourself. I never wanted anything until I wanted you. I'm not letting you go now."

It sinks into my soul: not the words, but their meaning. What he's tried to tell me before and what I couldn't understand.

"I love you too." I press my face into the divot where his neck meets his shoulders. Melt against him so there's no space left between us.

He shudders, like there's a crack in the earth, a fissure in the sky. "Truly?"

He was too afraid to say it first. I'll say it over and over again so he knows, so he believes that I finally figured out what I should've known for ages. "So much, I can barely stand it. I've loved you for years."

And it's too late.

I've found the love of my life when there's no more life left to live.

For once, I don't quail away from the pain. I let every bit of grief and regret hail against my heart. I grit my teeth at the ache, grabbing fistfuls of his shirt. He can't just hear this: He needs to feel the truth in every part of his body. "I really wish we could've had that workshop together."

The most agonizing thing is I can see it. A room overflowing with paper and paintbrushes, wisteria climbing over the front windows to dye the light purple in the late spring. There'd be two painters' stations downstairs but only one bed upstairs. Each day I'd be up before him, lay out the bread and jam for us both, my entire body waiting for the telltale creak above that means he's finally up too. I'd stop working, and we'd eat together. Perhaps we'd even lock the door, return upstairs. We'd get nothing done; we'd get everything done that mattered. It could've been ours. A perfectly imperfect life.

He tilts my chin up, his mouth a whisper from mine. "You see it too, don't you?"

Each heartbeat of mine feels like a too-big breath, so deep it hurts, but I like it. I want to remember everything about this for as long as I can. "It's incredible."

He smirks—that irresistible little smirk that's gotten under my skin for ages. "Of course. Anything we create together would be, tesoro."

He kisses me. Soft and sweet, but soon it turns hungry and hard. I push him onto the pallet the way he pushed me, and from the way his pupils flare wide, he likes it even more. Then we're kissing columns down each other's body, fumbling with laces with warm-honey smiles that melt away all the bad feelings. We try to stay quiet in case anyone's guarding the doors, but 'tis impossible to stop whispering, a stream of *yes* and *all right?* and *I love you, I love you so goddamn much.*

His face lies against my chest when we're done. I feel my heart pounding, and I know he can hear it too. I trace patterns on his skin, imagining a golden line linking all his freckles together. A map into his heart.

"It was nice to do this again without Lupa hovering over us," he says. "She told me she wasn't there, but unlike you, I do think she can lie."

I poke him and groan. "I do *not* want to think about her now."

"Too bad."

"Always need the last word, do you?"

"I love having the last word. It's my second favorite thing in the world."

Because I'm his first. I have to bite my lip to keep from smiling too broadly.

The sky grows dark through the ceiling window. Soon Leonardo's breath slows. His fingers go slack with sleep in mine. I hold him to me, wishing I could join him in slumber but watching the moonlight scythe across the floor instead.

My eyes flick over to the vial on the table.

I'll see you on the other side. That's what Lupa said right before she vanished.

What odd final words. And she was smiling as she said them.

Almost like she was happy about being torn from the body she possessed.

Almost as if she was trying to tell me something.

I press myself up on my elbows, suddenly wide awake.

Carefully I ease Leonardo's warm weight from me. I slip my pillow where I was, drooping with relief when his arm tightens, bringing it closer to his chest.

He's so beautiful like this, silvered in the shadows. He could be a statue in a royal garden. If he were, I'd go there every day and run my hands over the marble of him, even if stone would never do his freckles the justice they deserve.

I shrug on my crumpled doublet.

Then I move toward the waiting canvas, the palette knife already biting into my skin.

There's one final bargain I have to make.

CHAPTER FORTY-FIVE

I mix together my blood and the paints.

Then I lift a brush to the canvas and start.

The Medici didn't tell us how a portrait tethers a demon and a human, but they didn't have to. Their forearms are bare, unmarked. Lorenzo and Piero have never made a bargain in their entire lives. I've made dozens and dozens of them. Blood, a whispered wish.

Then, a bargain.

My very last one.

Leonardo can argue with me all he wants, but I know in my bones this is what I'm meant to do. I wish I didn't have to go, but dying to save someone I love feels like a fair trade. The period on a life well lived. The sort of end I can be proud of.

I'm painting for the first time in months with no inhibitions, no worries about what anyone else thinks. Fiery colors for the sky. Almost black for the trees. Two figures in the foreground, but not the ones you'd expect.

I pray Lupa is on the other side, waiting for me like she promised.

We can't defeat the Medici here. They're so certain they've already won. They banished Lupa and locked us in their highest tower and carried on with their days of wedding festivities like nothing had happened. Another ordinary day of destroying other peoples' lives to shore up their own power and might.

If I can get to hell, perhaps I can stop this. Lupa gave me everything I needed to bring myself there; there must be a reason why. There must still be a chance, or my heart wouldn't pound so fiercely.

My whole life, I wanted something that was just mine, except I kept letting other people tell me what that was. I cared too much about what they thought, learned to hide from my own wanting heart.

I know what I want now.

When I'm almost done, I walk over to Leonardo and smooth his hair from his face. Press a soft kiss to his temple. He'll remember me forever, I know he will. It was wrong of me to think he wouldn't. One day I hope he understands why I had to do it. I hope he knows I never, ever wanted to leave him.

"Please don't be too mad at me, caro."

I sit on my knees before the still-dripping painting.

Gray city walls beneath a red sky. A snarled black forest clawing at its edges. Two boys stand before a gate in the very center, so similar-looking, they can only be brothers.

I uncork the vial of Lupa's blood and tip my finger in gold. Trace a heart-shaped scar on one of the boy's faces. Linger there even as ichor bleeds down the surface.

Then I swallow back my fear and speak my last words. "Take me to hell."

CHAPTER FORTY-SIX

I wake up alone.

I push myself up, taking in the room.

'Tis the Medici's painting studio but . . . not.

The worktable and easel are missing, the earthy scent of linseed oil gone. Even the colors seem dimmer, like a faded canvas left in the sun. I glance to the corner—where a too-gangly boy sleeps in another world—my chest clenching when what I'm looking for isn't there.

The cut on my arm is healed, a black mark covering it. A long, shaky breath escapes me. I'm either dreaming, or I'm dead, but either way, it worked.

I ease open the studio's door—unlocked here—and step into an empty corridor, my footsteps strangely muffled. The silence is thick, stuffing my ears like wool. Each shift of my body feels like a warning, each step a step too far.

The Palazzo Medici shares the same, unnerving emptiness as the studio. The walls only seem to focus if I squint my eyes just so. There's a hazy, ethereal quality to it all, as if I'm looking through the bottom of a glass or stuck in the memory of a dream.

Downstairs, double doors loom closer and closer, more solid than anything else I've seen so far.

They open at my touch, as if pulled back by invisible footmen.

Leaving me to behold a ruined, gutted Florence.

My eyes slam shut, stomach roiling. *It's not real!*

But it looks like it could be, right down to the faded red duomo crumbling in the distance.

Buildings are upside down, entire walls missing. Some of the cobblestone streets run up their facades; others dead-end in a pall of mist that pours through the streets like smoke. Shapes flicker in the gray. Some seem human, but every time I'm on the verge of seeing a face, it dissolves in the haze. The air remains sepulchrally quiet, devoid of all the life and noise that belong in a city.

No, a *living* city.

I've entered a place that belongs to the dead.

Something flickers right beside me. The silence swallows my shout.

'Tis nothing but a lithe black cat. It sits and starts licking a paw.

A chill goes through me—one that seems to ripple on and on through the emptiness. I sidestep the creature and keep going.

There's a pinprick of pain on my calf. I gasp and turn.

The cat is up on its back legs, tail lashing furiously.

"Do . . . you want me to follow you?"

The cat's ears twitch. Shadow-fast, it races to the next corner, staring at me with an ancient, impenetrable gaze that stands my hair on end.

"I need to find my brother first."

His portrait is still whole. His body is not yet dead, but his soul is lost, drifting somewhere I couldn't find on earth. I have a hunch it's here. I don't know if I'm right, but I have to see if it's true.

The cat hisses but doesn't move. Are those . . . leathery wings slowly materializing above its shoulders? Not a cat, but a demon, then.

I swallow back a heap of nerves. I've made enough bargains in my life to know what happens next. I break the skin of my thumb against a jagged cobblestone and lower my hand.

The cat laps the blood eagerly, wings splaying for balance. Without a sound, it turns around and races through the foggy streets. I hurry after it.

The cat is always waiting for me when I round a corner, tail whipping impatiently. I have the oddest sense that if I took off in the opposite direction, I'd still find it waiting.

The deeper I go into the city, the narrower the streets become, as if this nightmare Florence has a hidden vanishing point like a sketchbook landscape. I'm about to tell the cat-demon I don't want to go any farther when I stumble into an open space and find myself dazzled by a strange golden orb.

It hangs in the piazza's center, so brilliant, I squint against it. It looks like the Easter Carro del Fuoco paused right as its fireworks explode, but smaller.

A gasp falls from my lips when my eyes adjust to the light. "Niccolo?"

He undulates weightlessly above the ground, gold pouring from every one of his pores. His eyes are closed, lashes two black fans against his cheekbones. I reach out with a trembling hand to touch him—

A force knocks me to the ground with a snarl.

The cat leers over me, the size of a lion now.

The meaning is clear: It's time for me to pay up.

Breath stuttering, I reach into my pocket and take out a handkerchief. "Will this do?"

A clawed paw the size of a cooking pot shreds it to ribbons.

I stand slowly. The demon-cat is so big, its wings blot out the sky above. Its fangs have grown longer, each one the length of a knife. A dark red gleam flickers in its black pupils.

I swallow and lift my arms. "I said I would pay you, but you never named your price, and so I get to name it now. The bargain has already been sealed with blood."

The demon lunges and roars. I wince as a wave of moist, rancid breath washes over me. Its teeth are inches from my face, saliva dripping down them in ropes. A drop lands wetly on my boot and soaks through the leather. I take shallow, steadying breaths, willing myself to stay calm. "How about the taste of freshly churned butter?"

The demon's ears flatten. Its mouth opens wider.

Before I can scream, a rough scaly tongue licks my forehead. A starlike speck flashes on the demon's tongue before it swallows.

I blink, and suddenly the demon is cat-sized again. With a final hiss, it beats its wings and zips off into the mist.

I pat my head where the cat licked me, but there's nothing there. I think of butter, anticipate the delicious sweetness melting across my tongue, the richness as I take a bite of thickly slathered bread . . .

But I can't. Each time I reach for the memory, it's like digging in an empty jar, my fingers scraping the bottom for something I know was once there. I can think of all the composite parts of fresh butter, see it and feel it, but I can't recall the moment the taste floods my mouth. It's as if I've never tasted it at all.

The memory is a small price to pay, but what else will I be asked to give up on this journey? Does the demon-cat have kinsmen?

The warmth of Niccolo's soul hangs just beside me, peaceful and quiet. A single candle left burning in the window to welcome me home.

Trembling, I touch his hand for the first time in years. "Volpone?"

His eyes open. "Volpacchiotto."

CHAPTER FORTY-SEVEN

His arms wrap around me. I fall into them like I always do. "It's you." Tears fill my eyes. "It's really *you*."

Niccolo flinches. He scrubs away my tears before they can fall. "Don't cry. It'll bring them closer."

"Bring what closer?"

He touches a finger to his lips and motions for quiet. I try not to let it bother me, how we're finally together and he's already telling me what to do. "We're not the only things here."

He's got the same black curls tumbling over his forehead, the same heart-shaped scar on his cheekbone. The gold gleam dances across his skin, growing livelier. It's as if my being here has awakened his soul. As if he were a sleeping cinder until I touched him.

He grabs my wrist, forcing me to look him in the eyes. "I'm sorry. I've missed you for—" He swallows down the emotion. Takes a breath and adds more quietly, "For a very long time. But you can't feel too deeply here. 'Tis dangerous."

The fog writhes between us, an unnatural cold leaching warmth from under my surface. "The Medici told me you were desperate to escape your life. That's why you became a host." I don't think it's true—I don't want it to be true—but I have to know.

Niccolo draws in a sharp gasp. Then he's squeezing me so

hard, I can't breathe. "No. Life was hard, but not because of you. *Never* because of you."

The words crawl into my chest, into my heart, where a crack I've carried for years finally fuses. I nod, unable to speak.

Not letting me go, Niccolo turns so we're standing side by side, looking at up at the sky. Lightning crackles along the gray clouds, silent and unsettling. "The Medici lied. They said if I agreed to work with them for a few years, they'd give back Casa delle Volpi. I agreed because it seemed simple. A few years of my life for everyone's else well-being. I didn't realize they were lying until it was too late, and when I did . . . they threatened you all."

"But why wouldn't you tell me?" The old hurt squirms its way to the surface again. Second son. Second best. "I begged you to. I could've kept a secret."

"They were *working with demons*," Niccolo says. "I couldn't let you face that too. When I came to the workshop, there was a guard around the corner. I said the meanest things I could to keep you away. I couldn't risk you following me and running into him. I've regretted it ever since." His gaze drops. "That's why I asked the printmaker to create a new version of Dante's *Inferno*. I thought you'd find the note and put it together."

My hurt grows bigger, biting me with sharp teeth, refusing to let go. "You should've told me yourself, damn the guard!" If he had, everything would've been different. We could've fixed it together like we were meant to.

"Virgil—"

"I thought you had *died*, Niccolo. Do you have any idea how your disappearance has weighed on us? I blamed myself for it."

He flinches. "Why?"

"What did you expect me to do when you never came home after I told you to leave?" My voice goes hot and high, and I'm too loud for this silent city, but I don't care. How could he think he could disappear without a word and everything would be fine? How could he decide that tearing our family apart was what needed to be done? I deserved a say. We all did.

"I didn't expect you to do anything. I was taking care of it!" His face shutters. His glow is suddenly grayer, darker. The last bit of color clinging to the landscape before a too-early winter sunset. "But I was wrong. I'm sorry. I thought I was doing the right thing." He laughs unexpectedly. "Papà really fucked us over, didn't he?"

Father. I inhale sharply and search the piazza, as if his shade already lurks to tell me how disappointed he is in me yet again. Oh God, is screaming at me from beyond the grave possible now? Have we moved from a place of metaphor into horrifying possibility? What if he haunts me forever in this afterlife?

"Virgil." Niccolo's hand is on my shoulder. "He's not here. I promise."

I nod once, grateful for the reassurance, even more grateful that I didn't have to voice my fear out loud.

Niccolo speaks again. "I know Papà was unforgivably cruel to you, but he got to me, too. When he died—when I was suddenly in charge of everything—I thought I had to do it alone, because he had told me so in a thousand different ways. When I turned away from you, I knew I should go back and tell you the truth, but I didn't know how to apologize for hurting you." His eyes bore into mine, green at the edges and sunbursts of copper around the pupils. I could be looking at myself. "I'm apologizing now. I shouldn't have shut you out. I was wrong, and I've very much paid for it. Can you forgive me? I love you so much. I never, ever meant to leave you."

Years of guilt, years of tying myself in knots over things out of my control. Trying to control them anyway and blaming myself when they didn't work out. Pushing people away because I thought the brokenness in me was my fault and not the fault of the world that broke me.

I thought I was doing the right thing too. We both did.

"Yes." I wrap him in my arms, ribs creaking. "I forgive you."

He hugs me back, body slack with relief.

My throat is tight—almost too tight to speak through. "In Florence, your body—"

He sighs and scrubs a hand over his chin. In this world, his ring is missing. "I know."

I think of the stranger wearing his face, how cruelly he laughed at us. The fear and rage and terror in his eyes when I spoke his name. "You don't remember who you are, and the Medici use you to do their dirty work. They've forced you to *kill* people—"

He shudders and presses a burning-hot finger to my cold lips. "You can't feel like that here."

"Feel like what?"

"Demons hunt souls." Niccolo's voice is low and quick, but even he can't keep the thread of panic from it. "Feeling too much, acting too human, it's like lighting a bonfire for—"

He stops abruptly.

An awful, icy feeling crawls over my shoulders. I turn slowly.

The demon-cat from before has returned and stares with gleaming red eyes. Another steps out beside it and sits on its haunches. Then a third.

Their eyes glow like embers, more and more of them burning from the gray each second. Surrounding us.

"Niccolo," I say carefully. "What happens when demons catch souls?"

His ghostly gold light has dimmed to a barely there caul over his skin. Niccolo has mastered the art of repressing his feelings, but I haven't. "Oh, the usual things you'd expect. Torture. Dismemberment. Boiled alive in a cauldron of blood."

I nod, mouth dry. "And souls can't die, so it goes on for eternity?"

"They get bored. Eventually."

One of the demon-cats licks its lips and creeps closer.

It tasted my soul, and it wants more. And now there's Niccolo's soul beside mine, glowing with . . . whatever it is lost souls glow with.

Side by side, I can't help but notice that my brother only has a few inches on me now, the head or so he once held above me no longer there. We've wronged each other. We've made decisions alone we should've made together.

But he's still my brother, my volpone.

And we were always better at getting in and out of trouble together than we were apart.

"You must be wondering why I'm here," I say conversationally as we edge toward an alley funneling into the endless gray. The one line from the piazza free of horrible little cat eyes.

"I *was* wondering, yes." Niccolo's voice stays light even as a demon swipes at his ankle.

"I need your help. I'm searching for a demon I met in Florence. She has a plan to destroy the Medici and needs me for it."

We can't change the past. We were wrong about each other, but if we work together, perhaps we can finally set things right.

Niccolo lets out a horrified gasp. "You befriended a *demon*?"

"I can handle demons." I fist my hands and turn my forearms toward him. Each one of my black marks looks freshly cut into my skin, even the oldest ones that faded to charcoal. "She's not like the others."

"You grew up." His face grows sad. "I wish I had been there to see it."

I bump his shoulder and smile, not wanting to tarnish however much time we have left with more dark feelings. "I had a good example of who to become. Even if he was a bit of an idiota sometimes."

"Maybe a lot of an idiota most of the time."

We pick up the pace. The cats all follow, some on foot, some flying from rooftop to rooftop. Behind, I hear the *whump whump whump* of something far larger than all the others pounding after us. I truly, sincerely hope that Niccolo knows where he's taking us.

"Don't be so hard on yourself! 'Tis the law of nature for older siblings to be bested by their younger siblings eventually."

His mouth quirks. "Oh, is that so?"

"Yes. Giovannia's become absolutely terrifying. Father should've made her his heir."

His face splits into a wide grin. His glow is so bright now, it's barely visible. "God, I wish I could see her again."

Then he grabs my hand and we run.

The demons screech—the cacophony like nails on stone, discordant and jarring, the wrongness rattling my teeth in their sockets. The *whump whump whump* grows louder, shifting to our left instead of behind us.

The giant cat-demon bursts out from the next cross street.

I gasp, only Niccolo keeping me from stumbling. The cat-demon is somehow even bigger than before, its black wings big as frigate sails. It lowers its head and snarls, tail lashing and punching a hole in the nearest wall.

I duck beneath a flying brick and cut to the right. My bones grind in Niccolo's too-hard grasp. My lungs burn, on the very verge of ripping.

The Arno River rises before us, a single, small boat bobbing at the end of a dock. But we're too slow, the demons all too fast. Some already hover over the dock.

WHUMP WHUMP WHUMP!

Fetid warmth streams over my skin. I hit a cobblestone wrong. A sharp, splitting pain twists my ankle.

I fall. My scream turns into a choking wheeze as the air is forced from my lungs.

The cat-demon hisses above me, another wave of its putrid breath making me cough.

I only see the curved claw for a split second before it plummets toward my heart.

There's socket-wrenching pressure in my shoulders, and then I'm blinking against the explosion of cobblestones, forced to my feet as Niccolo heaves me half over his back.

"Nearly there!"

My brother half drags, half throws me the last few feet onto the dock.

I flip over and scramble backward on my elbows, gasping

for air, still waiting for another one of the knife-claws to pierce my ribs.

But the giant cat-demon has stopped. It paces at the dock's edge, paws a millimeter from the wood. It hisses, tail lashing furiously.

"They can't come here," Niccolo pants.

"Why not?" I wheeze out.

A deep chuckle answers from behind.

"Because this dock belongs to me."

CHAPTER FORTY-EIGHT

I scramble to my feet, heart thundering.

The demon's shadow engulfs me. An elongated head swivels toward us, a pond-weed tangle of hair covering most of the grayed face except for a pair of lambent, pupilless eyes.

"Wh-who are you?" I stammer.

The mouth parts, revealing rows and rows of jagged, broken teeth. From behind the rotting fangs emerges a voice, deep and throaty, like something pulled from the bottom of a swamp. "A name is a precious thing. You won't be getting mine."

The voice rattles through me—a storm in the trees, a gale against a window. I have the sudden certainty that this being could end my life as easily as blowing out a candle.

Niccolo mouths, *Demon!* and falls into a flawless bow. "Could we borrow your boat, signore? We need to go deeper into hell."

I bow as well, a half second late. Being respectful has only occasionally gotten me in trouble, while being disrespectful has caused me trouble more times than I can count. "Thank you for sheltering us from our enemies."

"They want to devour you." From between the demon's horrible rows of teeth, a long, forked tongue appears. I gasp and wrench backward, but some unseen force holds me fast, anchors my feet to the dock. My chest heaves as the tongue gets closer, caresses my cheek. A coldness like I've never felt before slithers through me. With a moan, I sink to my knees, exhausted.

The tongue snakes back into that awful month. "I want to taste you too." A deep verdant light pulses behind those grayed-out eyes. "The devil used to feed us, but now he keeps all the tastiest morsels for himself. We're *starving*." A chorus of yowling screams agrees from the shore. "Will you feed us?"

My soul screams when those fathomless eyes lock onto mine. I let out a long, slow breath and try not to let it overwhelm me. "Will you let us take your boat if I do?"

Niccolo gasps, his golden light flaring. "You can't."

I don't know if what I'm asking for is possible. Dante went to hell. Aeneas went to the Roman underworld. But these were just poems—stories I very much assumed weren't real.

The demon licks its lipless mouth. "Such *fear*." A reptilian tail slashes in the water below, swirling it to a froth. "Such life." It inches closer, slitted nostrils quivering.

If we don't act soon, the demon will. There's nothing we can do to stop it if it decides to devour us. Nothing except for—

"Bargain with me."

My head whips toward Niccolo. *"No!"*

My brother ignores me. The demon has gone stone-still, the ancient words stopping its creep. "My soul for your boat. Then"—his throat bobs—"then you can eat me when I bring it back."

I force myself up on shaky legs, grinding out another *no*. My brother can't do this. I won't let him. This is my journey, my task.

I'm the one who's supposed to save him.

Niccolo cups my face. His heat shocks me, sends strength ricocheting through me. Not the warmth of a body, but the warmth of a soul, his love blazing like a shooting star through the cold. "I couldn't help you before. Let me help now. I can't die here, remember? Only the devil can unmake a soul."

I can't hold back a whimper. "It could eat you forever."

His mouth tips into a smile. "Like I said, they get bored. Eventually."

The demon shudders with want. A pleased hiss pushes through its teeth. "To feast on you? Yes, yes, I accept." Before we can move, its tail riots from the water. The pointed end spears into Niccolo's side. He doubles over, coughing blood. The demon yanks out the barbed tip and laps my brother's blood from it as I scream.

"I'm fine," Niccolo says through gritted teeth. "See?"

Where the mortal wound was, there's nothing, not even a rip in his clothes.

The nothingness is almost as unsettling as the blood splattering the dock.

Breathing hard, and trying to rein in my terror, I step into the boat and reach up to help Niccolo in.

The demon grabs his elbow, faster than a snake. "Not you. Only the dead can journey down the river."

Niccolo's brows become narrow slashes. "I've been here for ages!"

The demon lifts its hand, its webbed fingers pulling on a sleek golden thread. It runs from Niccolo's glow across the dock, through the horde of cat-demons, into the gray city back where we came from.

"That wasn't there before!" Niccolo says.

The demon gives the thread a firm tug. My brother stumbles

back, gasping. "Your soul is lost, but you are not yet dead." It grins a predator's smile. "You can't go deeper into hell."

Niccolo makes a soft, helpless sound, eyes sliding to me.

My brother, lost in two worlds. But how?

"You're a demon, yes? Why couldn't one of you possess my brother's body in Florence?"

The demon considers me thoughtfully, a pantomime of a smirk on its inhuman mouth. "His attachment to earth is too strong. He could not let go enough for one of us to take him. He remained anchored there, even as his soul was summoned here." It flicks the golden thread savagely. The force knocks Niccolo to his knees, but the thread doesn't fray. "I cannot break it. Only the devil possesses such power."

The struck thread vibrates like a liuto string. Not a song, but a single sweet note echoing strangely across the water. The cat-demons fall silent and cock their heads. Niccolo quiets it with a hand, glancing nervously at them.

My gaze latches onto the empty space of this Niccolo's knuckle. How curious for his ring to be missing when the rest of him is here. I think of the ring on the stranger's hand, how often he twisted it. My heart thuds unevenly. Surely something so small isn't enough for an entire soul to cling to?

"The ring I gave you. I think it's your anchor," I whisper.

Niccolo had offered it to me when he left. What if I had taken it? Would he have been lost forever? The old fear of getting it wrong swirls in me like smoke. I take a deep breath and let it out, let it go.

This isn't about what could've happened, but what *did* happen. My brother is lost but not yet gone.

He can still be saved.

Niccolo throws back his head and laughs. "It's not the ring. It's *you*, Virgil. You've always been my anchor. In any sea, through any storm."

The words settle in the deepest, softest part of me. My brother couldn't leave me even when he tried. Tears fill my eyes.

Niccole moves to wipe them away. As his hand crosses the dock's edge, the demon hisses, and green sparks crackle along the wood. They leap and burrow into his skin like worms. Niccolo winces, but he doesn't back off, doesn't stop thumbing away the dampness on my face before taking both my hands in his. "You've got to go. Demons aren't known for their patience."

I nod, even as my belly fills with lead.

A brother for a brother. A soul for a soul.

"One more thing." He drags me closer, expression stern. "Why did you kill yourself to come here?" His face crumples with sadness. "'Tis a sin, Virgil. You might be stuck forever. You had to know I wouldn't want you to do it."

A question with so many answers and not enough time. My brother is already fading, his color going pale.

"There's a boy." I swallow, the truth making me tender. "I had to save him because I love him."

His grip tightens. Behind him, the river demon heaves itself onto the dock, no longer mostly human but broad and scaled. Its eyes burn a horrible, fervent green. "What's his name?"

"Leonardo." Gold trembles through the air. "The Medici want him to paint for them."

Niccolo leans his forehead to mine, the pressure softer than a kiss. "If anyone can stop this, it's you." Hell's pale light burns through his ghostly form now. "I love you, Volpacchiotto."

"I love you too, Volpone."

His fingers squeeze mine one last time. "Be careful. Don't curse our bloodlines for generations."

"I won't," I whisper, voice thick with tears. "Our sisters would never forgive me."

My brother shoves the boat as hard as he can.

I don't see the demon lunge.

But I hear Niccolo's screams.

I curl in on myself and cover my ears, knowing he wouldn't want me to listen, trying to hold back my cries, knowing my fear and horror will only bring more demons closer.

Niccolo is gone.

I'm alone.

CHAPTER FORTY-NINE

I don't know how long I weep into my knees.

But eventually the tears burn themselves out; Niccolo's screams fade, settle in a deep, dark part of me I'll return to in my nightmares. I blink away the dampness and lift my head.

The boat glides silently down the river, into a thicket of gray fog. Eerie wisps of fire undulate across the water. I lean over the boat's side to get a closer look.

And scream.

There are *people* in the water.

Their visages are death-pale, a parade of grimaces. Their hands claw for me, shards of bone poking from splintered fingertips. I bolt upright. The boat wobbles, tipping to one side, water sloshing dangerously close to the edge.

I swallow and fix my eyes on the shore, trying to ignore the faces floating like weeds inches away.

Occasionally a darker, sinuous shadow swims beneath the boat, bumping the people out of the way. I clamp my eyes shut and wait for an eldritch horror to burst forth and demand a tithe to stop my boat with its awful power and shred my soul to pieces, but the water's surface stays still.

As if I'm destined for someone else.

Something else.

A black palazzo emerges from the fog, a snarling, hulking beast of a building with sharp curved turrets and jagged-teeth walls. A long, lonely quay pierces the river before it.

A hooded cloaked figure stands at the very end.

My heart crawls into my throat. The boat drifts closer and closer. From this far away, I have to hope, I have to believe. 'Tis all I have left in this dark, forsaken place.

The boat bumps against the black stone. My lungs stop working. I couldn't scream if I wanted to. There's nowhere to hide, nowhere else to go except the river filled with the dead. Their torn fingertips scrape the boat, as if they know I'll join them soon.

The figure turns, face hidden in the hood.

But the light catches the bow of a smile.

"I've been waiting for you, Virgil."

It's Lupa. Beautiful, fierce Lupa.

She's taller, sharper. More like the wolf I named her for. The hand she offers me is tipped in pointed black-painted nails. I stare at the paint, the practice unfamiliar and strange.

"It's me, I swear it." Her hand clenches into a fist, an expression almost like sadness flickering across her face. "I don't know what you've gone through to get here, but I promise you're safe with me."

I don't miss how she says *with me*, and not safe *for now*.

Her eyes are the same as before, the green gold of them brilliant behind dark pupils. I saw her ripped from the body she possessed, but she's here waiting for me. I trusted her before when I shouldn't have. Why shouldn't I trust her in hell—when she's all that I have?

I release a shaky breath and let her help me out of the boat. "I missed you."

One claw grazes the back of my hand, too gentle to hurt. "Me too."

With a soft, sibilant groan, the grabbing souls in the river fall back.

The black palazzo is the only object visible in the fog, as if it's the only thing in this world. A gruesome feeling of being watched walks across my skin, but every window is empty. The feeling intensifies when we go inside.

I expected opulence, an overflowing abundance of gold and gems and marble statues of fantastical creatures dripping with flowers. The luxury of the Medici run amok.

Instead the corridors are cold stone. A horrible, teeth-grating chorus of squeals echoes through the emptiness. I wince at a particularly offensive high note.

"The devil insists the music is close to human." Lupa looks embarrassed. "I can still remember what it's supposed to sound like, but barely."

The few portraits on the walls are ripped and fading. I linger before one that could be a Last Supper, except each person has been replaced by a monster. Wet oozes from the canvas, and the iron tang of blood fills my nose.

I shudder and pass underneath a chandelier made of bones. The candles drip thick rivulets of wax to the floor—wax that smells horribly of rendered fat. "Why does he bother? You remember enough to know this isn't right."

Lupa stops before a table made of polished, gleaming ice. It's so crystalline, my own unsettled face peers back at me. But in the background, the chandelier is missing. There's nothing but bare stone walls and barren torch brackets.

"Would you tell the devil he's wrong when this is the alternative?" Lupa steps behind me.

And my heart thunders.

There's a monster at my shoulder.

It's made of writhing shadows and scales. Twice as tall as any human, too thin and skeletal to ever be mistaken for one even at a distance. Twin green-gold flames burn in its eye sockets. A pair of what could be horns curves from its skull, the tips vicious.

"This is who I am." Lupa's hand with its elegant, painted nails creeps over my shoulder. In the reflection, a horrible, too-many-jointed appendage with gold-green flames dripping from its claws drapes over my ripped, soiled doublet. One sudden jab, and the claw would pierce my heart.

The head lowers beside my face, more ghostly flames spilling from its jaws. "The devil insists we pretend to be something we're not. Something mortal. Half-forgotten memories of beauty are the only thing left to us in this place."

I want to turn away from the ice. I wish I'd never seen Lupa like this so I could picture her as what she pretended to be instead of what she truly is.

Except . . . Lupa never turned away from me during my ugliest moments, and I won't do it to her now. I bend to kiss the scaled knuckles on my shoulder, slipping my hand up beneath them and braiding the fingers through mine. A pulse of gold shudders through Lupa's true form from the point of contact.

Only then do I turn away, toward the face she's chosen to wear tonight.

"That's not true. You have me now too."

She tilts her head, surprised. Then a close-mouthed smile. "Leonardo was right. You can be very sweet."

There it is again. The telltale whisper down my neck that there's something she's keeping from me.

Lupa ushers me into a chamber and closes the door. Even the window doesn't look out at anything: only a swirl of gray beyond the mullioned glass. There's nothing inside but an old, battered chair. On the ripped cushion, a large tortoiseshell cat—Fifi?—lifts her head and glares.

'Tis the sight of Verrocchio's cat that finally lets the truth sink in.

I'm in *hell.* With Lupa.

For an odd moment, it feels like I'm standing beside myself, separate from my body. I watch my back thud against the wall, see my unsteady fist in my sweaty curls.

"The girl you possessed died. Did you know what would happen to her?" I hear myself say.

Lupa slowly bends down to my level, her radiant eyes catching mine and holding. "Yes. I swallowed her soul to walk on earth. I was always a demon, even when I couldn't remember."

Does a wolf mean to kill? It's the question Leonardo asked me so long ago. I run my tongue along the back of my teeth and nod. I don't like her answer, but I understand it.

Lupa gently nudges the cat aside and motions for me to take the chair. "When I returned here, so did my memories. I've seen countless demons leave and come back filled with stories of art, of poetry, beauty, and love. I didn't understand until I was there myself that they'd seen it all from the corners. They hadn't *lived* it. They had spent years in your world, but learned nothing of what it was to be human." She strokes the cat's fur, glancing out the window of nothingness like it might become a view if she looks long enough. "Taking that girl's soul felt unsporting. Each time a bargain-maker asked me for magic, it was unsatisfying. Tricking a soul from a mortal is quite different from tormenting one who deserves to be here." She reaches up to graze the space behind her ear—the memory of a scar. "You helped me see why it felt wrong."

"Me?"

"After we became friends, I felt a foreign stirring in my mind. A memory from the girl whose body I had stolen. Her name was Maddalena. She was married against her will and fought to escape her husband." She traces the phantom scar again. "But not before he hurt her."

My hands clench on the armrests, a tension I feel down in my very core. I can guess what happened next. She heard rumors that the Medici could solve her problems. They promised her the world and destroyed hers instead.

Just like they did to my brother.

Tears fill my eyes again.

Deep in the palace, there's a long, ecstatic scream. I bolt away from the door, gasping. My fear is an overflowing cup, drenching me with cold. I'm feeling too much, and the demons know, but the way Lupa's looking at me now tells me that it's right. I'm doing exactly what I need to do.

"No soul should be trapped in hell unless they deserve it." Lupa's illusion slips, and I flinch seeing the dark, scaled flicker of her true shape. It only lasts a blink, and then her gold-green eyes are back on mine. "The devil's power comes from these ill-gotten souls, but it's as corrupt as his methods. This crumbling castle. Our monstrous forms. He says we're beautiful, but I still remember what real beauty is. I still remember *you.*" Her hand curls over mine, a deep smoldering fire in her eyes. "When I left that girl's body, I remembered why I wanted to come to earth. I remembered what I'd set out to do."

A force slams the door.

"Bring the mortal to me!"

My hands fly over my ears, but the voice rattles my brain, my very soul. It *hurts*. Tears sting my eyes.

Lupa falls to her knees, teeth gritted, bits of her dress dissolved to reveal flashes of sinew and bone beneath. "Your Majesty, I—"

"Now!"

The roaring pressure disappears. Lupa straightens, her glare harder than iron. "He knows you're here now."

I don't need to ask. I already know.

The devil wants me.

CHAPTER FIFTY

Lupa escorts me through the palazzo, bringing us to a vast ballroom as the awful music I heard before swells. Inside, demons lurch in a clumsy pantomime of dancing. They look more or less human—minus a tail, or a pair of wings or horns—but their clothes are all wrong. Some wear skirts on their torsos and corsets on the legs. Some are completely naked, save jewels dripping from their ears and fingers. Even though it's all an illusion, I blush and look away.

Lupa bows. "Here is Virgil, my honored guest for the evening."

The ballroom lurches to a stop.

A hundred pairs of eyes fasten onto me.

I force my face to ease into a smile, force my waist to bend, bowing to the crowd even though my entire body screams at me to turn around and run. "It's a pleasure to be here."

When I lift, I see the devil.

Young, handsome, more human than anyone else. He'd be the least monstrous thing here if it wasn't for the writhing shadows that blur his edges like dark fire. His power fills me, a nauseous, dizzying wave. A poison of the mind. I stumble and cough, vision wavy at the sides. Only Lupa's grip on my elbow keeps me upright.

The devil's voice is a silky pout. "We don't bring humans here anymore. Remember Hercules?"

The other demons murmur and hiss, remembering something so far gone, it's considered myth in my time.

Lupa ducks her head. "He's not merely a human. He's also my friend."

The devil flinches at the word "friend," shock fading away to mounting anger. "Why did you do this? Do you mock my rules?"

Lupa raises her hands, asking for silence. "Virgil is dead, Your Majesty. The dead cannot hurt you here."

Is it my imagination, or does her voice press into that "here" a little more than usual? A shiver races down my back.

If the devil can't be hurt *here*, then there must be a *there* we need to get to.

Channeling a confidence that would make Leonardo weep with pride, I stride closer. Past the shocked faces of the demons, past the gilded tables bowed with maggoty cakes and vases of molding flowers. One demon crunches a mouthful of roses, bloody streaks running from the corners of his mouth.

I stop at the edge of the devil's dais. I kneel, even though getting this close to him makes my stomach roll and head pound. In his human illusion, I see the flicker of something else. I swallow back an iron taste and keep my eyes on his crown, the only part of him that doesn't shimmer and shake. "I want to make a bargain with you." The words taste ancient and binding. "I want to put an end to the Medici's power."

The devil flashes a dazzling smile. "Is that truly why you're here?"

Up close, his beauty is painful to behold. Black, curling hair cascades into dark, drowning eyes. His olive skin shimmers with the faintest bronze glow. He looks like a sculpture made from living flesh. How could I possibly make someone so beautiful unhappy? I want to fall to the floor and kiss the hem of his cloak. I want to call him master and sit by his feet.

Why else would I be here, if not to spend forever at his side?

I clamp my eyes shut and take a deep breath, another.

With his beauty still searing the inside of my eyelids, I paint over the image with one of my own until bronze dust becomes freckles, until black curls become red waves.

Until all I can see is my Leonardo.

If I can't undo the Medici's bargain with the devil, he'll be forced to paint for them, to condemn people's souls to the same fate of his stepmother. It would break him. I can't let that happen.

"Yes," I say, lifting, clear-eyed, from my bow. The nausea is still there, but fainter. "The Medici think themselves your equal. They believe they're more powerful than you. They use *your* magic, *your* gifted power, to worship God!"

An unholy chorus of screams rends the air. Parts of the illusions curl away like peeling wallpaper, showing the shadows, the rot and filth, underneath it all.

The entire room shudders, and my knees buckle from the force.

The devil throws out a ringed hand, his fingernails suddenly black points. *"Enough!"*

The screams stop, dissolving into shuddering sobs instead. No one is dancing now. The demons huddle in sad piles, some of them bereft of their illusions entirely. Even Lupa is affected—her dark, curving horns now visible over her blond head, her eyes red-rimmed.

The devil doesn't tear his stare away from me for an instant. Slowly, so slowly, the illusions decorating the ballroom slip back into place. He claps his hands. The sound echoes strangely, too loud and layered to be anything but magical. "You, play louder!"

The musicians startle back to their feet and saw away on their uncanny instruments once more.

"You, keep dancing!"

The dancers slam into each other and start swinging their partners around so fast, it makes me ill to watch.

"And you." The devil hovers over me, terrible in his wrath, his eyebrows two curving daggers above his glare. "You're coming with me."

He snaps his fingers, and the last thing I see is Lupa's stricken face before the ballroom dissolves.

CHAPTER FIFTY-ONE

The ballroom disappears like the view beyond a rain-slicked window. I blink away the grayness and find myself in an opulent throne room. Dark walls and ornately carved chairs and tables dominate the space, the furniture too large to be comfortable. A portrait hangs across from the throne—its golden frame the only spot of color. It depicts a snarling, scaled creature with cloven hooves and curved horns.

The devil reclines on his throne and gestures for me to do the same on one of the chairs beneath him. I move to a seat, except my foot catches on an object.

A demon with too many legs sleeps sprawled under the chair. It's one of perhaps a dozen at the edges of the room. I watch the drowsy rise and fall of their sides, freezing like I've stumbled into a den of slumbering wolves. One more noise, one more step, and they'll wake up and tear out my throat.

"They're in Florence right now, aren't they?" I whisper. Their bodies sleeping here; their souls, or whatever passes as a soul for a demon, down on earth. The opposite of Niccolo.

The devil frowns, annoyed I've guessed right. His appearance has changed. His skin is fairer, his hair now a cascading gold curtain. He reminds me of angels painted in the churches, blond, beautiful, terrifying. The part of me that's all instinct and no thought doesn't know whether to shiver from fear or desire.

He wants you to find him agreeable, I remind myself fiercely. *He doesn't want you to fight him.*

The devil smirks deliberately, and I flush, knowing he can see all my thoughts as plain as written words. "Do you think me a fool? Of course I know the Medici are liars. All humans lie."

Flames suddenly erupt at the throne's feet. I inhale sharply, shoving away from the table. Where's Lupa? I don't like the final look she gave me. "Why not take away their power, then? You're a king. Surely you can outwit them."

The devil's cold eyes pass over me, a feeling like walking under icicles gathered thick and dangerous on winter eaves. "Who says I haven't?"

He snaps his fingers, and the image out the window changes. The river of souls that ferried me here. But the water looks different this time. No longer calm, but foaming white, rising higher and higher each second.

"I don't care about the Medici's lies, because I led them to believe they could control me. Portraits, hosts, tethers, bargains. They think they've won, but they've always been wrong. For generations, they've helped me accumulate the souls I need."

I take a step back. "Need for what?"

"To pass between worlds. Earth is wasted on you lying, small-minded mortals. I've lived for centuries and judged your sins." A sly, curving smile lifts his mouth. Pointed teeth break his human facade, a crack in his elegant armor. "Your mortal lives are but a spark in the infinite darkness, and you spend your brief time lying and cheating and killing for scraps of power. You are born into beauty and wonder, and devote yourselves to ugliness and cruelty. It is an outrage!"

He gestures to the window, which has become an image of the ballroom with its rotting splendor. "Tell me, if you could be here or on earth, which would you choose? Would you fight fang and claw for another second of the sun on your skin?"

It's not the sky I see but *him*. His red-gold hair all fire in the sunlight. It's a question without an answer. If I could bask in the light of Leonardo's love for a single second longer, I'd do anything.

The ballroom fades, the river view returning. "That's what I thought." The devil stands. His shadow hulks huge and horrible on the floor—all claws and horns and fangs. It doesn't match his human appearance. I shiver, a tendril of fear snaking around my heart and cinching tight. "I'll visit the Medici first. I want them to know what they've done before they drown."

The river surges from its banks. I fly to the window, remembering the eternal drowning power of the soul-filled waters.

But the land stays dry. Water wells from the riverbed but disappears as soon as it touches the banks.

As if it's going somewhere else.

Flooding a place I can't see.

"Or before they get torn apart." One by one, the devil touches the bodies of the sleeping demons. They jerk awake and disappear with a crack of fire.

Into distant skies.

The edges of my vision spot with black. Leonardo. My family. Thousands of innocent people, all there and unable to protect themselves.

"I'm taking Florence at last." The devil's human illusion

dissolves like paint in water. A muscular body covered in scales and fur, legs ending in cloven hooves, hands curling into sharp claws. "Your soul is the very last one I need to get there."

The devil towers over me like a stained glass window. He doesn't touch me, but he doesn't have to. His power is a vise, and I'm a grape betwixt two thick fingers. Any more pressure, and I'll burst.

"How does it feel, knowing your friend betrayed you?" A flame-slicked smile leers.

It takes me an agonizing moment to understand he means Lupa.

Lupa, with a dark trickle running down her chin in the workshop's corner. Lupa, her eyes flashing pupilless and predatory in the dark. Her too-sharp nails and too-pointed teeth. I think of the she-wolf I named her for, how she rose, ghost-pale and growling. How my brother and I fled before the promise of danger became real.

Didn't Verrocchio tell me not to trust her?

Even though my mouth is dry, even though my entire body quivers and I have nothing left, I spit at his feet. "You're lying. No better than a mortal, are you?"

The devil rears back, flames burning in the sockets of his eyes.

And the world becomes pain.

A headache cleaves my temples. Nausea surges in my gut, then sick splatters my feet. His power overwhelms me. I scream, falling to my knees, every nerve inside me shredding.

"I have seen your sins, Virgil Pitti, and you disgust me! You are sick with envy, gluttonous for recognition. You let fear make you small and mean, a rat biting at the hand that moves to crush it. You are nothing. No one. The world is full of millions like you."

I curl into a ball beneath the weight of that horrible voice. Fire rages all around me, inside me, the soul-blackening truth of the smallest parts of me impossible to run from.

Everything he says is true. I let fear turn my heart to ice. Put up walls to keep everyone out even as I was desperate to let someone in. Jealousy festered in me like an oozing wound. I wasted my time dwelling on the ugly, cruel darkness.

But would I have ever recognized the light without it?

Even though my bones still shudder, even though I'm drenched in stinking sweat and fear tears through my veins like glass, I lift my head.

"You're right. I was nothing." His stare burns, but I don't see it. I'm a world away, inside a future that'll never come to pass, in an ivy-faced home filled with art. The freckled, smiling boy at the center of it all. "But I was still someone's entire world—something you'll never be."

And then the devil *roars*.

The sound is a furnace blast, a scorching wave of sorcery. The blistering pain welts my skin, peels it from my very body.

It lasts only a second. I return to myself with a sob, still clutching my pounding head. The devil's monstrous form shrinks to a man with golden hair and a livid red face.

"You insolent mortal!" His scream lacks the echo of power, the skull-crushing might of his rage. He lifts me by the collar and slams me against the wall. I cry, shoulder crunching. He puts his face close to mine, his breath meat-rancid like a dog's. "I'm going to relish swallowing every shred of your rotten soul."

His fangs plunge into my neck.

CHAPTER FIFTY-TWO

There's an explosion of green-gold.

I hit the floor with a wheeze. The devil doubles over me, rubbing his mouth like he's cracked a tooth. I touch my neck, but there's no wound.

"You won't." Lupa storms into the room from a door that wasn't there before. Her red dress has become more ornate, silver brocade peering out from the slashes on her sleeves, a gossamer net pulling back her thick hair. She looks like a queen. As I think it, a silver-and-pearl diadem appears on her head. She looks at me and winks. "His soul belongs to me."

To *her*?

How?

Lupa snaps her fingers, and my pain vanishes. A gentle hidden force lifts me under my armpits and sets me on my feet. I touch my shoulder, tracing the ache of the snapped bone. 'Tis whole and hale. My lips part softly.

The devil scoffs. "Impossible! You collect souls for *me*. You cannot take them yourself."

A satin-and-silver padded chair appears across from the devil's throne. Lupa sits on it, grabs the armrests, and crosses her legs.

"Once, Virgil wanted to make a bargain. He was willing to offer me his very last scrap of soul for it. I sensed it was the end of something, but I didn't know what. I took it from him but refused to give him what he asked for. The bargain was made, but incomplete." She touches her bodice, the place over her heart. She pulls her hand away and draws out a glittering golden orb.

Her eyes meet mine, chagrined despite the ancient power pooling in their depths. "I shouldn't have kept it. Stealing is a crime."

My mouth twitches. The cakes she loved, the coins from my purse. Lupa was always a thief. "You can keep it." I wag my chin toward the devil. "As long as it helps you get rid of him."

Lupa smiles with every single one of her pointed teeth, and swallows the glowing orb whole. A frisson of power pulses, shaking the devil's portrait.

He rights it with a clawed finger, frowning. "You've defied me. And for what? A soul is as common as a worm. I'll get another soon and make my way to Florence." His features shift, become uglier and not entirely human. "I should make you a worm for this."

Before I can shout—before I can warn her—the devil draws a sword from a scabbard he wasn't wearing a blink ago.

And cleaves Lupa in two.

There's a burst of intense green. I block the glare, a scream tearing from my lungs that rattles every window in the palazzo.

The sound is still fading when the green glow diminishes.

When Lupa stands.

When I see she's caught the devil's blade in her clawed hand.

Gold gathers where the weapon touches her. It sweeps down her arm, building faster and faster, almost too bright to look at.

The devil's face waxes pale, Lupa's gleam refracted in his widening eyes. "No."

The gold arrests me—prophetic and strange. Have I slipped between the pages of a poem, one painstakingly hand-copied and passed forward century after century? "Lupa, what's happening?"

The devil staggers back. "This mortal named you?"

"Names are different for demons," Lupa says. "Secret. Private. Giving away your name gives someone power over you. Earning a new name, though . . ." She lifts her arms, growing taller and taller. Her horns appear, curving over the crown. Golden flames lick the hem of her dress. "A new name gives you power."

The devil stares at Lupa's gold gleam with smoldering hatred. "You *tricked* me!"

"A mortal's soul, freely given, is more powerful than a thousand souls stolen." Lupa's horns brush the ceiling now.

But the devil is growing larger too, his beautiful eyes burning crimson like the heart of a fire. "You think this is enough to best me? I was king of hell when you were still slithering on your belly."

Lupa grins unexpectedly. "Who said I was working alone?"

She punches through the ceiling.

A cloud of black pours in from the hole. The cat-demons, a screaming, endless horde of them. The devil shouts and lifts his sword again, but it does nothing. Each one he cuts down rises up whole in a moment.

The room flickers once. Twice.

And then I'm blinking at the top of a tower overlooking a raging river. Half the walls are missing, and an awful wind tears at my limbs. The sky is red; jagged, silent lightning streaks across it. The only thing left from the devil's throne room is his portrait, but the image has become a black, swirling vortex. The throne room was an illusion, just like the ballroom.

Behind me, there's a door. The clamor of approaching hooves and feet and paws builds on its other side.

"You call yourself a king, but you're only a demon like the rest of us." There's another flash—lightning?—no, Lupa in a full suit of gold armor. She snaps down her helmet's visor. "Some of us think it's time for a queen."

The devil roars and charges with his sword.

Sparks catch when Lupa parries it with one of her own.

The door shatters behind me.

The demons froth like dark, raging rapids, so fast, I can't make them out. I throw myself down and crawl into a corner where the floor meets one of the remaining walls. I want to escape down the stairs, but I'm afraid I'll be knocked off the tower if I stand. Among the demon horde flicker scraps of gold. I gasp when a woman appears, a baby with red-gold hair clasped in her arms. She looks at me, and I know her smile as well as my own heart.

Leonardo's stepmother.

Madonna santa. The trapped souls have come to fight for Lupa's side too.

"Do you trust me?" Lupa seizes my front. She's panting hard, weeping sluggish gold blood from the armored plates along her side. She sees me look and smiles tightly. "He can't kill me. He can only take me from this body."

"What about the souls?"

"He can unmake them, but they knew that was a possibility. I gave them the choice the Medici didn't." She nods toward what's left of the devil's portrait. "I need you to find that in Florence and destroy it. It's a portal that lets him use his magic on earth." Her clawed fingers slip under my chin, bite into the delicate skin.

"Will you do it? If I win, I will free the stolen souls. You'd get Niccolo back."

I stare at this demon drenched in gold. Who tricked me. Who saved me.

I nod, eyes burning. "Yes. I'd do anything for that."

She yanks the gold orb from her chest and blows it to me.

I gasp when it breaks against me and scatters like the seeds of a dandelion. The little pieces sink into my skin, a dusting of embers without the sting. I blink, lifting my arm as it starts to limn with gold.

Just like Niccolo's trapped soul.

Just like Lupa.

Who shoves me off the tower into the burning sky.

CHAPTER FIFTY-THREE

I jolt awake, engulfed in white.

For a moment I'm stunned, overwhelmed by the roughness against my skin, the pull of pressure along my arms.

I'm alive.

Wild, beating, beautifully, *here*.

But I can't move a muscle.

Fabric. I'm wrapped in a funeral shroud. I'm about to be buried in the dark earth forever, where no one can hear me scream.

My pinned hands claw at the muslin, nails digging holes in the tough weave. One hand rips free, and I kick the rest off with a frantic movement.

The Mary over the altar gives me a patient, knowing smile. I'm back inside the Medici chapel again. My ragged breath is the only sound.

I'm alone.

I don't know how long I lay beneath the shroud, but my body is whole and unharmed, my clothes the same as the ones I died in.

I start to leave, flinching when my foot sends an object skittering across the floor. I pick it up, see the glint of the beads and their dangling crucifix in the guttering candlelight. A rosary.

My skin prickles. These are Clarice de' Medici's beads. She said the chapel was the only place she felt safe.

Now she's not here.

A faint scream echoes from beyond the chapel door.

My head whips up. I pocket the rosary and find a paintbrush I tucked away and forgot about. I almost throw it aside, but think better of it.

I ease the chapel door open. The creak is swallowed by the ceaseless pounding of the rain. I cross the empty corridor and peer out the window.

Water sluices down in torrents, washing the streets and buildings a dull winter gray. The clouds press low, bruise-purple and tinged with pink. Dark heavy shadows flit through them, larger and faster than any bird. One emerges on the corner of a building across the street, something horrible and dangling caught in its grasp. A guard. I flinch and turn away when the body drops to a growing pile on the street below.

The devil wasn't jesting when he said he'd destroy Florence. He's already started.

I clench my jaw to stop my teeth from chattering, try to smooth away my fear.

Lupa told me to find the devil's portrait and destroy it. If I do, the rain will stop, the violence will end. My brother's soul will return.

I don't know how much time I have, but I won't do it without Leonardo. I've got to find him first.

Not bothering to close the chapel door behind me, I set off for the hidden painting studio.

The Palazzo Medici looks like it was ransacked by an army. Serving trays shattered on the floor, frescoed walls smeared with cake. The eye-watering burn of spilled alcohol fills the air. The corridors are devoid of guests. A few guards huddle outside barricaded doors like cowering boys; most have fled their posts entirely. None of them bother to look at me, all focused on the rain pummeling the earth outside, straining to hear something far worse. The palazzo is under siege from divine beings. No one gives a damn about someone stupid enough to wander around at a time like this.

Passing the windows overlooking the gardens is the hardest. The tables and chairs are all abandoned in sodden puddles. Broken bodies dot the lawn, wedding guests and guards, their eyes open and staring at the unnatural gray sky. One demon with a vulture's wings and sharp talons plucks the eyes from the corpses one by one. When its head jerks toward me, I freeze.

Its stare burns a fiery, flagrant red. Just like the devil's.

I rip away from the window. I ascend one staircase, then another, following a half-remembered map, praying I'm right.

When I spot a familiar door on the highest floor, terrifying hope sinks its teeth into me. I brush the prayer beads in my pocket and surge down the hall.

Unless he's gone—unless I'm too late—I'm almost certain the Medici's painting studio is right there.

Is Leonardo still inside? Is he safe?

My hand grazes the doorknob—

A sharp point digs betwixt my shoulders.

CHAPTER FIFTY-FOUR

Niccolo.

"*You* again." The words are rough, unsettled. "I dreamed I was in hell last night. You were there." His blade digs in deeper, voice hardening. "You *knew* me."

"Yes." I turn around slowly.

Niccolo's hand flexes, his black-garnet ring catching the light. His knife is level with the hollow of my throat. "Why do you keep following me?"

I swallow, the pulse pushing my skin to the tip of his knife. "Because I knew you once."

Then I see it. Niccolo's portrait. One eye glaring at me from his pocket. He's ripped it from the frame, the edges torn and frayed.

He covers the painting with his free hand. "When the angels attacked, Lorenzo de' Medici ordered me to destroy all the portraits in a private room. I found this there." His gaze drops to his ring, a pang of fear flashing through his eyes. "I don't remember sitting for one."

My voice cracks. "Don't let *anything* happen to it." I need him to believe me. If his portrait is destroyed, will he die like the girl Lupa possessed? I'm so close to saving him. My fingers curl, wanting to reach for him but knowing they can't.

A ripple goes across his features. Not surprise, but knowing. "Are you my brother?"

The words wash over me, through me. I can barely breathe. I've wanted to hear them for so very long.

He sheathes his blade. "When I see your face, I can almost remember who are you."

"It's all right," I whisper. "I can remember for both us."

Everything I want to remind him of fills my lungs to the brim, but there's not enough time. He deserves more than a few stolen seconds on the threshold of the door I need to get through. He deserves a lifetime.

When I destroy the devil's portrait—when I end the bargain the Medici made decades ago—Lupa will send him home. She promised me and she's never broken a promise.

There's a clamor at the end of the hall. A guard bursts out from a closed door, eyes ringed white with terror. "Signore! The angels are attacking the doors! What should we do?"

Niccolo frowns, and his face shutters like a window that has been fastened shut. He flinches at the sight of me. "How did you get in here?" He glances around the corridor fearfully. "Who are you?"

The distrust in his voice is a knife in my chest. I've lost him again. Slowly I tug the folded-up canvas from his pocket. He inhales sharply, hand leaping to his sword hilt. But he doesn't draw the blade, doesn't cut me down like he knows he should.

I take the paintbrush from my pocket. Even though the paint is mostly dried, I can still eke out some color. I flip the canvas over and write an address on the back. Casa delle Volpi.

"You'll find answers here," I say softly. If I fail, perhaps

Giovannia can help him remember. Even if he never does, Niccolo deserves a home where he's known and loved. I want to give him everything I can. He's always done the same for me.

Feeling like I'm wrapping up part of my own heart, I refold his portrait. "You were telling me what you wanted me to do with the prisoner. Remember?"

Tricking my brother after he's been lied to for years feels low, but I ignore the slippery feeling. Without Leonardo's help, there might not be a home for him to return to. *I'm fighting to bring you back,* I promise those familiar hazel eyes. *Please just wait a little bit longer.*

I put the canvas into his hand. "Do you remember?"

He blinks down at it, lost. The expression looks so much like one of mine, I could be looking in the mirror. "Can you remind me again?"

I do.

CHAPTER FIFTY-FIVE

I wait until Niccolo leaves with the guard to turn the key he gave me in the painting studio door.

My heartbeat crescendoes, loudest in my temples. It takes my shaking hands two tries to twist the key, and then I throw my shoulder against the door with all my might.

Inside the studio, the pallet is gutted and weeping straw, the bedclothes are ribbons, the workshop table lies in splintered pieces—

And a figure slumps on the floor beside it.

"Leonardo!" His name bursts from my chest, from my very soul. I pull him onto my lap, smooth the rust-gold tangle from his face. He's my last second of sunlight, the person I'd give anything to see again. He's finally here in my arms.

His eyes open a sliver, bloodshot and swollen. There's a cut on one cheek, like he was nicked by someone's ring. The thought of anyone hitting him fills me with a feral, vibrating rage.

He blinks, focusing. "Virgil?" His fingers hover just over my cheek, like I'm a painting too fresh to touch without ruining. "I didn't think it'd take so long."

I comb through his hair, searching for injuries. "What are you talking about, caro?" This confusion isn't him. He's the smartest, quickest person I know. My anger coalesces into a fiery throb in my center. If they hurt him—if anyone touched a single goddamn freckle—

His mouth tugs sideways, like I ought to be smarter than this. "Dying and coming back to life. I've been terribly bored without you."

I laugh, the sound echoing all around us until it ends in a sob. "I missed you too."

His fingertips trail over my face, down my neck, softer and colder than snowflakes. They push at the flutter in my neck, counting my heartbeats. "You're alive." He clutches my wrist with sudden violence, eyes filling with relieved tears. "It *worked*."

I kiss them away, savoring every taste of him I can get. A shadow creeps over my heart, eclipsing my happiness. I want to clean his bloodied face and feed him castagnaccio and tell him I saw his stepmother, and his baby sibling had his red-gold hair. I don't want to put him in danger again. "Lupa sent me back. We've got to destroy the portrait that sealed the devil's bargain with the Medici."

Something *slams* into the window.

A forked tongue laves the glass between three sets of gnashing teeth. Cracks spiderweb through the windowpane, spreading with each thrust of the demon's tongue. I cower, but Leonardo sits up and makes the sign of the cross. The demon *snarls*. With a baleful look, it bludgeons the window with a thick, scaly tail and disappears.

"It doesn't hold them off for long," Leonardo says. "Will destroying the portrait stop them?"

"Them, and the rain." My mouth twitches, almost smiling. "If we don't finish this soon, the city will flood."

Leonardo scrambles upright, one hand offered to me. "And I thought it was only raining because you had died."

I pull myself up, not letting go of him. "The rain reminds you of me?"

"It always has." He kisses me so softly, I could float away. "Everything a little sad reminds me of you."

My answering smile is its own sun. My thumb runs along the ridges at the base of his fingers, just above his palm. We have calluses in all the same places, and I still want to learn every single one of his.

Another *slam*.

The demon is back, a claw tip worrying into one of the window cracks. When we look, it goes stone-still. A cat stalking a mouse.

I swallow and stumble backward.

Leonardo's arm catches my back, stopping me from hitting the capsized worktable.

"Careful now. You don't want to jostle it."

"Jostle what?"

The room is a disaster, but on closer inspection, the disorder seems almost deliberate. The worktable isn't smashed, but broken and rearranged, its wooden pieces fastened together with hand-carved mortise-and-tenon joints. A familiar panic skitters down my spine—like Leonardo's ditched Verrocchio's morning exercises again, and I'll have to be the one to tell our master.

"You know that I'm not great at doing what I'm told." Leonardo moves a bundle of ripped bedclothes onto what's left of the table and starts tying the shreds to wooden pegs. "When the Medici told me to paint, I decided to make something else."

"Make what?"

Leonardo smiles up from his tangled hair. The expression is sly, flirting with a smirk. The infuriating one that's always gotten under my skin like a fever. He nods toward the inside of whatever the worktable has become. "Can you give me that jar near your feet?"

I step closer, seeing something that can be described as wagon benches, one behind the other.

And on the floor beneath it is the vial of Lupa's blood.

I draw in a soft breath. His cut-up hands, his bloodshot eyes. Leonardo hasn't been slapped around by the Medici or mourning my demise.

He's been working on a secret project.

With shaking fingers, I uncork the vial. There's still a single drop gleaming at the bottom. "Can whatever you made get us past this thing?"

Leonardo takes the vial with a wink. He snaps out a large paper fan from the table. Are those his sketches making up the webbing? "That's the plan."

A second fan snaps out. No, not a fan.

A *wing.*

Leonardo dumps the rest of Lupa's blood on the table's remains.

And the flying machine shudders to life in a wash of gold light.

Right as the window shatters.

With a triumphant scream, the demon thrusts its head inside the hole. Glass and water spray across me.

I turn toward the door.

"No!" Leonardo shouts. "Sit down. We'll be trapped if we go back!"

The demon strikes like a serpent.

I dive onto the second wagon bench, feeling a gust ruffle my hair.

The demon hisses, pulling back for another attack—

I thrust Clarice de' Medici's rosary in its face right as it snaps forward. It flinches away, eyes furious reptilian slits.

Leonardo gives the flying machine a push, thuds onto the bench in front of me, and whistles.

The machine shudders. Starts canting across the floor toward the demon occupying the window. If the creature doesn't move, we'll crash and lose our only way out.

"Throw it, throw it!"

I tighten my fingers around the prayer beads, the little golden cross at the end gleaming.

Then I hurl it with all my might straight at the demon's snout.

And it *howls*.

The demon recoils, clawing at its face with an outraged noise. The stink of burning flesh hits me.

It falls backward, taking out the rest of the window along the way.

And with a downward heave of its wings, the flying machine shoots out the open aperture.

The writhing demon gets smaller as we sail into the storming sky: Leonardo gives it a jaunty wave, whooping with delight. "Did you know there's magic in Lupa's blood?"

Laughter pours out of me, a torrent that streaks behind us like a comet's tail. My brave, brilliant inventor.

The flying machine cuts across the sky, skimming above rain-slicked rooftops. Its fragile wings shudder in the gale, but the magic holds them together. Gold crackles over the wooden body, little flickers of warmth that zip across me.

"Where to?" Leonardo shouts over the roar.

I reach out to him with a wild grin and squeeze his shoulders. "Where all this started. The Palazzo della Signoria."

CHAPTER FIFTY-SIX

The overwrought portrait of God in Piero's office isn't God.

It's a Medici.

Every unkind, unholy thought I've had about it is suddenly justified.

'Tis why the devil's throne room felt oddly familiar. I'd been there before.

Rain pelts my face, stinging and cold. I cling to the flying machine's frame with tense fingers, feeling each jolting wing beat answered with a queasy lurch in my stomach. As we get closer to the river, the streets become streams.

The piazza outside the Palazzo della Signoria is already flooded.

The palazzo's doors are already open, smashed to splinters, dark ink pouring inside the building in an endless, drowning gush.

"Watch out!" Leonardo cries.

A dark shadow arrows toward us: fangs and claws and fervid eyes.

The demon crashes into the flying machine.

The machine breaks apart, falling like a stone.

The gray-brown flood rushes to meet me. Water silences my

scream, pitches down my throat. I thrust my head above the roiling surface.

I can't see Leonardo.

A sudden wave bowls me over, drags me beneath again. It's not deep, but the current is too powerful, and I can't find my footing. My lungs sting, each wild movement burning up more and more air. Bubbles spurt from my nose. I'm getting swept away, I'm going to *drown*.

A hard pressure circles my wrist.

Pulls.

Leonardo helps me get my bearings. His hair is bronze-dark. The fall tore off his doublet, and water has plastered his tunic to every pane of his chest so he may as well not be wearing it at all. The locket with his mother's hair juts out proudly over his heart. He watches the demon circle and land on the palazzo's crenellated wall with a rueful sigh. "Perhaps 'tis for the best. I didn't have a plan for landing it."

Arms around each other, we wade across the piazza. My body shudders with each step, the current tugging at our legs. Each stomp up the slick stairs through the palazzo's smashed doors takes twice the effort it ought.

Then we're inside.

Wavering reflections ribbon across the walls of the palazzo's courtyard. The magicked frescos watch the water rise with panic-stricken expressions. The rain plummets down the courtyard's open interior, an endless gray screen, as if the water itself knows what the devil wants destroyed and is eager to do his bidding.

We slosh over to the doors leading inside. For once, they're unlocked.

When they close, the pummeling of the rain finally disappears.

Leaving us alone in the silence.

A portrait of angels regards us with stern, unblinking stares. Judgmental ones that remind me so much of my father, I rub my arms and look away. The sudden stillness unnerves me after the fervor of escape, makes me second-guess myself.

The devil's portrait is just upstairs.

One knife stroke is all it will take to destroy it.

So why can't I make my feet move?

There's no reason to hesitate. The lie of the angels' bargains was revealed the moment they became demons and attacked the very people they once obeyed. It's the end of an era. The age of holy beauty is over.

Florence will never be the same.

Leonardo drags his fingertips down one of the angels' faces, brow furrowed. He only ever made one bargain—and still never told me what it was for. Even when the rest of us fell over each other to sacrifice our lives and memories for magic, he stubbornly stuck to his methods. Every artist learned to create without magic, and then, once we were good enough to be apprenticed, we decided our hands and eyes and minds weren't enough anymore.

But it wasn't that we weren't good enough.

My perfect paintings are not what I remember best. It's my brother's delight seeing two foxes on a paper scrap. Leonardo's eyes going soft holding his misshapen locket. I dismissed those pieces as juvenilia, a beginner's embarrassing, earnest, amateur fumbles.

But that earnestness meant something. It showed the truth in my soul when nothing else could. I forgot that art isn't brought to life by magic: It's alive because of the impact it has on someone else.

What will it be like when the artists of Florence create only with their hands and hearts?

What would change if we believed in creativity and not magic?

What happens next?

"Virgil?" Leonardo shifts, his voice wary. "You're not having misgivings, are you?"

"No." I stoop to snag a jagged stone from the floor. Feel a thrill race through me at the thought of the canvas's give. "Not about this."

He grins at me—soaked, exhausted, but so beautiful that my chest clenches like a fist—and laces his fingers through mine.

We hurtle upstairs together.

The Medici office's doors with their panels of the Last Judgment grow bigger and bigger at the end of the hall.

Leonardo reaches them first. Throws the doors open.

The Medici portrait sneers down at me, the entire world narrowing to the stern face. The canvas's paint swirls strangely. A scaled foot with wicked claws emerges from the shimmer—

"Virgil, wait!"

But I've already leaped, stone angled to the canvas.

The very tip catches, and I *rip*. A force seems to rip into me at the very same time.

I fall to the floor, staring up at the torn edge of the canvas that starts curling upward, the dark red-black line that follows the spreading tear. The reptilian foot is sucked into the rip with a frustrated yowl.

Then I glance down at the dagger in my side.

CHAPTER FIFTY-SEVEN

Lorenzo de' Medici.

Deep burgundy stains his white wedding tunic. One of the sleeves is missing, torn off completely. Scarlet weeps down his thigh from a cut, and the hand that holds the slick dagger trembles.

It falls with a clatter. "You were dead."

I spit out a mouthful of blood. "Not anymore."

But perhaps soon again.

Crimson pours from my side in a dark rush, a thick, pulsing hurt. There's a high keening in my head, the terrified animal instinct of wanting to save myself and fearing it's too late.

I have to believe it's not. I have to keep going. I need to see my brother again and have him recognize me.

Leonardo grabs my shoulders and shakes. "Why didn't you listen?"

I cup his face with a bloodied hand, even though the movement sets all my nerves on fire. "One of us had to do it."

Better me than him.

There's a soft, disgusted sigh. Then Lorenzo flies across the room.

He slams into the wall, one hand clutching his throat.

Piero de' Medici erupts from his throne-like chair, stomping over to where his son is pinned against the wall with a scolding finger and a snarl. "You said you took care of them!"

Lorenzo winces, then gasps, finally able to breathe again. "I carried the boy's body to the chapel myself. The demons were attacking. I thought it would be enough—"

Piero scoffs and twists his hand. Lorenzo jolts up on his toes, both hands ringed around his neck. He gasps, the sound cut off with a sputter. As if a noose has slipped around his neck and all it takes is a single tug to strangle him.

"I told you to kill them both when the demons attacked. Does this look like enough to you?" Piero demands. Compared to his bedraggled son, the Medici patriarch looks well. His fine clothes are spotless, his hands steady. The only sign he bears of the siege assailing his city is a single scabbed-over cut under his eye. Piero makes another motion, and the toes of his son's boots scrape against the floor. He slowly rotates Lorenzo to face Leonardo and me. "Do they look *dead* to you?" Piero unfurls his hands, and Lorenzo stumbles to his knees.

"I'll do better next time," he pants. "I swear it."

I stare at Piero, hands pressed to my wound. Warm rivulets trickle through my fingers.

He still has his devil's magic.

But the portrait behind me is slashed. I destroyed it. His magic should be *gone.*

"You're not Piero de' Medici anymore, are you?" I say.

The old man smirks, a gleam shining predator-slick behind his pupils. "I don't need a portal. Each Medici was foolish enough to let my magic inside them deeper and deeper for the promise of more power. I possess this body entirely now." He examines his hands, the lines and wrinkles on them, grimacing. There's a wash of crimson over the skin, and they vanish. Red lingers in his eyes now, no longer hidden but two sweltering coals.

They burn right through me, a brand on my soul, black and spreading and more terrible than any nightmare.

We were too late.

The devil's here already.

And he's going to destroy everything and everyone I care for.

Piero snaps his fingers. One after another, demons land on the sills outside each window. They press their monstrous faces to the glass, all gnashing teeth and too many eyes.

An invisible force drags Leonardo to the closest one. He twists sideways, his frantic breaths fogging the windowpane. The demon mirrors the position, cheek to cheek with him if not for the barrier. Long strings of drool drip from its double-hinged jaws to puddle on the frame outside. The window starts to sizzle. A sharp, acrid scent fills the air.

"How would you like to see him die?" Piero taps his chin. "I'm partial to dismemberment myself, but I'd hate to ruin the room."

My vision pulses with heat, each beat in time with the agonizing throb in my side.

I've never wanted to kill someone before.

I don't like the feeling—a tangle of rage and desperation too big for my body. It feels choking, overwhelming. All the worst parts of me eclipsing everything else.

The devil smirks, his face a decade younger than before. The cut on his face starts weeping a dark, deep gold. "Ah, there's your darkness. Not so courageous without your demon friend, are you?"

I scoff, and even though 'tis hell, even though every movement screams with pain, I stagger upright and turn to the only person who can possibly still make a difference.

Lorenzo's face goes pale. He runs, plucking his dagger from the floor, knuckles white on the grip—

I raise my hands. "Wait."

I'm wounded, weaponless, out of ideas. I have nothing except the wild, furious rush of blood under my skin, a reminder of my second chance, my second life.

"You don't have to be like him," I say softly. "You can be someone else. Someone better."

I haven't forgotten how Lorenzo stood behind his father's chair like a servant. Piero's careless cruelty. It reminds me of my own father, how his voice boomed like God's, listing out all my failures and shortcomings. How my brother always reassured me that he was wrong. How I didn't always believe him. The worst things someone says about you are the words that linger, the ones that gnaw after midnight.

I don't know if Lorenzo has ever had someone stand beside him in the darkness.

But I'll try now. He should have a chance to change. I don't know if he deserves it, but I didn't believe I deserved one either.

Lorenzo squares his jaw and glances out to the window. The demons glare back, their red eyes smoldering through the mist.

"He's gone," Leonardo whispers. "You know it."

If this doesn't work, nothing else will. My brother will be trapped in hell forever. Florence will drown.

Lorenzo's eyes lift. Cut to mine.

He lifts his hand. Sends something sailing across the room.

Feeling like my heart might explode, I catch it.

The dagger.

Pain is a crushing, wailing force, threatening to gut me, but I grit my teeth and heave forward, my gaze tunneling to the metallic blood on Piero's face.

I plunge the dagger up into his belly with all my might.

He shudders, just as the old angel shuddered when Verrocchio's sword ran him through. I remember how my magic faded the moment those hungry, haunted eyes went dark. The demon inside the workshop's angel might've been immortal, but the body he possessed on earth wasn't.

The devil's eyes bulge wide. He slumps to his knees, pink bubbles frothing from his shocked mouth. He covers my shaking, blood-soaked hands with his and starts pulling the dagger from his body. The edges of the wound start to close—

Another force slams behind me, adds strength to my cause.

Leonardo pants in my ear, his body a furnace against my freezing back. "I can't believe Verrocchio's sodding morning lessons were useful!"

Together, we thrust the dagger deeper, higher.

And with a final spurt of blood, Piero falls against me.

Leonardo pulls me away, and Piero collapses face-first on the floor with a wet crunch.

The demons howl. One by one, they disappear in a scarlet blur. The roar of the storm becomes a growl, even if the oppressive sky remains. I hear hysterical footsteps race past and fade. Lorenzo fleeing.

Leonardo makes an awful, wounded sound. He gathers my broken body in his arms.

I murmur softly—the syllables of his name coming out scrambled—and brush his thigh, the only part of him I can reach. The edges of my vision wave and dance. "Find my brother."

"No!" He presses his brow against mine. "You'll find him yourself!"

I let myself hang heavy in his arms. He can believe whatever he wants, but the feeling in my hands and feet is already gone, the spreading numbness a dark shroud pulling over my sight. The warmth of him is a rocking boat, one to carry me into the afterlife.

I think I hear him begging someone.

A flare of light burns through my eyelids right as I'm about to tip over the edge of consciousness. I jolt back from the cliff with a pained moan.

"Leonardo da Vinci. I've come to honor my bargain with you."

That voice.

I know it.

The room is noon-bright, all the light coming from a figure that radiates gold power.

Lupa.

Gone are the horns, the bloodied armor. The face she wears is the one she had when I met her, the stolen girl's. *Maddalena.* The thought is a hazy dust mote. *Someone needs to tell her family what happened.*

Leonardo runs his hand over the black mark on his wrist, each breath a ragged pant. "I didn't think you'd come. I thought you'd already done it."

She bows her head, like an artist before an angel, begging for magic. "I gave Virgil his soul back before. Now I'm here for your bargain."

The one he wouldn't tell me about.

I gasp, iron thick in my mouth.

Lupa's burning gaze flickers, almost guilty. "You remember the price, do you not?"

Leonardo shudders. He cradles me closer, sweeps the matted hair from my brow with a long, lingering touch. "Yes. The memory of the person I love for their life."

I don't understand for a moment.

And then I do.

A blow of anguish follows the knowing, cutting deeper than my mortal wound. "You'll forget me."

He kisses my brow fiercely, making a broken noise that I feel everywhere. "Yes, but you'll *live*."

I comforted myself imagining his future, a glorious long life without me.

Never for a single moment did I consider living without him.

I'm not ready for it. What if I let this final gift of his sail past me? What if I don't make enough of it?

A cough punches through me—and something in my side crumples. I twist, gasping for air. The sounds and smells of the room fade. Charred linen, the soft low keen of my name over and over again, a wonderfully hot hand on my cold face. I want to catch those longer fingers in mine, press the heat closer, but I can't move.

"I can't feel his pulse!" The voice is frantic, near. But still so distant, it could be the wind whispering through the empty workshop. I reach toward it, a golden ribbon in the dark, but it slips through my fingers.

"Give him to me."

A mouth bruises my throat, a rose-sharp kiss. I gasp at the pain of it. "If you find a human who doesn't mind . . ." I feel a smile on my skin. "Don't forget about the second vial."

CHAPTER FIFTY-EIGHT

I wake up in silence.

Actually no, not quite. There are pigeons on the windowsill, their cooing noises coming in through the glass. And sunlight. I blink into the brightness, wondering if something went wrong and I'm dead after all.

A soft gasp brings me back to the present.

Leonardo da Vinci crouches on the floor, covered in blood, his eyes wide like he's seen a ghost or a minotaur or one of those frightening baby Jesus paintings where the holy infant looks like a middle-aged man with spider hands.

"Sorry," he whispers. "I didn't see you there."

My eyes burn. It's the very first thing he said to me, all those years ago, when he was just a too-handsome, too-bright new apprentice, and I was a storm cloud of a boy who had no idea that the love of his life had just walked into the workshop to set his world ablaze.

He takes in the rest of me, breathing unsteadily. "Did you know you're covered in blood?"

I drag a hand across my chest, feeling the edges of the rip in my shirt and the puckered new scar on my ribs beneath it. "Yes. I think I'll be all right, though."

He nods, the movement fast and jerky. “Good! That’s good. I, uh—”

“Didn’t need to deal with a stranger’s corpse on the strangest day of your life?” I say dryly.

The tiny divot I love appears between his brow, there and gone so fast, I barely catch it. I probably shouldn’t tease him. I have no idea how his memories have rearranged themselves, how his mind could rewrite the past day or years without me being in them. I don’t want to drive him mad.

At least not with this.

“Sorry.” He apologizes again. “My memory is a bit muddled.”

The corners of my mouth kick up. “I understand.”

I get to my feet. Golden sunlight slants into the office now, falling upon the empty ornate gold portrait frame with nothing but ripped canvas stuck to its edges. The water is already receding in the piazza below, the flood backing off as suddenly as it came.

Piero de’ Medici’s body is still lying face down in a burst of blood. Red and not gold. I touch the body with the toe of my boot, just to confirm he’s well and truly dead. I’m not taking any goddamn chances. “’Tis a pity he fell on his dagger, is it not?”

Leonardo startles, blinking in confusion. “What?”

I lift my eyes to his, enunciating each word clearly. “I said ’tis a pity he fell.”

His eyes widen, then narrow, finally figuring out what I’m trying to say.

If neither of us saw who killed Piero de’ Medici, then neither of us killed him.

"Yes, a shame," Leonardo says. "He was quite the patron of the arts."

I can't hold back a snort this time. "He had terrible taste, though."

In the piazza, guards wade through the water and head for the palazzo. It'll take them a while to get up here, but I have no doubt Piero's office will be one of the first rooms they check. We need to be gone before they arrive.

I turn back to Leonardo, wipe my bloodstained hand on my thigh, and offer it to him. "I'm Virgil."

He stares at my hand like he's never seen one before. There's that divot again. "Leonardo. I'm an apprentice at Master Verrocchio's workshop." He glances around the blood-soaked room, shaking his head. "And I have no sodding clue how I got here."

I bite back a laugh. *I know what you do,* I want to whisper. *I was an apprentice with you.*

He finally grasps my wrist and pulls himself up. "Sorry, but . . . do I know you? It feels like—" He bites off the rest of the sentence with an embarrassed laugh, dragging his other hand through his hair.

I smile, and the expression is so big, so dazzling, I can feel it lifting up my entire soul. "No, but you will."

I hold his hand a second longer than necessary before letting go.

FLORENCE, ITALY
OCTOBER 1469

CHAPTER FIFTY-NINE

Casa delle Volpi is utter chaos the day Niccolo and I sit for our portraits.

Footmen race up and down the stairs, arranging the flowers and paintings and candelabras just so. Mamma follows them with her list, cheeks rouged with excitement.

One of the first things Niccolo decided to do when he came home was redo every room in the place, and to my shock, Mamma committed to the plan like a knight on a crusade. Every reminder of Niccolo's absence, of Father's thunderous, commanding ghost, has been replaced with something different, something that feels more like us. The house is unrecognizable from the building I grew up in. It's almost starting to feel like home.

The last things to change are the three horrible portraits in the foyer. Father's will be brought to Mamma's parlor, and as much as I tried to dissuade him, Niccolo insisted that mine needed to hang next to his, right there where everyone can see it.

"I might be head of the household, but we do things together. I always want you at my side."

After years apart, I didn't want to argue with him anymore, so I just smiled and said yes.

On one condition.

A *very specific* condition.

I hold my breath when the footman announces the arrival of the painter.

He steps inside and stops beneath the three portraits. He frowns at the name placards—likely thinking to himself, *Surely there's been a mistake. There couldn't be three Niccolo Pittis in the same house, could there?*

He stares the longest at mine, eyes getting wider and wider. He tears away with a snort, clapping a hand over his mouth, but helpless giggles spill out the side anyway.

"See something interesting?" I ask.

The artist spins around. His rust-gold hair is slightly shorter now, falling around his face in soft, big waves. My fingers flex, wanting to know how it feels pulling my fingers through it.

Instead I cross my arms and stuff my hands deep in my armpits. I tip my head toward the deeply unfortunate likeness of my younger self. "My deceased father's doing. I think you can see why my brother and I have need of you."

His dark eyes snag on the pearl hanging from my earlobe before slowly dragging back to my face. He smiles, slowly, widely. As if he's not sure why, but he'll go along with it. "Someone summon the magistrate. I'd like to report a crime against a child."

I laugh and step closer. He's the same, but different. There's a new white scar bisecting the smallest finger of his left hand. One knuckle is stained with ultramarine paint. I wonder if the boys still have a bet going on how many Virgin Mary commissions Verrocchio will get before the end of the year. I want to know if he still skips the morning exercises, if he ever finds a half-drawn face among the piles and piles of sketches in his disaster of a room that makes his heart stop for no reason.

"Welcome, Leonardo da Vinci. My family and I appreciate you coming here."

"Of course. Niccolo Pitti, I presume?" His mouth kicks up in one corner, our own private joke. As if I could be anyone else.

That little smile does unspeakable things to my composure. "Virgil, actually. We met once before."

His smile slips. "We did?"

I swallow. An entire swarm of bees is trapped inside me, the stinging buzz more than I can stand. "Yes, the day the angels attacked." I don't know how his bargain works. Did it erase me from his future as well as his past? Will he ever remember? Or are we doomed to meet over and over again, leaving me forever gutted by the lack of recognition in his eyes?

He glances at his feet. "I . . . suppose I forgot."

This close, I swear there are more freckles on his skin now than there were before, a hundred little galaxies of them. I let out a rush of air, tearing my eyes away from his face. "Please, come inside."

He fumbles with his notes as we walk through the airy rooms. Though calling them notes is a generous stretch. More like an armload of paper scraps, each one containing some detail about the Pitti family portrait commissions in curiously large handwriting, except for one that just says *CATS!* and is underlined three times. I bite the inside of my cheek to stop from laughing.

He drops them once, twice, and even though I'm utterly, completely charmed by it, he's gotten so nervous, he keeps stammering apologies, so I force him to let me carry the stack while he goes through them.

"So the smaller pieces. Per my conversation with, erm, the

other Niccolo Pitti—your brother, I'm guessing? Right, then. So I'll do 'Giovannia, writing poetry at her desk,' 'Mamma in her rose garden,' and . . . 'Elisabetta with her sword'?"

"Emilo." I smile softly. It's compulsive—I can't stop it whenever I think of the day my little brother took me aside and asked me what it took to change a name. How my heart swelled so big, I thought it would pop right out from my ribs. In the end, one Pitti brother escaped the curse of Niccolo.

The church rightly declared the angels' monstrous transformation and flood an attack from the devil: an envious assault on Florence and her divine beauty. And the name of the brave hero who saved the city? They're calling him Lorenzo the Magnificent.

I'm not sure I quite agree yet—seems a smidge pompous—but perhaps it's a name he can grow into. When my brother's soul rushed back to him with his memories, he found and threatened the Medici heir at sword point. Said the price of Lorenzo's life was Casa delle Volpi and a fortune to make the Pitti family rich beyond compare.

I don't need to work anymore, but Giorgio assured me that Verrocchio would be happy to have me back. I decided to stay away. Not just because Leonardo's memory loss around me and only me would be horribly confusing for everyone, but because Niccolo wanted to take over Father's old business and I asked if I could help. I wanted to stay with my family, at least for a little bit. Leonardo gave me a gift, and I owed it to him to see who I was beneath the hurt I'd held close my entire life before trying to bring him back to mine.

The art can wait. I'm no longer afraid of losing that part of me. It's who I am, and whenever I decide to pick up a brush again, I know the spark of creation will be there, even more brilliant for my time away from it.

No one quite knows what a world without magic means for Florence yet, but I'm optimistic about it. Not that anyone would ask me, but it feels like a rebirth, a renewal.

A renaissance, if I may.

"We're painting you outside?" Leonardo hesitates at the open doors leading to the gardens. He frowns and riffles through his notes, losing a few of them to the chill-fingered breeze. "You know what? It doesn't say where I'll be painting you. With your brother and you having the same name, I didn't know—I'd assumed there was only one Niccolo."

I smile, so nervous, the expression barely touches my eyes. I must look deranged. "There is. I'm Virgil."

"Right. But . . ." There it is again, that divot on his brow. I want to press it with my thumb, rub it away until a scrap of me comes back to him. But I don't. Not yet.

"We met before!" he blurts out, eyes big and wide as bronze coins. "The day of the flood."

I bite the inside of my cheek, a terrible ache opening under my ribs. *Please don't go. Not yet.* "Yes. I remembered you said you were a painter." I gesture grandly to the hedges beyond. "Shall we?"

Leonardo hesitates for a long, long moment. Then his body swells with a big breath, as if he's made some sort of decision, and he walks past me.

There's a crispness in the air, the edge of Florence's too-hot summer finally tipping into fall. The trees burn ocher and crimson, a flame-colored carpet strewn between the deep green hedgerows. Leonardo walks through it with eager eyes and twitchy fingers. He's so distracted, he doesn't notice when we come to the rose-filled grotto. "Have you ever wondered why leaves change color? I know it's supposed to be God's doing, but I can't help but notice it always happens right when the air turns cold."

Madonna santa, he's so *him*. How did I ever keep him at arm's length? How did I ever once fail to recognize how the cinders in my chest flared to life for him and no one else?

I press my mouth together, desperate to hold the smile back. "How interesting." I let out a long, shaky breath as we round the last corner, as I bring him to the place I want him to see.

"Do you really think so? My master says it's a waste of time and—*oh*."

He stops so suddenly, I nearly walk into him.

"Your family . . . keeps your art outside?" He stops at the first canvas. A night over the city's skyline. The duomo is front and center, two faceless silhouettes before it. The artist has clearly used his fingers to paint, and he's massacred the details of the piece with his clumsy prints. It's unquestionably terrible—too personal, too strange.

It's my very favorite of the new paintings I've created.

"Not always. But when the occasion calls for it, yes." I gesture for him to follow me deeper into the roses. There's another finger painting of two faceless boys at a river bridge, pigeons flying off with their food.

Then a red-roofed workshop with ivy crawling up its face.

He lifts a finger to that one, mouth going slack. "I think . . . I think I've been here."

"You haven't," I say softly. "Not yet."

Around the next corner, it's just a sketch of me. *His* sketch.

He makes a soft sound when he sees his name in the corner.

"You might be wondering why my brother and I chose you among every other artist in Florence. I'm not sure if you remember, but you've drawn me before."

After Leonardo lost his memory, I bribed Giorgio to go through Leonardo's room and bring me any sketches the Medici had missed.

He only found one, hidden under the mattress, just beneath the spot where Leonardo dreamed each night.

I framed it myself, like it was a holy masterpiece destined for the grandest church in all of Europe. Like each long-faded line was a tender fragment of my heart.

And now it's hanging in the farthest corner of the garden.

Unlike all the other sketches he made of me, I'm smiling in this one.

He goes marble at the sight of it, cold and still. I know what he sees—how unsettling it must be. No one can look at these drawings and not see that the artist loved the subject. I can't look at this and not realize he once loved me.

I dig my nails into my palms, willing my anxiety down into the smallest, darkest place in me. It's going to be fine. Bargain or not, he still has an uncanny memory. He's going to remember. He has to.

He touches his signature with a single finger. "I drew this."

It's not a question, but I answer anyway. "Yes."

His eyes flicker to me. "Of you."

Tears fill my eyes. "Yes."

A minute passes, a century. My entire world narrows to that furrowed line on his brow. He's looking less like someone on the verge of being assailed by a feral creature, and more like the scholar I know and love, the boy who once asked me in complete seriousness if centaurs and insects were the same.

Do you remember? Please remember . . .

My chest is airless, entirely made of hope. I draw up beside him and run my finger along the fading black mark on his wrist.

"You saved my life, but there was a cost." Not only my life, but my very soul. Would I be here, putting my wild, beating heart in his hands if not for him? Would I have taken down the walls I built to keep everyone out even as they imprisoned me like a tomb? Lupa told me to stay alive, but I wasn't living until I let him in.

Even if he never remembers me, I'll never forget him.

"A cost." His breath is steady and even, nothing like the riot in me. Does it quicken at my touch? Does his body know me even if his heart can't? A flower doesn't know why it unfurls for the sun. Something within it tells it to grow toward the light.

There's still a seed inside him that calls us together, I'm certain of it.

He catches my wrist in his elegant hand. I shudder as the cuff of my sleeve rises, baring my skin and the first of the black marks marching up my arms. He makes a bitten-off sound at the sight of them.

"Virgil." His voice is warm, breathless. It curls around my name like a quilt, like home. *"Virgil."* He brushes back my overlong hair, traces his thumb under my jaw, where my pulse leaps.

My tears are already falling, but I must ask; I have to make sure he's here before I let myself fall again. "Do you remember the last animal I painted with you?"

He presses his brow to mine. His laughter is a warm rain against my face, a stormy summer night spent tangled on a floor overlooking the sky. "That dog was a millipede. You'll never change my mind."

I can't tell if it's a sob or a laugh that splits me wide open, but I'm not in pieces for long. Our arms tangle, my head goes to the divot of his neck, and he's holding me together. Each gasping breath feels like the first one I ever took.

"You remember."

He tucks a black curl behind my ear, thumb lingering on my cheekbone, brushing away the tears I can't stop shedding. "Not fully, but bits and pieces. I know—I know you were important to me."

His dark, shining eyes are careful, but in them I also see softness. He hardly remembers who I am, but he trusts me. He *knows* me.

He deserves the truth even if it feels like too much. "Then know that I love you, Leonardo. I loved you for years and was too lonely to know it. If you'll allow it—if it's not too late—I want to earn your love again."

He blinks, then smiles, a slow, sly smirk I've seen a thousand times before. "Virgil." Cristo santo, will there ever be a day when my name in his mouth doesn't set every one of my nerves on fire? I hope not. I don't think so. I'll burn for him until I'm ash. "How can it be too late already? We've only just met."

I've spent so much of the year dwelling on my death, wondering what its cause would be.

I never expected it could be sheer, heartrending *joy*.

I push up onto my toes and kiss him.

He tastes like chestnuts. And honey. A cake, if I'm being honest, and all at once, I remember the feast I asked the servants to lay out inside.

"Did you know," Leonardo says, "there's people watching us?"

I turn and gasp. The spying scoundrels! My brothers and sister watching us from the third-floor windows even though I asked them not to. Beneath them on the second floor, Mamma, already weeping. She waves tentatively, clutching a handkerchief.

"My family." I pause, worrying I'm overwhelming him, and decide to leap in anyway. "They'd like to be yours, too, if you'd let them?"

He makes a soft sound, two fingers touching the place where I've kissed him. "I've always wanted a younger sibling."

"I know, caro, I know." My tears well up again. There's an ocean of feeling inside me, its shores hidden on distant horizons. I don't know how this will go. I don't know if he'll want to stay at Casa delle Volpi or leave, but I believe there'll be time enough for everything. To remember our history, to make the dreams we talked about real enough to touch. I have him here, and that's all I want for now. Niccolo is keeping everything else I need safe: a battered drawing of two foxes, a red-leather-bound copy of Dante's *Inferno*, and a little vial filled with gold.

"Can . . . we go inside? I'd like to meet them." Slowly, tentatively, he laces his fingers through mine. As if testing a lost key on a forgotten door. "I want to remember this old life of mine."

I squeeze his hand tightly, so he knows he belongs. "'Tis not old. It's barely started."

FLORENCE, ITALY
APRIL 1506

EPILOGUE

The wisteria vine is so ancient and huge, the workshop door is barely visible behind it.

The boy ducks beneath the cascades of lavender flowers and sets the pigments on the workbench. Master da Vinci is working, painting the same portrait of the woman with the odd smile he's worked on for years. It's been so long, the boy knows Master Pitti had to buy it from the man who commissioned it. Master Pitti is forever doing things like this for Master da Vinci: paying off forgotten balances with shopkeepers, closing drawers and cupboards, scrubbing paint footprints off the workshop floor. Every time the boy offers to help, Master Pitti waves him away, as if part of him likes doing it himself.

Master da Vinci gasps, noticing him. "Didn't we tell you to take today off?"

The apprentice ducks his head. They had, but the pigments were ready, and truth be told, he'd hoped for some time working with his masters all on his own.

The da Vinci workshop is one of the most prestigious in Florence, and he wants to be the very best. Sometimes, when Master Pitti gets all misty-eyed, he'll even tell stories about his days being an apprentice during the age of the angels. The old bargain marks on his arms are almost gone, but you can still count them, if you look closely. Master Pitti doesn't like it when anyone does that.

A hand clamps down on the boy's shoulder now. Master Pitti's smile isn't friendly. "Off with you, ragazzo."

Murmuring apologies, the boy slips out the door again and makes sure it slams loudly behind him. He waits until he hears the *snick* of the lock turning.

Then he races around the side of the workshop and through the open window back inside. He tiptoes across the floor behind his masters to crouch among the straw-filled crates alongside the door. Usually, he'd let himself be shooed off and think nothing of it, but today his masters are acting strange. He wants to know why.

Master da Vinci creaks back on his painter's stool. "It's ready. I have a good feeling about it."

"You say that every year."

"This time I mean it. Signora del Giocondo told me she's ready to move on. Her pain is getting worse."

Master Pitti reaches a shaking hand into his pocket and pulls out an old vial. "What if it doesn't work?"

"What if it does?"

"We try every year, and she never comes." A pause then. "We're getting old, Leo."

Master Pitti uncorks the vial. His hands shake so badly, Master da Vinci has to help him. He dabs a dot of whatever's in it on Master Pitti's fingertip. He drags it across the portrait's strange smile. Lingers on her cheek.

"Lupa." The word shakes with hope and yearning and a feeling the boy can't name. "Would you like to come home?"

"Please do. Virgil frets we're going to die soon," Master da Vinci says. Master Pitti nudges his side, and then they laugh, their hands finding each other.

For a long, long moment, nothing happens.

Then, behind the boy, the locked door opens.

ACKNOWLEDGMENTS

Nicole Ellul: Thank you for helping me find the heart of this story. I can't believe this is our third book together! Your enthusiasm, insightful notes, and willingness to chat through the most bonkers plot ideas made this book ten times better. (Special thank-you for letting me borrow your cat's name in this one!) Working with you is a dream.

Kari Sutherland, I could not imagine a better advocate for my career. You have an uncanny ability to know and ask for what I need before I realize how much I need it. You are an author whisperer, and I'm so incredibly thankful to have you in my corner.

At Simon & Schuster, tremendous thank-yous to Jess Egan (your editorial notes were so helpful!), Amanda Brenner, Sara Berko, Thad Whittier, Shannon Pender, Amy Lavigne, Sammy Yuen, Laura Eckes, Hilary Zarycky, and Sophia Lee. It takes an army to publish a book, and I am so grateful for all your hard work in bringing *A Dangerous Bargain* to life.

Thank you, Brian Luster, for the fact-checks and line edits.

Thank you, Yorgos Cotronis, for creating the most perfect cover.

Thank you to my friends, who made sure I looked away from my screen from time to time: Courtney Bertrand, Justin Bertrand, Sarah Brandt, Jeff Boruszak, Mike Capone, Dilara Cirit, Kyle Cocina, Jody Cook, Rebecca Dearlove, David Devine, Jason Durbin, Meredith Durbin, Reid Echols, Jesi Egan, Kaitlyn Farrell Rodriguez, Nick Farrell Rodriguez, Kaeley Ferguson, Emily King, Gretchen Hardin, Sarah Mathis, Claire Lines-Mattei, Pat

Lines-Mattei, Alicia Mauer, Rachel Mochon, Alyssa Morris, Jessica Piette, Kate Schoohoven, Sara Schoonhoven, Skye Simpson, Amanda Snell, Megan Snell, Sean Tucker, and Elliott Turley.

Carlie Sorosiak, Jamie Pacton, and Matthew Hubbard: In the wild world of publishing, y'all keep me grounded. To every other fellow writer who has cheered me on, thank you so much!

Thank you to the fabulous women of LLL, whose creativity and community have become a grounding force.

Thank you, Rachel Reid and Jacob Tierney, for creating *Heated Rivalry*, the world that got me through the end of this book and reminded me why I started writing in the first place.

Thank you, Jena Whitley, Nathan Breazeale, and the amazing PTAs at Austin Sports Medicine, who helped me come back from yet another injury.

Thank you to my family, especially my parents, Joyoa and Mark, for supporting me no matter what. I know I can do anything because you believe in me. Thank you to my brother, for the sibling antics, and to my Aunt Sheila. You were the first artist I knew, and I hope you would've loved this book.

To the activists and educators battling book bans, thank you for your tireless work to make sure diverse books stay accessible.

To my readers, you are the reason I get to do this at all, and there are no words to adequately express my level of gratitude. Thank you, thank you, thank you.

To the animals in my life, especially Tybalt and Hermione: You really didn't make writing this book easier, but you did make life better.

And thank you to Loren, for everything else. I love you the most.